"Did Chesney te   his mother does not know you are marrying him?"

"No, he did not tell me," said Constance.

"But this is terrible! She will cast you out!"

"I must take that chance." *For how could she admit that this marriage was but a device to take her to Dorset and there she would escape Chesney and flee to Devon?* "Anyway it's too late. The ceremony is about to begin."

The sonorous words fell dizzily upon her. *Cherish ...honor...obey...* words which had taken on such glorious meaning in Essex when she had looked deep into Dev's smiling green eyes and plighted forever her troth. *If God struck down liars with lightning bolts, I would be the first to go,* she thought as she said "I do."

She tried not to look ahead. To her bridal night. Soon the guests would be boisterously snatching away her bride's garters.

And then—!

Novels by
VALERIE SHERWOOD

This Loving Torment

These Golden Pleasures

This Towering Passion

Her Shining Splendor

Bold Breathless Love

Rash Reckless Love

Wild Willful Love

Rich Radiant Love

Lovely Lying Lips

AND COMING SOON:

Born To Love

Published By
WARNER BOOKS

Valerie Sherwood

Lovely Lying Lips

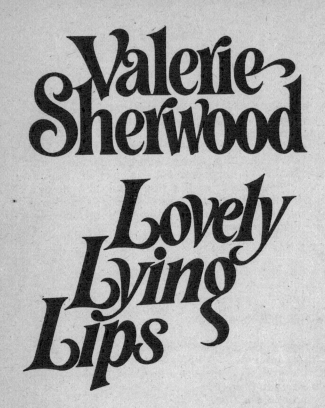

WARNER BOOKS

A Warner Communications Company

WARNING

The reader is hereby specifically warned against using any of the unusual foods or the cosmetics or medications mentioned herein. They are included only to give the authentic flavor of the times and readers are implored to seek the advice of a doctor before undertaking any "experiments" in their use. For example, the popular seventeenth-century cosmetic ceruse contained white lead, which is lethal; other concoctions of the day were often as bad, and the "cures" used for illness were sometimes worse than the disease itself.

WARNER BOOKS EDITION

Copyright © 1983 by Valerie Sherwood
All rights reserved.

Cover design by Gene Light
Cover art by Elaine Duillo

Warner Books, Inc.,
666 Fifth Avenue,
New York, N.Y. 10103

W A Warner Communications Company

Printed in the United States of America

First Warner Books Printing: December, 1983

10 9 8 7 6 5 4 3 2 1

DEDICATION

To lovely Spicy, who came to us as a bedraggled thrown-away waif of a kitten peering out of an empty barn and won through to box and cushion of her own; Spicy the indomitable, surmounting all her misfortunes with a proudly waving tail; Spice the cynic, who learned to trust only us and ever viewed the world with scathing watchful aquamarine eyes; dear Lady Spice who mated with our beautiful long-haired Fancy, a real "puss in boots" of a fellow, and gave us six lovely kittens; Spice, whose story is as "rags to riches" as any of my tormented heroines and whose spirit is as reckless and dashing as any of them; brilliant Spicy, whose vivid imagination is in constant evidence; lighthearted, playful, brave and loyal Spicy, our beautiful Calico cat, grown fragile with age but ever loved and loving, this book is dedicated.

Author's Note

In the magical world of the 1600s, no single summer was perhaps more eventful than the stirring summer of 1685 when England's West Country rose in rebellion in a desperate attempt to place Charles II's illegitimate son, the handsome young Duke of Monmouth, upon the English throne. My characters and their tumultuous lives are purely fiction, of course, but the settings and the times are as authentic as I could make them—from snowy Yorkshire with its romantic ruins of Fountains Abbey, rising like upflung stone lace above the River Skell, to the green loveliness of the Valley of the Axe, to the wilds of Dartmoor with its far gray-green vistas and ancient granite-topped tors.

Old hourses have always been for me a consuming interest and the great houses that I have described herein are all based on actual houses from England's storied past that still exist, although I have made certain changes within and without to better suit the action of my story.

Thus "Axeleigh," home of the lovely and tempestuous Pamela, will be observed to be strikingly like beautiful Wilderhope Manor in Shropshire—that Wilderhope made famous by the dramatic escape of its owner during England's civil war by a great leap on horseback over Wenlock Edge, which is still today called "Major's Leap."

"Claxton Hall" in Yorkshire's remote West Riding, where so many dramatic events of Constance's early life take place, will be easily recognized as East Riddlesden Hall in

Yorkshire's West Riding—and it seemed a perfect choice, for its early owners, the Murgatroyds, were as wild a lot as the Daceys who inhabit it in my story. Imprisoned, fined—even excommunicated—it is said that below the house the Aire River actually changed its course to protest the Murgatroyds' myriad debaucheries!

Noble "Warwood," home of the redoubtable Captain Warburton of my story—beloved by two of my characters—is really Buckland Abbey, the home bought by another adventurous gentleman, Sir Francis Drake, after his remarkable buccaneering voyage on the *Golden Hind* which took him round the world—and I have transported it, along with part of its history, practically unaltered from Devon to the Valley of the Axe.

For "Hawley Grange," whose flirtatious daughters make Pamela so jealous, I could not resist recreating one of the ancient and enormous stone tithe barns with their baronial architecture and churchlike "naves." Such barns in medieval times used to be scattered all over England—and why should not a "wool-rich" country gentleman transform one into a home for his family?

I was so beguiled by Moseley Old Hall in Staffordshire, where Charles II was hidden during his escape from the disastrous Battle of Worcester, that I have transported it practically intact to the lonely wastes of Dartmoor to become my "Tattersall," which shelters the tragic but indomitable "Masked Lady."

For the "Huntlands" of my story, with its great balls and its debonair and dangerous owner, I have combined two famous Cornish homes—Trerice and Cotehele—magically recreated in Somerset, while beautiful Blickling Hall in Norfolk (suitably transformed from red brick to typical gray-brown Kentish stone) is whisked away to Kent to become romantic "Wingfield," the lost heritage of Deverell, my story's wild young highwayman.

The dates of particular trials during England's Bloody Assizes have been adjusted slightly, the better to suit my story—and Christmas in 1684 actually fell on a Monday, not on Sunday as my story records. But I have tried to truly recount Essex as it was then with its ancient hornbeam forests and lighthearted "penny bridals." Before the Norman Conquest, Hatfield Forest was a royal hunting demesne, and the Old Doodle Oak, some sixty feet in circumference, beneath whose spreading branches Constance and Dev spend their wedding night after their wild "penny bridal," still exists (although it no longer greens in spring) and who is to say this eight-hundred-year-old giant is *not* the oak shown on the Domesday Survey made for William the Conqueror?

Gibb's bizarre burial is based on an actual case in Surrey. And smallpox was the true scourge of the day. While the Black Death claimed many victims, the Red Death was ever present and there were few whose lives were untouched by it (even Queen Elizabeth I, for all her precautions, contracted smallpox and upon her face at her death was measured half an inch of permanent makeup to hide the scars). Whether the Red Death's scarring was ever minimized or eliminated by a "red glow" is entirely a matter of conjecture—it has been so claimed.

And the timeless Valley of the Axe with its silvery river is real as well, as is the deep green gash of the Cheddar Gorge where Constance nearly plunges to her death. Real too is the George, that quaint half-timbered inn at Norton St. Philip where a sniper fired on the ill-starred young duke on the morning of the Battle of Sedgemoor, which would decide his fate—although of course the identity of the sniper has been changed to suit my story. Monmouth, Lord Grey, Lady Alice Lisle, Judge Jeffreys and the Bloody Assizes he held at Taunton and elsewhere were all real enough, although the story I have woven around them is entirely my own invention.

But I yearn to believe that this tale of dazzling ladies in riding masks and their reckless loves, of sword-swinging plumed-hatted gentlemen and their desperate ventures, might really have come to pass. Even if it did not, *it should have happened,* and so, dear readers, I commend it to you with all my heart.

And as a benediction for those thrilling times, gone alas

forever, and for my story of flaming passions, bright honor and dark despair:

> Let the sun shine in at last
> And illuminate the past!
> Let the World That Was be with us once again!
> Let the lovers who are dust
> And the swords that all are rust
> Come back to shining life and live again!

Valerie Sherwood

CONTENTS

PROLOGUE   *The Impetuous Lie*   15
           Somerset, England, June 11, 1685
BOOK I: *Daughters of Eve*   21
  Part One: The Daffodil and the Iris   23
  Part Two: The Dangerous Lover   49
BOOK II: *The Lovely Outcast*   105
BOOK III: *Lightskirts and Lovers*   125
  Part One: First Love   127
  Part Two: The Lightskirt   157
  Part Three: The Wild Reunion   193
  Part Four: The Highwayman's Bride   223
BOOK IV: *The Masked Lady*   249
  Part One: The Gallant Lie   251
  Part Two: Midsummer Madness   283
BOOK V: *The Conspirators*   325
  Part One: The Tangled Web   327
  Part Two: The Strange Wedding   399
BOOK VI: *Of Death and Moonlight*   445
  Part One: Midnight Silk   447
  Part Two: The Beautiful Liar   499
EPILOGUE   568

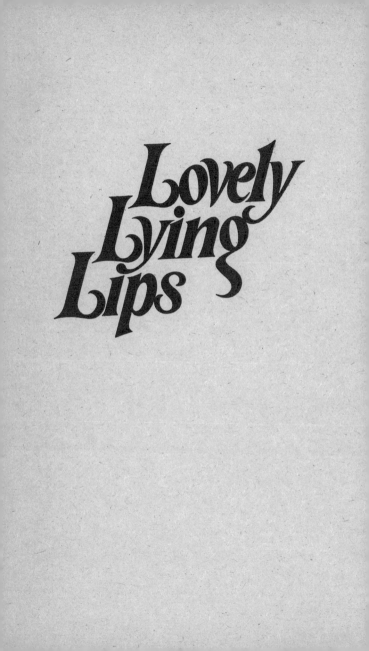

PROLOGUE

The Impetuous Lie
Somerset, England,
June 11, 1685

Truth shines abroad, its rosy glow
Lights up another summer,
Yet a wild sweet lie is on her lips—
And the lady's lie's a stunner!

It was a glorious day for a hanging. In the bright sunshiny weather people had been filtering into the market town of Bridgwater since morning and now a motley collection of carts was clustered in a circle around the hastily constructed gibbet. For a gentleman was to be hanged this day for murder on the Bridgwater road, and hangings were great social occasions. Now, as the moment approached, satin-clad aristocrats jostled with country fellows in rough homespun, and ladies who had arrived in open carriages with big silken skirts billowing waved their ruffled parasols next to rude farm carts. From all about they had come and now their fascinated faces peered upward at the scaffold where a green-eyed gentleman in russet was about to be hanged.

Outstanding in the crowd was a new arrival, a girl—perhaps sixteen—of striking beauty. She had ridden into town on a dancing white mare whose long flaunting mane was almost as silky as her own daffodil yellow hair. Her grip on the reins was firm, her bearing reflected confidence in her wealth and position, and many turned from regarding the scaffold to gaze admiringly at her. Her lovely figure was encased in one of the new mannish riding habits that had become so fashionable—this one of thin scarlet taffeta that shimmered in the light. A burst of expensive white lace was caught round her neck with a small ruby, and lace cuffs spilled over her riding gloves. A sweeping hat, afloat with vivid tulip red plumes, flamed in the sun above her cascading daffodil yellow hair. The hat's wide brim shadowed a face both piquant and charming with a flawless pink and white complexion. But anyone who looked closely would note that it was a restless face, that there was a certain tension around the soft mouth, and that the wide crystal blue eyes had a reckless gleam.

Her name was Pamela Archer, and although she detested hangings, she had a good reason for attending this one—she was looking for Tom Thornton, and the butler at Huntlands had told her Tom had ridden off for Bridgwater as if the devil were after him.

She was certainly *not* looking for the young fellow in gaudy yellow and violet satin some distance away who was jumping up and down and waving his yellow-plumed hat to attract her attention.

Dick Peacham.

Pamela's crystal blue gaze considered him levelly—and with enormous distaste. No wit, no flair, no gallantry, no wild impulses, no deep-throated laughter, no dangerous reputation—in short, none of the attractions that golden-haired Tom Thornton of Huntlands possessed in such abundance. But he was her betrothed, was Dick Peacham, the banns were already being cried and her father had sworn that she would marry him in a fortnight. She gave Peacham a curt bow, just the barest nod of her lovely head—which she hoped would

16

not encourage him to join her. Anxiously searching for Tom, she had hoped to avoid Peacham today of all days.

Her maid, Tabby, who had ridden into town with Pamela as became a young lady of wealth and fashion, muttered that they could not see from here and with a sigh Pamela plunged her horse's head forward, easing through the throng.

Of a sudden her breath caught as a wild thought occurred to her. There *was* a way to rid herself of Dick Peacham once and for all, no matter how her father raged! She was at the moment urging the mare forward past a gaily painted farm cart when her bright head swung back and she regarded the condemned man with such a lively interest that a nearby lady nudged her companion and was heard to mutter tartly that the Squire of Axeleigh's daughter seemed quite taken by the prisoner!

Indeed he was something to look upon, was the tall fellow just now mounting the scaffold. His clothing was nothing remarkable—serviceable russet broadcloth suit, dusty wide-topped russet boots. His gleaming shoulder-length hair was russet too. It was his arrogant manner that caught her attention. Indeed, he might have been mounting the steps of a throne, thought Pamela with a queer little tug at her heartstrings, rather than climbing toward death at the end of a hempen rope. Sinewy lean, he moved almost contemptuously to the platform with the light-footed grace of a prowling tiger. The daunting look in the cold green eyes that raked the assemblage made the hangman wonder nervously if the prisoner might not try at the last minute to break free—and he felt the ropes that bound the prisoner to make sure he was well shackled.

Now it was time for the customary speech made by every condemned man on the scaffold just before the rope cut off his breathing forever, and the crowd quieted expectantly.

At that moment, Pamela would have given much to know his thoughts.

This truly put the crown to a wasted life, he was thinking sardonically. *To die for a murder he didn't commit!* He cast a

17

last thoughtful look at the blue skies that rode over Somerset—the last blue skies he would see this side of hell. He knew he could perhaps buy his life—at least for a little while, until they discovered that he was in reality a famous highwayman, wanted dead or alive all over England—by naming a certain lady whose face, he noted regretfully, he did not see in the crowd below. *But name her he would not!*

"I say again that I am innocent." His grim voice carried over those upturned faces. "I repeat that I had spent the night in question at the Rose and Thistle in the company of a lady—"

"Name the lady!" cut in a raucous voice from the crowd.

In the sudden expectant hush, Pamela rose in her stirrups. The sun shimmered on her scarlet taffeta riding habit and the breeze ruffled her scarlet plumes.

"You have been very gallant, sir, in protecting my reputation"—she gave the prisoner a smile as sunny as her daffodil yellow hair, and her calm voice rang out across the throng—"but I cannot let you die for it. It is true, good people, what this gentleman says. He did indeed spend the night in question at the Rose and Thistle in Bridgwater. With me. In my bedchamber."

Around her there were gasps. Townsfolk and countrymen alike gaped at her. Satin-clad ladies dropped their fans from nerveless fingers. Gentlemen choked on their snuff.

For the golden-haired lady in scarlet was one of the beauties of the county. Indeed she had turned up her dainty nose at proposals of marriage from half the eligible gentlemen here. They could not, they felt, be hearing her aright.

And then they remembered—she was a lightskirt's daughter. Had not her gorgeous but willful mother slept with half the county both before and after wedding the Squire of Axeleigh?

On the wings of her reckless words, the lady in scarlet had become on the instant a scarlet lady!

Pamela ignored their shocked mutterings. "So I demand that you release him," she added, heedless that she was shredding her reputation with every word she spoke. "For I can swear that on the night in question he had no part in any murder. He was"—the slight flush on her soft cheeks deepened—"otherwise engaged."

Above the excited twitter that greeted this revelation, her brilliant crystal blue eyes met the narrow green gaze of the condemned man—met and locked.

From the scaffold the man about to be hanged concealed his astonishment with difficulty.

For the lovely challenging face he gazed upon was one he had never seen before. This lady, just now occupied with saving his life, was a complete stranger.

He wondered, even through the shock wave of relief that went through him, whatever had induced this lustrous wench to lie for him.

And how she came to do it makes a tale worth the telling.

BOOK I
Daughters of Eve

If you would be true, love,
This is what you do, love:
Hide your head and stay in bed,
Else you'll learn to rue, love!

PART ONE
The Daffodil and the Iris

Other loves may hold her, other arms entwine
But they will be no bolder than the arms she left
  behind,
Other men may stir her, other vows endure
But she will not forget him—that at least is sure!

*The Valley of the Axe,
Somerset, England,
December 22, 1684*

CHAPTER 1

A cold wind was sweeping down from the Mendip Hills. It brought with it the promise of snow and a white Christmas at Axeleigh Hall, and the two young ladies in their fashionable velvet riding habits clutched their plumed hats lest they be swept from their heads and sent skittering across the meadow or perhaps lodged in the winter-bare upper branches of a nearby wych elm that soared a hundred feet and more above them.

They made a remarkable pair: dainty Pamela, in her slate blue velvet habit with her wealth of golden hair and blue and white plumes, sitting proud and erect in the saddle and controlling with practiced ease her white Arabian mare who wanted to dance sideways down the road. And her father's ward, Constance, tall and reed slender in her violet velvets, swaying with unconscious elegance and with a cloud of midnight dark hair beneath her wide-brimmed violet-plumed hat.

The two girls could not have been more different in

appearance but they shared two traits in common—impetuous-ness and reckless hearts. And both would lead them into trouble.

Pamela Archer, who talked a great deal, was speaking now.

"I don't care how wealthy Melissa Hawley's father is!" she told Constance energetically, and her strikingly beautiful blue eyes, so light in color that they were near to crystal, sparkled with annoyance. "She isn't good enough for Tom. He needs—"

"Someone like you?" hazarded Constance, her lovely but slightly jaded face turned toward sixteen-year-old Pamela.

"No, I mean she's out to get him any way she can!" sputtered Pamela, giving the older girl an angry look. "When I spied them last night at the ball at Hawley Grange, they were clutched tight together there in the dark buttery. Melissa's bodice was clear down off one shoulder and Tom was untying the riband that held her chemise. I could actually see his hands on it—*fumbling*!"

The ghost of a smile hovered at the corners of Constance's pretty mouth. "You could see all that in the dark?"

"I had brought a candle," said Pamela stiffly.

"Naturally."

Carried away by her subject, Pamela missed the irony of that comment. "Indeed had I not chanced upon them, a moment more and he'd no doubt have borne Melissa to the floor and her father would have insisted the fool marry her!" She sounded indignant.

Constance's calm gaze was fixed on a distant line of willows that, she knew, hid from view the silvery ribbon of the River Axe as it wound through this lovely valley. "And what," she wondered, "were you doing in the buttery at that hour? Surely the ball was not taking place *there*?" She swung her amused gaze around to the younger girl.

Pamela gave her an injured look. "Of course the ball wasn't taking place there, Constance! Don't be dense! Melissa's mother had organized a game of hide-and-seek for the young people while the musicians rested and had some ale," she explained huffily. "As you might very well have guessed."

"As I might indeed have guessed," agreed Constance lightly. She was thinking of that huge barnlike house at Hawley Grange—indeed it had been a medieval tithe barn and had fallen into disrepair before wool-rich Nathaniel Hawley had decided to remodel the old stone structure to house his growing family. That he had done so neither tastefully nor well in no way diminished the value of the 125-foot-long building with its 40-foot gabled ends and its rabbit warren of rooms, for playing hide-and-seek. "And while the rest of them were hiding, *you* were seeking Tom, I take it?" she could not resist adding.

"Nothing of the kind! I was searching about for a clever place to hide, and it occurred to me that the dark buttery—"

"Was exactly the place where Tom might be hiding with Melissa?" suggested Constance with gentle irony.

A high color rose in Mistress Pamela's cheeks and she reined in her white Arabian mare so sharply that Angel reared up indignantly on her hind feet. Constance, not the superb rider that Pamela was by half, managed to bring her gray to a restless halt.

"Oh, you can't think *I'm* after Tom Thornton!" cried Pamela passionately.

Constance wondered suddenly if golden-haired Pamela was the only person in the county not to know it. Had she really managed to deceive herself into thinking she was *not* in love with Tom? At the sight of Pamela's flushed indignant face and snapping crystal blue eyes, she concealed a smile with difficulty. "Oh, I wasn't saying that," she managed vaguely.

"I should hope not!" cried Pamela with so much energy that Constance fought back an almost uncontrollable desire to laugh. " 'Tis just that I've grown up with Tom, being neighbors," she added in a prim voice.

And you're mad in love with him, and he still sees you as the tomboy you were, the rampant little girl he took fences with as a boy, and climbed trees with—and not as the beauty you've become! thought Constance wryly.

"Well, Tom Thornton's a fickle fellow, not bent on marriage," she told Pamela with a shrug. "You know that very well, yet every time he takes off after a new girl, you near burst your bodice with worry. I'm not implying that you *need* stays," she added hastily to mute the black look Pamela gave her. "Not with a waist like yours that's near to nothing!" For dainty Pamela's waist was indeed as slim as her own.

The compliment breezed right past Pamela, who had but one thing on her mind. "Tom's like a brother to me," she insisted with a righteous air. "And I can't bear to see him make a mistake and ruin his life."

"Some would say 'twas no mistake," countered Constance, "to court the daughter of a man as rich as Nathaniel Hawley!"

"Oh, that's ridiculous," sniffed Pamela. "Melissa's father is wealthy enough with all those sheep grazing, 'tis true. But there are lots of girls could bring him more!"

Yourself, for instance, mused Constance. *You, the heiress to Axeleigh Hall, could bring him manors and farms, and the dairies and cheeses of Cheddar, which your father owns as well, to add to Tom's home estate of Huntlands.* . . . Aloud she said, "Weren't they surprised to see you, dashing in on them like that? I mean, I suppose they felt safe from prying eyes in the buttery. What did they say?"

"Tom turned and glared at me," admitted Pamela, aggrieved. "Melissa just stood there giggling away, and when I told them everybody was wondering where they were and her mother would no doubt be searching the house for them, Melissa pulled away from Tom, making sure that I could see the state her bodice was in, and she sort of swaggered toward me, just *flaunting* her bare skin at me as if to say 'Can't you see he's mine if I want him?' "

"Did she say that?"

"No, she said"—Pamela gritted her white teeth—"she *said,* in a sort of plaintive wail, 'She's found us again, Tom!' As if I was searching the house looking for them!"

Constance, from her slightly taller height, gave the younger Pamela a commiserating look. "That must have been irritating for you," she agreed.

"Irritating? I was about to box Melissa's ears for her when Tom stepped between us and said in a truly *icy* voice, 'I hope if I should chance to run into you again this evening, Pam, that you will be in better humor.' And dragged Melissa away with him! I followed along after because I realized of course by then that the game of hide-and-seek must be long over."

Of course, since you'd no doubt spent quite a while searching the house for Tom and his newest light-of-love, thought Constance, amused. "So what happened then?" she asked.

"Oh, the dancing had begun again and before Tom could get Melissa on the dance floor, that gawky Landwell fellow claimed her and swung her out on the floor."

"And did Tom ask you to dance?"

"No, he spun on his heel away from me and asked somebody else—Lydia Wilston, I think." How galling *that* had been showed plainly in Pamela's voice.

Lydia Wilston, undoubtedly, thought Constance with a wry look at Pamela. *You probably could catalog with complete accuracy every partner Tom Thornton had in the dancing and where he was at any particular time during the evening.* Pam was nothing if not thorough in these matters. She sighed.

"I wish *you* had attended the ball, Constance," said Pamela plaintively. "I don't know why you pleaded you were sick and stayed at home. You weren't sick, you couldn't have been or you wouldn't be so fit today!"

"I—do feel somewhat better today," admitted Constance. Her dark winglike brows drew together in a frown that shadowed the deep purple of her eyes. It was not illness that had kept her from last night's ball at Hawley Grange, but Ned Warburton. Ned was pressing his suit with too much heat and she was growing uneasy lest the Squire, her guardian, point out to her bluntly that she had already turned down half the young bucks in the county and bid her to choose one of them forthwith—perhaps even Ned. Indeed it was to elude Ned who, she sensed, might dash over today from Warwood on his big gelding to inquire about her health, that she had ridden out with Pamela. For Constance was not, like the Squire's daughter, born to the saddle. She detested riding and she was rather afraid of horses. Indeed she was having trouble handling the spirited mount she was presently aboard.

"Ned was there," Pamela volunteered with a slanted look.

"Was he indeed?" said Constance grimly.

"Yes, he asked about you and when I told him you weren't well he seemed very concerned and we had a long talk in the dining room."

"Really? What about?"

"About Tom and his unconscionable behavior!"

"And did Ned agree with you?"

"He said I'd bring him to heel! Can you imagine?"

Constance very well could but she forebore to say so.

"I am *furious* with Tom," announced Pamela hotly. "In fact, if he shows no better judgment than to pursue lightskirts like Melissa Hawley, then I may decide to wash my hands of him!"

"Oh, I wouldn't call her a lightskirt," demurred Constance. "A little foolish, perhaps. And if you're washing your hands of Tom Thornton, may I ask why you've headed your horse so determinedly toward Huntlands?"

Pamela caught her breath. "Why, I wasn't aware which way we were going," she said with an airy toss of her golden curls. "I suppose we *are* headed toward Huntlands but that certainly doesn't mean—"

Constance caught that argumentative note. She didn't want to quarrel with Pam, for whom she held a warm affection. She managed to veer the conversation into a discussion of marriage, and whether they should fly into it on their own or wait to be pushed and cajoled into it by well-meaning family members—meaning the Squire.

It was a subject Pamela enjoyed discussing.

"My old governess wrote me last week from Bath, where

she's teaching a whole brood of youngsters," she told Constance. "It was a very gloomy letter. I had told her you were here with us now and she urged us both to marry!" Pamela's laughter pealed; her laugh had an infectious ring that made all the world seem better.

"And why, pray, should she urge that?" wondered Constance, looking blank.

"She says that at seventeen you are already past your first bloom and can hope for little enough," Pamela told her on another ripple of laughter. "And that I am still in my prime—but just barely—and I should take the first man who offers!"

Constance looked amazed. "If those are her opinions, I'm surprised your father had her in the house!"

"Oh, she was very mousy when she was here and never expressed any opinions. I take it she's rather come out in Bath. What was *your* school like, Constance? I mean—Mistress Waldegrave's, was it? Did they strap you to a backboard to make you straighter and pile books on your head to make you hold your head just so? My old governess was always threatening to do things like that but she never did."

"Oh—no, they didn't," said Constance vaguely and Pamela shot a sudden look at her. There was something rather mysterious about Constance, she thought. Daughter of an old friend of her father's of whom Pamela had never heard until the day last summer that Constance arrived in their midst, Constance seemed to have a reluctance to discuss the past. Not that she didn't answer with apparent openness anything you asked her, but she never volunteered anything. And she must have had a bad time, all those years in that school for girls, for her violet eyes were often so sad. You'd think she'd want to tell someone about it, but she never did. She'd just fall into those long silences and stare pensively out the window and when you spoke to her she would give a sudden start as if she'd been miles away.

It had been worse lately. Tabby, her maid, muttered sometimes that the Squire's new ward was "given to the sulks," but somehow Pamela thought that wasn't true. Something had happened in Constance's past, something that didn't bear speaking of. Something that had Marked Her Childhood! But *she* would find it out! Her crystal blue eyes sparkled.

"Perhaps my old governess will find a match for each of us in Bath," she chuckled. "And send them riding posthaste here to Axeleigh!"

"I doubt that!" Constance was adjusting the plum velvet skirts of her narrow-waisted riding habit as she spoke and wondering if the sudden wind that had come up and was whipping across the brown-and-straw-colored meadow grass would tear loose the long hatpin that held her hat. Even as she reached for it, on a sudden wild gust the hat tore loose and went skittering into the meadow, its violet plumes ruffling as it sped along, as if it were alive. "Oh, no!" she wailed in dismay.

Pamela, superb rider that she was, immediately touched Angel with her knee and launched herself into the meadow. Hanging onto the horn of her sidesaddle and putting her weight precariously on one stirrup, she swung down and swept up the quivering hat with one gauntlet-gloved hand. Laughing, she rode back to Constance, who had reined in her horse and shuddered as she watched the performance.

"I couldn't have done that," sighed Constance. "I'd have catapulted headfirst into the meadow and garnered a headful of burrs!"

"So nearly did I," laughed Pamela. She had a sweet clear voice with a ring to it, like the clear chiming of church bells in the distance—none of the lazy languor of Constance's dulcet tones. "But 'tis not so hard to catch the knack of. Here, shall I toss it back and you try it?"

Constance gave her such an affronted look that she laughed.

"*You* were born on a horse—I was not!" Hastily retrieving her hat from Pamela, Constance tried vainly to pin it more securely to her thick dark hair. "I was a city child and there were always plenty of sedan chairs or hackney coaches about!"

Pamela nodded contentedly. She was glad she hadn't been brought up in the city, viewing life from the stuffy confines of chairs and coaches. She loved to feel the wind in her hair and her skirts blowing as she cleared a stone fence. And she wanted a man like that, someone to ride beside, laughing and carefree.

She shot a sudden look at Constance. "What kind of man would you choose for yourself?" she challenged.

Around Constance the world seemed to still suddenly. She *had* chosen a man for herself, although curious Pamela was not to know that. Before her, from the slight rise of ground over which they now rode, stretched the broad Valley of the Axe, with the river flowing silvery and sparkling down through meadowland and woodlands, shadowed on the north by the blue beauty of the Mendip Hills—but she was not seeing any of that. *She was seeing instead the beech and birch trees of the glorious Essex countryside, and the leaden skies of winter that rode the Axe River valley had changed for her to the blue and white rhapsody of summer. The months had magically melted away and she was floating as a bride on a sea of joy. Her light feet hardly felt the cobbles, warm underfoot from the brilliant sunlight. So dazzled were her eyes on that, her wedding day, that she had seen no pitfalls— none at all.*

"You have that same faraway look again," complained Pamela as Constance gave up on her hat and clasped it under her arm as she urged her horse forward in an effort to keep up with Pamela's dancing mare. "As if you've gone some place I can't follow. I always feel you're seeing demons, that there's something lurking, waiting to jump out at you!"

Constance shot her a sudden look. Frank young Pamela was more perceptive than she had thought.

"You've never really told us about your past, you know."

"What do you want to know?" asked Constance warily.

"What was it like, living in London?"

"In summer, when the weather was fine my father would hire a carriage and we would all ride out into the country and stay at some inn. In winter there were frost fairs." No need to tell Pamela that the frost fairs and the country inns were all part of the early life that had degenerated as the pittance of money which Anne Cheltenham had brought to her marriage gradually dwindled out. No need to tell her about the lean years when they lived—no, existed was a better word—from month to month, managing to get by mostly on the grudging generosity of a distant cousin in Norfolk who sent a trifling sum and a scolding letter on the first of every month. Anne always cried when she received the letters and Hammond Dacey would go striding out and come home drunk. Running from his problems—he had always done that.

"And then you went to your father's people in Yorkshire? Claxton House, I think you said?"

"Near Ripon in the West Riding," Constance heard herself say.

"What was it like?"

It was a house of hatred. I thought to die there. Aloud, she said, "Oh, it was much as any other manor house, nothing remarkable."

"Like Axeleigh?"

"No, nothing like." *How could she describe that stone pile of a house to Pamela and not communicate the despair she had felt at living there? How every night she had wished herself gone?* She shivered. "It's getting very cold and I can't control this hat. Every time I move my arm, I'm near to losing it—and the wind is taking my hair. Let's go back."

"All right. It *is* getting awfully cold." Pamela wheeled her horse about. "I think when I marry I will wear a gold satin petticoat to match my hair," she declared suddenly, wrinkling her nose. "And have an overgown of cloth of gold to astound the county!" She laughed. "What do you think of that, Constance?"

"I think that will be—very nice with your yellow hair." There was a slight catch in Constance's voice. *She* had worn her dark hair combed down long and floating over her shoulders like some country dairymaid. Her wedding gown had been a faded lavender linen kirtle with a separate white bodice, low cut and with full three-quarter sleeves. And the wedding circlet she had worn upon her head was not the elegant arrangement of pearls and golden leaves that carefree Pamela would undoubtedly wear, but a simple wreath of daisies twined about her inky locks.

She had not cared. She had been happy that day. Happier those first weeks she had spent with her tall bridegroom than she had ever been before—or since for that matter.

Now he was gone. She had not seen him all these months past. She supposed she would never see him again. She was seventeen and no one knew about her secret marriage.

Axeleigh Hall, Somerset,
December 22, 1684

CHAPTER 2

Constance was still brooding as she rode beside Pamela down Axeleigh's long oak-lined driveway. Indeed they were almost blown down it by a ripping wind that whipped the branches overhead and kept them hard-pressed to keep their velvet skirts from flying over their heads. She lifted her eyes to the house—big and substantial, built of rough courses of Ham stone back in the Old Queen's time. Its long front rose three stories high to four tall gables and its stone-tiled roofs were surmounted by towering clusters of chimneys through which fragrant wood smoke was even now smudging the winter-gray sky. Huge airy mullioned and transomed windows made it light and bright.

Their approach was observed by a tall commanding gentleman somberly garbed in black and silver who stood before the drawing room window with a glass of port in his hand. He was Ned Warburton's brother, Captain Anthony Warburton, and he had made the long cold ride from Warwood, the ancient seat of the Warburtons in Somerset, to press his younger brother's suit for Constance's hand in marriage.

The Squire of Axeleigh, a vigorous sandy-haired man with a deep chest and keen blue eyes, was leaning against the carved overmantel. He had listened quietly to his friend, but in truth he was not paying much attention. He was studying in rather melancholy fashion the tall earnest Captain, who strode restlessly about, emphasizing his remarks with vigorous gestures. Tony Warburton had always had a nice sense of style, thought the Squire, whose own clothes never quite seemed to fit his strong body. Over the rich baritone flow of the Captain's words he noted the crisp cut of his guest's black velvet coat, wide-cuffed, deep-reversed, full-skirted and strikingly trimmed in silver braid and silver buttons. That coat's full skirts were slit from hem to waist in the back to facilitate riding—and riding was to the lean Captain second nature; the coat was slit up both sides to permit hasty withdrawal of the serviceable basket-hilted sword that peeked out from the gray satin lining as Captain Warburton roved about the room, his tall figure in dark trousers and riding boots moving with the lithe grace that proclaimed him the swordsman he was.

"And since I've no wife nor any intention of gaining one," Captain Warburton turned to fix the Squire with a pair of steady gunmetal eyes beneath straight dark brows, "that means Ned will inherit Warwood when I'm gone."

"Aye, 'tis a good point you make, Tony," agreed the Squire, mentally approving the fact that Tony Warburton, despite all those years away fighting foreign wars, still chose—like himself—to wear his own hair instead of one of those barbarous wigs which had become so fashionable. Indeed the Captain's hair made a very substantial showing of its own, for it was thick and straight and heavy and of so dark and rich a brown that to the casual observer it appeared black, although in sunlight it flashed a rich russet. It hung like a thick skein of gleaming silk to the Captain's broad shoulders.

Captain Warburton, frowning slightly that throwing the bait of Warwood into the conversation had not produced more enthusiasm, took another turn around the room and his saturnine face grew thoughtful. What *would* win the day for Ned? The boy was half out of his mind with love of the wench Constance! Mooning about, dancing attendance on her—and all apparently for naught.

The tall Captain lifted his glass of port and studied its fiery red color against the light. The gesture caused the lace that spilled from the cuffs of his full-sleeved white linen shirt to fall back over a pair of fine strong hands made for gripping a sword—or a woman.

"Ned would not ask ye for a dowry," he said, picking his words carefully. "In case the girl has little substance behind her?" It was thrown out experimentally, should that be the stumbling block.

The Squire of Axeleigh flushed. "Constance will have a handsome dowry," he said stiffly. "Provided by me."

"Ah, I'd thought as much," sighed the Captain, running long fingers through his dark hair. Another thrust gone wrong. He had been recounting Ned's good points now for a full fifteen minutes, and it was beginning to weary him. He downed his drink, perplexed.

The Squire gave him a sympathetic look. He was much accustomed to giving sympathy to suitors, for there had been many of late. But he and the Captain were friends of old—indeed he had once expected Tony Warburton to become his brother-in-law in the old days when, snared by her beauty (Tony had always had a great appreciation of female beauty), Tony had become betrothed to the Squire's younger sister, Margaret. They had made a handsome pair, he thought wistfully, tall regal flame-haired Margaret swaying gracefully beside her genial dark lover with his quick flashing smile and his arrogant military bearing. And the Squire had not held it against Tony Warburton at all when, on learning of Margaret's death, he had plunged—not into drink, which everyone felt would have been perfectly natural—but into the arms of that flighty little Weatherby girl, so frail she had perished a short two months after the wedding.

The blow of *her* death had seemed to shake Tony Warburton at last, and he had gone into a long period of grieving and restless nights during which, his housekeeper had reported in a scandalized whisper to all who would listen, in his sleep he had called out brokenly for Margaret as if the frail little Weatherby girl had never been. Clifford Archer, hearing of it, had felt he understood. Margaret's death had been such a massive blow to Tony that he had reeled from it into a marriage of convenience with a girl whose love he had not really returned. Her loss had triggered him back into reality, and grief for the girl he had really loved—and lost.

Since then the Captain, once he had got through the initial shock, had become as determined a widower as the Squire and had eventually managed to discourage even the most determined matchmakers. Both men would have been pleased had Ned showed an interest in Pamela, but he did not.

Not so with Constance! When Constance had arrived on the scene last summer, young Ned had noticed her immediately. And ever since had haunted her whereabouts.

And Ned's older brother at their womanless establishment at Warwood, having met the lass, approved the chase, thought the Squire wryly. For slender Constance passed like a bright shimmer before men's eyes, and the dark splendor of her glance brought a quickening of the heart, a vision of what might be, to even the dullest laggard.

It would have surprised the Squire to know that what most captivated Captain Warburton (although he took great pains not to show it) was her voice—that soft husky murmur like the rustle of taffeta petticoats, melting into sounds so soft they might have been the brushing of fine silk. Margaret had had a voice like that and its tones had rubbed his nerves raw with desire. *No wonder Ned felt as he did about the girl,* the Captain thought with sympathy.

And so he had gone this day to Axeleigh to arrange the match.

The Squire, good host as always, had heard his friend out. He had pressed on his lean guest more port.

" 'Tis rumored ye'll be going back overseas soon to fight in some other foreign war ye've no business in," he told the Captain bluntly. "Is it true?"

The Captain's dark intent face, with the long white scar on his cheek that lent itself to sinister imaginings, relaxed for a moment. " 'Tis false," he asserted. "I'm staying here until I get Ned's affairs settled. So can we strike a bargain on it, Clifford?"

The Squire fingered his empty glass and bethought him of a letter he had received only this morning, one of a string of letters, all saying the same thing. "Tony," he sighed, and, having said it, could not believe that the words had escaped his lips. "I had rather you brought your own suit, for the girl does not seem to favor Ned."

For once Captain Warburton was completely floored. If the winter sky had opened up and rained down apple blossoms, he could not have been more astonished.

"Did I hear ye aright?" he demanded and his voice was stern.

The Squire brushed a hand over his forehead and wondered what madness had inspired him finally to say the words that had been quivering on his lips for months. " 'Tis just that I've seen a certain light in your eyes when you look at her, Tony, and I just thought—"

"That I'd brush Ned aside and take her for myself? Ah, that's not worthy of you, Clifford."

" 'Tis just that she seems to have no special liking for Ned," pointed out the Squire weakly.

Captain Warburton pounced on that. "Ned tells me she blows hot and she blows cold, he knows not where he stands with her. That was why I came—to clear the air."

The Squire heaved a gusty sigh. "Young girls are inclined to be missish. I'll not pretend I understand them, Tony."

Captain Warburton swung away from him and his hard gray gaze swept round the long drawing room with its cross-legged chairs and handsome Holbein carpet, richly colored and full of angular arabesques, which the Squire called a "Turkey" carpet because, although made in England, it was hand-knotted in the Turkish manner. His gaze passed over the apricot damask drapes. Margaret had chosen those drapes herself in Taunton, he remembered, possibly because they went so well with her own coloring, and taken the fabric home to Axeleigh, where the Squire's wife had not approved them. But in one of the "minor triumphs" that Margaret laughed about, they had gone up anyway.

Behind those drapes he and Margaret had stolen kisses, he had felt her thigh pressed softly against his, her warm sweet breath on his cheeks, breathed the scent of lilies of the valley that always seemed to permeate her flame-red hair. Behind those drapes he had felt his body grow fevered and had to hold himself in check and remind himself that Margaret was young and innocent and not to be taken like one of the casual women of whom he had known so many.

He passed his hand rapidly over his eyes. God, this room held memories for him—all of Axeleigh did for that matter. Which was in the main why he managed to stay away from it, despite his long-standing friendship with Clifford Archer.

It was in this very room that he, having a drink by that fireplace against which Clifford was now leaning, had first laid eyes on Margaret, home only the day before from boarding school. A tall fourteen she had been, but already a woman, as anyone could see from the straining of her silken bodice and the enchantingly wild look in her vivid dark-lashed emerald eyes. She had come dashing into the room, where the two men were talking, with schoolgirl abandon, her burnt orange silk skirts fluttering and her wild flame-colored hair in charming disarray, waving two parts of a broken comb.

"Clifford, I have broken my comb again on this unmanageable hair—" she began. And stopped at sight of her older brother's debonair guest. "I am sorry, I did not know you had company." Her voice had the rustling quality of tall grass brushing sensuously, a voice that subconsciously tore at the senses. Tony Warburton had felt that voice play music all along his spine and he had stared at Margaret as if he had never seen a woman before.

Clifford hastened to present his "little sister, back home at last" and Tony had made her a leg, bowing as elegantly as he knew how. Margaret's smile had flashed with a winsome sparkle of white teeth and she had dropped him a delightful curtsy, learnt at school.

Tony had come back the next day bringing a gift of a handsome repousse silver comb—and his heart as well, although he had hoped that was not so obvious.

His restless gaze moved past the drapes to the green brocade sofa at one end of the long light room. It was before that very sofa, poised gracefully on bended knee, that he had asked fifteen-year-old Margaret to marry him. He had just brought her home from a ball at Huntlands and she was wearing her ball gown, of tawny peach satin with an enormous spill of lace at the elbows and a neckline cut so low that a man could bury his face in it and feel the soft warm pulsing of her pearly white breasts.

Margaret had stared at him for a full minute with her green eyes luminous.

She had said yes. . . .

Captain Warburton yanked himself back to the present. He had come here on behalf of Ned. For Constance. "I'm not in the running, Clifford." He could be as blunt as the Squire when the occasion arose. "But what of Ned?"

"I'll have to sound the girl out, Tony." Smoothly his host turned the conversation down another line, speculating on the state of the King's health, which was reputed to be worsening. Not surprising, they agreed, for surely some seventeen acknowledged mistresses plus a host of other less durable affairs of the heart would wear out even an iron constitution such as the King's! They touched uneasily on the growing unrest and frowned over the fact that the French King Louis XIV was advancing Charles money to keep him going—money that had enabled Charles to disband Parliament.

"That's the worst," declared the Squire gloomily. "A king

of England bought and paid for by France—it galls me, damme, it does!''

Captain Warburton's answering nod was grim. It galled him too—and he knew rather more about the situation than his host. Indeed the discovery of the deal Charles had made with the French king had been for the Captain a disillusioning experience.

"And revoking town charters good these hundreds of years so that he can confer offices on his favorites," grumbled the Squire. His big head gave a shake. "And his brother James next in succession to the throne and James an avowed Catholic! It would be terrible to see the days of the burnings come back like the times of Bloody Mary when a man could smell Protestant flesh burning all across the countryside!"

Captain Warburton nodded, for in politics he was a moderate man, like his host. But even in the midst of such sober thoughts, the cynical Captain had a lancing wit. It flashed now.

"So far Charles has managed to anger the Catholics almost as much as the Dissenters," he pointed out with a grin. "A man who irritates everyone can't be all bad!"

But his host was not to be cajoled into mirth. "James is worse than Charles," he grumbled.

But it was the Captain who coolly stated what they both were thinking. "It is rumored that if James gains the throne, the West Country will rise against him."

"I hope not." The Squire was disturbed. "In time we can surely work things out, if rash young fools don't dash about shooting off guns!"

At the mention of rash young fools, Captain Warburton resumed his pacing, for he had no doubt as to which rash young fool his old friend referred: Ned. This interest in politics had risen recently in Ned, who had never before shown the slightest interest. The Captain listened as the Squire muttered, "We'll need wise heads and a tight rein on our tempers if James comes to the throne." He broke off. "I see the girls are back from their ride. They chose a cold day for it—as did you!''

The Captain turned toward the tall windows that overlooked the long driveway. Through their panes he had a view of the two girls, laughing as they clutched their plumed hats, who rode toward him beneath the wind-whipped branches of the old gnarled oaks. They made a pretty picture with their hair and their velvet skirts flying and the Captain was prompted to exclaim enviously, ''You're a lucky man, Clifford, to have so much beauty in your house. Faith, you live in a veritable flower garden!''

''You sound as flowery as old Scoresby,'' said the Squire dryly. ''Dead now, God rest his soul.''

Tony Warburton laughed. It was a pleasant laugh, rather deep and low in his throat. ''I remember at the Hamiltons' ball this fall Old Scoresby, tipsy and tottering on his feet, proposed a toast to their eyelashes. Called them the Daffodil and the Iris.'' He stopped abruptly, remembering that that same Old Scoresby had once called flame-haired Margaret the Tiger Lily.

The Squire joined him at the window and they stood watching the girls dismount in the wild weather, laughing as they clutched at their blowing skirts, calling out merrily for grooms to take their horses to the stables and rub them down.

The Daffodil and the Iris . . . he'd forgotten Old Scoresby had called them that. But as he looked at his lovely daughter, leaping down from her horse in a single fluid motion, with her glorious daffodil yellow hair blowing in the wind, her wide crystal blue eyes clear as the dew and her fragile apple blossom complexion abloom, he could not help thinking that Old Scoresby had been right.

And was not Constance, he mused, a veritable iris? Hers was a long-stemmed, swaying beauty, and her lustrous cloud of almost blue-black hair surrounded a pale heart-shaped face dominated by enormous dark eyes of a rich velvety purple that could easily be compared to the violet-hued irises that bloomed so lavishly in the gardens of Axeleigh.

44

They both had the sparkle and freshness of spring flowers. But the toastmaker, the Squire thought wryly, had entirely overlooked the stubborn challenge of Pamela's daintily squared jaw and the jaded sophistication of Constance's shadowed glance. Clifford wanted them both to be happy, but he was not sure that was going to be easily achieved. Pamela, he understood, favored Tom Thornton, but Tom was a reckless chaser as yet, not ready to settle down—and Constance seemed bent on eluding Ned.

They heard the front door slam behind them as the wind took it; they heard Pamela's tinkling laugh. Then the two girls swirled into the room from the hall with a swish of velvet skirts and stood there pulling off their gloves, with their cheeks still flushed from the cutting wind outside.

"Captain Warburton, how nice to see you." Sixteen-year-old Pamela, self-assured in her position as sole heiress to Axeleigh Hall, stepped forward charmingly to greet her father's guest.

But seventeen-year-old Constance, heiress to nothing, hesitated a moment before stepping forward warily to greet the tall Captain, for she had guessed his errand.

The Captain's gray eyes kindled as he greeted Constance, struck as always by the feminine aura she radiated. Not true classical beauty perhaps as an artist might paint it, but the illusion of beauty, something compounded of fragility and poise, a sense of drama and an almost overwhelming femininity that held men in thrall.

"Mistress Constance," he said affably, making a courtly bow to her that brought his mane of dark hair sweeping almost to the floor. "Did you enjoy your ride?"

Pamela, when they had first entered and seen the Captain standing beside her father, had thought for a moment that Constance might break and run. For a moment there in the doorway her body had quivered. But now she had quite recovered and she gave him a graceful curtsy.

"Indeed, sir," she replied coolly, and the soft rustle of her voice, catching the Captain as it did in the depths of his bow, coursed through him like a flood. For a moment that soft whirring voice brought Margaret back to him, and the current of misery that went through him in that bleak moment made him hold his bow stiffly a moment too long.

He rose to meet Constance's level contemptuous gaze.

"Will ye stay to dinner, Tony?" asked the Squire.

Captain Warburton, risen from his bow and in control of his thoughts again, gave the dark beauty a regretful look, and explained that he was expected this night at Hawley Grange. This to alert the Squire that he had best be about making arrangements for the betrothal for there were three eligible daughters at Hawley Grange, and a father eager to see them wed!

The Squire chose not to understand the inference, but when the Captain had left and Pamela chuckled, "There goes a suitor for your hand, Constance!" he corrected her. "Speaking in Ned's behalf," he said.

"I don't favor Ned's suit, sir," said Constance quickly.

"Father," said Pamela, going over and giving her father an impulsive hug, "will not force either of us into marriage with anyone we don't want!"

Thank God for that, thought Constance bleakly. *For I'm apt to be on his hands a long time!*

"Captain Warburton does ride a horse well, doesn't he?" Pamela's voice from the window cut into Constance's unhappy thoughts.

"Tony Warburton does everything well," her father told her in some amusement. "And Ned, I don't doubt, is going to be just like him. Dashing fellows, these Warburtons."

"We must change for dinner, Pam." Hoping they had not noticed how this meeting with Captain Warburton had shaken her, Constance made for the door.

"It's beginning to snow," she heard Pamela say. "Look, it's coming down very hard. Someone really should run after Captain Warburton and make him come back—he could get caught in a blizzard and freeze to death, like my Uncle Brandon."

The Squire gave his daughter a stricken look and his gaze flitted to Constance. She stood poised in the doorway, her back rigid. She was glad they could not see her face because she wanted nothing so much as to dash heedlessly after Captain Warburton, to clutch at his stirrup if necessary, to clasp her arms around his riding boot and beg him to return.

But she would not do it!

She would let the lean Captain ride into a blizzard—or into hell if need be—before she would beg him to come back. And it was not just those marriage vows, taken all those months ago, that were holding her back, but something else—something she refused to face. She choked back a sob and would have run on into the hall but that Pamela cut in breathlessly with, "Oh, look who's coming down the drive! It's Tom, and Ned is with him. They've stopped to talk—now the Captain has left them with a wave and they're coming on." Her voice grew joyous. "We can have them to dinner!"

The Squire's face lightened at this glad acceptance of a potential suitor by his daughter but Constance's face grew stormy. Ned appearing hot on the heels of his brother, sweeping in with all the Warburton dash to claim her for himself! She made a little unconscious gesture of rejection for she was very wary of Ned. She found him attractive—but that was only because he was so like Tony. And she would *not* be forced into a farce of a betrothal with him!

Pamela ran to meet them as they came in dusting snow from their clothes. She skimmed over the floor with her slate blue riding skirts pulled up scandalously high about her trim ankles. Her father watched her indulgently. Pamela's exuberance was as much a part of her as her sunbeam hair and prismlike crystal blue eyes that seemed to reflect all the colors of the rainbow.

"Tom! Ned!" She greeted them joyously and all but dragged them into the room with her. "Look what we've snared for dinner, Father! Guests!"

The Squire gave them both a smiling greeting. Ned, he noted, looked worried behind that flashing smile. Like his brother, he had the wild Warburton stamp on him. Tom was a golden Viking with a face made for laughter, yet he'd be a good man in a fight. The Squire approved his daughter's choice.

With a pounding heart, Constance greeted their guests and tried to bear up under Ned's dazzling smile.

"Snow is always lucky for me!" murmured Pamela irrepressibly as she brushed by Constance.

Snow had not always been lucky for *her*, thought Constance, remembering the snows of Yorkshire. She had an uneasy feeling *this* snow would not be lucky for her either.

PART TWO
The Dangerous Lover

Bright honor always drove him, most dangerous of
* men,*
But her soft voice draws him ever back—to take her
* while he can!*
And his love's a goad on the icy road
And his burdened heart threatens to explode!
Can he square it with his conscience? Is he free to love
* again?*

Axeleigh Hall, Somerset,
December 22, 1684

CHAPTER 3

Having greeted Tom and Ned and given Ned a noncommital answer to the question that loomed in the younger man's anxious gray eyes, Captain Warburton parted from them with a wave and continued to ride his great charcoal horse Cinder down the driveway toward the gates of Axeleigh. His broad back beneath his wind-whipped cloak was arrow straight as became the excellent rider he was, but his dark head beneath its broad-brimmed plumed hat, which was now being dusted with snowflakes, was sunk in thought and his expression was stern. This was one battle he should have won easily. Ned was charming, attractive, all that a lad of his age should be and he and the Squire were old friends—there should have been no objection to the match.

But he had bungled it. He told himself bitterly that he had no talent for finding true love—either for himself or anyone else. And that when he did find it, he did not recognize it. Ned would have been well advised to get somebody else to intercede for him.

A good man in a fight, but otherwise he did not account himself for much, did Tony Warburton.

His was a checkered past. At thirteen he had run away to sea and been gone three years. While this had the advantage of keeping him away from England during the Great Plague, it had brought him home into the port of London immediately after the Great Fire and he had viewed his country's capital with some trepidation, seeing it as a charred and smoking city.

He had arrived back at Warwood at about the time six-year-old Margaret was being sent away to boarding school. For a time he had enjoyed a riotous life as a student at Oxford, but the ivied walls of academe were not for him and at eighteen he had departed Oxford for London and then the Continent, where the English ambassador to France had discovered his keen perception and information-gathering capabilities. In time he had become a focal point in England's sketchy intelligence network. At heart an idealist—and made cynical by Charles II's shifting policies—he had soured on the Stuarts all and returned to Somerset in time to meet, in the Squire's drawing room, Margaret Archer back from boarding school.

One look at her blazing beauty and Tony Warburton was aflame. Forgotten were politics and the fate of kings. He pursued the beautiful Margaret with single-minded devotion and before the week was out he had offered her his heart and his hand.

But Margaret, just bursting free of the bonds of a strictly run school for young ladies, was of no mind to settle down at once. She was flattered by the attentions of the dashing Captain and indeed assured him blithely that she felt she would *eventually* choose him from among her admirers—but that did not keep her from flirting with any bright-eyed young fellow who caught her fancy. Captain Warburton, who had loved and left so many women, was led on a wearying chase.

His temper grew short. Twice he called out suitors who, it seemed to him, had pressed too close for Margaret's hand—

and perhaps received encouragement—and nicked them both with his sword as a rebuke.

Margaret was delighted. It was very satisfying to have, as proof of her desirability, the clash of steel to prove that men thought she was worth fighting over.

So at fifteen she became betrothed to the dangerous Captain Warburton.

At fifteen, in the pulsing magic of first love, she let him kiss her in the garden maze at Axeleigh—and kiss her again. And let his fevered lips slide tingling down her bare throat and bosom, let his warm hands urge down the low-cut neckline of her orange lawn gown and kiss the warm bare flesh below.

With a little cry she had seemed to melt into his arms—and with that soft impact melted his up-to-now firm resolve not to take her until after the ceremony.

"Margaret," he had said in a strangled voice, "we can be seen from the house."

"Well, *I* know where we won't be seen—where they'll never even think to look for us!" Her rich laughter lilted and she seized his hand and ducked down, holding her loosened bodice to cover her bared breasts, and led him—for he followed willingly enough in his overheated condition—through the lazy summer air toward the walled private family burial ground.

"Margaret," he protested, laughing. *"Not* a graveyard, surely!"

"Why not?" She gave him a wicked slanted look from her green eyes. " 'Tis well overhung by trees and walled and safe from prying eyes—and besides there's a great blank space that's all myrtle and smells lovely. Clifford says that he and Brandon and I shall be buried there—but of course *I* won't, I'll be buried at Warwood someday. Beside you."

And now both she and Brandon *were* buried there, he thought bitterly, with moss slowly covering the damp marble of their headstones. Captain Warburton passed a hand over his eyes whenever he thought about it, as if to dispel cobwebs. Or perhaps nightmares. For it still seemed unreal to him that Margaret—so young, so beautiful, so reckless and so infinitely desirable—should be other than vividly wonderfully alive.

Certainly she had been wonderfully alive at that moment when she had pulled him with her from the garden maze into the walled enclosure and thrown herself down, laughing, into the fragrant blue-flowered myrtle and held out white arms to him, dimmed by the shadows of the overarching oak branches.

"Tony," she had whispered. *"Why should we wait?"*

Why indeed? Captain Warburton flung off his chivalrous desire to bed his virgin according to the tenets of church and law and flung off his restraint just as he flung off his coat, near tearing the seams as he came out of it.

From the bed of myrtle a winsome Margaret sat up and began coquettishly arranging and rearranging her skirts, making sure her dainty knees were well displayed. "I don't know . . ." she murmured, pulling off one of the blue myrtle blossoms. "Do you really think it is right?"

She had said it lightly, tauntingly, to goad him on—and she was not disappointed. Tony Warburton, down now to shirt and trousers, had fallen to the ground beside her and his strong arms—arms that had ached to hold her so—slid protectively around her.

"Margaret," he said in that soft rich voice that she had come to love so much, "whatever we do alone together is *right*." He kissed her forehead, her hair. "I only waited" —he kissed her cheeks, her soft square jawline—"because I wanted"—his lips found hers, turned sideways, pressed them gently apart, probed within them with a questing tongue that sent showers of feeling bursting through her—"to do what was best for you." He drew back, looked down gravely into her face. "I wanted to do you honor."

It was a simple declaration of love and the fiery girl in his arms responded to it.

"Oh, Tony, you do me great honor!" Her fingers twined into his hair, caressing the back of his neck, causing him to tense. They slid down his back, roving over his ropy back muscles so that the tension built. "You do me the honor of wanting to marry me!" Those fingers were trying to unbutton his cambric shirt now, so that they might quest inside, rove over the heavy satiny muscles of his chest. "And this—oh, *this* is best for me, Tony!" It was almost a wail.

And an invitation.

Tony Warburton was not one to let such an invitation go by. He swept aside the restraining bodice and chemise that only half covered her round young breasts and burrowed his face with a groan in the white valley between them. With expert fingers—for he had had many paramours and reckless adventures with women, married and unmarried, and had learnt all the clever ways that women's clothes were fastened together—he now assisted her skirts to ride up over her hips, slid them along gently, as his lips, now worrying one pink crested nipple and now the other, kept her occupied elsewhere.

So that it was almost with a start that eager young Margaret became suddenly aware that her bare bottom was resting upon a bed of cool damp myrtle in flower and that little grass blades that tried to thrust through the myrtle were tickling between her buttocks.

And with that sudden awareness came another—that Tony Warburton's hard masculinity was pressed against her, was—in a sudden thrust that brought a sharp short cry to her lips—claiming her.

"I'm sorry," he whispered, desisting for the moment even as his long body quivered. "Did I hurt you too much, Meg?"

"No," said Margaret sturdily. "Only get my skirt down under me, Tony—this grass and myrtle is tickling me monstrously!"

He laughed exultantly and in what seemed a single strong gesture lifted her up and swept her skirt down beneath her thighs, laid her gently back upon it. "Meg, Meg," he murmured.

And with those sighing words began an assault upon her feelings that Margaret to her dying day would never forget.

All the skill, all the expertise that he had learnt from a hundred women, Tony Warburton now brought to her—and with it all the gentleness, all the warmth of a lover who has found at last the One Woman to satisfy all his dreams.

Margaret, her senses assaulted on every side, thrilling to his gentle insidious touch, her flesh afire with newfound passion, felt herself swept away and transformed—reborn. No longer girl but woman—*woman*, tingling, thrilling, triumphant.

On the wings of his burgeoning passion she felt herself borne up and up. Her body was filled with delightful new explosions of feeling, each more tempestuous, more soul-shattering than the last. Until in a last great burst of wonder her wild spirit seemed to break free and join with his somewhere beyond the treetops.

Softly, gently, with kisses, he brought her back down with him, down to the flower-scented earth of this secret lair again. "Meg," he was murmuring against her passion-shivered skin. "Meg, oh, Meg."

He naturally presumed she would be willing to have the banns cried that week.

But he was wrong.

His spirited fifteen-year-old sweetheart was of no mind to marry just yet. She was enjoying too much having him as a lover!

And so began a relationship that with any other woman the Captain would have regarded as highly satisfactory. But with Margaret it chafed him, for to him Margaret was—*would always be*—different. He wanted to claim her before all the world not as a mere betrothed, a tenuous some-day arrangement, but as his wife to have and hold. In his heart the lean Captain had taken a mate, just as the lean gray wolves that roam the forest take their mates—for life. And he wanted Margaret to acknowledge that.

She did not.

Steadfastly she refused to have the banns cried. "Not just yet," she would say, with a witching look at the tall frowning Captain. "The Hamiltons' house party is next week." Or "the races at Taunton." Or somebody's wedding. Or christening. Or whatever. Always an excuse.

And the seething Captain had to be content with clandestine meetings and short wild bouts behind latched bedroom doors to which they had stolen away in other people's houses, with laughing intervals in the gardens at Axeleigh Hall, or beneath the trees at Huntlands—and even once beneath the great yew hedge at Warwood, where Margaret any day she chose could become mistress.

Heedless Margaret was driving him wild. She went her way with abandon and it seemed she could not get enough of dancing and parties. Captain Warburton kept hoping she would get pregnant and decide of a sudden to marry him—but she did not.

Instead she seemed to thrive on clandestine meetings and flaunting her lover. For her, nothing seemed really to have changed except that she reveled in having Tony Warburton clasp her to his breast and pour out his love for her. She still flirted outrageously and had it not been for the Captain's mounting reputation with the sword, which made most recipients of her slanted smiles extremely wary, she would have gotten into far worse scrapes than she did.

Tony Warburton ground his teeth as Margaret's satin skirts swirled gaily by him at balls—in the company of somebody else. As other encouraged swains drank impassioned toasts to her eyelids, her instep, her slippers, her flaming hair. And on a summer afternoon at Huntlands matters all came to a head.

It was a day when Margaret was at her reckless worst, for the night before in the attics of Hawley Grange, during a respite in the dancing, Tony had seized her in an ungentle grip.

"D'you think I'm going to spend my life creeping up dark stairs like a thief?" he had grated, bringing her lithe young body hard up against his own. "Don't you realize that sooner or later we're bound to be discovered in each other's arms? Do you want our first child to be born in scandal?"

Margaret, who had already come to the same conclusion

57

and who had actually lured him up here to tell him that she was ready at last to marry him, took exception to his tone.

"Don't hold me so tight!" she exclaimed. "You're hurting me!"

He relaxed his grip, fighting off the sweet opiate of the senses that always came over him just from touching her. She was like a strong drug, he thought bitterly. Addictive—and not good for him. But she *would be* good for him—once they were married!

"Hush," she cautioned nervously. "I think I hear someone coming. One of the servants probably—they sleep up here."

He shook her in frustration. "That's what I mean, Meg. We can't go on like this. I want you in my bed—at Warwood, where you belong."

His voice had a carrying quality. It irritated Margaret that he might be overheard. She was not listening to him—she was listening to those soft half-heard footsteps. Now they had gone away. She relaxed.

"Oh, Tony," she sighed. "Can't we just forget everything for a few moments of bliss?"

And Tony Warburton, victim of his own ardent desires, had indeed forgotten everything for a blissful joining that fulfilled his fondest hopes.

But afterward he had stood up while she—looking fetchingly disheveled—smoothed down her silken skirts and gave him a demure smile in the moonlight that lanced in through one of the vast dormers. "Meg," he said through clenched teeth, "you must *set the date*."

And something perverse in red-haired Margaret had caused her to skip away from him, crying back over her shoulder, "Oh, Tony, not just yet. Tomorrow is the picnic at Huntlands and after that there's—"

Tony Warburton had not followed to hear what came after that. He had picked up the old feather bed on which they had lain and thrown it against the low rafters so hard that it burst and feathers filled the air.

Margaret was already dancing down the stairs.

For the rest of the evening Captain Warburton ignored her, choosing instead to drink deep of his host's wine, and to watch from beneath lowering brows as his flirtatious betrothed whirled about the floor, favoring him from time to time with a tossed head and a malicious smile.

Reckless Margaret had not recognized her danger.

She had arrived at the picnic at Huntlands the next day determined to humble Tony. Indeed she had started out early so that Tony, when he arrived at Axeleigh Hall to squire her to Huntlands, would find her gone—as a punishment for pointedly ignoring her last night after their argument at Hawley Grange. On arrival at Huntlands she found herself immediately swept into a laughing crowd that included Ralph Pembroke, who was of a mind to wrest laughing Margaret from Warburton's grasp—after all, a betrothal could easily be broken. When the frowning Captain arrived, she merely waved at him.

Margaret flaunted her femininity that day with reckless abandon, and to some she seemed like a firefly, glowing with her own light, flitting and sparkling against the dark backdrop of foliage of the ancient oaks and holly.

Captain Warburton had not been amused.

In late afternoon, after a game of forfeits, there had been dancing on the greensward and Captain Warburton had been even less amused when Margaret in her light copper silk dress had whirled away with Ralph Pembroke and disappeared behind a screen of holly. He had left the dancers, lengthened his stride, and gone in pursuit. One or two of the guests had nudged each other and turned to watch him, muttering there'd be hell to pay if Tony Warburton found Ralph Pembroke taking liberties with wild young Margaret!

They were not disappointed.

What Tony Warburton saw on the other side of the thick branching holly caused him to spring forward with a growl in his throat.

For Margaret was standing clasped in Ralph Pembroke's arms and Pembroke was kissing her.

Ralph heard the crunch of Tony's boots breaking fallen twigs and holly leaves and broke free, almost upsetting Margaret, who staggered back painfully into the holly.

This time there was no gentlemanly slapping of gloves across the face, no exchange of challenges, no seconds called for. With a snarl, Tony Warburton, his nerves rubbed raw by Margaret's dalliance, leaped for Pembroke's throat. Pembroke went down, clawing at his sword. He brought his elbow up in the Captain's face and was happy to see that devilish countenance snap away from him, but a moment later the Captain's hard fist dusted across his jawbone with enough force to break an average jaw.

But Ralph Pembroke's was no average jaw. He was built like a castle keep. With a herculean effort he managed to throw his assailant off and stagger to his feet, dragging out his sword as he did so.

"So that's how ye want it, is it?" In an instant the Captain's sword had flashed out too.

"No, Tony!" White-faced, Margaret wrenched loose her hair from the spiny clutch of the holly leaves. Too late she realized what her recklessness had unleashed. "I was but paying a forfeit to Ralph for—"

Her voice was lost in the clash of steel on steel. Neither combatant heard her. They were concentrating with fierce intensity upon each other, for Ralph Pembroke had been nettled by the young lady's preference for the dashing Captain and was eager to down him, and Tony's gorge was up and at that moment he thirsted for nothing so much as for Pembroke's blood. In his left hand, Pembroke brought out a dagger, a wicked-looking twelve-inch blade, and the Captain retaliated by bringing out his own dagger, just as wicked.

The clash of blades alerted the revelers on the other side of the holly and they streamed toward the sound. They found the pair locked in combat, fighting with sword and dagger, circling each other warily, plunging in, parrying, leaping back.

"Warburton! Pembroke! Are ye gone mad?" cried the

elder Thornton, aghast. " 'Tis one thing to call a man out, formally and with seconds, but to skirmish this way in the bushes—if one of ye kills the other, he'll like as not be charged with murder!''

Neither combatant paid the slightest attention.

"As your host, I feel responsible!" roared Roger Thornton, pulling out his own blade.

He might have interposed that blade to separate them had not Margaret just then created her own diversion. No one had been noticing her, all eyes had been riveted on the duelists— Pembroke the heavier and stronger, Warburton steel hard, tempered and experienced and with a longer reach. Wagers as to the outcome were being murmured among the gentlemen, while the ladies gave little shrieks of horror every time the blades clashed and the two angry faces spun close to each other.

Having freed herself of the holly that had torn her light silk dress, ruined her coiffure and scratched her skin, Margaret had come to the same conclusion as her host—Tony looked in a mood to do murder and *she* had brought him to it. And Ralph Pembroke, who had been pursuing her for months, was in no mood to back down. Even as Roger Thornton bellowed his admonitions to the pair, she was taking action.

Looking about for what was at hand, she seized a heavy piece of wood, part of a fallen tree branch, lifted it high above her head and brought it crashing down on the swords just as they clashed again. Pembroke's blade skittered from his hand to the ground and Tony's was nearly knocked from his.

But Margaret was not finished. As she flung the wood she followed it with her body so that she seemed to fly at the flashing steel almost simultaneously with her missile.

Out of the corner of his eye, Tony saw her coming. Pembroke's angry and astonished face was nearly nose to nose with his own at that moment, for in his confusion Pembroke was not sure just what had hit him. He took a wild slash with his dagger at Tony's face in the same moment that

Tony brought up his blade and threw his right arm to the side in an effort to ward Margaret off and keep her from catapulting headfirst into the flashing daggers.

Margaret was thrown free and landed, skirts swirling above a froth of lacy chemise, some distance away.

But saving her had cost Tony something. It had put him in line for Ralph Pembroke's dagger and that jabbing dagger described a jagged course from just below his left eye down nearly to his mouth before Tony's own dagger plunged into Pembroke's neck and caused him to jerk spasmodically away.

Both men staggered back, covered with blood, to be seized and disarmed by the excited onlookers—Captain Warburton by his host and his host's sixteen-year-old-son, Tom, and Ralph Pembroke by two of his boon companions from Bridgwater.

Margaret, on her knees now on the grass where she had been flung, thought for a horrified moment that Tony had lost his eye. She was near fainting when she realized he had not, that he was holding a bloody kerchief to the wound and had shaken free of the two men who held him and was striding toward Ralph Pembroke, whose condition was serious.

"I had not meant to wound him so badly," Tony Warburton muttered. "I but meant to teach him a lesson."

"We all saw Mistress Margaret enter the fray," said Tom Thornton's father heavily, for the way Pembroke was bleeding, he half expected him to expire on the spot.

Captain Warburton, who had some experience with wounds in his eventful life, pushed through and insisted on trying his skill.

" 'Twas a fair fight," gasped out Pembroke, willingly submitting to the Captain's ministrations—or anyone else's who could staunch the flow of his blood.

Cleverly, Tony managed it.

"Hold very still," he counseled softly. "No, he's to drink nothing"—he waved away the leather flask of liquor someone held out—"for 'twill only excite his blood and make the wound bleed worse. I saw a worse wound in the Netherlands and the fellow who had it held it—so. He was determined not to die. He held rigid for hours and eventually the blood did clot by itself.''

The fellow had been himself.

A doctor was sent for—but who knew when he would arrive? In any event the battle was over and most of the guests wandered off to resume their revelry.

Margaret was not among them. Disheveled and pale, she crouched by Pembroke, silently willing him to live—not only for himself, although she liked him well enough, but so that Tony would not be accounted a murderer.

Tony Warburton mistook her silent vigil for real concern. A lover's concern. He watched her bitterly. Meg, *his* Meg—at least he had thought her his—and that blustery Pembroke fellow!

Eventually Pembroke was deemed fit enough to be carried from the site and Margaret got up stiffly, brushing holly leaves from her dress. She turned to Tony, who had also stayed nearby.

"I think he will live," she said tonelessly, for she felt exhausted, drained.

"Yes. I think so," he agreed, watching her.

They stood silently surveying each other for a moment. Margaret was about to blurt out a heartfelt apology, but Captain Warburton was the first to speak.

"I wish you joy of him, Meg," he said bitterly and whirled on his heel and strode away.

For a moment Margaret stood stock-still. Then, as what Tony had said sank in on her, she gathered up her skirts and began to run after him. "Tony—wait!" But a servant, ordered in an undertone while Margaret's gaze was fixed on the fallen Pembroke, had already brought up Captain Warburton's horse and before she could reach him the Captain had swung up into the saddle and galloped away without a backward look.

There wasn't a horse there that could catch Cinder. No use trying to follow! With a pounding heart she watched him go, for that afternoon had wrought a change in Margaret. She repented her teasing of Tony and promised herself she would surprise him by setting the date for their wedding—she would tell him tomorrow when he rode over as usual to Axeleigh.

But Tony Warburton did not ride over to Axeleigh on the morrow or for many morrows to come. Instead he rode for Warwood, but paused there only long enough to change horses and fill his saddlebags. He rode that night for London and took ship for the Continent.

His days as a lover, he told himself grimly, were over. He would take his women where he found them and leave them there when he left. No more flinging his heart beneath the slippers of some heartless wench who'd lead him to believe she loved him and then turn to somebody else!

But he thanked God most fervently when he was informed by letter that Ralph Pembroke was recovering nicely. Lord, he'd meant to best Pembroke, but not to kill him! And he laid that at Margaret's door too, that he had nearly killed a man for her—*and how she must love the fellow, to have hurled herself into the swords like that! It was a miracle she had not been hurt.*

Night after sleepless night as he roved the Continent he pondered the perfidy of women. He was out of touch with Warwood; his mail reached him infrequently and it was six months before he received Margaret's letter. His jaw worked as he stared down at the familiar handwriting and with a violent gesture he flung it unread into the fireplace and watched it burn. So much for Margaret, who was doubtless signing herself "Margaret Pembroke" by now and was writing to him only to clear her conscience!

He plunged again into his intelligence activities, which led him deep into France, for he was convinced that a French king who considered himself a "lieutenant of God" and was already persecuting French Dissenters, a king moreover who was assembling the most formidable army in Europe, would bring no good to his neighbors across the Channel. It alarmed Tony Warburton that Louis had invaded Dutch territory, and

April of 1677 found him at Saint-Omer, where the French were locked in battle with William of Orange, a man the Captain grimly admired for having opened the Dutch sluices and halting the French advance. But Tony Warburton, intent on making a full report, had edged too close to the battle. A stray shot found his thigh and he spent a slow time recovering. Fierce raged the seas and all of his mail went astray—or sank. It was months before he again received mail from Warwood and learnt from his father's own hand—along with belated news of the startling ''Popish Plot''—that Margaret was still unmarried, considered herself still betrothed to him, although ''deeply hurt'' that he had not answered any of her letters, and that Ralph Pembroke had been wed September last to a great heiress in Wiltshire (though nothing for looks) and had removed to her home there, reputed to be over a hundred rooms! Margaret had shrugged when told about Pembroke's impending nuptials and was quoted as saying that fortune hunters usually got what they deserved and Ralph Pembroke would be no exception, that his wife-to-be was as awkward as a scullery maid among the fine china, and that he would live to see all of his children trip over the furniture legs, elegant though those legs might be.

Tony Warburton had grinned at that. His Meg had always had a biting tongue! But it stunned him to learn that she was still waiting. *How had he so mistook her?*

Nevertheless, all the love he had ever felt for her rushed back to warn him and it was a restless Captain Warburton who, with one leg still moving a bit stiffly from his latest wound, took ship for England.

Having disdained to write to Margaret that he was coming—faith, he would deliver himself to her door instead of some scribbled parchment!—Captain Warburton arrived in his native land to find his world changed. William of Orange had married Mary, eldest daughter of that James, Duke of York, whose eventual ascent to the English throne was regarded by the Squire of Axeleigh with such foreboding. In Somerset he was shocked to learn that both his parents were dead and Ned returned from Oxford and trying to cope with matters at Warwood.

It was from Ned's lips that he learned that which turned his saturnine face pale beneath its tan: Margaret, *his* Margaret, was ill of the smallpox in Bath, caught while visiting some people named Forbush there. But, Ned assured him anxiously, the latest word was that she was expected to recover.

Tony Warburton, dusty from his journey, paused only to mount a fresh horse. "I'm for Bath," he called back to Ned. "And Margaret. Hold things here for my return."

"But ye cannot!" cried Ned belatedly. "Half the city is down with the pox!"

It is doubtful Tony heard him. If he had, it would not have mattered. Nothing would have kept him from Margaret at that moment—nothing short of death.

He was banging the Forbush knocker when he learnt the news—news told him through the door panels by a weeping voice he recognized as belonging to Margaret's old nurse.

"Ye came too late!" she cried. "My lady's dead." And burst into tears again.

The iron knocker pounded again. "Let me in! I will see her."

"No—oh, no! None are allowed in. This house is infected!"

On the verge of kicking down the door that separated him from his Margaret—alive or dead—Tony Warburton was gradually quieted by an outburst of words from the old nurse, which told him of the virulence of the disease that had quite exhausted Margaret's frail frame. A frailty, her injured tone implied, brought on by Tony Warburton's defection.

That Margaret had never been either frail or easily exhausted by anything never reached the level of his consciousness. He was borne down by one thing and one thing only—she was dead. His loved and lovely Meg was dead. And she had died believing the worst of him—that he had deserted her. She had died without ever knowing how much he still loved her.

In black misery Tony Warburton had ridden home to Warwood—a Warwood draped in the black cloth of mourning. In black misery he had sat himself down in the echoing reaches of the great hall and stared into the fire. It seemed to him in his darkness of the spirit that everyone he had ever loved was dead, snatched away from him. Troop movements, arms buildups, secret alliances, all seemed of a sudden trivial.

His life had ended: Margaret was gone.

Even his younger brother, Ned, with his jovial ways, could not jolt Tony Warburton out of the mire of despond into which he had sunk.

"If only he'd drink," muttered Ned to his friends, for Ned was convinced that with liquor to warm your blood, you could surmount anything. "But he doesn't even do that—he just sits there."

But when little Lucy Weatherby and her parents had come by the house to invite the gentlemen of Warwood to a ball, surprisingly Tony had risen up and accepted. He had gone to the ball as in a dream—indeed he felt he had been dreaming ever since his ship had docked in England, one long nightmare. But he had been seeking balm for his lacerated heart: he had danced with his host's daughter and had so turned the little Weatherby girl's head that she was madly in love with him before the evening was half over.

She had maneuvered him into the moonlit garden and—as she had hoped—he kissed her there, a perfunctory kiss, meaningless. But Lucy Weatherby had flung her arms around his neck in such a surprising display of passion that he had stared down at her in wonder.

And when the ball was over and the little Weatherby girl should have been in bed, she stole out to the stables, swore the stableboys to secrecy, and mounted up and followed him home, just shadowing the two men as he and Ned talked on their way back from the Weatherbys' ball.

She slipped into the house unnoticed, and when Captain Warburton, scorning a candle, came into the dark bedroom and moved about tossing off his clothes, needing no light to keep his shins from connecting with the familiar furniture, he noted nothing amiss.

Until he got into bed and felt a warm, naked, yielding shape beside him.

Captain Warburton recoiled with a surprised oath from whatever human creature he had touched and a small hurt voice said, "Tony, aren't you glad to see me?"

It was little Lucy Weatherby's voice, and although Tony Warburton knew he shouldn't do it, the state of his mind was such that he took what the gods—and little Lucy Weatherby—offered. He joined her in the big bed, and gained a brief forgetfulness in her arms.

The next day he did the Right Thing. He escorted a blushing Lucy back to her father's house, explained that in a gust of passion he had made off with her, offered for her, and hoped for an early crying of the banns.

Ned had told him gloomily that he was making a mistake, for to Ned's view supplanting Margaret with Lucy Weatherby was to exchange a lioness for a mouse, but the Captain was in no mood to listen to anyone. He wanted to wall off his past and begin again. And now he was going to do it—with sparrowlike Lucy Weatherby.

He gave it a good try.

But two months later, during a lingering damp spell, when his bride caught a deep cold that turned into pneumonia and she died in his arms, Tony Warburton looked up at the ceiling, and in his mind past the ceiling and through the roof into the leaden sky. He listened to the patter of the rain on the roof slates and tried to fathom what fate had in mind for him. It was obvious that a vengeful heaven meant to allow him no one close, no one of his own to love.

That night began his true bachelorhood, for he was a confirmed loner after that.

It began something else. His nerves, which had been shocked into numbness by the triple loss of Margaret and his parents, were triggered back into pain again by the loss of his frail young bride. At last, there alone in his bedchamber, by the fire, he could put his head in his hands and feel hot tears sting his eyelids.

But it was for Margaret, his real love, that he wept. . . .

And now his friend Clifford's quiet question had jolted him into facing his real feelings. He had felt a sense of shame when his bride had died—shame that he had not loved her more—but not a sense of loss. That aching sense of loss was reserved for Margaret. He had doomed himself to bachelorhood on that day, for—unlike the Squire, who felt women were false and not to be trusted—Tony Warburton felt that he did not deserve a wife.

When he had first realized how much Constance attracted him, Ned had been already so far gone on her that pursuing the matter in his own behalf would have seemed unconscionable—it still did.

But the Squire had seen through him. And now he wondered if others had—Constance herself for instance. And perhaps despised him for it. Certainly that was a cold look she had given him. Impossible to read anything in those velvet eyes of hers, he lost himself in their violet depths every time he looked at her.

It seemed ironic that after all these years the ice around his heart had melted and given him a new love—one who would be forever denied him. Loyalty to Ned demanded that. His jaw set as it had the day they were probing in his leg for the bullet and having trouble finding it, and the expression in his eyes was just as hard and mirrored as much suffering as it had then—plus spreading horror and a sense of shock.

He could have done much more back there! He could have tried to win the girl for Ned after she had arrived. There were ways to kindle interest.

But he had not, he told himself with remorse. Instead he had fled the scene the moment she arrived because in his subconscious he had wanted no one to guess what up to now he had not admitted even to himself:

He desired Constance. He wanted to clasp that velvet form in the crook of his arm and bend back that slender waist and let her dark hair fall like a cloud of silk over his arm while he showered her with kisses. He wanted to sweep her up and carry her away and tear off her clothes and bring her breathless and enchanted to his bed. He wanted to hear the silken rasp of her voice—like the whisper of bedsheets—as he made love to her. He wanted her body. He wanted her soul.

Dear God in heaven, what manner of man was he that he would *allow* himself to feel so about a girl of whom his brother was so deeply enamored? Better had he been struck down on the battlefield than face so shameful a realization.

But having faced it at last he felt, along with a pervading sense of doom, almost a feeling of relief. The dark cloud that had been overhanging his spirit had been identified.

Its name was Love.

He was in love with beautiful Constance.

CHAPTER 4

With unexpected guests for dinner—and one of those guests Tom, which in itself was enough to set her young heart pounding—Pamela dashed up the massive Jacobean staircase that had been installed by her grandfather, well ahead of Constance.

"Tabby!" she called impatiently down the dark servants' stair that wound down toward the big kitchen.

At her call there was a clatter of feet on the stair treads and a young fresh-faced girl and a big long-haired tabby cat erupted into the corridor, almost colliding with Constance, who stepped aside hastily to let them pass.

"Oh, Puss, I don't need *you* to help me dress! I need *Tabitha*!" She swept the big coppery brown cat with his dense black markings into her arms and carried him into her bedchamber. Puss, happy to be held in those arms, purred loudly. "I wonder why he always comes when I call you?"

Tabitha, swishing her brown homespun skirts in Pamela's wake, refrained from telling her that cook called "Tabby!"

when she wanted to feed Puss, since he was usually in her company.

Pamela tossed Puss lightly to the feather bed, where his weight promptly made him sink down into the coverlet until only his broad furry head with its tufted ears and round full cheeks, decorated outrageously with sooty black swirls, stood out. His green eyes adoring, the cat gave a spring from bed to floor and sidled over on his short striped legs to rub his massive furry body, brindled and smudged in black and copper, against Pamela's velvet riding skirts.

"That cat's leaving his long hairs on your skirt." Tabitha eyed the slate blue velvet doubtfully.

"Oh, it's no matter, Tabby," laughed Pamela. "Puss just wants to show his affection."

The little maidservant smiled. Puss, she knew, could do no wrong where Pamela was concerned. He had the run of the house.

Puss had arrived at Axeleigh as a half-grown kitten on the same day as Tabitha—a day of quick drenching spring rains and sudden sunshine. They had arrived from different directions: Tabitha walking sturdily on her worn leather shoes from Wells, where she, youngest of ten children, had quarreled with her parents and vowed she'd not endure being bound for seven years to a gray-bearded baker whose interest in her was hotter than the cakes in his ovens. Half-grown Puss had strolled in from his most recent residence, a dairy farm where a whole platoon of sturdy black and white tomcats, all of them built like barrels, had threatened his life daily if he went near the wooden milk bowl, for they saw in genial Puss a future rival for the favors of the pussycats who sidled around the barn at milking time swishing their tails seductively amid the rustling hay.

Hospitable Axeleigh had welcomed both, and Pamela had been struck that day by the similarity in coloring of these two wayfarers—for Puss's coppery brown undercoat with its black overmarkings gave him sooty undertones near to the color of Tabitha's soot-stained brown homespun kirtle (for the girl has been cleaning out the hearth on the occasion of her last quarrel at home and Tabitha's coarse coppery hair exactly matched the shade of the cat's thick undercoat. They both had big expressive wary green eyes—Puss with permanent black furry markings etched around his, Tabitha with less permanent blackish purple markings given her by her father when she defied him.

Pamela, who'd been riding and was turning to go in through the big stone-arched front door, had caught a glimpse of Puss coming down the drive, a bit bedraggled and walking on tired paws but still with a jaunty wave to his fluffy ringed tail and with his head uplifted hopefully.

That hope sprang from the tired cat's near encounter with a careening cartwheel. Puss had darted into a bush to avoid the wheel and found there a delightful though small repast in the form of a half-eaten chicken leg which the cart's driver lost as he tried to keep the light cart from overturning between the stone gateposts that marked the entrance to Axeleigh's drive.

Thus encouraged, Puss sauntered down the long driveway where Pamela, who had gone swiftly inside after sighting him, met him with a wooden bowl of milk which she set down before him. Puss gave her a questioning look from his big green eyes and warily approached the bowl. No fierce tomcats leapt forward to cut him off. Hunger overcoming caution, Puss hurried to the bowl and swallowed the milk in big laps while Pamela gently kneaded his thick fur with her fingers.

When he had finished she was still petting him and Puss had decided he liked it. He purred and fell into step with her when she picked up the bowl and said, ''Let's go to the kitchen and get cook to give us some scraps!''

Midway there, they bumped into Tabitha, who had tried to take a shortcut across a meadow, lost her way in a fringe of woods and blundered by mistake into the gardens of Axeleigh.

Pamela had stopped in surprise. "Who are you?" she asked the defiant-faced girl with the sooty skirt and two black eyes who had just stumbled out of the box hedge.

Tabitha, tottering on her feet from fatigue, had still remembered to curtsy. "My name's Tabitha. I'm looking for work." Her green eyes flashed their defiance, for she'd been rejected for work all along the road: too young, too small and spindly, not strong enough—all uneasy excuses, for those bruises proclaimed her a runaway most like and no one wanted to be responsible for taking her in and then having some angry master reclaim her as his bond servant. Little and thin she was, but her lifted head and determined face proclaimed that if they'd not take her in here, footsore as she was, she'd just journey on until someone did.

Pamela, who had spirit, liked spirit in others. She gave Tabitha a sympathetic look. "Would you like a hot cross bun?" she asked. "Cook just made some." Seeing Tabitha's green eyes light up, she motioned her graciously to a long wooden bench. Tabitha ate a whole plate of hot cross buns and downed two brimming tankards of milk while Pamela watched and the big brown tabby cat washed his paws and purred. Afterward, Tabitha told her earnestly about her problems and how no one would take her in because they guessed she was a runaway.

"Then we'll say you're an orphan and don't want to be sent to an orphanage and so you seek employment. I'm sure Father will let you stay and help cook in the kitchen. Would you like that?"

At that point Tabitha's green eyes were fixed on Pamela as adoringly as the cat's.

They both stayed. At first Pamela wanted to call them both "Tabby" but her father insisted some distinction must be made. Why not call the cat—

"Puss!" cried Pamela.

"But the cat's a tom," protested her father. "Why not call him Tom?"

There was only one Tom in Pamela's world and that was

Tom Thornton. "I'm going to call him Puss," she said stubbornly. And Puss the young tomcat became.

That was four years ago and now both tomcat and servingmaid could scarce remember having lived any other place. Tabby sang as she worked and Puss, now a full-grown, full-furred and formidable tomcat with a thick cobby body, a deep chest, long wavy whiskers and a set of handsome claws which he kept meticulously clean and razor sharp, strolled on broad paws beneath the oaks, scouted out the big stables for rats, occasionally warred with the peafowls, and sunned himself on the wide sills of the big mullioned windows.

Puss was "Mistress Pamela's cat" according to the servants, who spoiled him just as they spoiled the Squire's daughter, and when Constance arrived, Tabitha unofficially became maid to both girls, helping them in and out of their enveloping overdresses and wide petticoats and tight bodices with their myriad hooks. She was even learning to do coiffures—Constance, who had a knack for such things, was teaching her. But her first loyalty was—and always would be, just like Puss's—to Pamela. For it was Pamela's open-hearted kindness that had welcomed them to Axeleigh and given them both a home.

Now Pamela turned to Tabby. "I want to wear my best-looking gown down to dinner, Tabby."

"Yes," said Tabby wisely. "I saw Master Tom come in."

Pamela gave her a chiding look. "Nothing to do with Tom Thornton," she insisted. "I want to dress well in celebration of—of my father's birthday."

"Oh?" muttered Tabby, who had heard cook say the Squire's birthday was next week. But if dainty Pamela wanted to keep up the fiction that she wasn't interested in Tom Thornton, she, Tabby, would help her. "Your pink damask perhaps?"

"Oh, yes!" Pamela dashed over to the big cherry clothespress that stood in one corner of the room and pulled out a stiff strawberry pink damask alight with silver threads. "That's a wonderful suggestion!" Nudging her judgment was the

75

interest Tom had shown in Melissa Hawley at Hawley Grange and how only last week she'd seen him gallop his horse to catch up with Nellie Haycock's carriage—and both girls had been wearing pink at the time, although neither of them so sumptuous a gown as this.

Her crystal blue eyes sparkled like prisms as she and Tabby searched for exactly the right petticoat—and found one, of stiffened deep rose velvet heavily worked with silver flowers. When she had donned both, the stiff material stuck out in angular lines from her young figure. Tabby gave her a doubtful look. "Can you walk down the stairs in all that?" she wondered. "Me, I'd trip!"

"So long as I keep the train behind me," caroled Pamela, kicking aside the small train with a satin slipper. She'd have risked it even if there was no railing, for the mirror gave her back a sparkling sight of rich eye-catching material. She twirled, the better to view her magnificence. "Don't you think I should add velvet rosettes at the elbows where the lace falls away? I don't want to look *plain,* Tabby."

Tabitha nodded and rummaged for rosettes to pin onto the already overladen gown. If lovable Mistress Pam wanted to be bedecked like a queen, she'd help her. They were still pinning on rosettes and ribands at strategic places when Constance stopped by to collect Pamela and go down to dinner.

Constance herself was garbed in a lissome gown of plum velvet, cut with dramatic simplicity. She gave Pamela's glittering effect a slightly startled look, but chose not to comment, and together they walked down the broad Jacobean staircase into the great hall where the gentlemen stood waiting to take them in to dinner.

The dignity of Pamela's elegant advance was somewhat marred by her sudden shout of "Puss! Oh, no, Puss!" And her sudden swoop upon the big tabby cat who had leaped onto the pile of Christmas greenery the servants had brought in and was busy sharpening his claws there. She carried him mewing down the hall and handed him to Tabitha, who took charge of him with a wide grin.

Tom, with the others, watched this little tableau tolerantly, then turned, quirking a burnished gold eyebrow at the Squire.

"Stebbins tells me Lord Peacham's coach has been cutting up your driveway recently," he observed.

"In and out, in and out," agreed the Squire in a dry voice.

"I'd heard he'd been struck down with gout these last five months and never left Taunton?"

" 'Tis not the father but the son who haunts our gates," his host hastened to assure him.

"Indeed?" Tom gave Ned a droll look. "Come to pay court, has he? Constance, is there anyone has *not* asked for you?"

Conscious of Pamela's sudden frown, Constance spoke up. "Oh, 'tis Pamela, not me, he comes to see."

"And indeed I may take him," put in Pamela recklessly, furious at Tom's calm assumption that it would be Constance Dick Peacham was after. "For he'll be *Lord* Peacham when his father dies!" Her lifted chin invited Tom to match that.

Tom's gaze focused on her in amazement. "You'd want a title enough to marry a fellow who stumbles over his own feet? And who can barely stay astride his horse?"

"The Honorable Richard does not need to stay astride," laughed Constance. "He travels in his father's coach."

"Which must jar his teeth loose," interposed Ned equably. "The roads to Taunton being what they are." For discovering that Constance was not the attraction, he had warmed to Dick Peacham.

"Ah, but consider his magnificence," mocked Tom. "A gilded coach wheeling up to the door—see, it has already snared Pam!"

That he should take this bantering attitude! Pamela flushed. "Dick is but one of my suitors," she declared airily.

As they went in to dinner, Clifford Archer gave his daughter a thoughtful look. Interested in young Peacham, was she? Well, the name was old, the family wealthy, and if she chose to marry a bumbling lad, he supposed he would not stand in the way. Of course, he'd always hoped that Tom . . . In his reverie he did not notice that Tom laughed a bit uncomfortably as he studied Pamela, whose pretty face seemed to emerge from her stiff high-necked finery like a little girl's dressed up in her mother's clothes.

Tom bent over her as he pulled back her chair. "You're not ready for marriage, Pam," he said almost roughly.

"Oh, am I not?" she challenged him. "Well, I'm going to let Dick Peacham propose to me twice more. And *then*—" She tossed her daffodil golden curls and let the words drift off, trying to give Tom the clear impression that she would accept Peacham.

The Squire heard that. "I will be glad when they have both chosen and have done with it. What's the gossip, Tom? In your rovings, you always glean some."

Tom shrugged his broad shoulders. For some reason he was at a loss for conversation tonight.

That evening was a nightmare for Constance. Pamela, forgetting she was angry with Tom, became her usual self again. But Ned Warburton, driven to mightier efforts by the Squire's refusal to award him Constance at once—which had been tersely reported to him by Captain Warburton on the driveway—kept his attention riveted on the graceful dark-haired girl who sat stiff and pale, only toying with her roast capon and oysters.

"I know you went to school in London but were you born there?" he asked.

"Yes," replied Constance, and the very name of London brought back in a rush the narrow streets, the crowded overhanging half-timbered houses, the noisy hawkers and the creak of carts and coaches, the heavy pea-soup fogs and the ever-present smell of wood smoke and sea coal. And the magic of frost fairs on the frozen Thames and blooming gardens in the spring—it had been an exciting place for a child, had London.

"Your mother's people, were they Londoners?"

Constance sighed. "My mother's people were all dead by the time I came along. They had perished of the Plague while my mother visited in the West Country."

"Ah-h-h . . ." Ned's voice hovered on a sigh, for although he had been but four years old when the Great Plague stalked the land, there was hardly a family in England but whose lives had been touched by it. "So your mother was left with an empty house when the Plague marched on?" he prodded helpfully.

"She was left with no house at all!" Constance's voice was tart. "For the Great Fire that ravaged London the next year burnt her house to the ground and destroyed everything in it. Nothing was saved." Her mother had been bitter about that. She had been in the West Country herself, but it had seemed to her that the servants—who had fled at the first whiff of smoke—should have saved something, some of the plate, some of the fine vellum volumes her father had collected, her mother's delicate embroideries—*something*.

Ned's bland young face was sympathetic. His mouth was not as firm, his hands not of the same fine cut as the Captain's, she thought. But for all of that he was a fine-looking young man in his scarlet coat and buff vest and trousers. A man any girl would be proud to have—except herself, of course.

"Your father's people, were they from London too?"

"No, from Yorkshire." His questions were getting too close. She saw the Squire's gaze fixed upon her at the head of the table and said quickly, "Do you think it will snow all night? Pam is mad to build a snow fort and pelt us all with snowballs!"

"It will be Tom and me against you and Ned," declared Pamela merrily from the other side of the table.

"Good, I'll take you on," laughed Ned, looking at Tom.

"Before breakfast, then?" Pamela was eager to keep them for the night.

Constance grimaced inwardly. The thought of doing anything before breakfast always appalled her. She had a reluctance to rise, inherited no doubt from her father, that made her a child of the night, at her best in the evening hours, while sunny Pamela was the very opposite, a true daughter of the light.

The Squire cleared his throat and brought the conversation briefly around to politics, but his guests backed warily away from that. Pamela brought up the subject of parties, and then a heated discussion of which was the fastest horse in the Valley carried them through dessert—custard and the delicious little pastries whose making Pamela always supervised.

Pamela was a charming combination, thought Constance, studying the golden girl who sat across from her. Half tomboy, half homemaker, part child, part woman. In her stiff pink damask gown, so heavily stitched with silver thread that it blazed silver in the candlelight, she looked strikingly young. And yet, in her own way, she was deeply in love with Tom. She worshipped him.

And Tom loved his freedom and flirted with every attractive skirt that flirted by. Constance sighed. She was not the only one who had trouble.

After dinner she pleaded a headache and would have fled up the broad Jacobean staircase to the safety of her room where no one would ask her about her shaky past. But Pamela, who had never had a headache in her life and whose health was always glorious, merrily brushed off her excuses. With childish exuberance she seized both of Constance's slender hands and fairly dragged her into the drawing room, where the servants had lit a pair of branched candlesticks and a fire blazed on the hearth. Pamela flopped down on a stool before the delicate rosewood harpsichord, arranged her silvery pink skirts about her, struck a key dramatically and urged Constance to sing to her accompaniment "because your voice is better than mine and we all know it." She dimpled at Tom as she spoke.

There was nothing for it but to sing, but Constance's thoughts were chaotic. She leant against the polished rosewood with her slender back slightly arched and tried to compose herself as Pamela's clever fingers ran a scale or two. She was unaware of the picture they made: Pamela with her silver dusting on pink and her golden hair glinting in the candlelight like a freshly opened Maiden's Blush rose sprinkled with dew, and Constance in her figure-hugging plum velvet, its wide skirts swaying and rippling about her long slim legs, her white bosom and the pearly expanse of her upper breasts barely covered by the sheer "pinner" of almost transparent white lawn. Her head was thrown slightly back from a swanlike throat and crowned by a cloud of darkness lit by the red-violet glitter of brilliants that flashed like fireflies from her hair. She did indeed resemble a tall-stemmed purple iris, soft, velvety, a miracle to touch.

Ned's gray eyes glinted as he looked at her. His brother Tony had not been eloquent enough—he'd have a go at the Squire himself after the girls had trundled off to bed! For have her he must. He'd decided that the moment he first saw her at the Midsummer Masque at Huntlands last summer. She had winged into his life like a swallow, borne on the wind. He'd been bowled over by her beauty then as now. The Squire would come around!

His imagination raced on, making short work of a betrothal, skipping past the ceremony to the wedding night when Constance, with a circlet of gilt flowers and pearls around her gleaming dark hair, would stand there looking radiant while the guests snipped riband favors from her costume—this very dress in his vivid imagination. And after all the toasts to the bride's health, he would at last be alone with her in a big canopied four-poster.

He imagined himself in that warm darkness removing her nightclothes with his own hands, letting his palms slip over the smoothness of her skin, letting his yearning lips rove at will over her bare pulsing breasts. And then he would draw back the heavy hangings that draped the big four-poster and let the moonlight in—and devour with his eyes the delicate beauty of her naked body.

She would make a soft protest at first at being thus

exposed, her body would quiver—and then she would hold out her arms and welcome him. *And then*—beads of sweat had appeared on Ned's brow, although the big room at Axeleigh was drafty. His breath came unevenly. *Then he would explore all the sweet mysteries, all the delicious secrets, of her woman's body!* He looked at the swaying reedlike velvet figure before him and was engulfed by desire.

He had tried to tell Tony how he felt about her, but his brother had only regarded him with a troubled gaze. Ned could see no reason for that. Constance was but toying with him—as girls were wont to do. Before long she would be his. Forever.

But the velvet beauty avoided his gaze. She looked instead past the roaring fire across from her out to the snow swirling down past the windowpanes through the midnight blue outside. To Pamela's tinkling accompaniment, she lifted her voice in song—and fought to keep her thoughts from Captain Warburton, who was out there somewhere riding through that blue and white world. She sang to please Pamela—and saw, stricken, that she was pleasing Ned, who sat watching her raptly with his heart in his dark gray eyes.

Constance's singing had a misty quality, intimate, beguiling. Like her speaking voice, it had a soft sensuous rustle, like the whirr of wings, and it rose lightly to heights that had an angel chorus ring to them. It was not a strong voice, nor yet a cultivated one, but in the long drawing room of Axeleigh Hall that night with the snowflakes dusting down over a magic landscape, no one remained unmoved by it. It enchanted its hearers.

"Beautiful," breathed Ned, rising to his feet and coming to stand beside her. "Sing another."

Pamela cast Tom a wickedly laughing glance. That glance said *she* would bring the lovers together even if Captain Warburton and the Squire failed. Tom's friendly answering smile said he hoped it worked.

Constance, miserably aware of both glances, felt Ned's

breath warm upon her cheek as he bent over to arrange Pamela's music for her. She edged away slightly.

"Don't stand so close," she chided.

Ned gave her a wicked look, from that face that was so like his brother's, as if to say, *So my nearness affects you, does it?* And for a moment his grin might have been Tony Warburton's.

Constance didn't want to sing—she wanted to scream.

Somehow the evening was got through. Somehow they were off to bed, but for Constance there was little sleep. And when she did sleep she was nagged by troubled dreams in which Tony Warburton and his lighthearted brother rode in and out of her life, exchanging places.

*Axeleigh Hall, Somerset,
December 23, 1684*

CHAPTER 5

Constance woke, heavy-eyed, to Pamela's shake.

"We're all going out into the snow before breakfast—remember, we decided that yesterday? Hurry and dress, lazybones!"

"Oh, do go without me." Constance tried to wriggle back down under the covers but Pamela wouldn't let her. "You're already dressed and—"

"Tabby can get you dressed in no time!"

And so it was that Constance, still sleepy, found herself propelled protesting into the corridor with half her bodice hooks hooked wrong by a hurrying Tabitha. By the time they reached the stairs, Pamela cried, "Oh, bother the hooks—we'll throw a cloak over your shoulders and no one will know whether they're hooked right or not!" Tabby, taking her cue, promptly gave up the endeavor and tossed a fur-trimmed hooded cloak over a protesting Constance, mismatched hooks and all. In the lower hall—its floor littered by Christmas greenery where a roguish Puss had scattered it—the girls were greeted by Tom and Ned, already dressed for the outdoors. Pamela was wearing riding boots and waited impatiently as Ned helped Constance on with her high pattens.

So, willy-nilly, Constance found herself venturing out into the snow beside Ned Warburton, whose scarlet coat made a brilliant patch of color against the dark shrubbery, the black and gray tree boles, the white glitter of the snow. Warily she avoided a snowy mound that concealed a sturdy example of the lovely Maiden's Blush rose, that pink cousin of the famous White Rose of York which had graced English gardens these hundred years and more.

Tom and Pamela immediately began throwing snowballs at each other, laughing and shouting like children as they darted about under the big trees.

"I didn't bargain on this!" Constance ducked a snowball. "Pamela said we were going to build a snow fort!"

"She'd rather make war," chuckled Ned. "Pamela's a real tomboy. I always think she'd be happier wearing trousers than a skirt!"

And riding astride instead of aside. Tempted to agree with him, Constance dodged another snowball, and Ned laughed. "We'll have to leave the scene if we're to avoid them. Would you like a snowy walk through the maze?"

"Anything would be better than this!" Constance gave a small scream as two snowballs struck her, neither very hard but both spattering her plum velvet cloak with snow.

Glad of a chance to get his lady alone behind tall box hedges, Ned escorted her to the entrance to the maze, and to the accompaniment of a disappointed wail from Pamela, who had hoped to engage them in mock battle, they disappeared into the snow-frosted boxwood maze.

Pamela's crystal blue eyes followed them thoughtfully. Perhaps Constance was not so averse to Ned as she seemed. . . . Pamela jumped at a sudden demonic scream behind her, then laughed as she realized it was only the harsh cry of a peacock that, careless of the snow, was strutting along the snow-covered top of a low stone wall nearby with his great train of tail feathers dragging along behind him. He was moving at a leisurely pace toward a peahen. She chose to ignore him, concentrating instead on the grain that had been spread by a servant along the top of the low wall to feed the brilliant ornamental birds. He screamed again and the peahen looked up and gave him what Pamela considered to be a most scathing look.

Undeterred by his lady's indifference, the handsome crested cock executed a series of intricate steps, whirling about so that his back was turned to her and suddenly opening up the great fan of his tail feathers and flashing it aloft.

"Watch this," Pamela told Tom, and he straightened up from rolling up snow for the snow fort and followed her gaze. The enormous fanned tail, held stiffly erect, seemed almost to overpower the sleek iridescent blue-green body of the bird, and as the peahen pecked nearer to the edge of that fan he swirled about suddenly to face her and the beautiful overarching plumes of his burnished green tail, dotted with beautiful "eyes," hovered over her, rustling seductively. He was a sight to take the breath.

Except to the peahen. With studied disinterest she concentrated on her breakfast, pecking at the snow even when there was no food there.

Instead of being put off by this, the crested cock redoubled his attempts to interest this disdainful bird, making an even more gorgeous display of multihued glittering feathers.

Pamela chuckled. "They remind me of Ned and Constance. The more she ignores him, the more he pursues her!"

" 'Tis lucky there's no other peacock about," said Tom dryly. "Else this gaudy fellow would go after him with his spurs!"

Pamela shot Tom a swift look. "You're saying he'd fight for her?"

Tom gave a laconic shrug. He had no need to answer—indeed Pamela often understood his slightest gesture more clearly than words. Ned was itching to fight for her, was the implication, to show his lady the depth of his regard!

"I'm not sure how Constance feels about Ned," she said, going back to helping Tom roll up the snow and mound it for the sides of the fort. "Sometimes I think she's mad about him and just refuses to show it and other times I think she'd be glad to be rid of him!"

Tom frowned. Ned had asked him to find out through Pam how Constance felt and this was a most unsatisfactory answer. "You're saying she doesn't know her own mind?"

"It isn't that exactly," puzzled Pamela. "She just seems to—veer, if you know what I mean."

"Missishness!" laughed Tom, suddenly flipping a bit of snow down her neck.

Pamela squealed and—regardless that the snow fort wasn't finished—they went at it, with herself crouching behind the snowy barrier and heaving snowballs at Tom and he running about trying to "take" the fort. It was all grand, lighthearted fun—the kind of fun they had had together as children and enjoyed so little of, of late, and they both lost themselves in it.

Meanwhile, inside the maze, Ned was lightly brushing the snow from Constance's cloak. "Of course there's really nowhere to go now we're in here," he told her. "There used to be a narrow way cut through to the family burial ground, but it's grown up solid now."

"I've already seen that," said Constance hastily, forestalling an offer to view it in the snow. "I think the family burial ground was the last thing Pamela showed me when I came here—the first was the stables!"

Ned laughed. "It would be! Like Tom, the stables come first with her. Not a better rider in the county than Pamela." He grinned. "Did she tell you there's a jingle for the headstones there?"

"No, she didn't."

"Well, you know how schoolchildren try to keep straight the confusing line of French kings?"

"Yes, I do," laughed Constance, picking at random: "Louis

the Pious, Louis the Bearded, Louis the Sluggard, Louis the Fat, Louis from over the Sea!"

"For the Archers there's a jingle too. It goes—beginning with the present squire's grandfather: *Alger the Strong*—because old Alger once lifted the back end of a loaded wagon out of the mire when a team of horses couldn't pull it out. *Alfred the Long*—that was the Squire's father, who towered over everyone. *Richard the Pate*—the Squire's uncle, who went bald at twenty. *Brandon the Late*—the Squire's brother, who was never known to be on time for anything. *Virginia the Inquisitor*—she was Pamela's mother and she was always asking questions. And *Margaret the Visitor*—she was the Squire's younger sister, who died in Bath."

"Why," asked Constance, "did they call her 'Margaret the Visitor'?"

"Because she was never at home—at least after Tony left. You should see Warwood in the snow, Constance. It's beautiful."

"I know it would be," she murmured. "All those lovely ash trees."

She thought of Warwood—*Tony's home*—as it would look frosted by snow. The long approach through an avenue of stately ash trees, set wide apart like meadow trees so that the full sweep of their graceful branching arms could be seen. She had been to Warwood but once, arriving in a carriage last fall when the Squire paid a call on a distant neighbor and took the girls along, but she remembered the ash trees' pale gray trunks and pale gray branches. It had seemed to her, fancifully, that she was riding down a double column of Roman pillars, the white marble grayed by time and a leafy bower added overhead. In spring, Pamela had told her, large clusters of flowers would droop from the sides of those branches. Big lance-shaped leaves would follow and the horses would nibble them—Angel found them delicious!

Ned seized on her mention of the ash trees. "Did you know that portions of our barns were built of young ash timber from the estate? Finest wood for beams you can get—ash timber will bear a greater strain than any other wood."

"No," said Constance absently, her mind still picturing beautiful Warwood, which had once been an abbey. Looking as if it had been built around a huge square crenellated medieval keep, the great stone house rose loftily, a strange combination of church architecture and country gentleman's home. Some of the windows had a gothic tracery of stone lace such as she remembered at Fountains Abbey, while the newer ones were mullioned and transomed like those at Axeleigh. She remembered suddenly that cook (whose oldest sister worked in the kitchens at Warwood) had told her of an ancient curse that was put on future owners of the abbey by the departing monks. "O' course it only hurts the Warburtons and not them as works there," cook had shrugged. Now that curse flitted unbidden through Constance's mind: *If brothers live here, one will not survive . . . for they will be as Cain and Abel*. So had the abbot cursed the place as he walked away from it in 1539.

But surely, surely it was not true!

She told herself that Warwood's big echoing rooms lent themselves to such stories. The house had a strange, half-forlorn, half-formidable air—a flavor all its own, rising four stories to its eaves and six stories in its massive and somehow forbidding square tower. Indomitable it rose above the countryside, a determined house—fit abode for the dangerous Captain Warburton.

"I did not know ash timber was so valued," she said hastily, for Ned was looking at her.

"Oh, indeed! In ancient times the Anglo-Saxons used ashwood for their spear shafts. That was how the place came to be called Warwood originally—because it had produced so many of those ancient spears!"

Ancient spears had little interest for her today.

"I hope Captain Warburton made it home safely through the snow yesterday," she said—a bit stiffly for Ned was leaning so close it made her treacherous heart skip a beat. A pigeon, flying back to its dovecote, swooped by and her gaze followed it up into the winter sky—a gunmetal sky, exactly the color of Tony Warburton's eyes.

"Oh, Tony always makes it back all right," said Ned with an airy shrug. "No need to worry about him."

"But his horse *could* have gone lame," pointed out Constance, nettled. "Any number of things could have happened to him!"

"Not to Tony—he always gets through. If *I'd* ridden out into the snow yesterday, would you have worried about me?" he asked teasingly.

"But you'd only have been riding as far as Huntlands, where you were staying! And besides, you'd have had Tom with you."

"Oh, so Tom's to protect me, eh?" Ned's brows shot up. "I can look after myself, thank you!"

Amused at his chagrin, she laughed. "I've seen blizzards in Yorkshire that would daunt the bravest!"

"Was it in Yorkshire that you got your political views?" wondered Ned. "For they don't sound much like London."

No, her views didn't sound like aristocratic London's. . . .

"Look out," he said, taking her by the arm. "Puss is coming through. He may overset you!"

As he spoke, Puss dashed past them, his cobby body and short legs taking powerful leaps through the snow. Whatever he was pursuing had vanished into the thick box hedge and after it went Puss in a flash of brindled copper, only his fluffy ringed tail remaining in view for a while as he struggled through the boxwood.

But taking hold of her had sent showers of sparks zinging through Ned.

"Marry me, Constance!" he muttered hoarsely, and before she could frame an answer, he seized her and drew her to him with a force that lifted her pattens from the snow. She struggled indignantly at first, and then with her soft breasts crushed against his hard chest, her own hot nature triumphed treacherously and she seemed to melt in his arms. Exhilarated as he had never been before, Ned felt her soft mouth part beneath the eager assault of his kisses, felt her slender body tremble in his arms—and then she was returning his kiss with a turbulence that seemed to overpower her slight frame. Her velvet arms went around his neck, her kidskin gloves entwined themselves in his shoulder-length hair, her fur muff was tickling his ear, he could feel the tingling urgency that was surging through her.

Elated by this surprising turn of events—for he had at best hoped to be pushed away halfheartedly—Ned held on to his lady. Until with a gasp and a violent wrench she twisted away from him.

Her face was very white, her eyes enormous and dark. For an unguarded moment there she had lost control and surrendered herself to wild abandon. She had let her eyelids flutter shut so that her lashes were dark wings against her cheeks as her soft mouth tingled under Ned's kisses but—*it was Tony Warburton she kissed*. And now, looking up into Ned's face, the shame of that burnt through her—that her treacherous body could respond to Ned when in reality her mind and thought and heart were all centered on his absent brother.

"How dare you take such liberties!" she cried, choked with anger not so much at the mystified young man standing before her in his scarlet coat, but at herself. And as she spoke, in a reflexive gesture of refusal she swung the velvet arm that had so recently twined about his neck so that her gloved hand cracked across his cheek.

Ned took the blow unflinching. He never moved as a red weal slowly grew across his suddenly paler face. Only his dark gray eyes were watchful, uneasy, mirroring the alarm he felt. For the lady blew hot and cold, as he'd complained to Tom. One time her smile would seem to beckon, luring him on—another time her violet eyes frosted over in rebuff.

But how was he to know how much that brief contact with a man's strong body had shaken her? It had been so long, so long. . . . And she was young and her blood was a red fire in her veins. How was he to know that for one reckless moment she had forgotten the past, forgotten vows spoken in Essex, forgotten honor. How close she had been to saying "Yes!" and by that one short word assuring that she would spend her life at Warwood where Tony Warburton's booted feet strode in and out! Oh, it was a shameful thought that had swirled through her mind and it had rocked her to her foundations... *to consider marrying one man so that she might be near another!*

And her reaction, her revulsion from what she had so nearly done to him—for Ned deserved better—had given added strength to the blow that had left that red mark across his white face.

But the gentleman from Warwood was not finished with her yet. His hands shot out and roughly pinioned her shoulders even as she reeled away from him. She could feel his fingers digging through the velvet of her cloak in a grip she could not unloose.

"Admit you love me!" he cried, almost in panic. "Stop fighting me, Constance. You *do* love me—your kiss told me that just now!"

"I *don't* love you," she said unsteadily, for there for a moment those eyes had looked at her like Tony's and even being held at arm's length was too close. Her senses reeled. Ever since the Midsummer Masque at Huntlands last summer when she had first met Tony Warburton, she had known he was right for her—and she was right for him. *And it could never be!* "I don't love you!" she almost shouted. *"I don't!"*

Ned's strong fingers eased their grip. "I'm not giving up, you know," he warned her.

"Well, you should! Your brother has already asked the Squire and he said the decision was up to me. He won't force me to marry you!"

A deeper pallor came over Ned's already pale countenance and the red weal seemed to darken. Abruptly he released her. "I should hate to think you were 'forced' into marriage with me," he said slowly. He stood regarding her steadily, and his gray gaze seemed to burn into her like hot ashes. She stood her ground with lifted chin, giving him back her defiance. Then, "I'll be back when you're in better temper," he said shortly and spun on his heel, tramping off through the snow. At the end of the maze aisle, where he would turn a corner and be lost from view, he turned and flashed a cold smile at her. "You need not worry about me," he called softly. "We Warburtons can always find our way home—in the snow or otherwise!"

Constance stared at him stonily. But when he was gone she covered her face with her hands and her shoulders rocked with agony. What was she doing to herself, to him? That she should so mislead him as to where her true feelings lay—she who had been so careful to dissemble, to be cold, distant, reserved, where Tony Warburton was concerned. And now she had led his brother to believe that *he* was the one for whom she burned, and he would be back as surely as the sun would rise tomorrow. She found herself shaking—and not from cold.

From one of the tall mullioned windows on the second floor that overlooked the gardens, Clifford Archer, looking out to gauge the depth of the snow and consider whether his horse could make it to Cheddar over the rutted roads, observed this little pantomime with unconcealed wonder. The girl had gone into Ned's arms willingly enough so far as he could judge, she had flung her arms around Ned's neck—and then she had torn away and struck him. A hard blow. The Squire shook his head in puzzlement. Was this the new flirtatiousness, he wondered, to blow hot and blow cold at such a rapid pace? If so, he was well out of the courting game, for he'd not have understood the rules!

CHAPTER 6

Ned strode up to the stamped-down area of snow where Tom was just "taking" Pamela's snow fort. He stood surveying the merry pair for a moment, observing Pamela in her enveloping scarlet cloak with a snowball poised in her hand and devilment in her merry crystal blue eyes. He waited while she launched her snowball and Tom ducked and then suddenly ran forward and seized a heavy oak branch over her head and half buried his laughing lady in a great fall of snow.

Pamela came up out of the snowfall with Tom brushing her off in time to hear the last of Ned's remark: "—so if I'm to reach Warwood before nightfall with the roads buried this deep in snow, I'd best be starting."

"But you can't leave before breakfast!" cried Pamela. She was shaking the snow from her hair and trying vainly to get at those frozen bits which were melting down her neck.

"Sorry. Expected home. Things to do." Ned made a courteous leg that almost dusted his plumed hat with snowflakes. "Make my regrets to the Squire, won't you?"

By now they had both noted the red weal across Ned's rather set face, and Tom offered hastily to ride with him a ways. "Say our good-bys for us, won't you, Pam? We'll breakfast at Huntlands." He set off beside Ned toward the stables.

A moment later Constance ran from the maze with her velvet skirts held up, hurrying toward the house. Pamela, thinking how Constance's slap—for that mark on Ned's face must surely have come from a blow—had ruined her day with Tom, hoped sincerely that every branch Constance passed under would shower her with snow.

None did. She watched Constance run lightly into the house and marched in to find her bent over, removing her pattens in the hall.

"What did you do to Ned?" she demanded, throwing off her red cloak and shaking it as she stamped snow from her boots. "He dashed off saying he had to get back to Warwood."

"Maybe he did," countered Constance coolly, straightening up. "There's snow all over you, Pamela! What did you do, take a header into a snowbank while you flung snowballs at Tom?"

"Almost! Tom showered snow on me by shaking a tree branch over my head."

They were like heedless children, Tom and Pamela, thought Constance. And at that moment she would have given *anything* to be like them.

She remembered snowy times from her own childhood. Frost fairs on the frozen Thames when their fortunes were better and the money not all spent. Vendors' and hawkers' stalls upon the ice, sleds and laughing skaters whirling over it—and even horses, some drawing carriages carrying ladies and gentlemen in plumed hats and fur-trimmed cloaks.

In a white fur hat and muff and a wide-skirted little dress of purple velvet, little Constance had essayed to skate for the first time on double-bladed skates. And then her father, an accomplished skater from the North Country, had picked her up and placed her on his shoulder and winged with her across

95

the ice while her mother, no skater at all, laughed and clapped her gloved hands from the shore. And then he had come back and set Constance down on the snowy bank and swept her mother up, holding her slenderness like a rag doll clasped to his lean body, and with her feet never touching the ice had executed an intricate ice dance that had caused feet to tap and heads to bob and hands to clap in pleasure. And after that they all sat around a bonfire and ate sweetmeats and little hot sausages and drank a scalding liquid her mother had told her with a laugh was chocolate.

She had loved snow then.

But gradually the money had run out, and life had lost its joy. Constance remembered how cold their lodgings were in winter when they could not afford enough sea coal to warm them, how cramped and hot in summer. She remembered days when they ate but little—and days when they ate not at all. She remembered how anxiously her mother's clever fingers had mended every rent and tear in their precious clothing, for new ones were not to be had. The distant cousin in Norfolk died, and little by little the pittance that kept them alive (through the sale of the last of her mother's little trinkets) dissolved away and they were forced at last to make what little Constance called in her own excited mind The Great Decision—to go north and throw themselves on the mercy of Hammond Dacey's father at Claxton House in Yorkshire's West Riding.

Constance had secretly wondered why they did not do so long before, for her father was always spinning her stories of his boyhood in the West Riding. He told her that Yorkshire was the largest county in England, so large that it had been divided into "thryddings," or thirds, and that the West Riding alone was so large as to be second in size among English counties! He took her upon his knee and told her how it had always been a divided country, the West Riding—divided in the Wars of the Roses, and, later, in the Civil War the east hewed to the king but the western part was for Parliament. The child didn't understand these things but she thrilled to his stories about Mother Shipton, the witch who was conceived of the devil and born in a cave among terrible rocks and died three years before the young Elizabeth became queen. Mother Shipton had predicted the end of the world, that men would fly in strange machines, and that a vast horde of gold would be discovered in a frozen land in the far north across the ocean sea. The child listened raptly as he told her of the eerie Dropping Well near Mother Shipton's cave, where water fell from a rocky ledge and slowly petrified everything dropped into it, and how in the limestone areas south of her cave wild orchids grew, one of them—the dark red helleborine—as dark a red as her father's worn mended coat. He told her of pools in the Vale of York where he had watched great flights of teal and widgeon and tufted ducks and swans as lovely as any they had seen on their one short excursion up the Thames.

He told her—and his voice softened and had a wistful twang to it—what life had been like for him as a boy in Claxton House when his mother—Elizabeth, the first Lady Dacey—was alive. Warm, lovely lady that she was, she had taken him with her on long rides and they had galloped laughing across the wild high-heathered moors.

"You'll tire the child," Constance's mother had told him, smiling wanly as she listened. Anne Cheltenham as a young girl had been sought after and feted; her world had spread out before her like a bright carpet of flowers wherever she chose to tread—and one by one those flowers had been snatched away until she stood, it seemed, knee deep in thorns with nowhere to turn. Sometimes she combed Constance's cloud of dark hair with a wooden comb (the filigreed silver comb had long since been sold) and told her gently of her own girlhood in London, and how the fountains had run wine when Charles II was restored to his throne and all of London took one long mad holiday. She made it all sound very lovely and there was a catch in her soft musical voice as she spoke.

Constance was to understand that everyone had seen Better Days but her; they were now living through The Worst.

That was in London.

The real "Worst" was yet to come at Claxton House in York.

Constance had been totally unprepared for that, of course. Listening untiringly to her father's stories, she had built up in her mind a magic picture of the majestic edifice that was Claxton House, a place of wondrous joy, set in a fairyland and ruled by Sir John Dacey, Baronet, her own grandfather! For there was a luster to Hammond Dacey's descriptions of his home and boyhood that painted for the child word pictures of luxury, ease and secure position—all that they did not have in London.

And then they had sold their meager possessions and with the money that brought had traveled north one fall by stagecoach—and all Constance's illusions about Claxton House had collapsed one by one.

London and faraway Yorkshire faded as Pamela's voice cut into her reverie.

"Whatever did you do to Ned to make him run off like that?" Pamela sounded plaintive.

Constance gave her a hard look. "Nothing. Ned has offered and I've refused—that's all." She began to beat snowflakes from her muff.

"Sometimes I get the feeling you really care for Ned but you just won't admit it." Pamela was still clawing at the bits of ice and snow that had slid down her neckline and were dripping an icy trail down her back as she followed Constance up the stairs. "Or"—she gave the dark-haired girl beside her a slanting speculative gaze—"is it Captain Warburton you care about?"

Constance bit her lip. Could she really be so transparent? Or was this just woman's intuition speaking?

"I don't care for either one of them," she shrugged. "What about Tom?" she demanded, desperate to change the subject. "Did you scold him for hiding in the buttery with Melissa Hawley?"

"No, I didn't," confessed Pamela, giving her wet hair a shake that scattered droplets all over Constance. "Indeed I forgot all about it. It was so like old times, having Tom chase me with snowballs, gamboling like children over the snow. Constance.'' She grew suddenly serious as they reached Constance's room and she turned in with her. ''What do you think Tom sees in Melissa?''

''An easy conquest,'' Constance told her in a jaded voice.

''Do you really think that's it?''

''Certainly. You're *much* prettier.''

But being prettier hadn't seemed to matter in the darkness of the buttery.

''I can't stand Melissa Hawley!'' Pamela's light young voice was indignant. ''She goes around with that sleepy, heavy-lidded look, as if she should be in bed. And her clothes all somehow look like chemises! Tell me, how do you think *this* dress looks on me?'' She twirled about and her heavy indigo woolen skirts—damp at the hem from trailing in the snow—whirled stiffly.

''I've been meaning to talk to you about that,'' murmured Constance, determined that the conversation should not veer back to the Warburtons. ''That dress is warm, I'll allow, and it's serviceable—''

''And it's a good color for me, don't you think?'' asked Pamela anxiously. ''This deep blue?''

''With your cheeks red from the cold, yes, it is. But it's very plain—''

''Well, it's woolen. I like plain woolen dresses for outdoors. And my eyes do pick up color from it, don't they? I mean, they're so *pale*.''

''What I'm trying to tell you is that I don't think anybody will turn and look at you twice in it. It completely hides your figure. You veer from dresses so plain and heavy that you might as well be wearing a sack, to gowns so—so ornamented with ruchings and tucks and braid and ribands and embroidery that nobody can see the real *you*!''

''Men always turn and look at you first anyway!'' Pamela stopped whirling and regarded willowy Constance indignantly. ''Although for the life of me,'' she added in a burst of frankness, "I can't understand why. Blondes are much more striking than brunettes—Tom says so."

That ultimate authority—Tom! Constance resisted an urge to point out that Melissa Hawley too was a blonde, but she did not. She had guessed that Pamela's urge to overdress came from a basic sense of insecurity. Outdoors Pamela's childhood world had been complete—and outdoors even now she cared not what she wore, so long as it was serviceable. But life indoors had been more complex. Her father had had reason to shun the house while his wife Virginia was alive and had had little time for Pamela since; her mother, the lightskirt, had been forever retreating behind closed bedroom doors with a variety of men and had left young Pamela with a succession of nurses and governesses. Pamela was trying to bolster her damaged ego by getting herself up like the decoration for a wedding cake!

"I'm only trying to point out that your clothes are too stiff," she told Pamela gently. "Sumptuous, I'll grant you—but stiff. And you do wear your necklines cut too high."

"I'm high-busted," countered Pamela defensively. "If I cut my gowns any lower, my nipples will show!"

Constance shrugged. She went over to the big press in the corner and pulled out the gown Pamela had worn last night, of heavy strawberry pink damask alight with silver threads. "Take this thing you wore last night." She shook it negligently at Pamela. "As you can see, it practically stands alone—it doesn't *need* you. How can you expect your figure to survive *that?*" She cast a scathing glance at the heavy indigo wool dress whose wet hemline Pamela was vainly trying to wring out. "No one knows what you look like, Pam!"

Pamela straightened and surveyed critically Constance's flowing velvet dress that moulded her every line and flowed with her as she walked, gracefully suggesting slender hips and long beautiful legs. She bit her lip. "But I *like* silvery pink things," she complained.

"Then try silver tissue over thin apple blossom pink silk—you'll be surprised what it will do for you!"

Pamela frowned at her but her expression was wavering. She phrased her next words carefully. "You're saying I'd be—*noticed* more if I wore what you suggest?"

"By Tom, at least," said Constance ruthlessly, going directly to the point.

The Squire's daughter flushed, for they both knew that this whole exercise had to do with Tom and Tom only. "Well," she said doubtfully. "I'll *think* about it." She brightened. "After breakfast."

It began to snow again during breakfast, which kept them inside. Afterward Constance curled up with a book in the window seat of one of the big overhanging bays and read a novel while Pamela spent a happy morning in the hot kitchen supervising the making of plum pudding. And listening to cook recount her early days in Torquay as she stomped, heavy-footed, back and forth before the steamed-up windows. According to cook, she had seduced half the young sailors in Torquay! Pamela listened attentively, hoping she'd learn something. Cook, sensitive to Stebbins the butler's muttered warning about making her stories too broad, cheerfully cleaned them up for Pamela's dainty ears. And while the scullery maids giggled (for they didn't believe a word cook said) and Puss contentedly gorged himself on cold mutton, a plum pudding came into being.

The afternoon was spent decorating the house for Christmas, for tomorrow would be Christmas Eve. Pamela was adept at making the big holly wreath which, with a red satin bow tied by Constance, graced Axeleigh's front door, surrounding the big iron knocker. They placed evergreen boughs behind the heavy gilt-framed family portraits and arranged holly across the mantels and hung mistletoe from the big chandelier in the hall.

As they worked they discussed clothes, and together they selected the gown Pamela was to wear that night at dinner. It was to be a sort of trial run, they would try the gown out on the Squire and see if he commented on it.

The gown was a new one that Pamela had never worn. It

was of thick undulating ice blue satin, trimmed in ermine tails that swayed with every movement, calling attention to Pamela's delectable bustline. It was so low-cut that Constance felt called upon to remark accusingly, "The reason you haven't worn it is because you're afraid you'll pop out! But you must stop being afraid. With forty whalebone stays holding you rigid, there's no chance for such violent motion!"

"*You* don't wear stays at all," accused Pamela, who hated anything that even resembled a corset. She often looked with horror at those whalebone instruments of torture, corsets with unyielding pointed horn busks that reposed in trunks of her mother's things, imagining those busks—that reached from the décolletage to run the full length of the bodice to be tied into place by something called a busk lace—cutting into her flesh.

"Well, *I* have plebian tastes," sighed Constance. "I like to be comfortable. *You*, on the other hand, want to dazzle everyone in sight."

Pamela gave an irritable nod. "This dress may be fashionable but I can't move about in it," she complained.

"You're not supposed to take violent exercise in it," retorted Constance. "And it doesn't weigh as much as your pink damask by half!"

Pamela glared at her. *Her* idea of a proper ball gown was a gown as stiff and ornate as possible—but loose-fitting so that one could move around nimbly in it and at the same time look splendid! She tried an experimental wriggle of her shoulders. Nothing much happened because the sleeves were sewn in so low on her upper arms that they reached the deltoid muscle. The oblique-angled seams at the shoulder were far back on her trapezius muscle, which made elevating her arms very difficult and reaching the top of her head impossible.

"I won't be able to push back my hair if it falls over my eyes," she announced dolefully.

"So *that's* why all your dresses are cut wrong?" Constance pounced on that. "This one makes you look the way you should. See that sloping line? It's very fashionable this year!''

Gazing at her reflection in the mirror, Pamela had to acknowledge that Constance certainly had a flair for style. She looked elegant—and sophisticated. But she wailed when Constance went about with a pair of scissors, mercilessly snipping off a riband here, a rosette there, deleting what Pamela had thought to be interestingly placed bits of braid or lace.

''Now we'll catch the skirt up at the sides with a pair of jeweled clasps to display your petticoat—no, *that* petticoat definitely will not do''—this as Pamela indicated one of rose taffeta heavily ornamented with metallic lace laid out in a geometric pattern over the narrow flat braid called ''galloon.'' ''Here, this one would be perfect.'' She held up a thin petticoat of delicately embroidered silvery silk that caught and reflected pale blue lights from the ice blue satin.

''It's quite old,'' objected Pamela.

''No matter. See how it undulates as you walk.''

Pamela tried it on and took a couple of experimental steps in her smart long vamp, high-heeled blue satin slippers. The heels were set almost in the center of the foot and narrowed in the center like little hourglasses. They were the latest thing.

''Now with your hair parted in the middle and your curls swept to the sides—''

''Like spaniels' ears,'' giggled Pamela.

''And glittery earbobs and a string of pearls, and a blue satin riband—*just one!*'' This as Pamela, deciding if one riband was a good thing, three might be better, picked up three. ''One blue satin riband peeking in and out of your golden curls—there.'' Constance stepped back. ''Now if only the point lace on your chemise cuffs could be a little daintier so more of your arms would show through—you have good arms, Pamela. Do you think you could tug your neckline down a little farther in the front?''

''Oh, no!'' wailed Pamela. ''I'll be *out!*'' She was awfully glad Tom wasn't going to be here for dinner tonight for she was sure she'd forget and reach up to toss back a falling lock and bring her arm up—and hear a terrible ripping sound as the seams gave way!

"Now," said Constance, "we'll see what your father thinks. And then you can try it out on Tom." She put down the scissors and brushed bits of riband and lace from her skirt. "I must dress for dinner myself," she said and left the room.

She had not cleared the door before all her problems were back again, nagging at her. And as she went into her own room to change into something that would complement Pamela's "new look," she pondered bitterly on what she had been— and what she would become.

From the corridor she could hear Pamela calling to Tabitha to catch Puss, he had made off with some of the Christmas greenery, and she smiled wistfully. *Pamela, safe in her sheltered world* . . . Outside, the blue-gray winter dusk was fast closing down. A few flakes of snow were falling and while she stood there they became a great swirl that obscured the oaks and turned the world to a white whirl outside the tall casements. And she was reminded of another day, and another snow that would always linger in her memory. Now those memories she had fought to push away rushed back unbidden to overwhelm her and she was back again at Claxton House in Yorkshire's wild West Riding.

BOOK II
The Lovely Outcast

Memories come and memories go,
Shadows flit across the snow
And she'll remember he loved her so
That winter's eve so long ago.

Claxton House,
The West Riding, Yorkshire,
November 1679

CHAPTER 7

A great November ball was in full swing at Claxton House, family seat of the Daceys. Usually a gray forbidding pile of stone, standing like a sentinel in the middle of its lands, the great house was tonight a miracle of light with candles winking from all its windows and the great Banqueting Hall glowing in the radiance of myriad chandeliers. The guests were to stay the night—and maybe longer because, while it had snowed only fitfully throughout the day, it was now snowing hard. Great flakes drifted down, giving a new frosting of white to an already white world. Frost glittered on the small panes of the massive stone edifice's mullioned windows, and the smoke from its banks of tall chimneys were smudges that disappeared into a snow-drifted sky.

The great house was filled with merriment, for guests had come from far away, many of them making the hard slow progress across the snowy Yorkshire moors for this occasion, although most had arrived by sled and were from the environs of nearby Ripon. Laughter rippled above the tinkling music, toasts were being drunk, satin skirts swished by heaping tables laden with great pastries, hams, every kind of dainty, and upon vast silver chargers rode peacocks and swans in full plumage.

But in the great stone stables—almost as large as the house—where the horses, including those of the guests, were already bedded down for the night, a strange tableau was taking place.

By the light of a lanthorn set on the hard-packed floor, a little girl—she could have been no more than eleven—was carefully mimicking the dance steps she had seen in the great house a short time before—seen through the carved balusters at the top of the stairs, for the child was not allowed to mingle with the guests whose satin skirts and breeches were swirling to music in the Banqueting Hall. She swooped earnestly about on shoes and stockings wet with snow, fluffing out the much-mended and faded indigo blue homespun of her too-short skirts.

She thought she was alone.

She was not.

From behind a tall mound of hay, a boy watched her. He was fifteen, although he looked older, and his rapt young face, watching her graceful swoops and swirls, was grave and intent. Indeed he thought her the most beautiful creature he had ever beheld.

She must have felt the intent pressure of his gaze, for she turned suddenly and stopped dancing.

"Who's there?" she asked uncertainly.

" 'Tis only I," he said, coming out and showing himself so that she might not feel frightened.

Little Constance looked uncertainly at this tall lad in clothing even more disreputable than her own. She had seen him about, of course, but she had never spoken to him. Her position in the family was a strange one. She lived in the great house, was accepted as kin—and yet not as kin. Although she was included in the lessons that Henriette, the French governess, taught young Hugh and Felicity, she was not included in most social functions. She took her meals in the servants' hall. The ball just now taking place in the great Banqueting Hall was definitely not for her. Even had she had a proper gown to wear for the occasion—which she did not—she would not have been allowed to attend.

It was all part of the same pattern that had emerged almost immediately when she had—wearing the same indigo gown in which she was dancing by lanthorn light tonight—arrived through a blinding snowstorm at the Daceys' ancestral home. Their journey north had been arduous for they had not been able to afford a coach past Lincoln and had had to bargain with local farmers along the way for transportation in carts and uncomfortable nights spent in the lofts of cottages. Indeed it was a lumbering farm cart that delivered them to the main entrance of Claxton House.

Seated, half-frozen, in the cart, the child had brushed the snow from her hood and stared at the building in fascination. Of heavy ashlar masonry, it frowned down upon her from its many gables. Its numerous small-paned windows seemed to peek out at her like a rodent's eyes. Her awed gaze swept upward to the lofty finials crowning the battlements like watchful stone guardians atop the massive square stone projection that formed the entrance. Two stories tall and with an enormous circular window of eight lights rising above the yawning arched entrance, it presented a picture of menace to her childish eyes.

She did not want to leave the cart.

"Come, Constance," urged her father. "We're home." He caught his wife's eye and a look of foreboding passed between them.

The child caught that look and in a sudden flash of intuition she knew that nothing good was ever going to happen to them here. She hung back stubbornly.

"Constance," said her mother with a catch in her voice. "Stand straight when we go in and remember to give your best curtsy." She took the child's hand, and they followed her father as he went to bang the heavy iron knocker.

Constance gave a last wistful look back at the snowy landscape as they stood beneath the shelter of the carved stone entrance. Somewhere back there across the endless miles was London. *That* was home. Not this place of cold stones and shrieking wind and snow that struck at you like pellets.

And then the heavy door had swung open and they were ushered in.

Her mother, frail, lovely creature that she was, had been shivering as they entered, for the chill of this last leg of the journey had pierced through to her slight bones. She had held Constance to her, almost defensively, when they had arrived at last in the vast echoing hall that stretched about them in medieval splendor and were being looked over coldly by the Dacey clan.

Sir John Dacey, Baronet, Hammond's father, old and stiff and grim, with a lock of gray hair sticking out from under his rumpled sandy periwig, came forward to greet them, leaning heavily on his cane. Beside him his gaunt second wife gave a faint sniff and a disapproving rustle of her maroon skirts as she surveyed their worn luggage and threadbare clothing. Standing on Sir John's other side, rather like a watchdog determined to ward off interlopers, young Hugh Dacey glowered. Three years older than Constance, Hugh stood stolidly, balanced on heavy legs spaced wide apart, his big head and shoulders already giving promise of the massive man he would become and his little piglike eyes darting over the newcomers with a kind of half-human intelligence that chilled the little girl shivering against her mother's skirts. Half hiding behind her stepmother was Hugh's sister, Felicity Dacey, two years older than Constance, a painfully thin, pallid little girl with pale sad eyes and a crushed demeanor. Felicity was richly dressed in persimmon velvet ornamented with creamy lace. When their parents had met their death in a careening coach that shattered in a ditch, the old baronet—newly married to a raw-boned frowning woman named Elvira—had taken on the task of rearing his older son's children.

And now his younger son had brought his little family home to him.

There was no joy in the air, no spirit of welcome.

Constance curtsied mechanically when she was presented to Lady Dacey, who gave her a curt greeting and a scathing glance.

When she trudged up the massive stairway with the others, being escorted to the rooms they would occupy, Hugh Dacey surreptitiously managed to trip her and Constance fell forward with a little cry to bark her shins against the wide parquetry stair treads.

It was a portent of things to come.

Constance never forgot that first week at Claxton House, the big damp echoing rooms, the strange unfriendly atmosphere, the long hours her father spent closeted with Sir John behind a closed library door, the heated voices that issued from it, never quite distinguishable, and sometimes what sounded like someone pounding on a table for emphasis. Constance had lurked near the door but only twice had she managed to hear anything. Both times it was her mother's name and the word "mistake" almost shouted. It didn't make sense to Constance.

Her father always emerged from these sessions gray-faced and looking years older than he was. He would dash up the stairs to their rooms and go to her mother, and her mother would bury her lovely appealing face in his chest and they would whisper and comfort each other—the child, watching, puzzled, never knew what about.

That winter her father died. He came in out of a biting gale, his lips blue, and clutching his heart. He made wild groping motions, clawing at the air, and fell to the floor writhing. Frozen in terror, Constance heard behind her her mother's scream. Anne ran past her to Hammond and sank beside him in her worn voluminous skirts—and, while she wept, he died in her arms.

After that her mother wore black. The mirrors were covered with black drapery and black hangings were substituted

111

for the apple green sarsenet window hangings. Even the bed wore a black coverlet. Constance was a pale shadow of herself in mourning clothes.

Now the family, cold enough toward them during her father's time, seemed to draw away from mother and child even further. Once after Hugh snowballed her with big chunks of ice and she came in limping, Constance asked her mother in a whispered sob, *"Why?* He *wanted* to hurt me. *Why?"*

And her mother, paler now than she had ever seen her and with a racking cough that would not seem to leave, held her close in protective arms and said huskily, "Don't ask. Don't ever ask."

More bewildered than ever, little Constance watched her mother drift away from her in the spring, gliding almost imperceptibly into the Land of Death.

The casket closed over Anne Dacey when the northern buds were sprouting and apple blossoms bursting all about. For Constance there was no joy that springtime. It seemed to her that they had all come north to die.

Her life changed abruptly that summer. Sir John had taken to his bed in March with the gout, and by summer Lady Dacey was in firm command and running the house with a merciless hand. She made Hugh and Felicity toe the line—but she was fierce in her rebuffs to Constance.

The mourning draperies all came down. Constance was relegated to a sleeping alcove off Felicity's large bedchamber. Her handsome mourning garments were taken away and she was reduced to wearing her old tattered clothes or garments made over from the pitiful remnants of her mother's wardrobe.

"Be of some use," her step-grandmother was fond of remarking crisply whenever she passed Constance.

The child, bitter at the great gap in treatment between herself and those luckier children, Hugh and Felicity, managed to hold her tongue. It was wise that she did so, for Lady Dacey was as quick to box one's ears as she was to criticize and give orders.

And so life for little Constance settled down at Claxton House into a drab routine enlivened only in the schoolroom by Henriette Ladoux, the plump, lively, black-haired, black-eyed French governess who had been brought all the way from Paris to instruct young Hugh and Felicity in her native tongue.

Clever Henriette was her only friend in the house. Attracted by the wistful dainty child, it was Henriette who had brought the idea to the lord of the manor that his granddaughter might learn faster by having a female companion at her lessons— and it was Henriette's delight to teach the girls dance steps and social graces and watch Constance excel over Felicity.

Henriette was always bursting with gossip about the household and its visitors: The Penningtons had been near to killing each other when they arrived—had Constance but looked out the window she would have seen Lady Pennington strike her husband in the face as they dismounted. And the reason was not hard to find. Did Constance know that doelike Mary Audley had crept into Lord Pennington's bedchamber when they had spent the night here? That was while his wife was off visiting the Stantons. Oh, yes, indeed she had! And she had come out of that bedchamber at an unfortunate moment— just when her husband, that great bear of a man, was strolling down the hall. But Mary Audley, caught outside her lover's door in her nightdress, had been equal to it! She had thrust her arms straight out in front of her and stalked down the hall, pretending to be sleepwalking! Plump Henriette fell into gales of laughter. And then she had given Constance's dark head an affectionate pat.

"You will do well in life, *ma chère*," she assured Constance in her soft whirring French. "You could well end up a great lady for you have a *flair*. Not like—" She gave Felicity a hopeless look, for Felicity was apathetic in the classroom.

Felicity did not care that "Mademoiselle," as the children called Henriette, despaired of her. She was consumed by her one great passion: the making of delicate webs of spider-fine point lace. All her energy she poured out upon the lacy magic that appeared beneath her clever fingers. Just now she was creating a miracle of diaphanous scrolls and flowers in Venetian rose point lace.

Henriette gave her charge a jaundiced look. "My mother was very expert at making point *d'aiguille,*" she told Constance. "I learned to do it. See the *réseau*—these fine threads of the groundwork? And these slender threads that connect the patterns are called *brides;* the spiky little knots are *picots.* Would you like to learn how? I could show you."

Constance shook her head. With all the great world beckoning, she had no desire to spend her days crouched like Felicity over needlework.

Henriette gave her an understanding glance. "It was the same with me." Her smile deepened a trifle. "Perhaps you would like to learn some new dance steps, no?" And as Constance brightened, the French woman whirled about, her feet tripping lightly over the floor. "Come, Felicity," she commanded. "You must learn too."

Regretfully, Felicity laid down her lacework and stumbled indifferently through the dance. When it was over and Constance wanted to try it again, Felicity shook her head and slipped away from them, back to her window seat, back to her lace.

"I wonder what they have done to the child in this terrible household to make her retreat like this," wondered Henriette, her dark eyes suddenly filled with pity. "They are *sauvage* in this place—savages." She gave her striped tabby skirts an angry twirl. "They treat me like dirt! Barbarous English!" She lapsed into French, muttering. "What do they have against you?" she asked suddenly of Constance. "Allowing you to go around dressed in rags! And where is that Hugh? He should be here, learning to dance!"

Constance flushed. "I suppose he is angry that you took a switch to him for putting a snake in your writing desk yesterday."

"I suppose so," sighed Henriette.

Constance, who was the special target for most of Hugh's vicious tricks, was overjoyed when he did not show up for lessons. She had had her hair pulled, water spilled on the floor so that she would slip, her quill pens all broken, nasty things written on her copy paper, molasses substituted for her ink. Hugh had splashed her dress with a variety of things which would not wash out, had jumped out at her at the head of the stairs, startling her so that she nearly fell down the entire flight. She almost wept with relief when one day Hugh told Henriette belligerently that he was too old to be taught by a woman anyway, and abandoned the classroom altogether.

With Sir John indisposed, Henriette took the matter up with Lady Dacey, only to be told she should watch her own deportment, that Hugh had reported to her that she was deliberately displaying her ankles as she taught them dancing.

"She implies I am trying to seduce the little beast!" Henriette told Constance stormily—and retaliated by teaching Constance to make potpourri and attar of roses and pomades and to dress her hair fashionably. As a result, Constance went about in her shabby clothes with elaborate coiffures and smelling like a flower garden, which greatly irritated Lady Dacey.

"You had best be in the kitchen learning housewifely tasks," she would scold. "For there'll be a whole lifetime of cleaning and scrubbing and cooking ahead of you!"

Those words sent a chill through Constance. Their meaning was painfully clear. They told her that no matter what her expectations as a daughter of the house might be, she was not to achieve every young girl's dream of a Great Marriage.

Not here. Not among these people who hated her.

The months went by, enlivened mainly by spirited Henriette, who was fond of comparing everyone about her to animals. "Look at Felicity in her white dress," she would mutter. "With her white stockings and that long pale riband thrusting out at an angle toward her lacework, she could well be a unicorn!" And again, from a window, indicating Hugh, who was charging across the lawn, "Is he not a perfect example of a vicious wild boar? Indeed he needs only tusks to make him complete!"

Constance wished Henriette would not poke fun at Felicity, for whom she felt a puzzled sympathy. She tried to help her but Felicity—although she occasionally gave Constance a shy smile—wanted to remain remote—with her lace.

"What will become of us all if Sir John dies?" Henriette worried one day. "He is like a great antique stag, dying, with his big head almost ready to be stuffed and mounted! And if he does die that dreadful woman will take over entirely—it is only the fear that he may recover that holds her back!"

But the old baronet did not die. Instead his obnoxious second wife, leaning over the upstairs railing in an attempt to peer down and see if a too-pretty chambermaid (whose loose behavior she had already decried) was really huddled at the bottom of the stairwell kissing the butler, leant too far and with a wild scream pitched over the bannisters. She landed on her head on the polished floor of the hall, her neck broken.

Sir John was too ill to attend the funeral. The entire house, by his orders, was draped in black for three months and then the black hangings were all removed—Sir John was not one to mourn overlong, and especially for a wife who had not turned out as he had expected.

By fall his condition had bettered, he had sent Hugh away to school, and under the urging of old friends who came to call, he was persuaded to give a ball in November. A ball that had somehow managed not to include Constance, who had viewed the proceedings in the Banqueting Hall, bright-eyed from between the spokes of the second-floor balustrade. She had watched the guests arrive in their velvets and furs, she had watched them dance—and when she saw a new dance, she memorized the steps carefully. Henriette being confined to her room with a cold, Constance might have practiced the steps at once in the upper hall but as a bevy of guests ascended the stairs, she fled down a back stairway, seized a lanthorn and ran through the moonlit snow to the big warm stables to practice the remembered dance steps before she forgot them.

And found that she was not alone—a stableboy was watching, studying her across the hay-strewn earthen floor.

"You're Sweep, aren't you?" she asked uncertainly.

"My name is Deverell Westmorland," he said, stepping forward into the light. His dark russet hair gleamed red in it. His eyes, green as emeralds, held an admiring gleam. In the distance she had noted his stance, his bearing—and wondered privately that he should be only a stableboy. Now, close up, even in his shabby clothes his lean hawklike face and arrogant bearing gave promise of the man he would become.

"Then why do they call you 'Sweep'?" she wondered.

A tinge of bitterness colored the boy's voice. "They said 'Deverell' was a gentleman's name, and not for a lad like me. And they called me 'Sweep' because I was thin enough when I came here to worm my way inside the chimneys and clean them. Since then my shoulders have broadened, so they decided I might get stuck there."

Constance thought of those banks of vast upswinging chimneys, tall against the sky, and shuddered. She had a fear of heights. "I would not like that," she said simply.

"I've seen you often," he volunteered. "And wondered why you did not come down to the stables."

"Oh—I'm not allowed to ride," she told him. " 'Tis not an accomplishment I will need, I'm told." Her soft lip curled.

"But you do take lessons along with young Mistress Felicity, I've heard?"

She nodded and laughed. "That's because Felicity is slow at learning and 'twas discovered that I'm not. 'Tis thought that I will be of help to her and that is the only reason I share her schoolroom."

He was quick to detect the bitterness of her tone, the slight flush that darkened her delicate cheekbones. Although he had often paused to watch her from afar, he was unprepared for her blinding beauty at this close range. Never had he dreamt that a pair of eyes could be of so deep a violet, a skin so sheer, a tumbling cloud of dark hair have such a rich sheen.

"Do your people live here on the estate?" she asked.

He stiffened at the suggestion that his people might be tenants of Sir John. "My father was Haverleigh Westmorland of Wingfield, Kent," he said a trifle frostily. "He was the second son of the Earl of Roxford." He did not know why he had blurted that out—he had been careful to tell nobody, for he would only have been laughed at, and scorn was something the youth did not relish. But he wanted to gain stature in the sight of this slim elfin miss who stood at last within range of his voice.

She gave him a startled look, half disbelieving.

Sensitive on what was to him a tender subject, he added in a defiant tone, "Hard to believe that I'm an earl's grandson when you see me like this, isn't it?" He indicated with a shrug his shabby trousers and worn leathern jerkin and mended woolen hose.

"I believe you," Constance said gravely. For who would believe, to look at her, that she was a baronet's granddaughter? "How did you come here?" she wondered.

"My father's family and my mother's were old enemies," he explained. "And when they ran away and got married, both families cast them out. My father took what little he had and purchased a cottage on the outskirts of Maidstone, but it burned down and they both died in the fire."

"How awful!" breathed Constance.

"Yes, wasn't it?" It had happened long enough ago that he could speak of it without flinching. "They could only afford one servant—catch-as-catch-can help. And the fellow got drunk and was careless with a candle, went to sleep leaving it too near the hangings, it's thought, and the place filled with smoke and smothered them all while they slept."

"Everything *my* mother's people owned vanished in the Great Fire of London!" exclaimed Constance. "Their house and everything in it!" She looked at Deverell Westmorland more warmly. Somehow this shared disaster seemed to establish a bond between them.

"When my father's debts were settled there was nothing left. My grandfather had died meanwhile; I was sent on to my

118

father's brother, the new earl, who had inherited the family seat of Wingfield in Kent.''

"So you were all right then?"

"For a while. But I fell afoul of my uncle's new bride and she turned me out of the house."

"Whatever did you do to merit that?" wondered Constance, fascinated.

"She laid my back open with her riding whip for running in front of her horse," the boy remembered grimly. "I was scooping up a puppy that she was about to run down but she cared nothing for that. Said I could have caused her to be thrown. That night I put a frog in her bed."

They both laughed.

"And she turned me out for it." His voice was rueful.

"And your uncle stood for it?" Constance looked indignant.

"That he did," sighed Deverell. In point of fact, there was more to the story. His uncle, the new Earl of Roxford, had been away at the time, and his mistress-turned-bride had made the most of it—with one of the grooms. It had been the boy's misfortune to witness one of their passionate partings with herself near naked bidding the groom good-by at the door of her bedchamber around dawn. Her face had gone ugly at sight of Deverell hurrying down the corridor for an early morning ride and she had slammed the door. Later she had tried to ride him down on the driveway and narrowly missed the puppy. When Deverell's uncle came back, she had been first to corner him lest Deverell tell of her doings. She had laid it on rather thick, insisting that she had indeed been thrown as a result of the boy's darting in front of her, and had suffered a miscarriage. The new Earl of Roxford had frowned mightily at that, for the main reason he had let himself be bullied into marriage with his erstwhile mistress had been the necessity of a legitimate heir. He had called Deverell in and thrust into his hand a couple of guineas and suggested vaguely that he run away to sea, that the life of a cabin boy might just suit him. Deverell had learned the truth later, but by then it was too late. The mistress-turned-wife had already borne a son and he knew he would not be welcome at Wingfield. But he felt no need to go into all that now beneath that glorious violet gaze.

"So I've been on my own since," he added crisply. He did not tell her of the awful hardships he had endured as a young lad in London, having his pocket picked the first day, the street life in the alleys—no, he would not tell her of that. He would tell her of the better times. "I worked for a peddler for a time, and that was how I came here. The peddler was seized in York. Had he not given a shout, I'd have been seized too."

"*Why?*" breathed Constance.

Deverell shrugged. "It was claimed he'd stolen something in the last town we'd been. I never believed it, but his horse and wagon and all his merchandise were confiscated—even my wages which were owing." *And they had whipped the peddler until he bled, before a sullen milling crowd at the Whip-ma-Whop-ma-Gate, as York's "street of punishment" was called. And before half the lashes were applied the peddler's eyes had rolled back and he had had a seizure and died.* He would not tell her that; it would horrify her. Instead he said, "It had begun to snow that day, I had nowhere to sleep that night and no money, so I took the first thing offered."

"Chimney sweep?" she guessed.

He nodded gravely and told her how Old Hays, taller than a scarecrow and as thin, with his height emphasized by the sooty tall-crowned beaver hat he always wore, had just lost his helper. Deverell had seen it happen. He had been walking through the snow down Spurriergate, the "street of spurmakers," for "gate" was the old Danish name for "street," and he had seen a lanky man dressed all in black, a man so tall he seemed to be walking on stilts. The man was accompanied by a reed-thin, soot-smudged boy slightly older than himself, and Deverell had realized they must be chimney sweeps. As he watched, the tall man's high-crowned beaver hat was taken by the wind and, as it went sailing off, the boy flashed into the narrow street to retrieve it. A heavy cart was just then lumbering by and a smaller one attempting to pass. It was all over before the horses could be brought to a halt. The boy was caught between them, crushed by the cartwheels in the fast-falling snow. Deverell had stood stunned—and then realized that he was in luck. A job opening had just come his way.

"And you ended up here, at Claxton House?"

"Where Old Hays died midway through the job, yes."

"Well, I can't call you 'Sweep,' " decided Constance. "It doesn't suit you at all. I think I'll call you 'Dev.' "

The boy would have been enchanted to be called anything by this fairylike creature. All he wanted was for her to stay within sight.

"Why are you practicing dancing?" he asked curiously, for he knew as well as she that she would not be allowed to dance in the Banqueting Hall and these steps she had been executing with such grace and precision were hardly the stuff for farmers gone a-Maying.

"Because"—Constance drew herself up—"someday I'm going to be a lady of fashion and have a big house of my own to manage. And I must be ready." Overcome by the folly of what she was saying, tears suddenly sparkled on her sooty lashes and her breath caught. "Of course—it won't happen, I suppose," she whispered.

"It will!" declared the boy's strong voice. "*I'll* get your house for you!" He spoke almost fiercely.

"You?" She gave him a wondering look.

He had spoken on impulse, but now he affirmed it recklessly. "You've my word on it! The word of a Westmorland!"

She smiled at him then, a slow sweet smile. Reaching out, she trustingly gave him her hand and they walked, boy and girl fashion, over to a low mound of hay and sat down upon it companionably. She was not to know how the touch of her soft hand affected the fifteen-year-old boy. It set him afire and lit in him strong new passions. He hardly dared look at her lest she see how he felt, and his guilty flush lit up his strong young face.

But they were now farther from the lanthorn and the girl could not see him as clearly. She noticed nothing amiss.

"Why do you make me this great offer, Dev?" she asked softly. For offers such as his—empty though it might be— were beyond her experience.

"Because you deserve it," he said ringingly. And looking at her, he knew with a pang that he was not the only man who would think she deserved a great house—she read *that* in his eyes and bridled.

"I am considered of no great worth here." Calmly.

"Then they are all either blind or mad!" he declared with such heat that again she considered him in wonder. For the world had yet to tell her that she had the kind of beauty to stop a man's heart.

"Perhaps you would like to dance with me?" she said tentatively.

Dev felt suffocated with joy. "If you will teach me?"

"We will learn together," she told him with her grave sweet smile.

In the days that followed she saw much of Dev. She basked in his kindness, she shared her innermost thoughts with him. And because he was thin and she was afraid he did not get enough to eat, she took food surreptitiously from the big kitchen and brought it to him in the stables wrapped in linen squares. She managed to bring him bullets too from the great store of bullets her grandfather kept in his study, for Dev had a grand ambition—he wanted to be "the best shot in England." He practiced his marksmanship out on the moors with the one legacy Old Hays had pressed into his hand before he died— a pistol. She, who was so hard-pressed and unhappy herself, tried her best to make Dev's life a little less hard.

Dev worshipped the ground she walked on.

There came an awful day when Hugh, home from school for a fortnight, seized her—for laughing when he slipped and fell inelegantly into a mud puddle—snatched out his hunting knife and hacked off part of her hair.

"I'll kill him!" muttered Deverell when he found her sobbing in the stables over a handful of long dark hair.

"No—Dev, you mustn't!" She clutched him, full of fear for there was murder in his eyes and he had already picked up a pitchfork. She thanked God he had used up all the bullets in his pistol.

He would have wrenched away. "I know how he treats you! I've seen him at it!"

"No, Dev, no!" She clung to him, white-faced. "Sir John dotes on him and—"

"I care naught for that." With the pitchfork firmly in hand, Dev started toward the big stable doors.

She managed to run around in front of him and block his exit. "If you fight him, they will send you away," she gasped. "And what would I do without you?"

Her lovely imploring face was very close and Dev was brought up short by her words: *What would I do without you?* How that tore at his heart!

"I can't let him hurt you, Constance," he said huskily.

"He hasn't hurt me, my hair will grow back."

Dev looked back at the dark lock she had dropped as she sought to hold him back. "Could I have that?" he wondered. "I'd like to weave it into a bracelet to wear round my wrist."

She flushed with pleasure. "I'll weave it for you," she promised eagerly.

Dev gave her a wistful look—and promised himself that he would deal with Hugh. Someday.

She looked up, her eyes luminous—and it was then that Dev gave her his first hurried kiss. A boyish kiss, swift and sweet, that caused them a moment later to spring apart in embarrassment—Dev busying himself with putting away the pitchfork and Constance quickly addressing herself to weaving a bracelet for Dev out of her own dark hair.

And so it was that Dev wore around his wrist a narrow braid of silken hair, as dark and shining as the cloud that framed Constance's sweet face—that cloud that was fast growing back again. Just as Constance was growing into young womanhood.

"I have always been an outsider here," she pondered one day to Dev. "Yet I'm of their own blood. Why do the Daceys treat me so?"

Dev could have told her, but he forbore. She would learn the hard truth soon enough.

BOOK III
Lightskirts and Lovers

Drink it slowly now, the wine,
Clasp the moment, rich and fine,
Let the golden hours pass
Like a torrent through the glass!

PART ONE
First Love

They've plighted troth so true today
And sealed it with a kiss,
Their love is fresh and new today,
A glorious season this!

Claxton House,
The West Riding, Yorkshire,
Spring 1681

CHAPTER 8

At Claxton House, the lord and lady of the manor were Church of England, but the servants were stubborn Dissenters all. They grumbled about the harsh repressive Acts that made life so hard for Dissenters, and as she ate the coarse food in the servants' hall or helped make butter in a big wooden churn or dipped tallow candles, Constance listened. In the drafty kitchens and buttery of Claxton House, she was learning Dissent—and politics. Discovering the real world.

But her most wondrous discovery was the magnificent ruins of Fountains Abbey, stretching along—and over—the river Skell.

At Claxton House she had often heard cook inveigh against the white-robed monks who had established their great Cistercian abbey near Ripon early in the twelfth century. "Fat abbots dressed to kill, riding on prancing palfreys with great silver crosses—and them supposed to have taken vows of poverty!" she was wont to remark in derision, drawing the back of her fat hand across her broad sweaty face. Then she would return

129

to basting with a long pewter spoon a shoulder of sizzling venison that turned on a long iron spit—or bend over a steaming pigeon pie.

"Where *is* Fountains?" Constance asked Dev one spring day.

"Haven't you seen it?" His brows shot up.

"No, never."

"I'll take you there, first chance I get," he promised. He was seventeen now, tall and rather startlingly handsome. All the younger chambermaids bridled when he passed by. Long-limbed, hard-muscled, his strong young face—for all he was but a stableboy and at Claxton House not likely to rise above it—mirrored authority. His voice too—and it was an attractive voice with rich timbred undertones—had a ring of authority to it. Already the other stableboys deferred to him, and not just because of his increasing prowess with his fists or his skill with a pistol, but because of something inborn, some innate sense of leadership that called out to them. He had come from a long line of commanders that reached back to that first Sir Deverell, chain-mailed knight, who had fought at the Battle of Hastings to gain for William the Norman an island empire.

"Is Fountains very far?"

"Not so far we cannot walk it," he assured her. "But we must skirt the thorn hedge that was planted by Sir John's grandfather to keep 'those pestilential monks' at a distance."

"Who told you about that?" she asked in surprise.

"Garn, the stable master," he grinned. "His people have tilled this land for generations."

"He must be as big a gossip as cook," Constance smiled. "To hear cook talk, you'd think those poor monks raped the country!"

"The abbey was rich, the people were poor," he said shortly. "And some of cook's people were burned to death in the time of Bloody Mary—just for the crime of being Protestant under a Catholic queen. You can't blame cook for being vengeful."

Constance wondered suddenly if cook's bright-eyed young daughter might have told him that. "But of course we live in more enlightened times," she said quickly. "Such a thing could never happen again. Could it, Dev?" Her young face was troubled.

He gave her an uneasy look. "Who knows?" he muttered. "When a religion comes to you from overseas, what feeling has it for the local people? How does Rome know what it's like here? I was brought up Church of England," he added. And then grimly, "But I'm a Dissenter now!"

Constance too was a Dissenter. At Claxton House she had aligned herself with the servants instead of the master.

"And Fountains—"

"For miles around this land was ruled from Fountains Abbey. But it's long deserted. You'll see."

It was on a spring afternoon with the ground soft and yielding underfoot that they set out across the fields, Dev's long legs walking strongly with their springy stride, Constance moving along beside him in her faded lavender kirtle with a light blue shawl thrown about her shoulders against the cool wind that swept down from the heather heights of the far-flung Yorkshire moors. They walked fast, talking and laughing. Caught up in conversation, Constance saw the great abbey all at once just at dusk and she missed a step and paused breathlessly to drink in the sight of it.

The timeless ruins, slumbering in the wooded valley drained by the River Skell, caught at her heart. Unroofed, deserted, its doorless openings and windows devoid of panes revealed the magnificence of the evening sky. Great and gray, it loomed before her, so lovely it seemed unreal. Begun early in the twelfth century, a scant seventy years after William of Normandy conquered this land, it had been unroofed, its treasure scattered, by order of a later lord, Henry of England. But in the centuries intervening, grown rich on vast church lands, immense flocks and commerce in wool, this remote and ancient seat of the austere white-robed Cistercian monks had flourished in grandeur. Even in its ruined state, it took her breath away.

They had reached Fountains just as the setting sun turned the western sky to brilliant rose madder, shading upward to pink and lavender and purple. And now with the changing of the light the clean massive lines of the somber gray walls and upflung stone lace of its gothic tracery became a rhapsody in stone. As they watched, those massive walls changed from dove gray to pinkish French gray and then to a heart-stopping rosy lavender.

As she stood there enraptured, Dev's arm stole around her. She shivered beneath his touch and turned toward him with her eyes wide and dark and wondering. Something quite magical had happened when he touched her, something she did not quite understand, but her body for a moment had seemed to want to reach out to Dev with a will of its own.

Blushing and suddenly shy, Constance turned away, to look back at the abbey, changing now at last to a cool whited purple as the sun went down and clear white moonlight from a pale greenish moon flooded the scene.

"It's beautiful," she breathed, watching the moonlight turn the wide expanse of intervening grass a mysterious deep viridian green even while it silvered the winding expanse of the River Skell. And then, almost accusingly, "No one said it was so beautiful!"

Dev, who had let her go reluctantly and was thinking how radiant she looked standing there, laughed. "That's because all at Claxton House shun the place!"

"Well, I'll not shun it!" declared Constance fervently. "I'll come here every chance I get!" Beckoning Dev forward, she picked up her skirts and ran over the parklike green turf, ran toward the magic that waited for them along the silver river. And Dev, smiling because he loved her, followed— and caught her, and kissed her in the moonlight. A long lingering kiss that made them both draw back in wonder, shaken by the glory that seemed to beckon just ahead.

"It must be—this place," said Constance unsteadily.

"It isn't," he said in a low rich voice. "It's you." He was toying with her hair as he spoke and now he ran his fingers playfully down the back of her neck, now he was caressing her soft pulsing throat.

"Don't," she whispered.

And Dev, sternly reminding himself how young she was, let his hand drop away and stepped back. He told himself sternly that he would do no more than hold her, kiss her now and then, he would give her no cause for alarm. But . . . her fresh young body, her elusive flower scent, her trusting face—she was like a lodestone drawing him. He wondered dizzily how long he could hold himself in check.

It was late when Constance—her body alight with strange new yearnings but her virtue still intact—crept up the stair and let herself into the bedchamber where Felicity lay sleeping. Tiptoeing not to awaken the sleeping girl, she slipped into her own cubbyhole—but not to sleep. To dream.

And so the vast complex of Fountains Abbey became their special retreat, to which they fled to heal the wounds of the spirit that life at Claxton House was inflicting on them every day. Together they explored the lofty unroofed church which stood just north of the Skell, together roamed the nave with its eleven great bays, hand in hand stood in wonder in the lovely Chapel of the Nine Altars. They frolicked through the *cellarium*'s magnificent double avenue of arches and lunched on whatever scraps Constance had been able to glean that day from the kitchen. There in that noble unroofed shell they sat on stones that, they agreed, had known feudal lords and mounted knights and medieval splendor—yes, and fat abbots too, they told each other, laughing. Together they wandered through the abbey's cellars, its brewhouse, its prisons, its buttery. Constance gazed in wonder at the magnificence of the Abbot's House and said it was amazing that with empty land all about, so much of the house should have been built on arches over the Skell.

"Amazing," agreed Dev, and bent to kiss her.

Constance, who was learning caution in such things, pulled away. "How large do you think this room is?" she exclaimed to divert him, for her cheeks were still flushed and her lips still burning from that kiss.

And Dev, transported by the gossamer touch of her silken mouth, dutifully paced off the great hall and found it to measure some 170 by 70 feet. Like the great hall at Winchester Castle, it was punctuated by eighteen stone pillars and arches. It had many rooms and even its vast kitchen dwarfed to insignificance the sizeable kitchen of Claxton House, for the abbot's kitchen measured 50 feet by 38 feet.

"And they called these monks 'austere'!" laughed Dev, moving toward her for he was eager to kiss her again. "Why, except for castles, this must have been the largest private home in England when it was built!"

Still breathless, Constance avoided him nimbly. Only this morning Henriette, spying grass stains on her dress, had cautioned her to "Stay clear of that handsome stableboy, *ma chère*. He is too much like a hawk—one day he will fly away and break your heart."

But of course, she told herself, *he would not*.

She knew more about Fountains now, for she had inquired about. The Abbot of Fountains, who had lived so richly, had been hanged at Tyburn like a common criminal at the time of the revolt. But bad or good, she could not bring herself, like cook, to hate his memory.

Staid Claxton House was where young Constance laid her head at night, Dissent was her religion and rebellion ran in her blood, but Fountains Abbey, so beautiful in its ruined state and indestructible forever in her memory, had become in a strange way her home of the heart.

"Oh, Dev!" She whirled about, and over him washed the purple glory of her sparkling eyes. "Wouldn't it be wonderful to have a home *half* as grand as this?"

"Wingfield is more than half as grand," said Dev sturdily. "And more than half as large as this Abbot's House."

"Is it really, Dev?" Constance was taken aback. "Perhaps one day you'll take me to see it," she said wistfully.

He shook his head and stubborn pride rang in his voice.

"The day my uncle cast me out, I swore I'd not return save as a belted earl!"

And that would never be, she knew, *for his uncle had a son of his own to inherit. Dev, the outcast, would never inherit Wingfield.*

"But we have this," she said quickly. "Our make-believe manor—Fountains!"

He caught her mood. "And to my chatelaine, I give the key to my new-won castle," he said, bowing in exaggerated fashion and presenting her with a horseshoe which he picked up from the ground.

She laughed and with a deep curtsy accepted the horse-shoe. "Just the right size for doors such as mine—if my castle had doors!" For Fountains' doors and windowpanes, like the roof, like the gold and silver it had housed, had been carted away long before they were born.

It was at Fountains that Dev told her of his boyhood in Kent. Lying on his back on the grass with his head on her lap, his voice had richened, deepened, as he described to her the garden land of Kent with its blooming orchards, its fields of hops dried in conical oasthouses, its thatch-roofed villages, its foggy winters and its glorious summers. He told her how the rakish half-timbered wattle-and-daub cottages were built, their timbers prefabricated in the forests where the great trees were felled, shaped and fitted by adz and numbered for reassembly on the site.

And he told her, with an ache in his voice, of Wingfield, built of the gray-brown Kentish stone, approached over green velvet lawns between tall hedges of clipped yew. Listening raptly, she could almost see its dramatic gabled roofline, its banks of mullioned and transomed windows, the vast sweep of its eastern front with a tall steeple in the center and at each end square towers surmounted by pointed roofs which formed the farther end of a great U-shaped design down which one passed between five steep gables on either side. It seemed far away and unreal. Like Fountains, it was part of her dream.

But she loved to hear Dev talk about it, loved to hear the

sound of his voice as he lay beside her, or sat with an arm flung lightly around her shoulders while she leaned back in the crook of that arm, looking outward at the silvery glitter of the river as it wound by.

She needed these fancies as a respite from the harsh unending grind of her life at Claxton House, just as Dev needed his fancies about someday achieving his own impossible dream—to become as his grandfather before him had been, Earl of Roxford. Children of adversity both, they would sometimes sit in silent communion while the breezes drifted down the Skell, ruffling their hair and bringing with it from the moors the scent of rain.

Sometimes on hot summer evenings they undressed with their backs to each other and swam naked in the River Skell, frolicking about the arches and foundations of the mighty stone structure looming above them. Constance, frailly built and never a very strong swimmer, would seek the shallower places and suddenly with a sweep of her arm direct a splash of water at Dev, showering his laughing face with glistening droplets. And he would retaliate by diving under and pulling her down into the depths until both their heads emerged, laughing and sputtering, from the water.

Once when she slid into the water too soon after devouring the lunch she had brought, Constance doubled up with a cramp and would have drowned but that Dev realized her difficulty, swam toward her and bore her competently to shore.

She lay there trembling and sick, her slender body pale and gleaming. And Dev, hovering over her, dripping wet, saw her as he had never seen her before—not as a shining silver mermaid half seen in the water but as a naked girl, totally desirable.

The sight made him sway on his feet.

Constance, doubled up with the cramp, was hardly aware of his rapt surveillance.

He did not touch her—not then, although he ached to. When she felt better, she dressed modestly, beyond his sight, and was sober as they walked home across the meadows, for she knew that on this day he had saved her life.

"Dev." Her voice was a gossamer whisper as she looked up at the tall youth striding along beside her. "I'd have died back there but for you."

His face was shadowed as he looked down at her. The moon had risen and its glow silvered the fields but cast his face in darkness. "I shouldn't have let you go in so soon after eating," he said roughly. "I knew better."

She sighed, a long-drawn-out sigh that seemed to sway her whole being, like a long-stemmed meadow flower swaying before a sudden breath of wind—and then her white arms twined round his neck and she drew his face down to hers for a swift sweet kiss.

This small tribute to his prowess, so freely and so gently given, rocked Dev to his foundations. He clutched her to him with such fervor that she gasped, and he bore her to the meadow grass in his enthusiasm.

" 'Tis only because you're so young I've held back," he said huskily. "We could stay till morning—we'd not be missed." His hand was caressing the silky skin of her bosom as he spoke, straying down beneath her bodice to explore the delicate texture of her round breasts.

A flood of feeling went through her.

"No, I—we must get back!" She pushed him away in panic and scrambled up, afraid suddenly of she knew not what. Of becoming a woman too soon, perhaps. Of Henriette's warning that Dev was a wild hawk who would wing away and leave her. She wanted this lightness of youth to last. . . . "Catch me if you can!" she cried and streaked off like a will-o'-the-wisp across the flowering meadows.

Dev, realizing that the time was not yet, ran lightly after her, fighting back the overwhelming desire that roared through his veins like a torrent. He caught her playful mood and frolicked with her—indeed they might have been two young colts running through the moonlight—all the way home to Claxton House.

But Midsummer's Eve was another story.

Bonfires had been built. All the servants were dancing round them. The merriment might well go on till dawn and no one would notice where a pair of waifs were tonight.

She and Dev, caught by the magic of summer, carried a kerchief of cakes along with them to Fountains Abbey and ate them there, talking of the future and what would one day be. They drank deep of the clean cold water of the river that once had watered the abbey gardens, lying full length in the grass to drink, scooping up clear handfuls of water in their cupped hands and laughing as they drank.

The moon had come up. Its pale radiance shimmered the stone lace into a place of wonder against the deep blue blush of the night sky. Constance lifted her head and rolled over on her back away from the water so that she might study the delicate stone tracery that always fascinated her.

She found instead a dark head obstructing her view and Dev's warm lips pressed down upon her own.

This time she did not stir or fight him, but lay quietly with her arms outflung as his long body came down to rest lightly against hers, his weight supported on his elbows. He seemed part of the magic of the night and she knew she loved him.

Perhaps she had always loved him, from that first day when he had found her dancing on the stable floor. It was as if she had overnight become a woman and Dev had discovered it before she had.

"Oh, Constance, I want you so." Dev's words came to her borne on a gusty sigh and she knew he was asking—not forcing.

When she made no response, lost in the loveliness of her surroundings, in the warmth that seemed to cascade from his strong body to hers, he toyed playfully with her ear, nibbling it, and let his lips wander over her face and throat. Then he shifted his weight to the side and with questing fingers gently eased down the neck of her bodice where her young breasts strained against them, released them from the taut material and kissed them too, worrying the pink crested nipples with his tongue until a soft little moan escaped her.

And suddenly, borne on a gust of desire, she wrapped her arms around him and pulled him down to her, returning fevered kiss for fevered kiss, letting the world slip away into oblivion.

Dev was her future and she would hold him to her heart.

Through the golden shimmer of her dazzled senses, she felt the sudden thrill that went through Dev at this open-hearted acceptance of his love, she felt the pride in him as he brought his youthful manliness up hard against her feminine softness, and she forced herself not to cry out when he entered her with a sudden thrust that brought tears of pain to her eyes and wet her lashes.

She was his and she wanted him to know it.

For his part, Dev felt that he was born to love her. His lean body fitted itself to her fragile slenderness as perfectly as a hand fits a glove. Her silken skin was a madness driving him on—and on. Clothes were something to be brushed away. Time had no meaning. Her body was alight with new discoveries, swift sensations of rushing feeling at his touch, mounting, ever mounting. Like enchanted lovers, there beside the silver river, they strove and murmured and loved and kissed and let themselves be swept onward by a river all their own, a river of endless desire on which they tossed like drifting leaves, uncaring of their destination. But their river built to a raging torrent, a wild uncharted stream that of a sudden burst its banks and swept them with it madly to thrills undreamt of.

And when it was over, when they lay there side by side, bodies touching in the pulsing tremor of the afterglow, their spirits seemed to mingle even as their bodies had done.

Not till the moon was on the wane could they bring themselves to leave—for they knew they must return before the sun was up.

Constance rose first. She smiled at Dev as she tucked her round young breasts back into her straining bodice and smoothed down her skirts around her slender hips. She looked lovely standing there against the background of the silver river, Dev thought dreamily. He still could not believe that she was his.

"We should exchange our vows," she told him softly.

"I would we could have the banns cried," he told her in a husky voice. But they both knew that would mean dismissal for him and God knew what for her.

"No matter," she said raptly. "This is a holy place. Time has hallowed it." *Holy—and beloved by me.* "And besides," she added haltingly, "it is where we first..."

"I know," he said, catching her mood as always. He rose and took her hand, there beside the ruined abbey beneath the open summer sky. "On this day, Constance, I do plight you my troth and swear to be ever true."

Her own voice caught as she softly echoed his words, and her eyes, looking up trustingly into his face, were velvet pools in which he sank and was lost. "On this day, Deverell, I do plight you my troth, and swear to be ever true."

And there they kissed, beneath the stars of Yorkshire.

And for them, the ancient stones they stood before were an altar fashioned for them alone, the upflung walls, rising magnificently in stone lacework against the sky, a cathedral of their love, and the faint murmur of distant thunder rolling down from the Cleveland Hills to the northwest, a soft benediction, pronouncing them man and wife.

Constance would always consider it a marriage, that simple clasping of hands and exchanging of vows that only God had witnessed. For on that night of stars, deep in her heart, she gave herself to Dev, and she knew her feelings for him would never alter.

Afterward they drank deep of the cold waters of the Skell and walked back hand in hand, awed into silence, to Claxton House, both of them with the feeling that life had changed for them, momentously.

Claxton House,
The West Riding, Yorkshire,
Midsummer's Day 1681

CHAPTER 9

The cock was crowing as the lovers reached the dark pile of Claxton House, and Dev, after a last swift kiss, went his way while Constance slipped into the house through a kitchen door that was left unlocked by kindly cook so that the scullery maids might slip back unobserved after trysting with their lovers.

At the top of the stairs she was suddenly confronted by Hugh. He was wearing dusty riding boots and his face was almost comically thunderstruck at sight of her, disheveled and with meadow grasses tangled in her rich dark hair.

"I—didn't know you were back," she gasped.

"Just got in," he said, and then with a nasty laugh, "and find you just getting in too. Well, if you get yourself pregnant, you won't be so lucky as your mother!" he added brutally.

"What do you mean?" she cried indignantly. "My mother—"

"Was well along with child before my uncle married her."

She stood quivering. "So what if she was?" she demanded

141

angrily. "She'd not be the first to visit the marriage bed before the preacher!"

"But the child was not his," he mocked. "He admitted that to my grandfather. Haven't you wondered about the way you're treated here? You're an embarrassment, we don't know quite what to do with you! You bear our name, yet you're not of our blood."

"I don't believe you!" she cried sharply. But even as she spoke, she knew it must be true. Like the missing piece of a puzzle, it explained everything. And now she knew why her mother had clutched her to her, whispering, *Don't ask, don't ever ask.* . . . With a sob, she ran past him.

"I wouldn't let on that you know," he called softly after her. "For then Grandfather might decide to put you in the kitchen permanently—and forget you." His mocking laugh rang out again and she felt it go through her like separate points of a pitchfork.

She was not one of them. But then, who was she? Who had her father been? She could not ask grinning Hugh, and she feared to ask that fierce old man, whom she had thought to be her grandfather.

When she darted past a sleeping Felicity and reached her own small sleeping alcove at last, her body—which should have been tingling with newfound wonder—felt cold and watchful and frightened.

She leant against the wall and her thoughts pounded at her. *Who am I? Who was my father? My real father?*

Constance kept out of Hugh's way throughout the day. But it was late afternoon before she managed to catch Dev alone in the stables. She blurted out the whole story and wept on his shoulder.

"I knew about it," he said quietly.

"You—*knew*?" she whispered, pulling back from him.

"Yes." He kept his hold on her, protectively. "But none of the servants know, not even the governess so far as I can tell. Hugh probably wasn't supposed to tell you."

Her world seemed to be tilting. "How *could* you know?" she cried.

"I found some papers," he told her briefly. "Last year when all the house servants were down with colds and I was sent up to the main house to clean out the fireplaces. As I was cleaning the hearth in Sir John's bedchamber a brick came loose and when I pulled at it, a metal box fell down and papers spilled out. I saw they concerned you so I took the box and hid it and replaced the brick."

"Where—where are they?" she asked uncertainly.

"I'll get them for you," he said. "I've hidden them up in the rafters where it's dry."

She climbed up to the hayloft with him and took the box he handed her in trembling hands. She was almost afraid to open it.

There were two letters in the box:

The first was a letter from her father, written to her grandfather from London. She read the pertinent parts twice: *I know you disapprove of me, sir, and that you will have heard rumors by now about my marriage. They are quite true. Our child*—she noted that he said "our child," which meant surely that he claimed her—*was born but five months after the wedding and but six months after I met Anne. You are not to concern yourself about that as I intend to make no claim upon you nor upon the estate.* Brave words from a man who had been forced to come crawling back bringing with him his threadbare family! Besides the love she bore him, Constance felt a quivering sympathy for this foster father who had claimed her so bravely.

The other letter in the box was also addressed to Sir John and it was the most surprising of all. It had come from Devon and was written in a hasty scrawl:

Although we have never had occasion to meet, I have had word of how you feel about Hammond's marriage to Anne, the letter began. *But the child is not to blame, whatever her mother has done. I feel that you should know that my brother Brandon was on his way to marry Anne Cheltenham when he died. (Brandon,* thought Constance. *My real father was named Brandon. Brandon Archer.) And consider that it was your son's love of Anne,* the letter continued, *that caused him to marry her even though he well knew she was with child by my brother. It has come to my attention that not only are the child's true parents dead, but your son as well, and I have a solution to what you must consider a difficult problem. If you will send the child to me, I promise to care for her as if she were my own. You may write to me at Tattersall House, Dartmoor.*

It was signed with a flourish *Margaret Archer.*

Obviously there had been no reply. Or at any rate a negative one. Sir John had preferred to keep his shameful secrets on his own doorstep. *He meant to hide me away forever!* Constance thought with a shiver. Her eyes glistening with unshed tears, she looked up at Dev. "You've had these all this time? Why didn't you show them to me before?"

He flushed scarlet. "I thought that if I showed them to you, you might leave," he admitted sheepishly. "And I couldn't have stood that."

She understood in that moment how very much she meant to him and was silent as it all sank in.

Dev loved her, had always loved her.

"You can see that this—changes everything," she said quietly.

"Does it?" His suddenly wary glance never wavered from her face. "You don't have to stay," he urged. "I'll take you away from here—to Devon if you like." He didn't point out the obvious—that Margaret Archer's letter was undated, it could have been written years ago! No matter, he told himself recklessly, he'd take care of Constance in any event!

Amethyst lights played in Constance's purple eyes as she thought about that. *To Devon with her lover* . . . They could be married on the way! Married in some hamlet where they could find work for a while—perhaps in a dairy or on some farm, to earn enough to let them move on to the next shire.

"Oh, Dev, do you really think we could?"

"Yes!" He took her by the shoulders and she thrilled to the touch of his strong fingers. "We could leave tonight."

"I was hoping we could spend one more night at Fountains," she said wistfully. "Because we'll probably never see it again."

No, they wouldn't dare come back—Dev knew that. For while Sir John didn't want her, she was still his ward and he wanted no one else to have her—lest her real story surface. And Hugh was always a danger. Every wary instinct he had warned him they should leave at once.

But his face softened at her pleading. One more night spent at magical Fountains . . . Was that so much to ask? "Tomorrow then," he agreed. "But tonight—Fountains."

"Oh, Dev!" She threw her arms around him rapturously. "We could go to Fountains now!"

"We'd be missed," he said. "Best wait till dusk." And rumpled her dark hair with affectionate fingers.

Constance was light of heart as they strolled through the dusk beneath a rising moon. And full of plans—she would tell Henriette, she would ask her advice, did she not think that was a good idea? Henriette was worldly, she would make suggestions.

Dev smiled down at her fondly and his arm tightened about her shoulders as they walked. She was so young, so fine, so right for him. God had shown him mercy the day He had brought Constance into his life. Silently he vowed that he would be worthy of the gift, he would love her, cherish her, bring her at last to all that her feminine heart desired.

The problem was he had no idea how to accomplish it.

He was frowning, perplexed, when at last they reached the sprawling complex of monastery buildings, rising in deserted grandeur above the sheep-cropped sod.

Constance led him to a place where the grass was very soft near the silver river's edge. It seemed screened from the world by the wide bulk of one of the abbey buildings, more ruinous than most. Above tumbled falls of stone, high up in the massive walls were sightless openings that had once been windows—and outlining them pointed arches of delicately wrought stone lace, giving a heartrending hint of what this once had been.

"It's perfect here," said Constance softly, surveying its beauty, its serenity. Around them the night noises were muffled. Somewhere there was the sleepy chirp of a nesting bird, and over there the rustle of a clump of taller grass as some little furry creature, perhaps a ferret, stole through on its way to a night hunt within the ruined walls. Above them stars sparkled.

She sighed. "Our last night here." Her voice held a note of melancholy.

"Then we must make the most of it," he rejoined cheerfully. For the very sight of her slim bewitching figure was already driving him wild. He yearned to get his arms around her, to hold her, have her—but she made a little gesture as if to ward him off and—sensitive to her every change of mood—he resisted the urge to seize her and smother her with kisses.

"Tonight will be different," she told him dreamily. "Tonight we will take our time." She kicked off her worn shoes. And sat down on the soft grass and removed her stockings and garters.

He watched, fascinated.

In a single supple gesture she rose. Then slowly, with her violet eyes locked to his, she took off her lavender kirtle, letting the faded linen slide down over her worn chemise. And then she unhooked, one by one, the hooks of her faded linen bodice, asking for no help. This was a little pantomime she had promised herself as they walked home last night.

Dev made a little sound in his throat, almost a groan, as she loosed the riband that held her chemise and let the material, worn thin from many washings, glide down around her fair young body.

And stood before him in all the perfection of her gleaming nakedness.

Dev's gaze was rapt. He reached out his arms for her.

Suddenly there was a loud "Bravo!" from behind the broken wall and as Dev whirled, a large stone grazed his ear.

He leaped for Constance and pulled her down behind a fallen pile of masonry. She gave a gasp of pain as her ankle turned under her, then huddled there shivering as more stones cracked against the barrier behind which they sheltered. And now she recognized Hugh's voice, hoarsely hurling epithets at them, calling her all manner of filthy things.

"Stay here," whispered Dev, taking off his shoes and picking up a stone. And when she would have held him back, he put a finger to his lips and gently unclasped her fingers from his arm. Moments later he was easing around the corner of the building, keeping to the shadows, his bare feet making no sound on the sheep-cropped turf.

The rain of stones and howls continued while she quailed in her refuge behind the pile of masonry.

Then suddenly there was silence.

Constance opened her mouth and no words came out. Was it Hugh who had been silenced? Or Dev?

And then she heard Dev's voice and in her thankfulness almost fainted. "You can come out now," he called calmly.

She picked up her kirtle and held it pressed against her trembling body as she limped over on her hurt ankle to join him, for suddenly she felt very naked, very defenseless.

"Is he—dead?" she asked fearfully, staring down at Hugh's great bulk, spread-eagled on the grass.

"No, just knocked unconscious. I got him with this." He kicked at a stone that lay near Hugh's head. "Don't worry, you won't be a party to his murder."

"I wasn't thinking of that," she murmured, trying hard to stand straight on the ankle that she had twisted so painfully. "I was thinking about what happens when he comes to!"

Dev was thinking about that too. There would be hell to pay. He had struck down the son and heir of Claxton House and Sir John was not likely to forgive that. If they caught him, punishment would be swift and sure.

Instinctively she had come close to him and now she leant

against him for support and clung with her fingers to his shirt front. His arms went protectively round her, and his hands, so gentle, so yearning, caressed her naked back. "We haven't— time," he muttered hoarsely and desire flickered in his eyes.

Constance's mind was working furiously. Her ankle was so painful that she could barely stand. Walking anywhere would be an agony—and very slow. And Dev could not carry her for any great distance.

But she knew he would try. And that was what made it all so terrible. Every fiber of her being screamed to go with him—but she dared not yield to that mad desire. Dev would take her with him, injured as she was—and he would be conspicuous doing so. Her twisted ankle would hold him back. And in the hue and cry that would be raised for them throughout the countryside, that could well prove fatal.

She knew by now that her looks were very striking. She would be readily found, identified, dragged back. And so would Dev.

But their fate would be different: *She* would be delivered back to an uncaring Sir John, who desired only to hide her away.

But Dev—Dev had raised his hand against the old baronet's grandson, had perhaps near killed him. He would be formally charged, perhaps hanged. At the very least he would be publicly whipped—perhaps a hundred lashes or more. In her terrified fancy she saw him strung up, held by chains while a cat-o'-nine-tails throbbed rhythmically along his back, each blow biting deeper, bringing blood—and a groan. She saw him fight back the agony of it, saw him fall mercifully at last unconscious—and still the lash kept tearing at his flesh. Blood pounded in her temples at these terrible imaginings, and the sound of her heartbeats were the sounds of the whip, never stopping, going on and on. . . .

He would take her with him, no matter what the cost, and her heart yearned to let him do it. But if she went, she would only bring him death.

"I'm not going," she heard herself say.

He was aghast. "I can't leave you here—with him!"

"Of course you can!" she cried in panic. "And you must! Oh, Dev, can't you see? The way we planned it, it would have been different. They might even have let me slip away, glad just to forget me. But now that you've struck Hugh down, there'll be a scandal and no way to keep it quiet because servants gossip, and Sir John will know that and he'll have to hunt us down for his pride's sake—"

"Constance—"

Her voice rushed on. "Don't come back for me—just keep going. Oh, for heaven's sake, Dev—*go now!*"

Beneath her clutching fingers, she felt his body stiffen. "I thought you loved me, Constance," he said slowly.

"Oh, I do, I do!"

"If you loved me"—his voice was stubborn—"you would come with me. You would not stay here."

"I intend to write to Aunt Margaret," she improvised hastily, and suddenly that seemed like a very good idea. "I'll be all right, I promise you! At the worst, they'll lock me in my room for a while to repent my wild ways. Oh, Dev"—her voice rose to a wail—"I could never make it, running, hiding. Please, please try to understand."

"It's your ankle," he guessed, looking down at her keenly. "You're afraid you can't walk on it."

Oh, God, if he thought that, he would stay—try to brazen it out and perhaps die for it. She could not let him do that. Desperately she cast about in her mind for something that would send him on his way—and found it.

"I never really meant to go with you," she whispered, turning away from him so that he might not see the hot tears that were coursing down her face now, splashing unnoticed onto her snowy bosom, running in tiny rivulets down her round white breasts. "That's why I wanted to spend the night with you at Fountains. Because I wasn't going."

He took hold of her then, spun her around fiercely to face him. His young face mirrored a kind of despair. "I don't believe it," he said savagely. "You gave yourself to me last night. We plighted our troth!"

She hung her head. "Oh, don't think badly of me, Dev. Last night was lovely—but it was make-believe. Now I've had time to think and I'm not sure Aunt Margaret would take me in if she thinks I've been living with—with—"

"With a stableboy," he supplied accusingly, and she saw his lean body stiffen.

"Yes," she said hurriedly. "And—and Aunt Margaret may have a nice house in Devon. If she sends for me, I could have clothes and satin slippers and—and brilliants for my hair." She hated what she was doing to him, but she knew the knife must cut deep or he would never leave her. "I'm sorry, Dev, but—I want my chance at those things. Things you could never give me. Please try not to hate me too much . . . ." Her voice trailed off.

He cast a quick glance down at Hugh's fallen body and she knew instinctively what he was thinking.

This I did for you, he would be thinking. *I may have thrown away my life this day for you. And you do not care! Dear God, it must be coursing through his mind like a shout: You do not care for me as I care for you!*

He stared at her, baffled and angry. Abruptly he tore the kirtle from her hand and his hot gaze raked up and down her young nakedness—but she saw no desire in his face, only a kind of grief.

"Good-by, Constance," he said, and turned on his heel and left her, walking fast away.

Through tear-blurred eyes she watched him, as long as she could see him. And when he had disappeared over the horizon she felt a terrible emptiness, as if her world had been swept away. She had driven him away with lies. And he had left her with bitterness in his heart. She had faced a terrible choice and she had made it. By driving Dev away, she had given him back his life.

She looked up into the night sky. The moon still shone, the stars were still as bright—but not to her. To her they had dimmed, for she had lost her lover.

She crumpled up, weeping, on the grass.

She was roused from her grief by a slight stirring of Hugh's body nearby and she sat up in alarm. Hugh must not wake to find her like this—naked! God only knew what he would do to her! She dressed with the speed of panic and found a rock, set it down carefully near her hand, and sank down beside Hugh to wait. If Hugh staggered up and went charging off after Dev, she meant to bring him down—no matter what he did to her later!

Time passed slowly. The white moon moved across the sky. She sat there surrounded by beauty, staring at emptiness. Her future seemed to spin out before her—a world bereft. She wondered if she would ever see Dev again.

Beside her came a groan. Her fingers tightened on the rock. She leant down. "Are you all right?" she asked, trying to make her voice sound anxious, for there was nothing to be gained by further antagonizing Hugh.

The body prone on the grass beside her gave another groan and a writhing of green satin garments. Abruptly Hugh's eyes snapped open and he looked up at her in bewilderment. "What happened?" he demanded. "How did I get *here*?"

He did not remember! Joy surged through Constance. Perhaps it would be a long time before he recalled what had happened, how he had been struck down—and in the meantime Dev could make good his escape!

"We came here together," she said gravely. "We were dancing. You were teaching me a new step and you slipped on the grass—you can see for yourself how slippery the dew has made it. And you fell and struck your head on a stone and I have been trying to rouse you ever since!" And as he came to his feet, "Come, we must get your wound attended to." Of necessity, she clung to his arm, letting him bear her weight like a crutch, as they set out for Claxton House.

"Why are you limping?" he demanded. "Did you fall too?"

"No, you bore me down with you when you fell," she said ruefully. "No matter, it will make us walk slowly but that

151

will be the better for you as well, after your knock on the head.''

He trudged along beside her, his bull-like body uncaring of her weight. ''I thought—there was someone else here,'' he muttered in a dazed voice and shook his head dizzily to clear it.

''No one,'' she corrected him tranquilly. ''Only ourselves.''

By now Dev would have made it back to Claxton House. He would have collected his pistol and his few belongings. He would be on his way.

''And you say we were *dancing*?'' Hugh sounded as if he could not believe it.

''Dancing,'' she echoed firmly, and tears glittered in her eyes.

The servants were stirring about when they reached Claxton House and several of them stopped to gape at the sight of Constance and Hugh limping in with the dawn. Her ankle was agony and she felt exhausted, drained—but she felt a stirring sense of triumph too, along with her sense of loss. Dev would be well away by now. And she could cover for him as long as Hugh's mind remained confused—she would say Hugh had sent him out on some errand, oh, she would think of something!

There was a great to-do about the young master's injury, and Constance abetted it, explaining glibly how it had happened. Eyes were round and there were gasps at her story. Swiftly exchanged glances told her that everyone assumed the worst, that she was having an affair with Hugh—and at Fountains! They all looked shocked.

Sir John had been roused and told about it. He had ordered Hugh put to bed, a doctor fetched.

The doctor did not reach Claxton House until afternoon and Hugh slept heavily until then. His head was carefully bathed and a poultice applied. The doctor looked wise and—since Sir John was wealthy and the doctor wished to retain his custom—he told them to change the poultices and call him at once if there was any change; Hugh would probably spend most of his time sleeping for a while.

Hugh did. He slept the better part of three days.

On the third day he sent for Constance.

She found him alone in the handsome room, lying back, propped up against the pillows in the big canopied bed. He looked resentful and rested. His little piglike eyes glittered evilly at her.

"I remember everything," he told her in a low vicious tone. "Naked strumpet! You've let that stableboy have you!" Overcome by rage—for he had meant to have beautiful Constance first himself—he leaped from the bed and threw out his arm and sent her spinning violently across the room to crash into the farther wall.

Constance's scream as her body struck the wall brought the servants running.

"Mistress Constance has had a slight mishap," smirked Hugh. "She slipped on something. Be good enough to take her from my sight."

On an ankle that was mending, Constance fled. A little later a curious, bright-eyed Henriette reported to her that Hugh, elegantly dressed in puce satins and carrying a large pistol, was searching the grounds for a missing stableboy.

Sir John heard about that and his heavy brows drew together. It was as well the stableboy had run away—Hugh might have murdered him and made more scandal. *But the girl had become a beauty and that made her dangerous*. The old baronet sighed. He would have to think what to do with her. In the meantime . . .

"Tell Mistress Constance to lock her door," he directed.

Felicity looked up from her lace as the key turned in the lock. "Why are you locking the door, Constance?" she asked in an indifferent voice.

"Because Sir John sent word to do it," said Constance grimly.

Felicity seemed to be content with that explanation.

Two days later Hugh was sent away on the Grand Tour. He

would be gone a year, perhaps two. Constance breathed easier—and had more time to mourn Dev. And now she remembered—she had told Dev she was going to write to Margaret Archer and she would do it! And she would ask Henriette to post the letter for her.

From information I have lately received, she wrote in the stilted manner of a schoolgirl, *it would seem that I have been misinformed as to my parentage. My mother was Anne Cheltenham and until recently I had believed myself to be the daughter of Hammond Dacey, her husband. But now it has been flung at me that such is not the case, and I have chanced upon your letter written no doubt years ago to Sir John Dacey, in which you state that I am your dead brother's child. I realize that much may have changed in the meantime but*—and here she poured out her heart more eloquently—*the bitterness against me here is such as will destroy me, for Sir John grows feeble and his grandson Hugh, who will succeed him, hates me from his soul. I would come to you at Tattersall, if you will receive me.*

And she signed it *Your obedient niece, Constance Dacey.*

She was half a mind to scratch out "Dacey" and substitute "Archer" in her signature, but after some hesitation she decided against it. "Dacey" was after all her legal name and Hammond Dacey had claimed her against the world as his own—she would honor him for it. Her eyes misted over as she remembered how he had swept her up on his shoulder at the frost fair and glided with her over the ice. How gallant he had been! And what if he had not been there at her conception? He had been a true father in all ways and she would never reject him, never!

Henriette, on her next journey into Ripon, dispatched the letter. It was taken aboard a cart hauling furniture into Leeds, where it would be given over into the care of a stagecoach driver. But the letter never reached Leeds. Sudden rains flooded the roads and swelled the rivers. The supports of a wooden bridge gave way and cart and furniture, driver and letter, were all dumped together into the swirling muddy waters. In his anxiety to retrieve his cart and the valuable furniture, the carter forgot all about the letter and never mentioned to anyone that he had lost it.

Sir John, had he known about it, would have informed Constance crisply that it did not matter, for when he had received that letter he himself had made inquiries. He would have told Constance, young and full of hope, that she had written a letter to a woman over whose headstone moss had long been growing.

The headstone of Margaret the Visitor.

PART TWO
The Lightskirt

*The blazing fires of yesterday are banked now, sad
  and cold,*
No longer do they shimmer her pale hair into gold,
*No longer do her arms reach up and twine around
  him so,*
*And heaven's where it always was—but hell is here
  below!*

Axeleigh Hall, Somerset,
December 23, 1684

CHAPTER 10

Although neither girl had so much as a glimmering of it, an event would happen that night at dinner that would change their lives.

Bent on providing only a background for Pamela's new splendor, Constance had slipped over her head a sinuous raspberry sarsenet silk and scooped the skirts up into panniers over a French gray satin petticoat. She told herself the effect was both festive and restrained as befitted a dinner on the brink of the Christmas season.

Across from her Pamela was talking very vivaciously, trying to attract her father's attention to the gown Constance had insisted would suit her even though all the way down the stairs she had complained that she couldn't move her arms properly in it.

"Aunt Margaret chose the living room drapes but Mother chose these." Pamela indicated the handsome pale blue damask hangings. "She said Aunt Margaret was never home to eat in the dining room anyway, so why should she care about the drapes?'' Her laughter tinkled. ''Mother was always asking Aunt Margaret where she was going this week. They didn't get along. Mother called her 'Margaret the Visitor.' ''

So that was where they got that derisive last line for the tombstone jingle that went:

> *Alger the Strong,*
> *Alfred the Long,*
> *Richard the Pate,*
> *Brandon the Late,*
> *Virginia the Inquisitor,*
> *And Margaret the Visitor!*

And what did Margaret call your mother? Constance was tempted to ask, but she forbore, looking down and studying her plate.

At the head of his table, the Squire listened to the music of Pamela's lilting laugh and looked upon his spirited daughter with pride. She was very like him in many ways—their coloring was identical, so was the steady way they both looked at you out of their crystal blue eyes, and Pamela would have a good head on her shoulders when she steadied up a bit. Marriage would do it, he told himself, and for that he favored Tom Thornton, once Tom settled down a bit. But there was a recklessness in the girl that troubled him—a recklessness that lovely Pamela had inherited from her mother.

Her mother . . . He had not thought of Virginia in years and now he looked down at his trencher and saw not the food on it. Instead he saw a woman with Pamela's dainty features and fetching ways and intriguing figure. A light woman. His mouth hardened. Virginia had always been a light woman, born to stray—and of all the county only *he* had not been aware of it, it seemed.

''Father.'' Impatiently, Pamela interrupted his thoughts. ''Have you noticed anything *different* about me tonight?''

The Squire, who was brooding meditatively upon his roast capon, looked up with a start and considered his daughter.

"You do look a bit flushed," he hazarded. "Aren't coming down with a cold, are you? D'ye think ye should be wearing such a low-cut gown in this drafty room?"

Pamela flung Constance a comically rueful look. *So much for this undulating dress that Constance had recommended!* that look said. For the sinewy fabrics and startling décolletage urged on her by Constance had only given her father the conviction that she might catch cold!

Constance's brows elevated as if to say the Squire's opinion was not necessarily the world's, but Pamela chose not to notice. Actually she much preferred her stiff and handsome ball gowns that seemed to stand at attention and glide about by themselves. She *liked* looking like a Christmas ornament on which one could always stick another flounce, or add a saucy riband or a bit of lace!

"Oh, I'm not the least bit cold," she assured her father cheerfully and launched with a ravenous appetite into a platter of eels.

The Squire smiled at her. Surely no one could be ill with so healthy an appetite!

He looked up. Stebbins, the butler, was bringing him a note and Stebbins's lined forehead was wrinkled in perplexity. " 'Twas found by one of the maids on the front hall table just now, sir," he said in a somewhat aggrieved tone. "Although none will confess to hearing the knocker and when I looked outside there was no one about."

Clifford Archer took the note without comment. He broke the red wax seal and scanned it rapidly.

And reading it, his world melted away—all the safety and security he had built up for himself and his daughter vanished on the instant and it was Midsummer's Eve fourteen years ago.

As in a slow-moving nightmare he saw himself as he had been then, married but three years, rushing home unexpectedly to the young wife he loved—and pulling up with a frown in the driveway at sight of a strange horse tethered to the hitching post there. Which was odd, for at this late hour some groom should already have taken the horse to the stables. And then he remembered that this was Midsummer's Eve and the servants would have been given permission to attend the great bonfires that always burned at this time, for there would be dancing and drink and much carousing tonight—and many a foolish maid would lose her virtue beneath the summer trees. No doubt the horse belonged to someone who had chosen to attend the bonfire in a cart with the others, and had been left there forgotten.

Not sure yet what to do about the animal, he stabled his own tired horse, gave him a fast rubdown and left him with food and water. The stableboys, when they returned from their frolic, could do a better job.

He had smiled and hurried inside, hoping against hope that Virginia would not have accompanied the merrymakers—for she loved dancing and pleasures and had been annoyed when he had told her regretfully that his business in Bristol would keep him gone for a fortnight. But he had arranged to ship the cheeses much faster than he had thought possible and had near worn out his horse in his eagerness to get home to her.

They'd have a late supper together, was his thought as he bounded, tired and dusty, up the moonlit stair. And he'd tell her how he'd bought an interest in the ship that was taking the cheeses, along with crockery and woolen socks and iron farm implements, to America, and how there'd be a great profit. He was thinking how he'd tell her of his plans to extend into buying up woolen cloth and cutlery and ship them to the Colonies too, for those merchants in Bristol were making a mint!

"Virginia!" He flung open without ceremony the door to his wife's bedchamber—and froze.

There, leaping up from the big rumpled four-poster were two figures—not one. And the moonlight revealed in stark detail the stricken face of his young wife as she scrabbled at the covers to shield her nakedness.

In that single moment his world had exploded. He was conscious only of rage and shock—and of pain that began in his knuckles and shuddered up through his arm as his fist smashed into the frightened face of the man who had leaped up from Virginia's bed and tried to make his escape. There had been the sound of bone striking bone and Virginia's scream as that loose-limbed figure crumpled senseless to the floor.

Then—and only then—had he turned his attention to his young wife.

She was out of bed now, and she would have run toward the fellow on the floor but that he solidly blocked her way. He took Virginia's bare shoulder—that shoulder he had loved to stroke and run his lips across—in the fingers of his aching hand and ground down upon it with a pressure that made her wince.

"Who is he?" he heard himself rasp.

"His name is Alfred Soames." She sounded tearfully indignant and he realized for the first time that tears were coursing down her face. And he, who had once been reduced to trembling jelly by even a woeful look from her, remained totally indifferent as he stood above her, judging her.

"Why?" he managed at last, and it was a cry wrenched from the depths of him.

"You were gone!" she cried. "You are always gone when I want you—selling cheeses, buying cattle, God knows what else!"

You were gone! Was that a reason for *this*? Surely it was not the reason he had expected. He had expected some tearful claim that this man, this Soames, had been her lover before, that she had been wrenched from his arms into an arranged marriage. Or that she had conceived a passion for Soames and nurtured it in secret. But no! He had been gone and therefore someone else must be found to occupy his bed!

He must have made some involuntary movement toward her for she shrank back. "You'd best check him, Clifford—he isn't moving." Her voice had a fretful note that amazed him—as if he were somehow at fault.

But he had turned his head slowly and seen that there was a

certain quality of stillness to that figure lying on the floor in the moonlight. And he had bent down and touched him—and then in alarm listened for a heartbeat and found none.

He had straightened up then and looked full at his wife, who had clutched a blue dressing gown and was struggling into it. Her pale hair streamed down and she looked very frightened.

"The man is dead, Virginia."

Her hand went to her lips to stifle the little cry that rose there. "Oh, God, Clifford, why did you hit him so hard?" she moaned.

"What is he to you, Virginia? Where does he come from?"

She shook her head miserably. "He was a traveler, lost and seeking directions. He came to the house after I had let all the servants go to the merrymaking at the bonfires. He seemed pleasant and I gave him some wine and—and we—" Her voice choked off.

Another thunderbolt struck him squarely between the eyes. *Not even someone known to her—a stranger!* He stared in disbelief at this woman he had courted and married, who had borne his child—a child sleeping peacefully, no doubt, in the next room in a crib more suited to a princess than to a plain country squire. *A stranger.* Virginia had taken to her bed a stranger! And all because *he* was not at the moment occupying it!

Without another look at Virginia, he slung the stranger's limp body over his arm, scooped up his clothes—the man was not naked like Virginia, he was still wearing his smallclothes, shirt, and opened trousers and stockings although he had—thoughtfully—removed his boots. But a gaily plumed hat and a short cloak, a handsome doublet, a small dress sword and a pair of riding gloves lay across a chair. He now realized that the stranger had been darting toward that sword even as he had struck him. He swept them all up in his other arm without even breaking stride, for he was a powerful man. And realized bitterly as he did so that the reason this plumed hat and cloak and gloves were not downstairs was because his Virginia was careful—the caution of long practice, no doubt—lest the servants remark this evidence of a guest, disappeared above stairs.

Only the horse would betray his presence and she had probably not thought of that, so used was she to grooms who came out and magically removed the horses from their hitching posts to some more pleasant spot where hay and water waited.

Down the stairs he clumped in his dusty boots, trying to think above the great despairing ache in his chest and the dry sorrowful lump in his throat. He had struck the fellow in anger—and he had struck hard. It did not seem enough of a blow to have killed the stranger but it had. And now he must face the consequences of that.

Or must he? He paused for a moment on the stair and made a quick decision. In his writing desk in the drawing room lay the key to the wine cellar. He deposited his burden in the hall, detoured by the writing desk, lifted its polished walnut lid and removed the key. He would need a candle now—and he lit one. Having done that, he took his unexpected guest to the wine cellar.

There was an open hole dug there into the foundation, for he had only this week been meaning to enlarge the wine cellar. The hole was not very large, for work on it had been stopped almost immediately when a summer storm had blown off part of the stable roof. Now he studied that hole. *Indeed it was of a very convenient size,* he thought grimly, as he deposited the stranger's body in it and heaped upon it the cloak and doublet and sword and gloves and hat.

Having done that, he went back upstairs.

Virginia met him at her bedroom door, her hazel eyes wide and terrified. "Where is he?" she whispered.

"Gone," he said briefly.

"Gone?"

"So far as you are concerned." It had never been his custom to involve women in his affairs and although Virginia was certainly involved in this one, it was in his nature—now that there was danger—to shut her out of it. For although he felt at that moment only revulsion for the young wife who cringed before him, he was automatically protective of her. For him it was an automatic reflex.

She swallowed and looked away. "There will be a terrible scandal when he is discovered," she whispered.

"He will not be discovered." He had had time to think about that as he bore the body down the stairs. He had thought what this would mean for him, for Virginia, and for the lovely golden child he had fathered. For himself, a trial and possibly death by hanging. For Virginia—it was what might happen to Virginia that had shaken him most, for despite the shock he had received tonight he still loved the lovely incontinent woman who now stood before him in a hastily donned robe. Many things might happen to Virginia— all of them bad. At the worst was death by burning—for the law was fiercer to women than it was to men, and a woman would burn for the same offense for which a man would be hanged—at the least she would suffer public humiliation and ostracism. And it would—and there his square jaw had hardened to stone—be used to cast doubt upon his daughter's parentage. Of that parentage at least he was sure, for Virginia had been menstruating on her wedding day—it had been a source of terrible embarrassment to her, he remembered—and all the week after. But they had made up for their enforced abstinence by such a wedding trip as would have made the gods blush. They had ridden far and stayed at strange inns and made love by the seaside and in forest glades—he had been with her every minute. And the child had been late in coming and she had had his coloring, even to the unusual crystal-blue eyes that looked so calmly from her sweet face.

Oh, Pamela was his, all right, whatever Virginia had become afterward! And Pamela, child of his own loins, must be protected at all costs.

"Stay in your room," he commanded Virginia. "Answer to no one. Sleep late—and forget this ever happened. You did not meet this stranger, you had gone to bed with a sick headache. When did he arrive?''

"Late." She moistened her trembling lips. "I had dismissed the servants some time before and I heard a banging on the door. I went to answer and he swept off his plumed hat with a flourish and begged my indulgence. He told me he had lost the road to Taunton.''

Taunton . . . That told him the road the stranger would take.

"Latch this door behind me," he said and departed.

Downstairs he walked past the wineglasses Virginia had left carelessly on the table—then frowned and returned to them, stuck them in a cupboard.

Then he climbed aboard the stranger's horse and, leading one of his own, took the road to Taunton, hoping against hope that he would meet no one this night.

He did not. Ten miles down that road he paused in an open glade and went through Alfred Soames's saddlebags thoroughly. They contained nothing to help him, only extra clothing, a razor and a little money. He replaced them all carefully just as they had been, gave the horse a slap on the rump and watched it canter riderless down the road to Taunton.

With luck the horse would keep going, for the hedgerows here crowded too close to give much food and several miles on there would be a stream just at the edge of a town. The horse would pause there for water and to munch the green grass growing at the stream's edge—and he would be found, and the missing rider inquired into. And hopefully presumed drowned for at places the road had bordered the river.

Clifford Archer's face was very set at that point. For if this Alfred Soames turned out to be a person of some importance, there'd be a stir raised throughout the countryside, a search instituted. God willing that search would not lead to Virginia— he could only hope she had been telling the truth when she said that Alfred Soames was a stranger to her—if he was not, if they had been carrying on a secret affair, then they were lost.

Feeling that he'd aged ten years, he climbed onto his own

unsaddled horse and rode back to Axeleigh, eyes and ears alert for returning merrymakers.

Now too late it occurred to him that he could have made the "drowning" real—he could have dumped Alfred Soames's body in the river. But that would have entailed riding down the road with that body conspicuously draped over the saddle— perhaps he had been wise not to risk it. His mind still roiling with what he perhaps *should* have done, he reached the gates of Axeleigh, dismounted, and sent the saddleless horse on his way with a light slap on the rump.

Dawn was breaking as he started down the drive. Forcing his thoughts away from the nightmarish events of the night, he strode down it jauntily, feeling the morning breeze blow across his sweaty face.

A groom walking by the front of the house looked at him in some surprise, for the Squire was not addicted to walking— he was a riding man.

"Did you see to my horse?" he called, to distract the fellow's attention. "Brought him in last evening, you must just have gone."

"Oh, aye, to the bonfire, sir. Give him a good rubdown, I did, first thing when I got back." He still looked curious at having found the Squire walking down the drive.

"Lost a gold watch out there somewhere," he told the groom in an easy voice. "Thought I might have lost it riding through the gates last evening"—he nodded behind him— "but I've searched the whole drive, couldn't find anything. Have a look for it, will you, there's a good fellow. There's a shilling in it for you if you find it."

The groom grinned and hurried down the driveway. He turned as the Squire called, "I heard a horse whinny out there just now. Could be one of the horses got out of the pasture— can't have them out in the road."

"No, sir," agreed the groom. "I'll have a look about, I will."

The Squire stood for a moment and watched him go with narrow crystal blue eyes. Then he relaxed. There'd be no suspicion there, just a lost watch that would turn up later and a horse that had jumped the pasture fence—for he'd been careful to choose a good jumper.

Now there was only one thing left to do to end this night's business—and it would take some doing. He went inside—and froze suddenly.

The wine cellar! He had forgotten to lock the wine cellar!

With unhurried steps, in case he was being observed from the hall above—and he was always to feel that every one of the casual footsteps that carried him there cost him a year off his life—he went and got a candle, lit it, and made his way to the wine cellar. The door stood open and unlocked just as he had left it and he cursed his folly—he must have been more excited than he knew. A few strides took him to the dug hole in the foundation from which a pile of stones had been removed—and he felt his heart lurch.

The clothing had been disturbed—the hat was in the wrong place.

And then, even as he took an involuntary step forward, he realized that the cloak and doublet and gloves that concealed the body stuffed into that narrow hole were still in place—the plumed hat had merely slipped down. A quick look around the wine cellar showed him nothing else had been disturbed. The candle he had left earlier had long since guttered out. He heaved a sigh of relief.

That morning the Squire became a stonemason. He shed his coat and shoveled back dirt into the hole to cover the hat and cloak and other clothing of Alfred Soames that showed, and then he lifted the heavy stones one by one and mixed mortar and somehow got them back into place. And stacked a large pile of kegs in front of the newly mortared stones.

By afternoon, aching in every bone, he had got the job done—and fairly creditably. But he could take no pleasure in his work. His hands were filthy and bleeding in several places, his fingernails broken. Wearily he put on his travel-stained outer garments, locked the wine cellar door carefully behind him, and as he went out through the many storerooms that honeycombed the cellars of Axeleigh he stumbled against a barrel of molasses and its contents spilled out over the floor.

When he reached the hall he bellowed for Stebbins. "I've been inspecting the cellars and a fine mess they are with molasses strewn about! See to it—and send me up a bath!"

The serving maid Stebbins sent to clear the mess passed the Squire going up as she made her way down and she told cook later that she had never seen the Squire's eyes look so bloodshot—he and his lady must have made quite a night of it!

After that night Clifford Archer had slept in his own room and had not visited Virginia's bedchamber. He felt a reluctance to touch the young wife who had led him to murder—a murder for which he could still be hanged.

Virginia was crushed at first, gazing at him across the long dining table with woeful hazel eyes, fixing her long pale hair in exotic new ways to tempt him, leaning across the table in gowns cut so low that her breasts threatened to pop out. When he still remained cold, she became aggrieved, resentful. And then she had tossed her fair head in a gesture very like Pamela's and taken a lover—one that he knew about, although how many others there were he could only imagine. Grimly, Clifford Archer had looked the other way. For she was Pamela's mother and he would have no scandal roiling around Pamela's pretty head.

It was only what he might have expected of Virginia, he told himself, for she was at heart a lightskirt. Amoral. He knew that now, what his friends had tried so hard to tell him in the days when he was courting her. God help him, he had near broken Lambert Beall's jaw when Lambert had made some too broad hint about Virginia's virtue! And Virginia had faked virginity, oh, so well! She had winced and cried out and clawed at him with her fingers and entreated him to stop. He had fallen eagerly into her every trap.

But still he could not hate her.

His ardor for her had cooled, and he made do with tavern wenches and an occasional willing chambermaid. He knew well what his young wife was doing, that she took her pleasure here and there and roundabout, but he let her go her own way.

It was, he felt, partially his own fault for not having seen her more clearly. She was a lightskirt and lightskirt she would always be. He was no more to her than any of the others, he had merely pressed his suit harder and been more acceptable to her parents because of his wealth.

It was a bitter cup to drain but he must drain it. But in the draining his desire for Virginia had ebbed away. . . .

When Pamela was ten, Virginia had taken a sudden cold. It had turned into pneumonia and she had died despite doctors from as far away as Bristol.

The Squire had mourned her in his fashion. He had sat up late of nights drinking and remembering the good things—the light in Virginia's hazel eyes when first he had asked her to wed him and she'd said yes so softly against his doublet, the beauty of her in the mornings when she stood naked at the window and stretched her arms and let the rays of the morning sun kiss her slender white body. He had lain in his bed those mornings, waiting for her to rise before him, just so he could view that morning ritual. He would lie there marveling at her piquant rose-tipped breasts, at the heavy pale hair that moved so languorously along her dainty back and fell past her waist to tweak at her soft round hips. His eyes had traced her shapely limbs and he had felt—always at those times—a tightening of his loins and a mad desire for her sweep upward through his whole being. "Come back to bed," he would say huskily, and she would turn and smile and come.

He remembered her at other times, riding through the rain beside him on their wedding trip and seeming not to mind. And smiling at him over breakfast. And looking so tired but so happy when she presented him with Pamela.

And he remembered the feel of her, sensually pressed against him in the big bed, and the fragrant flower smell of her, and the tingling touch of her.

171

And—reluctantly now that she was gone, he remembered all those other men—especially the first, at least the first that he had known about, the man he had killed. Fool that he was, he'd had no inkling that Virginia's skirts would flutter lightly up for any man who caught her fancy!

And *that* memory warned him off marriage. Virginia had made him wary of women.

So to everybody's surprise, the Squire of Axeleigh did not replace his young wife with another. And they whispered that it was because his heart was buried with her in the churchyard.

But that was not what had happened.

Clifford Archer had built a wall of stone around that heart, as surely as he had built a wall of stone to hide the body of the man he'd killed. And no woman's charms had ever been enough to pierce that wall. They were all lightskirts, he knew bitterly. Under their ingenuous smiles and their endearing ways they were all lightskirts.

Except Pamela, of course.

Now at his dinner table, he shot a glance down toward his lovely daughter. Save for that recklessness which she had inherited from her mother, Pamela was breath of his breath—she had his directness, his optimism, his valor. But it always amazed him that she could *look* so like Virginia. Except for her coloring it might have been Virginia sitting there smiling at him.

And she had slept that whole terrible night through. . . .

But now that night had come back to haunt him—and it was not the first time it had happened.

Last summer, the day before the Midsummer Masque at Huntlands which had brought Constance to him, he had received another blackmail note—the first. He had found it when he had reached into his saddlebag for his water flask as he returned through the summer heat on the dusty road from Bridgwater.

Reading it, he had sat at gaze until a farmer coming by in his cart and tipping his cap respectfully to the Squire had brought him back to the present. After the cart went by—and he never knew later what he said in response to the farmer's bluff greeting—he had reread the note with sweat pouring down his face.

The note had demanded ten gold guineas to keep silent about the matter of Alfred Soames and gave directions as to where the money should be placed. He had followed those directions to the letter and he had not heard from the blackmailer again—he had thought the matter was over and done and had heaved a great sigh of relief.

And now it was all happening again.

For this note read—and in the same cramped handwriting as the first: *I know all about what is buried in your wine cellar—and how it happened.* And it instructed the Squire when and where to leave ten gold guineas.

Nothing else. The note was unsigned.

"What's the matter, Father?" asked Pamela. "You look pale."

The Squire looked up. It always astonished him that Pamela, who was like him in so many ways, who had his unflinching pride and courage and steady loyalty, should not only look but *sound* so much like Virginia . . . that same sweet voice, those same endearing tones. He managed a laugh. It sounded hollow to his own ears but quite normal to the others. "I've not been feeling too well today," he admitted. "Think I'd best not eat any more." He excused himself and rose from the table. He needed time to think and he couldn't do it engaging in light conversation with his daughter.

"Was there something in the note?" wondered Pamela, stabbing intuitively at the source of the trouble.

"Of course not," he told her easily. "Just a receipt I'd forgot to pick up, for some wool. Fellow needn't have bothered—I could have got it later."

Hours later, pacing back and forth across the floor of his green-painted bedchamber, he would try to reconstruct that night, to think who could have written this note, who could have *known*.

The chilling fact was borne in on him that someone in his

173

own household must have placed that note on the hall table. And Stebbins had said all the servants denied putting it there. Assuming they were telling the truth, that left Stebbins himself—but he could not believe it was Stebbins. Stebbins had been butler here when he was a boy, had taught him to fish—Stebbins was as loyal as any man alive. No, it could not be Stebbins.

He thought back. It had surprised him at the time that he had heard nothing of the riderless horse. But he had assumed that some country fellow had simply stolen it and ridden away—a stroke of luck for him!

That had been a summer of storms and repairing damaged outbuildings naturally took precedence over some whim to expand the wine cellar. By the next year expanding the wine cellar was forgotten and when eventually the pile of kegs he had used to shield his work got moved and the new masonry was revealed, it was not remarked—everyone had assumed someone else had done it for it was none so big a job.

He had thought he had covered his tracks well—until last summer. And now again today.

He was now forced to confront the chilling possibility that that first blackmail note had not been slipped into his saddlebag at Bridgwater, that it too had originated at Axeleigh. If so, it was reasonable to assume that whoever had penned that note had been employed here the night he had accidentally killed Soames. That included all the house servants except Tabby, for Axeleigh was a happy household. Those fortunate enough to be employed here usually left feet first at the end of a long life of service—or retired to pleasant cottages from which they wished the Squire well and drank his health.

He ran a hand through his hair—he must be missing something. He was! Of the servants in his household, only Stebbins could read and write—and his half-literate writing was nothing like the cramped style in which the two blackmail notes had been penned.

Which added another panicky conjecture: Could an illiterate servant have *dictated* the first letter? And could the scribe who wrote it have penned the second? For the tone was slightly different, more confident somehow. As if it were written by a different person, or that person had subtly changed. . . .

But that note had appeared in the front hall without any banging of the knocker, without any horseman riding up. Good lord, *could there be an accomplice from within*? The very thought made the back of Clifford Archer's neck prickle slightly.

He would have reeled with shock had he known that it was Constance's hand that had set that note upon the hall table.

Claxton House,
The West Riding, Yorkshire,
Spring 1683

CHAPTER 11

April had come to Yorkshire, bringing rain and apple blossoms, and all of England was agog over the discovery of the Rye House Plot. Revolt had been brewing, for discontent with Charles II's high-handed policies was widespread, but a handful of extremists had decided to resolve the matter more simply—by murder. The plan was to cut down the King and his unpopular brother, the Duke of York, at Rye House, a farmstead owned by one of the conspirators, which the royal entourage would pass on the way back to London from the Newmarket races. With the King and his brother both dead, they would then set the Duke of Monmouth (the King's eldest illegitimate son—for he had no legitimate heir) upon the throne. But the plan had been discovered and Sidney and others of the "council of six" who favored revolt but had no part in any murder scheme were arrested and charged with high treason.

At Claxton House, cook—serving up steaming Yorkshire

pudding to one and all in the servants' hall—summed up the popular view.

"Ye should all mourn, ye should," she told the kitchen help impressively (with Constance listening, as eager for her portion of the crisp, gravy-topped baked pudding as the others), "for 'tis the country that lost out that day. Mind ye, King Charles is bad enough, but if James comes to the throne we'll all feel the pinch, for he's bound and determined to make us all Catholics and if he can't, he'll light the fires of Smithfield once again and burn us all for heresy! Ah, the Protestant duke—though the King won't admit 'twas a legal marriage that begot him, and him the son of the King's own body!—he's our only hope and now who knows if he'll ever reach the throne?"

She fetched a deep sigh and the servants all looked uneasily over their pudding at one another, for they were to a man Dissenters. They had no desire to see Protestants brought to the stake and burned again as had been the case in the time of Bloody Mary!

But by evening North Country humor had asserted itself and the scullery maids giggled when one of them reported that cook had burned the mutton to a crisp—made it black enough for mourning!

Now that Dev was gone, Constance no longer slipped away from the forbidding Yorkshire mansion to run across the close-cropped pastures in her faded linen kirtle and bodice to Fountains. She had not been back to Fountains since Dev left. She would go there again, she promised herself. Someday . . . with Dev. Fountains would still be there. It would always be there, like the moors, like the sky.

But she could not face its heartrending beauty now. Her memories were too fresh, they would crush her. She might break down and weep and perhaps never stop weeping.

Such are the pangs of first love.

She had heard nothing from Dev—and nothing from Margaret Archer either. Constance, every day hoping to hear, had plunged into politics—the politics of Dissent. She listened avidly to kitchen gossip, she attended surreptitious meetings with the servants when itinerant dissenting preachers came by—and she felt with the others a tingling excitement at the discovery of the Rye House Plot. Although she did not condone murder, she had learnt in Claxton's kitchens to be wary of the lords of the land. All her leanings were toward Dissent, for she had a deep and burning sense of injustice and her blood stirred easily to rebellion.

Henriette, the governess, had another view:

"La la la!" she cried when she heard about it. "Would it not have been a great joke, *ma chère,* if these insurgents *had* managed to butcher the King and his brother? Then"—she tittered—"England would have had to the throne a likely gentleman not even of the blood royal!"

"What do you mean?" frowned Constance. "The Duke of Monmouth may not be legitimate but he is certainly of the blood royal—King Charles himself accepts him as his son! Oh, I cannot believe he was in the Plot in any way. For a man to scheme to murder his own father!" She shuddered.

"Pish and tush!" cried Henriette, "Call him James Crofts! He was not born 'Duke of Monmouth'—that only came later when King Charles was duped into believing the lad his son!"

"He *is* his son—by Lucy Walter."

Henriette pounced on that. "Indeed he is Lucy Walter's son—no one denies that. *But not by Charles!*"

"Cook says the King actually married Lucy Walter while he was an exile living abroad—before he was restored to the throne. Married her secretly in Holland."

"What would cook know about it? Was she in Rotterdam when the child was born? No! She is a fat cow who will believe anything she is told." Henriette's gallic shrug dismissed cook. "Why, Charles himself denies they were ever married!"

"Yes, but 'tis said that is because the King is a secret Catholic and he wants the throne to pass to his Catholic brother and not to his Protestant son—and by denying the marriage he can achieve that!"

"I doubt me Charles cares enough about religion to go to such lengths," sniffed Henriette.

"Maybe not, but you'll agree that he loves money enough to go to *any* lengths! And 'tis a Catholic king—your own Louis of France—who has bought him! You'll have heard no doubt that is why Charles need not depend on Parliament for levies? Because he's receiving all the money he needs from the King of France!"

Henriette looked undecided. She was a woman of no religion. In France she had been a Catholic. Here in England she was Anglican. If Fortune took her to Spain she would become Catholic once again. Cynical, worldly Henriette changed her religion as she might change the color of her gown, shrugging it off as it suited her. It was not the politics of the Rye House Plot that interested her, but the personal gossipy side. Her mouth went stubborn. "I tell you Lucy Walter was Robert Sidney's mistress and Monmouth is the spitting image of Sidney! I have seen them both and the resemblance is *striking!* And is it not interesting that this other Sidney—this Algernon—plots to place his blood relation—Monmouth—on the throne? Ah, can you not see it, *ma chère*? Where are your wits?"

Like the others, Constance wanted to see Monmouth on the throne, rather than fanatical James. Why, Monmouth was a moderate—look at the clemency he'd given the Scottish Covenanters when he'd defeated them at Bothwell Bridge in '79! And besides he was young, a romantic figure.

"You are wrong, Mademoiselle," she said curtly and left Henriette blinking at this rebuff.

They made it up, of course—they always did. For who else was there to talk to? Dev was gone, Sir John ignored them, Henriette held herself above the servants—who were wary of friendship with Constance—and Felicity was no more communicative than ever. She had become so expert at making lace that none could excel her.

"Have you seen what Felicity is working on now?" Henriette's striped tabby skirts fell into step companionably

179

with Constance's faded lavender ones later that afternoon. "It is lace so fine and delicate that I told her she should save it for her wedding night—and do you know what she told me? She said 'I will never marry. I will throw myself from the roof first and die upon the stones.'" She shuddered. *"Mon Dieu!"*

"Perhaps she will not receive any offers," countered Constance. "For she never goes out and now that Sir John is so ill, hardly anyone comes here."

"True," agreed Henriette, rolling her black eyes. "You knew, of course, that Hugh has been sent for?"

Constance came to an abrupt halt. "No, I didn't know," she said slowly. "When was that?"

"Oh, last week, I think—I am not sure. I heard the doctor mention it as he brushed by me this morning but this talk of the Rye House Plot pushed it out of my mind. He was muttering that he hoped young Hugh would arrive in time."

"Then he's sure? Sir John is dying?"

Henriette nodded. "There can be no doubt, I am afraid." She sighed. "And horrible Hugh will be master here and you and I will have to endure it."

Endure it . . . *but she could not endure it*. She could only hope that Sir John, relenting on his deathbed from his perennial disdain of her, would leave her some pittance— enough that she could get away. She tried to see him, but the frowning nurse would not allow it.

And then, arriving much sooner than expected, Hugh came home. He had, it seemed, received no message. He had just decided to return and here he was.

Constance could see no change in him except that he was heavier, older, better dressed—for he had learnt much about clothes on the Continent. He took snuff with studied elegance but he still eyed people with the same contemptuous gaze from his little pig eyes.

Hugh had arrived in time. Sir John died that night.

The house was draped in black. Strict mourning was being

observed—but Hugh, returning from the funeral, strode forward to detain Constance.

"I suppose ye've bedded half the county since I've been gone," he said, giving her a bored look.

Constance recoiled and glared at him. She was looking pale and aristocratic in her black mourning attire, so striking against her white skin and violet eyes.

He laughed, taking her silence as an admission. "Well, I've a mind to try *my* luck with you too," he said casually. "You can share my bed tonight."

Constance was white to the lips. "I will not do it!" she cried.

"I am lord of this manor now," Hugh reminded her in a low brutal tone. "I am Sir Hugh Dacey, Baronet—and I will do as I please with my servants and chattels. Come to think of it, I suppose you are become my ward!" He laughed. "Convenient, isn't it?"

She had somehow not expected such an immediate attack. She had expected Hugh to wait a decent interval, to observe some period of mourning, however short. Which would have given her time to plan.

But it was plain he had no intention of waiting. The new baronet intended to exercise all his powers—and at once. She little doubted that he had raped his way across Europe, leaving a trail of weeping scullery maids and chambermaids behind him. And he was bent on having *her* tonight.

She had but one alternative—to run away.

Frowning, biting her lips, she paced about the empty library thinking how that could be done.

She could steal a horse—but she was no great rider, indeed she had not ridden since her London days. She could well be thrown, lamed and brought back in that condition. Her face paled at what that would mean, for Hugh would consider a broken leg no obstacle. Indeed to him it would be an advantage. She could easily imagine him twisting that leg, trusting excruciating pain to win her compliance.

She could make her way to Ripon easily, but she knew no

one there and the Wakeman would find her if she tried to sleep in some alleyway or loft. If she tried the moors, she was certain to lose her way—and Hugh would have no difficulty following her with dogs tracking her scent. He would find her and bring her back.

One of the crofters might take her in and let her sleep in a barn loft while she decided what to do. But dogs would follow her there too and she would have brought ruin upon whoever befriended her as well as on herself.

No—she needed a way out that could not be tracked, that would not be noticed until too late. As she pondered the problem, it was resolved for her by a great commotion outside the library windows.

Hearing angry voices raised, she ran to the window and peered out. There before her on the lawn was Henriette—and Hugh. Henriette had her arm raised dramatically as if to strike him and Hugh was leaning toward her menacingly with his jaw jutting out.

"*Mon Dieu,* that you could break the news to me so! And with your grandfather not yet cold in his grave! 'Twas he who hired me—how dare you give me no notice? I don't care if you have ordered the cart sent round, I'll *not* leave here today!"

"You will!" thundered Hugh, his face turning a mottled red. "Girls need no education. Constance has had too much already and Felicity cannot absorb it. You are dismissed, Henriette!"

With a sob, the French governess broke and ran for the house.

Constance dashed to Felicity's room. She found Felicity bent over her lace but the girl looked up with a smile as she entered, for she liked Constance.

"Felicity, Hugh has dismissed Henriette!"

Felicity nodded tranquilly. "I knew he would, when he came home."

"But you must stop him! He must give her proper notice and a good reference, Felicity!"

Felicity's pale face looked up at her. There was that vacant look in her eyes again that always appeared under stress. "Hugh is a baronet now," she sighed. "He will do what he likes. I cannot stop him."

Constance was brought up short by the sudden realization that that was true. As the new baronet, Hugh held all their futures in the palm of his hand. *All but hers! She* would not be cowed by that monster!

"You will leave now, I suppose?" Felicity said it with tragic conviction.

"You could not expect me to stay! Hugh has promised to rape me—tonight."

Felicity nodded as if that too were to be expected. From her crushed demeanor, Constance knew she would put up no resistance to anything Hugh proposed—short of marriage—so long as he did not take her precious lace away from her. "I have a gift for you," Felicity said suddenly, and drew from her basket a gossamer-sheer length of Venetian rose point and offered it to Constance. "Wear it at your wedding."

Constance was touched. Never had she owned anything so nice. "I've no wedding plans, Felicity," she said sadly, thinking of Dev.

"You will have." Felicity nodded her head firmly. "I think even Hugh would offer for you—if you could hold him back long enough." She peeked through her lashes at Constance hopefully, as if trying to plant a suggestion in the other girl's head.

Constance was not sure which would be worse—to be raped by Hugh or bound to him in marriage. On the whole she thought to be married to him would be infinitely worse. It would last longer.

"Thank you, Felicity," she said softly, folding the lace and pushing it down her bodice. At the door she turned. "Come with me," she urged. "Get away from here. Anything would be better than life with Hugh at the helm!"

But Felicity shook her head. "I'm not like you, Constance, eager for new experiences. As long as I have my lace, I will

183

be all right and Hugh would never dream of taking *that* away from me, for he regards it as valuable, something that could be sold.''

Constance had never realized how much shy, silent Felicity understood of those about her, or how deeply cynical she was. Her pity deepened, but with it her impatience. ''It may be your only chance, Felicity. If you do not come now, you may never get away.''

''I would never get away anyway. I would be found and brought back—and Hugh might punish me then by taking away my lace. I would go mad and they would hurl me in a pit among the snakes.''

So she knew about that, she had envisioned it. Constance felt herself shrink away from the thought. ''Felicity . . .'' she pleaded.

But the girl was adamant. ''I will lock my door after you go,'' she promised. ''I will make them break it down. And then I will tell them that I saw you run away westward into the moors.'' She gave Constance an anxious look. ''You will not go *that* way, will you?'' And when Constance shook her head, ''You are going with Henriette, I suppose. I am sure she will be glad to take you with her, for she hates Hugh— she hates us all.''

''Oh, you must not say that, Felicity! Henriette doesn't hate you!''

''She does,'' said Felicity stubbornly. ''I saw it in her eyes that first day—and I have heard her call me a dolt when she thought I could not hear! Oh, Constance,'' she wailed suddenly. ''I will miss you so. You are the only person who has ever liked me! I was a great disappointment to my grandparents— and I never knew my mother and father. There's only been you who's ever cared two pence about me!''

As upset as Felicity, Constance threw her arms about the other girl, noted how her thin shoulder bones protruded through the handsome fabric of her dress. Poor frail Felicity, Hugh would be the death of her! But nothing would shake Felicity in her determination to remain. She was afraid of the outside world. She would stay with the known evil—and her lace.

"I will write to you," Constance told Felicity huskily. "When I get to—wherever I am going."

"No," said Felicity in a mournful voice. "Do not do that. For Hugh will be sure to get my mail and he will tear the letter open and find out where you are."

"You have thought of everything!" cried Constance, amazed.

Felicity looked up at her with great solemn eyes. "Yes, I have thought it all out because I knew this day would come. You have befriended me, Constance, and I am going to help you to escape my brother. It is"—she said simply—"my going-away gift to you."

Constance felt her throat close up. She could not speak. All this from shy little Felicity, who had shown so little interest in her!

"Go now," said Felicity. "I will remember you." She seemed to withdraw into herself even as Constance gave her a last impulsive hug, and as she left the room she saw that Felicity was already bending in rapt concentration over her lace.

Henriette looked up from her packing as Constance entered. Angry tears sparkled in the Frenchwoman's eyes and she was muttering *"Sauvages!"* She raised a silencing hand before Constance could speak. "Do not ask me to take you with me for I have no money to carry you to London with me—and that is where I am going! I will shake this English soil from my feet!" She slammed down a trunk lid. "I will take ship to France!"

"Hugh would not let me leave openly," sighed Constance. "He has reminded me that I am now his ward—and has told me that tonight I will sleep in his bed."

Henriette gave her a measuring look. "You could find Hugh's strongbox and take what you need." She gave one of her hatboxes a vicious tug. "Surely no one could blame you for using his money to save yourself!"

But if she were caught, she would be a thief—and thieves

were hanged. Even for stealing so small a thing as a pin or a loaf of bread. She could imagine a triumphant Hugh promising not to bring charges if she would let him have his way with her. She repressed a shudder.

Suddenly her eyes lit on a wicker trunk in one corner. "Oh, Henriette, do take me with you!" she entreated. "Let me travel in that wicker trunk! There would be air for me to breathe, for the trunk could be tied to the top of the coach."

"Surely you are mad! You could not travel to London cooped up in there like a trussed-up chicken!"

"But you could say the trunk contained your 'necessaries' and have it set off with you whenever we stop."

"One shares a room at most inns," Henriette warned, but her black eyes gleamed at the thought of balking Hugh of his quarry. "Still, I suppose we could manage."

So Constance, who had arrived at Claxton House in a farm cart, left it stuffed into a wicker basket.

Henriette had warned she would be miserable. Even with the bottom and sides of the wicker trunk padded with quilts to keep her from being bruised too badly as the coach's big wheels lumbered over the rutted roads, the journey quickly became a nightmare. Luckily their first day's travel was short and Henriette managed to get a private room and had her supper sent in. Constance was still fairly fresh and game to try it again next day.

That day was a long one and she was stiff and groaning when she managed—with Henriette's help—to get out of the box.

When they reached York, Henriette said sensibly, "You cannot go on like this. Look at you." For Constance, with her hair disheveled, barely able to straighten up so long had she been crouched in a cramped position, did look woebegone.

"I have no choice," said Constance. "Hugh may look for me as far as York. Oh, Henriette, do take me as far as you can!"

Henriette sighed. She did not like to admit it, but having Constance with her in her room was cramping her style. Had she been alone, she might have found a gentleman to while away the time. Still, she liked Constance and thoroughly sympathized with her desire to put as much distance between herself and Hugh as possible.

And so the big coach that left York next day lurched along, its driver little dreaming that he carried one more passenger than he had bargained for.

Her last day on the coach was in many ways the worst. They were two days out of Lincoln, riding south on the Great North Road, when they had a day such as coach drivers dreaded. Everything went wrong. First a wheel came loose and had to be repaired in a tiny hamlet.

Henriette, who had pretended ill health throughout the journey, promptly demanded a room at the only inn "to rest," and insisted her wicker trunk of "necessaries" be brought up.

Constance, glad of the respite, crawled out of the wicker basket and threw herself across the hard mattress to rest until someone knocked on the door to tell them the coach was ready to leave. Tired to her bones from this difficult journey, she listened dimly to Henriette's steady tide of conversation.

"There is a tax collector on the coach," Henriette tittered. "A dried-up old goat! I asked him if he carried much gold and he looked shocked. But I think he fancies me!" She twirled her fan.

"Who else is on the coach?" mumbled Constance. "I thought I heard women's voices."

"Oh, a mother and daughter on their way to London to receive an inheritance. Their noses twitch like rabbits and they are very lofty with me because I am a mere governess! And an old gentleman from Leeds who will leave the coach at Peterborough, he tells me. He sits slumped over, rather like a large gander—and waddles when he walks. I think he is well past it! They are not the best of companions." She sighed gustily.

"Perhaps you will do better when we reach Peterborough," Constance consoled her.

The wheel fixed, the coach rolled on—only to have trouble again and with the same wheel. They stopped again, this time for supper, and the fuming driver informed them that to make his schedule they'd have to be on the road later than he liked.

It was growing dark when they left the roadside tavern that had supplied them with supper, and to the driver's immense relief, the moon came up and shed a clear white light over the road ahead. He drove cautiously, trying to miss the deeper ruts, lest the wheel come loose again—for he had no faith in the competence of the last man who had fixed it.

Stowed in her wicker basket atop the coach, trying to brace herself against sickening jolts that threatened to wrench her bones from their sockets, Constance had lost interest in where they were. All she knew was that they were lumbering south and that it was night, for through the chinks in the basket top that gave her air to breathe she could see stars winking from a dark sky.

She was wondering what a woman without money or a trade and bruised black and blue would do in London, when the coach came to a sudden violent halt and Constance, almost knocked senseless, heard Henriette scream.

It came to her dimly that something terrible had happened down there on the road, for there were shouts and curses and horses neighing. She thought they must have struck something—collided with another vehicle perhaps—when piercingly, carrying to her through the wicker even in her dazed condition, she heard Henriette cry, "No, for the love of heaven, do not throw the wicker basket down—there is a woman in it!"

After that things happened very fast.

She was aware of the basket being lifted down and set upon the road, she felt the blast of cool night air as the top was jerked open and then Henriette herself, babbling now in French, pulled her out to stand shakily upon her feet.

The scene before her was not a promising one.

The coach had come to a sliding halt and the horses were hopelessly entangled in the reins. The passengers were huddled together while the driver and his helper stood helplessly with their hands up regarding a man on a horse who held a pistol pointed very levelly at their heads.

Wavering on her feet, Constance stared at him. He wore a broad-brimmed black hat that shadowed his eyes, and a black silk scarf was tied around his face so that all that showed was a gleam where his eyes must be. Below that he was clad in an enveloping black cloak through which an arm stuck out holding the pistol. He was riding a rather nondescript horse that looked to be brown and he had an equally hard-to-identify horse attached on a lead to his saddle. She suspected he carried a knife to cut that lead quickly should the occasion arise.

It was the first time she had ever seen a highwayman and she regarded him with some awe.

"Now the rest of those boxes—down on the road with them." The voice came from behind her and her head swung round to see what must be the "old gentleman from Leeds" that Henriette thought was "past it" suddenly detach himself from among the passengers. He seemed to have grown younger for he now leaped about very nimbly, giving orders. And to enforce those orders he had pulled out a pistol almost as wicked-looking as the mounted man's.

They had been ambushed, she realized. Tricked! A little thrill of fear went through her—there must be a gang of them!

The driver and his helper were of that opinion too. They were quick to obey and soon the contents of everybody's boxes were spilled out on the dusty road, Henriette's among them. The tax collector groaned as one of his boxes was found to contain a false bottom and a horde of gold coins spilled out. Constance, standing motionless in her faded lavender kirtle and bodice, thought she saw a gleam light up the eyes of the black-cloaked highwayman who sat so impassively in the saddle.

She had not heard him speak until the "man from Leeds" advanced upon the ladies.

"No," he said in a voice of cold authority, somewhat

muffled by the scarf. "They'll keep their baubles. The gold is enough."

The "man from Leeds" hesitated, then shrugged.

"You." The barrel of the mounted highwayman's pistol swung suddenly toward her. "Up behind me."

Henriette gave a shriek and clasped Constance around the middle. "Oh, do not take her, *Monsieur*," she pleaded. Nearby the mother and daughter began to wail.

The "man from Leeds" looked astonished. "But we can't take her with us!" he protested.

"Up!" cried the highwayman, brandishing his pistol fiercely at Constance.

Constance extricated herself from Henriette's arms. "He will shoot us down here on the road," she muttered. "I'd best go with him."

Henriette fell back. She looked as if she might faint—which was entirely in keeping with the delicate state of health she had projected on the journey. "God keep you, *ma chère*," she whispered, and sank to her knees on the road, muttering, "A young girl—ah, *sauvage, sauvage. . . .*"

Moving slowly, and feeling as if she were in some nightmare from which she soon must wake, Constance walked toward the mounted black-clad figure.

Growling, "There'll be the devil to pay for this," the "man from Leeds" boosted her up and of a sudden the highwayman changed his mind and took her up in front of him, throwing an arm around her slim waist.

Constance vaguely considered trying to knock that pistol from his hand, but there would still be the "man from Leeds" and anyway both passengers and driver were scared out of their wits.

"Good-by, Henriette," she called, and then the highwayman muttered something to his horse which, for all its lackluster looks, seemed to be remarkably well trained, and a moment later he and his henchman were galloping away to the north.

Constance felt the wind on her face, felt it blow back her

hair, saw the dark trees rush by in the moonlight and wondered what would be her fate. She had no money, so he could be taking her along for only one reason.

She had gone from Hugh's clutches to—this.

They were out of sight of the coach now, thundering down a road whitened by moonlight. The highwayman stuck his pistol into his belt and yanked the black scarf from his face and Constance swung her head around to view the face of her captor.

It was a daunting face that she looked into. Hard and young and resolute. On it now a wicked half smile that would have chilled most men. Green eyes as brilliant as emeralds—and as cold.

But to Constance no face had ever been more welcome.

"Dev!" she breathed, and her heart gave a lurch.

In his dreams the young highwayman had pulled this girl out of many a coach in which she had been riding in her jewels and her furs, had carried her away protesting to his lair, had taunted her, made love to her, scorned her as she had once scorned him—and ravaged with fierce delight her perfumed softness. In his dreams he had made her pay for preferring the world's gifts to those he could give her, made her pay for his broken heart. He had imagined her gone far above him, dressed in silk and lace and jewels, languidly waving an ivory fan—not frightened and bruised and disheveled and being scooped out of a trunk! And now here she was, bedraggled and tired and overjoyed to see him—his own Constance, back in his arms again!

His hard green eyes softened, grew deep as the endless sea, and the arms that gathered her to him were tender arms, the arms of love.

"Is it really you?" she whispered. "I can't believe it!"

For answer his lips crushed down upon her own and Constance, spinning out of a harrowing night, felt that she had somehow risen from hell into a special heaven. She was galloping beneath the stars with Deverell, and no matter what happened now, she would always feel that God had been looking out for her this night.

PART THREE
The Wild Reunion

She knows he's out on the road tonight
With danger ever near,
And she loves him so that her eyes are bright
With many an unshed tear,
And she prays that the dawn will find him safe
And fast hooves bring him here!

The Great North Road,
Spring 1683

CHAPTER 12

Those rapturous first kisses after their long separation seemed to have no end. They clung together, unable to get enough of each other. Not a question did either ask—it was enough that they were back in each other's arms in a world made suddenly for love.

His henchman galloped up beside him, said "Johnny" on a disapproving note.

Dev lifted his head. "What is it, Gibb?"

"We're almost there. Got to turn just ahead." Gibb snorted. "The way you and the wench are goin' at it, I thought you might miss the turn!"

"No chance," said Dev laconically and eased Constance's warm body fractionally away from him.

"He called you 'Johnny,'" she whispered.

"I've taken the name John York. On the road I'm known as 'Gentleman Johnny.' Only Gibb knows my real name—and I trust Gibb."

She digested that slowly as they turned down a dark lane,

shadowed by tall unkempt hedges. They crossed a brook and paused to water the horses—and Dev swung her down and they cupped their hands and drank the cool rushing water.

"Nell, this is Gibb," said Dev in a matter-of-fact voice. "She's an old friend of mine." And Constance managed to hide a start that she'd been rechristened. A name for the road!

"I figured as much," said Gibb. "Once I got over the initial shock—'Gentleman Johnny' abductin' women from the highway!" He chuckled and turned to Constance. "Smart of you, Nell, not to let on as you know'd who Johnny was."

"Yes," said Constance in a small voice. "Wasn't it?" As they remounted, she asked, "Where are we staying?"

"You'll see," grinned Gibb. "Not anywhere's as ye'd expect!"

Dev smiled at her and when his arm went round her again she found she didn't really care where she was going—so long as she rode with Dev! Soon they were working their way down a narrow path that wound through a thorn thicket. When they broke out of that she saw ahead on the crest of a low hill the towering remains of an old windmill. It was a forlorn structure with its tattered sail and she was astonished when Dev urged his horse forward.

"We aren't staying there?" she asked in astonishment.

"Best hideout in this part of the country," he smiled, dismounting and handing her down.

With some foreboding she approached the ruined structure. It was a quiet night, but as they went in, one of the battered sails creaked a greeting. Inside, the place was a shambles, but, among the fallen stones at one side, makeshift stalls for the horses had been created. There was grain and hay and Gibb began vigorously currying the horses. "Guess you'd rather *I* did this tonight?" he grinned, with a meaningful look at Constance.

Constance blushed and Dev said, "We'll want some privacy tonight, Gibb. Would you take the tower watch?"

Gibb nodded and Dev began heaping up fresh straw for a

bed. He pulled out a linen tablecloth and upon it spread bread and cheese, apples and two bottles of wine.

Before he had finished, Gibb slouched through. He was a big man, carelessly dressed. In silence he hacked off some bread and cheese and stuffed them into his shirt. Then he picked up one of the bottles of wine and climbed on a wooden ladder up through a hole in the floor above and disappeared.

"Where is he going?" asked Constance, amazed.

"This is a Dutch-type mill," Dev told her. "Only the top part, that they call the head, revolves. Through the broken chinks of the dome up there Gibb will be able to see the whole countryside—and give us a head start in case anything's coming our way. We'll stay here for a day or two, till things have quieted down."

"Can't he see us from up there?"

"Not when I get this canopy set up," said Dev, propping up the tablecloth with pieces of lumber so that it would form a screen from above and yet let the breeze through.

He turned to look at her when he had finished and Constance felt suddenly shy. She looked down, picking at her skirt and began to tell him all that had happened. She saw that he was beginning to undress and it made her feel suddenly nervous. After the first joy of greeting, he now seemed a stranger, someone she did not know well enough to—to join on that heap of straw.

"Sir John died," she said, desperately making conversation.

"Did he?" Dev had flung down his pistol and cloak and was tugging off his boots.

"Yes—and Hugh came back."

Dev removed his last boot with unnecessary force. "What do you mean 'came back'? I didn't know he'd left."

"He said I'd have to go to bed with him."

Dev's hot eyes smouldered over her for a moment. About to remove his shirt, his hands suddenly came to a full stop. "And—?"

"That's when Henriette stuffed me into her wicker trunk and I rode that way until you found me."

His bunched-up muscles relaxed. "If I'd known that, I'd have given Henriette my share of tonight's gold." His shirt came off as he spoke and his naked torso gleamed in the shaft of moonlight that came down through chinks in the half-ruined wall.

She felt rising panic course through her. He was removing his trousers! Quickly she turned her head away. She had been sitting on the straw and now, convulsively, she got to her feet, turned as if to run. Dev was instantly beside her. He took hold of her forearm, felt the slight shiver that went through her at his touch, the flinching away.

"Constance," he murmured. "I'm afraid I've shocked you. This life on the road—one forgets how to behave." He looked down at her. "Can't you pretend we're at Fountains again?"

Here inside this dark frightening windmill with a strange highwayman high above them possibly looking down through a hole in the ceiling at their makeshift canopy which might collapse?

"Fountains was—a long time ago." Her hurried voice held a quiver. Gently he stroked her forearm. "You have forgotten?" he asked wistfully. "I thought, when I found you—"

"Oh, no, I've not forgotten!" she said quickly. "It's just—"

"Constance, sit down," he said in a low tone. And when she had sat back down, he left her and went and got something made of leather that was heavy when he placed it in her hands. "This is a pouch of gold," he said. "It's from my share of what we got from the tax collector tonight."

Shocked, she tried to push it back at him. She didn't want his gold!

"No, keep it," he said quietly. "Think of it as a dowry." His voice deepened. "If ever I do anything to displease you, if ever you're sorry you came away with me, you're free to take this gold and go wherever you choose. There's enough to carry you all across England.''

She was touched at the depth, the sincerity of his tone.

''Oh, Dev,'' she said. ''It's just that—'' *That I feel shy. It's been a long time and I—I feel so awkward about this.*

But she didn't have to tell him. ''Hush,'' he said. ''I understand. It can't have been easy to be pulled out of a box and find me pointing a gun at you. You haven't had time to get yourself sorted out. But I haven't changed, Constance. I'm still the same fellow I was at Fountains.'' He drew her to him and began gently to remove her shoes.

''But it's all changed,'' she said. ''Now I'm Nell and you're—''

''John York.'' He was pulling off her stockings, she could feel them leaving her legs. ''That's what you're to call me now—'Johnny.' We met in London, which is where we're both from. Duck any questions you can. Remember, half the people you meet would sell us both for a reward.''

''John York,'' she said with a shiver as his hands caressed her bare legs.

He leaned down and kissed her knee. ''I took the name York because Yorkshire was where I met you, Constance, where the best part of my life began.''

It was a simple declaration but it broke the bonds that had held her back.

''Oh, Dev!'' Suddenly she was hurling herself against him, suddenly she was crying, she didn't know why. It had been so long since his arms had held her, it had been a long bruising journey from Claxton House, and she had thought never to see him again, and now to discover that he was a highwayman, keeping company with rough dangerous men, with the law hot on his heels.... *''Oh, Dev...''*

He recognized in her voice that wild appeal, that surge of emotion that spoke of loneliness and love—and, beating toward them from the distance, desire.

''It's all right.'' His hand stayed on her knee as he nibbled gently at her ear. ''I won't rush you.''

199

She laughed a little, through her tears. "I feel like a fool," she said shakily.

"You don't look like one." His voice was rapt as he worked deftly with her hooks and eased off her bodice. "You look beautiful." He pushed down her chemise and cupped one of her breasts with his hand and smiled down at her, his teeth a white flash in the darkness.

More relaxed now, she let him undress her, felt herself go tense again as her chemise departed and she was naked beside him, lying on her spread-out kirtle and chemise. Dev's exploring fingers were wandering over her body, caressing her shoulders, her firm young breasts, tingling the nipples to hardness, sliding his hands down around her slender waist and easing them down to her ripe young hips. He made a soft sound in his throat as his hands dropped lower and caressed her thighs. She squirmed and caught her breath as his fingers twined in the silky dark triangle of hair between her thighs and made as if, playfully, he would pull her toward him by that.

"Dev," she murmured chidingly.

He laughed and drew her toward him, scooped her up in one great playful hug. It was so wonderful to hold her in his arms again! He wanted to kiss her, to fondle her—he wanted the dream never to end!

But she held him off—there was something that must be said first. "Dev." Her voice was soft and grave. "I lied to you that night at Fountains. I knew my ankle would hold you back." And she told him how she'd sat by Hugh with a rock after he'd left, meaning to strike him down if he set out in pursuit, how she'd lied for him, given him time to escape. Dev looked away from her as she told him those things for there were tears in his eyes. *And he had thought her a mercenary little chit who'd left him because she might get a better offer!* Hot shame washed over him.

"I just—wanted you to know," she said haltingly. "Before . . ."

"I don't deserve you," he whispered huskily, and drew her to him tenderly.

And then, suddenly, he was caught up by the maelstrom of his own emotions, driven too far by the tormenting touch of her sweet flesh, inundated by love of her. Overcome by desire, he caught her round buttocks one in each hand and drew her to him irresistibly so that his masculine hardness came up against her femaleness and, with a sudden lancing thrust, he entered her.

To Constance, shivering raptly in his arms, the whole thing had a strange headlong quality as she was suddenly held fast in his hard grasp. But she met him unflinching and, even though her own emotions had not peaked, she felt him go over the brink and clung to him, trembling.

"I'm—sorry," he gasped. "I know better. It's just that— oh, Constance, how I've missed you!" He pushed her away a little and began to kiss her hungrily. His yearning lips moved over her face, ruffling her eyebrows, her lashes, sliding down over her cheeks and chin, moving softly along her neck. "I want you to enjoy this," he murmured and bent his head, letting his lips slide fierily along her white pulsing bosom.

He lingered over her breasts, treating them with delicacy, with tenderness. His hands moved expertly between her legs, causing her to give a little moan of expectation. He seemed to be everywhere, nuzzling, caressing, tweaking where she least expected, rousing her to tingling desire and expectancy, and then carrying her upward to farther and farther reaches of desire until she felt she could not bear it. Her whole being seemed focused upon him in a terrible burning concentration that was lifting her to the heights but never quite over the precipice.

She felt rather than heard the soft laugh deep in his throat, felt on a spasmodic thrilling tremor his male hardness slide into her again. And this time there was no rhythm too fast for her, this time she could match him ardor for ardor, sigh for sigh, touch for tingling touch. This time, fueled by bursts of passion, they spun together toward the farther stars, whirled as one toward infinity. Locked together, panting in soul-shattering ecstasy, they went over the brink together.

And drifted down, down, down from rosy undreamt of heights, back to their windmill.

Constance had never felt so alive, so wanted, so thrillingly fulfilled. It was Fountains all over again, only better. And that, she knew suddenly, was because Dev was a better lover.

And how had he learned?

Surfeited now, sleepy but still awake enough to feel a stab of jealousy, she murmured, "You didn't know how to unhook my bodice at Fountains but now you're very good at it!"

"Aren't you glad?" he countered mischievously, and she gave him a playful cuff. If other women there'd been, he'd forget them now that she was back!

On that happy thought, forgetful of their precarious circumstances, forgetful of the fact that she was now consorting with highwaymen and could well hang alongside them if caught, forgetful of the fact that by her side forgotten lay a purse of highwayman's gold for a dowry, Constance fell into a deep and dreamless sleep.

From which she roused to Dev muttering, "Get dressed—quick. Gibb is coming down. I think he's seen something."

Confused for a moment as to where she was, Constance rolled over and got her chemise down around her. In the filtering pinkish light of dawn she saw Dev bolt into his clothes. By the time she had fastened her kirtle around her waist and was struggling with the hooks of her bodice, he was pulling on his boots.

"Horse and rider," said Gibb laconically, vaulting down from the last rungs of the ladder.

Constance felt her alarm mount as Dev stood up booted and picked up his pistol. "Only one?" he asked.

"All I could see," answered Gibb. "He's coming close. Could be he's a scout with others following."

"We may be leaving fast," Dev said over his shoulder as he strode off with Gibb toward the horses. "Stuff everything into the saddlebags—food and all."

Constance made haste to do it. She had the saddlebags packed and was standing there holding them when she realized in panic that she had left something behind. The gold— she had forgotten the gold! She snatched up a leather thong she found on the floor and tied the leather pouch of gold around her waist, up under her skirts.

Now, she thought, *Nell, the highwayman's doxy, was ready to travel!*

A moment later Dev was back. "You can unpack," he told her briefly. "He rode on by, apparently headed for one of the farms east of here."

So keyed up that she was trembling, Constance felt almost a sense of regret that they were not leaving.

"Calm down," said Dev.

"Where—where would we have gone?" she asked, troubled.

"Oh, several places," he shrugged. "There's an inn not too far from here that caters to such as we. Well, shall we have breakfast?"

Constance tried to treat their near miss with danger with the same aplomb Dev did, but found she could not. This was a new, bewildering way of life to her and she still jumped at every slight creak of the windmill's sail as she spread out their "canopy" again for a tablecloth.

During that long day, a day during which the highwaymen lounged about, she learned much. Dev had not come by his nickname of "Gentleman Johnny" for nothing, Gibb told her. The rough lot who made their living from the road had christened him that because he was too selective about those he robbed. No women, no children, no elderly, no one feeble. Tax collectors, government officials and the like—those were his meat. *And there weren't enough of them,* sighed Gibb.

"How do you decide where to strike?" she wondered.

"We can't stay long in one place," Dev told her. "Mostly we work the outskirts of the larger towns where there's considerable traffic."

"You learn the schedules and lie in wait for the stage-coaches?"

The best jobs, they told her, were the result of planning. Gibb had found out about the tax collector through a man in Lincoln, who specialized in such information—and required a cut of the take for it. In their case, since they were new to him, he had required a fee in advance—but it had been worth it.

" 'Twas me who slowed down the coach,'' Gibb bragged. "I had a devil of a time fixing that wheel so it would give trouble and yet not quite come off—for that would o' wrecked the coach and maybe killed us all!''

"But it broke down more than once!''

"I bribed them as fixed it.'' Gibb winked at her.

When they were alone, Dev told her, "Gibb took up this life out of desperation, as I did. He was a soldier and when his company was disbanded they didn't pay him. He came home to Norwich, to his little farm, half-starved, and found it had been sold for debt, his wife dead, his daughter gone to London. He followed her there but he never found her.''

"But couldn't he have got his army pay eventually?''

Dev shrugged. "We have a king in the pay of the French. He does as he likes—it's nothing new.''

"We should get rid of him,'' she cried, "and put the Duke of Monmouth on the throne!''

"Monmouth's illegitimate.'' He gave her a jaded look.

"Maybe not. Cook at Claxton House swears he married Lucy Walter.''

"That's as may be.'' Dev's shrug consigned the wayward duke to oblivion. "Most people prefer a king conceived after a celebrated marriage to some other monarch's daughter.''

"You've become cynical! England deserves a better king— and people like us should see she gets one!''

He looked into her earnest flushed face. "Don't let people hear you talk like that,'' he laughed. "The world out there is an easy place to find a gibbet.''

And especially for highwaymen, thought Constance with a pang.

"Gibb and I must go out again tomorrow," he told her, ruffling her hair affectionately.

"Another tip from the man from Lincoln?"

He nodded.

"Oh, Dev, don't go! We don't need the money."

"Yes, we do." He gave her a rueful look. "Life is hellish expensive on the road. 'Safe' inns charge double, triple. Money melts away—you'll see."

"Who—who is it this time?"

He gave a short laugh. " 'Tis a lofty churchman whose purse we'll be lightening—we hope."

"Church money?" She was scandalized.

"Tithe money," he corrected her. "Seized like any other tax from the unwilling. Money extorted by a church that has the force of government. D'ye wish to marry? 'Tis a fee you'll pay. D'ye wish to—what is it, Constance? You're laughing!"

For the moment his dangerous mission was forgotten. "Oh, Dev, you agreed with me all the time!" she cried, looking with delight at her cheerful young rebel.

He swept her up in his arms. "Not quite but near enough. I'm in sympathy with setting a better king on the throne. I just lack your confidence that we'll be able to do it."

Constance chose not to argue. She was content just to nestle in those strong arms.

Later though, when they were lying naked and warm beneath their makeshift canopy, with their bodies touching during an interval in their lovemaking, she broached what she had been thinking all day.

"Dev," she murmured. "Couldn't you—stop all this? It's a dreadful way to live, always being pursued!"

His hands roved gently through the pale valley between her breasts, wandered up to the pink crested peaks beyond, lingered there. His fingers felt light on her flesh and enticing. She felt her breath catch.

"I mean it, Dev," she said steadily.

The fingers left her abruptly.

"What do you suggest I do?" he asked dryly. "My main talent is that I'm a good man with a pistol."

"I don't know—but there must be *something* you could do."

He kissed her. "We'll think about it in the morning."

And eased his body once again against her naked softness and slipped his long leg between hers, sliding his loins against her thighs in a way that excited her senses and sent little ripples of feeling racing through her in scattered bursts. He stilled her lips with kisses and won her body again as he transported her through the Gates of Desire into a beautiful unreal world where time was meaningless and only passion ruled.

CHAPTER 13

A sense of foreboding hung over Constance all the next day. From the moment she woke, she felt it. She pleaded with Dev not to go—or at least to let her go with him, but he was adamant. "You'll wait here for us, Constance," he told her as he mounted up. "We'll be back by dawn."

And left, riding away through the dusk beside ginger-haired Gibb.

Constance stared after their departing figures. She felt as if her life were ending.

Briefly she considered following them, for Gibb had gone out and bought her a horse that morning.

"A sorry-looking nag she is," he told her apologetically as he handed her the dappled mare's bridle. "But she runs like the wind."

"I only hope I can stay aboard her," said Constance uneasily.

Dev had spent the better part of the afternoon trying to teach her horsemanship—and discovered that she had little aptitude. For all that she was graceful as a gazelle on her own feet, on a horse she was awkward.

"And you can't expect me to ride astride!" she wailed. " 'Tis unladylike!"

Dev and Gibb exchanged glances.

"Constance," said Dev. "Gibb has brought you something else—men's clothing."

She recoiled at that.

"Put the things on," he directed her sternly, "and we'll see how you look. They won't fit you very well, but we must hope you can pass for a boy with this wig." He handed her a comb. "I've hacked off the curls to the right length for a countryman and you can comb it out straight."

Constance looked at the nondescript wig in dismay. Awkwardly cut as it was, it looked limp and infinitely dejected. "I won't wear that!" she cried.

Dev sighed. "It's either that or cut your hair. Boys don't wear long tresses."

Angrily she snatched the wig from his hand.

"If you ride with us, you may be riding for your life," Dev warned her wearily. "In 'safe' inns you may dress as you please, but on the road you're safer as a lad."

Glumly she tried on the trousers and shirt and boots and light cloak Gibb had brought her. Not a single item was a very good fit and she was sure she did indeed look like a country bumpkin when Dev adjusted the hacked-off wig, clapped a battered wide-brimmed hat upon her head, and stepped back critically to view her.

"Keep your hat pulled well down over your eyes," he counseled. "Your eyes are too memorable. And try not to smile—your smile is memorable too."

Constance gave him an irritable look. "Am I permitted to breathe?" she demanded.

He grinned but his gaze was steely. "That's what I'm trying to ensure—that you keep breathing."

Somewhat mollified, she turned to Gibb. "What do you think, Gibb? Don't I make an excellent boy?"

Gibb shrugged. "I'd know ye for a wench by the way ye walk. Lad's hips don't move like that."

"Gibb's right," muttered Dev. "Don't—"

"Walk," supplied Constance crisply. "How am I to get into inns and taverns? I presume we will eat and sleep in such places sometimes?"

Dev considered that, his green eyes thoughtful. He went out and when he came back he was carrying a stout staff. "Ye'll swing in on that, holding up your right leg as if it pains you."

"Oh, you *won't* make me carry a cane?" She was dismayed.

"Why not? It may come in handy in case we're attacked at close quarters."

That last remark silenced her. She eyed the staff doubtfully, wondering if she'd be able to swing it to advantage.

Gibb laughed and clapped her on the shoulder. "He doesn't mean it, lass," he declared cheerfully. "Johnny here may be loath to shoot a man down on the road so's he can take his purse from him—but he'd blow the head off any man who threatened *you!*"

She flashed a sudden look at Dev and his grim expression told her Gibb had spoken the unvarnished truth.

To her dismay, she was told to wear the men's clothing Gibb had brought until they got back—and to keep the saddlebags packed and ready. Constance understood. She was to be ready to run.

"Not that there's apt to be any need," Dev told her, dropping a light kiss upon her forehead before he mounted up. "But it's as well to be ready for anything."

Oh, Dev, she thought, clenching her fingers—and her teeth too to keep from blurting out what she thought. *How can you live like this?*

That night was for Constance one of the worst nights of her life. Clouds scudded fitfully over the moon, turning the surrounding countryside pitch black. The wind had come up and the great sweeps of the windmill creaked aimlessly around and around, the slip-slapping of the tattered canvas of those sails making an appalling noise that would cloak any arriving hoofbeats.

Uncomfortable in her unfamiliar men's clothing and alarmed by the unfamiliar noises, Constance could not sit still. She kept pacing about, constantly running to peer out. Watching for Dev.

At last he came, streaking through the night. Fear struck her when she saw he was alone.

She was outside before he had leaped from his horse. "Dev, what's wrong? Where's Gibb?"

"Drawing them off," he said tersely. " 'Twas an ambush but we fought our way out of it. Gibb knew I had to come back for you, so he led them in the other direction. We're to meet at Starbuck's."

"Will—will he be all right?" she whispered fearfully. For the first time she realized that Gibb, whom she had secretly disdained, might be giving his life for her this night. She felt ashamed.

"All right? God knows." Even as he spoke, Dev was tossing her saddle and saddlebags onto her horse, boosting her up. "Hang on," he told her grimly. "This isn't practice anymore. Your life *does* depend on your staying aboard that mare."

Constance never knew how she got through the next few hours. She clung to the saddle, she twisted her fingers into the mare's gray mane, she reeled as branches whipped her face down the twisted paths Dev led her. For they were going cross country, she knew not where.

To her credit, she did not fall off once.

When the sun was well up, they sheltered in a little woodland glade, green and with a woodsy fragrance permeating the clear morning air. Constance was too tired to eat, too tired to do anything but fall off the dappled mare into Dev's arms and crumple up with a groan on the grass. "I don't think I can go another mile," she said.

"You won't have to. We'll stay here till it's dark."

Dev went off to water and care for the horses and, mercifully, Constance fell asleep.

She awoke to having her shoulder shaken. "Time to start again," said Dev, and she stumbled up—and made it gamely through another wearying night.

On the third night they reined up in the fog-shrouded courtyard of a small country inn, a low stone structure well off the beaten track and so well concealed that it seemed to loom up before them suddenly out of the trees. Talk and raucous laughter drifted to them from the inn but there was no sign of horses about—she was to learn later that they were housed in a capacious stable which was reached not only from the outside but by a tunnel that could be entered by a trapdoor from the kitchen. A broken dangling wooden sign proclaimed the place the "Wind and Whistle."

"Safest place I know," Dev muttered as he lifted her off her horse, for by now she felt that all her bones were broken. "Just let me do all the talking."

A boy had magically appeared out of the fog to take their horses and Dev tossed him a coin. He caught it and grinned.

"Who's here tonight?" asked Dev.

A pair of thin shoulders shrugged and a young-old face, infinitely worldly above a mop of dirty tow-colored hair, looked up speculatively at Dev. "Not Charley," the lad volunteered cheerfully. "He's dead."

"What happened?"

"Got shot on the road two nights ago."

Dev sighed. "Is Gibb here yet?"

"With a wench on each arm!" laughed the boy.

"That's Gibb for you," said Dev dryly, and Constance thought fleetingly, *And Henriette thought he was past it!*

They found the smoky low-ceilinged common room bustling. There was a single long table and as the door opened every head swung round. There were faces there Constance would not have cared to meet even in sunlight on a crowded street; in the dim light of guttering candles they chilled her.

A husky female voice broke the sudden stillness. "Well, if

it ain't Gentleman Johnny!'' And an orange-haired girl of perhaps eighteen rose from someone's lap at the end of the long table. Her hips swayed seductively in her orange satin skirts as she started toward them and her tightly laced black bodice seemed about to spill out a pair of voluptuous breasts that were barely concealed by a white chemise with big puffed sleeves. ''We ain't seen you lately, Johnny!'' There was an intimate sound to that voice.

Before she could go a step, the man on whose lap she'd been sitting, a big fellow with a black patch over one eye and a scarred lip, reached out a long arm to detain her. ''Hold it, Nan,'' he said tolerantly. ''Johnny's got a wench with him.''

Constance felt hot color flood her face as every pair of hard eyes raked her up and down. She was to learn that life on the highways required an instant assessment of what was about and that these rough men, whatever else they lacked, were nobody's fools. At least one of them had seen through her disguise from across the room before she was well over the threshold.

Beside her Dev laughed and although the laugh was easy she was standing so near she brushed him and she could feel his arm muscles tense.

''Sure, I've brought my wench,'' he declared easily. ''Just as you've brought yours, Candless. Nell, meet Candless.''

Gibb broke into the awkward moment. ''Over here, Johnny.'' He waved a bottle at them. ''Sit here between Maudie and me.''

Moments later Constance found herself wedged at the long table between ginger-bearded Gibb and Dev. On Dev's other side Maudie—an elderly bawd with a friendly, loose-lipped smile, gave Dev's arm a playful dig and wheezed, ''So you've got a new doxy, Johnny? Nan here won't like that!''

Down the table Constance could see that Nan was not liking it. She tossed her orange head and scowled at them.

Constance was still covertly watching Nan when Starbuck, the owner of this establishment, came up. He was a barrel-chested man with a nose smashed almost flat and no expression at all in his pale eyes as his voice boomed, "Glad to see ye, Johnny. Gibb says ye ran onto a bit of bad luck on the road."

"And some good." Dev indicated Constance. "Nell, this is Starbuck," he told her. "Friend of all. We'll need supper and a bottle of wine and a room for Nell and me."

"Supper and wine ye can have, Johnny, but I've no rooms left."

"Yes, ye have," said Gibb easily. "Johnny's got him a room, Starbuck. Don't worry about it."

"We ain't seen you here before, dearie." Maudie leaned over.

"No, I'm from London," Constance remembered to say, but she was still watching Nan. *So it was Nan's bodice that Dev had learned to unhook so expertly . . . and Nan was far too pretty.*

Maudie followed the direction of her gaze and chuckled. "Don't you worry none about Nan," she said. "Candless'll keep her in her place!"

But Candless didn't. When he turned to argue over a wager with the man on his right, Nan got up off his lap and flounced forward. As she passed them her hand suddenly swooped and lifted Constance's hat from her head. She tossed it up and caught it by its broad brim, laughing.

Constance had started to rise but Dev's sudden restraining grip on her wrist stopped her.

"Nan wants a fight with your doxy," muttered Maudie. "Woops, here comes Candless!"

Down the table the big black-patched man was rising to his feet. Nan ignored him. "Watch this, Johnny!" she said. Seductively she pulled up her skirts and Constance saw that she was wearing a black satin garter far up on her white thigh. From that garter she now snaked out a knife and regarded Constance from glittering tawny eyes.

Constance heard Maudie draw in a wheezing breath and was sharply aware that Dev had interposed his body between her and Nan.

Nan tossed the knife in the air, caught it and laughed. "Afraid I'll carve my initials on your new doxy, Johnny?" she mocked. "Watch this!"

She tossed the hat in the air and with her other hand hurled the knife. Straight and true it went through the crown and nailed the hat quivering to one of the low beams of the ceiling.

It could as easily have pierced my heart, thought Constance, chillingly aware of her danger.

"That's enough, Nan." Big Candless seized the girl in a rough grasp, picked her up kicking and, amid gales of laughter and much banging of tankards, carried her back to his end of the table. Furious and snarling, orange-haired Nan still fought him and he gave a howl as her white teeth sank into his hand. "Fierce little devil, ain't she?" Candless asked the company at large. "Makes love the same way!" He suddenly seized both her wrists and proceeded to slap Nan's angry face back and forth with a whipping motion.

Constance would have cried out but Dev muttered, "Be still. She's *his* wench, they'll settle this between themselves."

Nan stopped screeching and stared sullenly at Candless, who pulled her back on his lap and resumed his argument over the wager as if nothing had happened. Dev got up and wrenched hat and knife from the beam. The hat he tossed to Constance, who clapped it back over her wig. The knife he tossed down the table to Candless with a laconic, "I'd hang on to it, if I were you—to keep Nan from carving you up tonight!"

General laughter greeted this sally—in which, surprisingly, Nan joined. She cuffed Candless's ear and then kissed him.

"I've got a better man than you, Johnny!" she called up to them.

"See if you can keep him," retorted Dev. A serving wench shoved past them to put their food on the table and he sat down to eat it as calmly as if nothing had happened.

Constance, unused to such outbursts, wasn't hungry.

"We're lucky to get this," Dev told her as he surveyed their cubbyhole of a room under the second-floor eaves.

Constance, looking around her, didn't feel lucky. "What was Nan to you?" she asked.

"A passing fancy," he said, surprisingly frank. "I got her from Charley"—*the man who was shot,* she thought—"who got her from Bo Ringle who was hanged last August, and now she's moved on to Candless."

But to her you weren't just a passing fancy, thought Constance, feeling jealousy gnaw at her. She would learn later from Maudie that doxies changed hands quite often on the road—she herself had been the doxy of half a dozen highwaymen since hanged.

"I see," she said coldly.

Dev gave her a restless look. "I'm going back to talk to Gibb," he said. "I don't like the way we were ambushed on the road. Could be the man in Lincoln plays both sides of the street."

Hardly had he left than the door opened and a blowzy serving girl came in carrying a metal tub and a big pitcher of water. "Johnny said ye'd be wantin' a bath," she smirked. "Ye'll want to make yerself pretty fer 'im!"

The hot bath made Constance so sleepy she barely remembered to latch the door. Afterward she pitched forward upon the bed and was lost to the world.

She came to in the morning, to a persistent knocking. "Constance." Dev's voice. She was disoriented for a minute, looking wildly about her. Then she realized where she was—Starbuck's. She jumped up and let him in.

"I latched you out," she cried in dismay. "Oh, Dev, why didn't you wake me?"

"I came up and you didn't hear me knocking," he said. "I figured you were so tired I'd let you rest."

"But, you, where did you sleep?"

He shrugged. "I was down in the common room, with Gibb."

"You mean he doesn't have a room?"

"This was *his* room," said Dev. "He gave it up to us."

Once again she was grateful to Gibb.

Constance thought Nan must have been lying in wait for Dev, for when they went downstairs—and this time Constance was wearing her own clothes and not walking awkwardly in ill-fitting boots—orange-haired Nan was standing at the foot. Today she was garbed in green and yellow stripes with large black and yellow bows. It was almost the loudest costume Constance had ever seen. Instead of letting them pass, Nan blocked their way. Hands on hips, she regarded Dev through her short reddish lashes.

"Last night was like old times, Johnny," she purred and flashed him a sweet, insinuating smile. "Glad to have you back." She passed by Constance with a laugh and a toss of her head and went on upstairs.

"Don't pay no attention to Nan," said Gibb, who had seen what happened from the common room. "She was born for trouble."

"I'm sure she was," said Constance, and, head high, sailed into the common room. There her newly revealed dainty figure and cloud of dark hair were regarded by the lounging occupants with such lively interest as they stripped her with their eyes that she reddened to the roots of her hair.

"Take no notice," muttered Dev. "From them it's a tribute."

In her embarrassment Constance regretted having changed to women's clothes. She had done it, she realized suddenly, to compete with flashy Nan. *Wild dangerous Nan, heroine of dozens of stormy affairs, who had spent who knew how many nights in Dev's arms.* . . .

They rested at Starbuck's a week and then drifted east. Outside Norwich they found meaner quarters—this time in the loft of a farmer's stable.

"There's better places to be had on the road," Gibb explained. "But Johnny's takin' you to the safest ones."

She had developed a fondness for Gibb and found she enjoyed talking to him. He had a colorful view of the world.

"Get Gibb to tell you how he wants to be buried," Dev suggested one day.

"On my head," said Gibb promptly. "I want a shaft sunk straight down, and I want to be lowered in headfirst. There's a Resurrection comin', sure as you're born, and everything on earth's gonna be turned upside down. And when that time comes, *I mean to be the only one standin' on my feet!*"

Constance blinked at this remarkable idea.

"Johnny here's promised to have me buried the way I want should I die before him," Gibb told her.

Dev's pleasant smile challenged her not to laugh. Constance gave him a quelling look. "If he forgets to do so, I'll be sure to remind him," she promised Gibb tartly and Dev's green eyes brightened. He was glad Constance and Gibb got on so well together. "Perhaps you'd like to show us where you used to live?" she suggested. "You said you were from Norwich."

"Can't show you the house," shrugged Gibb. "It's burned down."

"Oh." She was sorry she'd mentioned it, for a bereaved look passed over his face, and she hastened to change the subject, to ask about their next job.

They were free-lancing now, after the debacle on the Great North Road, trusting to their own instincts rather than to bought information. They weren't having much luck.

That night Dev and Gibb went out on the road and when they rode back she was waiting for them at the stable—as usual, dressed and ready to ride. She thought Gibb looked unusually grim but Dev grinned at her and from the saddle tossed her a clinking purse. " 'Twas a bishop whose purse we lightened tonight."

Constance caught the purse. But there was something in Dev's voice, a slight waver. . . . She ran forward just as he slipped from the saddle and Gibb, who had just dismounted, caught him and eased him to the ground.

"He caught a rifle ball," explained Gibb.

"It's nothing," said Dev airily. "I but lost my balance. Here, help me up, Gibb, we're frightening Constance."

He made to rise and fell back, unconscious.

The farmer came at Gibb's hoarse call. He asked no questions but brought the hot water and clean cloths Gibb asked for.

Gibb took out his knife and washed it in the hot water. "Don't watch this," he told Constance.

"But I want to help."

"As you like. Don't faint on me, though." Gibb nodded to the farmer, a powerful man who stood impassively by. "Hold him down for me. When I cut out this bullet, it'll bring him to." And to Constance, "Try to hold his head down if you can."

Constance took Dev's head in her arms. Silently she began to pray.

As the knife cut in, Dev came to with a hoarse cry and Constance cried, "Gibb's got to get the bullet out of your shoulder!" as she wrestled with him. "Oh, please hold still, oh, please—" She was crying now, her tears falling hot on his face, which was a mask of agony beaded with sweat. She felt his strong neck muscles rope up and she moaned even as a great groan escaped his clenched teeth.

His body writhed suddenly in agony and Gibb cried triumphantly, "I've got it! Just wait now, Johnny, I've got to cauterize the wound."

Constance watched in horror as she saw Gibb pass his knife through the flames of a little fire the farmer had made out of hot coals he brought from the house. She shuddered as it began to glow.

"Don't watch," advised Gibb, and Constance turned her face away.

There was a horrible burning smell, Dev gave a hoarse cry, his body wrenched convulsively free from their grasp—and fell back, unconscious.

" 'Tis done," said Gibb calmly. "We'll get him to bed now."

Constance felt sick. She staggered to her feet and leaned against one of the posts that supported the stable roof. "There's no pursuit?" she gasped.

"None. We got away clean." Gibb gave her a sympathetic look. "The lad's survived worse than this, lass—and will again."

Oh, never let this happen again, she prayed, trailing along as the farmer and Gibb got Dev bedded down—this time not in the stable loft but in his own bed in the cottage. The farmer's wife gave Constance a hostile look as she saw her bed being taken by an injured highwayman.

"It's only for a little while," babbled Constance, desperate to placate her—for suppose the farmer's wife in pique let it be known that a highwayman was sheltering in their farmstead? She could gain a reward and Dev was in no condition to flee!

She was learning, the hard way, the perils of life on the road.

All that week Constance nursed Dev, but by the third day when no fever had developed he managed to climb the ladder back to the stable loft and she felt easier. Gibb had given the farmer's wife a gold coin and she had smirked her thanks.

Now Constance began to understand why Dev was always in need of money. Their accommodations here were worth only pennies—yet must be paid for in gold. They were buying not merely shelter, they were buying silence. And silence was costly.

She moved her pallet away from Dev's so that he might rest better. If he tried to embrace her, he might start his shoulder bleeding again and, despite Gibb's bragging, she was not sure how good a doctor he really was.

It gave her many a long hour to think and consider her situation, and what lay ahead: inns like Starbuck's, full of hard-eyed men and their bawds, places where fights erupted suddenly and violently, where hard money changed hands easily and life was cheap. Farmsteads like this one with sullen wives turned friendly by gold. Wild nights on the run, careening through the darkness with branches whipping her face, trying to stay aboard a plunging horse. And then the worst: nights with bullets whining through the darkness—and Dev hurt again. And maybe hurt some way that Gibb could not help him. She thought what it would be like to sit by him some place where they dared not send for a doctor, what it would be like to sit and watch him die.

Dev was feeling better. He stood on his feet and stretched his good arm and pronounced himself ready to ride. "And tonight we'll sleep together again," he told Constance with a grin. "I've a good arm will hold you even if I do have to be a bit tender with this shoulder."

She had been trembling with fear for him and now that fear gave way to anger.

"I can't live like this," she cried. "Never knowing whether a bullet has found you or not! I want a home, children—*a husband who will be there when I wake!*"

Dev stepped back. His face, transformed of a sudden, had lost its boyish wickedness and was very grave. "I would that I could give you those things, Constance," he said. "For they are all things that you deserve. You deserve more—a fine home, servants, luxury. I would that my uncle had died instead of my father and then I would be the Earl of Roxford and able to offer you one of the finest country seats in England. But I am not. I have no trade—nor any hope of one. Naught but my pistol."

She stood there shaking with the terrible truth of it sinking in. Dev was not a highwayman by choice—and indeed, as Gibb said, he was "dreadful dainty of who he robbed." *Dev was one of the lost—like herself.*

"Oh, Dev." She caught at his good shoulder, clung to it. "Couldn't we start again? Go to America?"

He looked down at her with a torment of emotions playing over his face. "All right," he said huskily, stroking her hair. "America it is. But first—Gibb has a brother over at Bury St. Edmunds he'd like to visit while he still has gold in his pocket. And I can give you the last of your three wishes now.'' He straightened up and his grin flashed at her. ''We're riding south, Constance—just the two of us. And''—his green eyes softened and deepened—''I'm going to put a wedding ring on your finger!''

PART FOUR
The Highwayman's Bride

Beneath the light of a waning moon
On thundering hooves he'll ride,
For he's taken a purse of gold tonight
And seeks a place to hide!
Some day he knows in his reckless heart
That the law and he must collide,
But till that day comes he'll drink deep of life
And toast his lovely bride!

Hatfield Forest, Essex,
Summer 1683

CHAPTER 14

White moonlight shone down upon the massive hornbeams and oaks of Hatfield Forest. It glimmered down upon the lovers through the leafy branches of that most monumental oak of all—the Old Doodle Oak, whose giant girth had seen uncounted generations come and go, and of whom men said it was the very oak marked on the Conqueror's Domesday Survey.

They had said good-by to Gibb outside Norwich. Dev had been for riding daringly into London and being married swiftly in Fleet Street, but Constance—more cautious—had insisted on a village marriage, under assumed names. And so in a tiny village near the ancient forest of Hatfield, whose thousand acres with its wide green chases had been a royal hunting preserve six hundred years before, Dev and Constance had the banns cried in the village church.

A much-changed pair they appeared, for Constance had gone back to wearing her faded lavender kirtle and homespun bodice; she wore her glorious hair bound up and stuffed demurely into a white linen cap—as became the chambermaid out of London she professed to be. And Dev was become overnight an impecunious scribe, whose pistols rested in his saddlebags, and who affected a pair of spectacles and a solemn demeanor. To the world they were a young pair planning to join relatives in Nottingham, who would give them shelter until the young man could find a patron. In the meantime, Dev ingenuously offered to write letters for a penny for any who felt the need—and found few takers.

The innkeeper at the tiny, half-timbered, wattle-and-daub inn where they stayed took a fancy to them. He even employed Dev to write a letter to his sister who had six years earlier gone to America "and hadn't been heard from since." And on the day they were married he insisted that a penny-bridal be held at his inn.

Constance, aware their safety lay in being inconspicuous, was wed in the same faded kirtle and bodice in which she had fled Claxton House. She didn't want a penny-bridal but the landlord insisted.

"I'll foot the fee for the wedding dinner myself," he told them gustily. "And make it all back in the trade in wine and ale that will come my way from it!"

Afraid to protest too loudly lest they seem strange—for penny-bridals were all the custom here—Constance agreed. She who had worn so many names since she had taken to the road with Dev had spoken her vows as "Mistress Penelope Goode" and been joined in marriage to "John Watts," as Dev now called himself. And had immediately repaired to the common room of the inn, where a motley collection of roisterers were assembled to drink her health in ale they paid for out of their own pockets.

"We'll get away as soon as we decently can," Dev muttered into her ear and Constance flashed him a grateful glance. But after dinner the fiddler called out like a town crier and she found herself plumped down at the upper end of a table while, according to custom, a white sheet was thrown over Dev's shoulders as he stood by. One by one, the wedding guests—by now for the most part drunk—staggered up to toss coins upon the table before her. Constance felt like a beggar—and a fraudulent beggar at that—as the pile of coins, mostly pennies, mounted before her. Her cheeks were already red with embarrassment when the most beribboned pair of gloves she had ever seen was ostentatiously laid upon the table and auctioned off.

"Don't bid, they won't like it," she whispered anxiously to Dev, laying a quick hand upon his arm, for his shoulders had given a slight lurch as the smirking auctioneer reminded his audience that the prize was not only the gloves, but a kiss from the blushing bride.

The bidding waxed hot but in the end it was the burly landlord, drunk on his own wine, who won the gloves and seized Constance with delight, swooping her entirely from her chair and planting a moist kiss—for she had dodged his lips—on her hot cheek.

He laughed as he set her down. Then Dev shrugged off the white sheet and they had a dance together, while everyone stood about and applauded. And then they made their escape.

"Oh, Dev, let's not spend our wedding night *here*," Constance said anxiously. "People will be singing and caterwauling all night, and banging on our door!"

Dev gave her a smiling look. "The horses are saddled," he told her. "I explained to the landlord we were leaving tonight."

And he had brought her here by moonlight to the wide green chases of Hatfield. Once as they rode through the night a red deer—one of the descendants of the red deer that William the Conqueror and his sons had hunted here—burst out of the brush and darted across their path. And once a badger, broad and furry night hunter that he was, caused their horses to rear up and Constance nearly lost her saddle. And then they saw before them the mightiest tree of the forest—the Old Doodle Oak that had seen kings and conquerors come and go.

And it was upon the soft grasses beneath that oak that Dev

had spread his cloak. And Constance, the banns and the vows and the penny-bridal behind her, had shed her clothes and lain down on that cloak in the soft warmth of the summer night and watched Dev undress.

A tall proud figure he cut in the half light that filtered down through the branches. Changed, she thought, from the boy she had first known. A man now, with a man's desires.

And a man's finesse as he took her lightly in his arms.

"I'm a bride at last," she murmured.

"You were a bride before—at Fountains," he pointed out, his voice reaching her through her tangled hair as he nuzzled her ear.

"A make-believe bride," she said.

"Bride enough for me."

She stirred in his arms. "But not for me. I wanted to be your bride not just in *our* sight, but in the world's sight."

Dev lifted his russet head and brushed back her hair and smiled down into her eyes. His face against the branches and the moon was in shadow but she could see the gleam of his eyes and his white teeth as he smiled. "*You're* my world, Constance."

That he should state it so calmly took her breath away.

"Oh, Dev!" She flung herself into his arms, eager to consummate this longed-for marriage as she would have done had she been a duke's daughter and a virgin and he an earl's son to whom she had just been wed. "For us this will be—a first time."

He laughed softly, but he caught her wistful yearning mood and his arms were gentle as he drew her close. Ardent lovers they were, but tonight they knew a lingering tenderness that was new to them. A kind of heavenly peace had descended upon their restless lovemaking, a blessed harmony of the spirit, a repose. It made Constance realize suddenly what it would be like to spend her life with him, to grow old with him, to be not only the first but the last woman he would ever hold in his arms.

And then her fanciful thoughts were swept away in the wild

ardor of his lovemaking. Like the pealing of a great bell, her body joined with his. Rapt, breathless, their bodies locked together, they shuddered in harmonic unison to the symphony of their rising passions, until in a mighty carillon of bursting joy they reached the far unreal peaks of ecstasy and silvered down like the moonlight to the green sward below the spreading branches of the oak that had watched England change hands at the time of the Conquest.

"Dev," she whispered in wonder, hushing her voice to the felt majesty of the night. "Will it always be like this for us?"

"Always," he murmured. And with a last long lingering kiss that began at her throat and wandered down her slender quivering form in a way that swept away questions and memory together, he rolled away from her and slept.

But for Constance, whose violet velvet eyes were wide open upon the moonlit night, sleep was not yet. Now that the afterglow had faded to a lovely memory, she lay there in all her naked loveliness, sated with lovemaking, dreaming, and wondered what their lives would be like...in America. There they could go through another wedding ceremony— under their own names. She quailed at the thought of the long voyage, for the sea had never been to her liking. She was a daughter of the land, an iris meant to bloom in some sunlit garden—not a sea sprite meant for the sea's wild winds and hard bright glitter. America...land of dreams.

And on that thought she drifted off to sleep.

She woke to warm sunlight to find her naked body being pelted with wild orchids, which Dev had found growing abundantly on the marshy ground nearby. Flowers were tickling her breasts, sliding between her thighs. She sat up laughing, fending off the barrage of flowers and tossing back her long tangled hair as she rose. She scooped up handfuls of the brightly colored orchids and tossed them back at him. As he ducked and dodged she leaped up and ran after him, chasing him to a deep pool hidden in the trees, where they stood knee deep in rushes and water plantain and bathed, smiling at each other.

Afterward he carried her through the dappled sunlight, through wild thyme and primroses, back to their "home" beneath the Old Doodle Oak and laid her down on the grass and tickled and caressed her to laughing delight. She would pretend to try to escape him, rolling and tossing and turning and flailing her arms, and he would catch a flying ankle or a rolling thigh and ever turn her back to face him. Their lovemaking had a free lighthearted gaiety this morning very different from the sonorous elegance of the night before. Last night they had been Lovers Who Had Taken Steps—formal wedding vows. This morning they were again the lovers of Fountains Abbey, gamboling children bathed in the beauty of a newfound world.

Constance dragged her fingers lovingly along his chest and felt his hard muscles ripple, she leant her head against that chest and heard the strong beating of his heart, she let her soft body be brought up fiercely against his own and felt his maleness enter her and knew that life would always be good and that they would always be together.

Such is the golden summertime of love.

They lingered in the beautiful forest of Hatfield through the golden days of summer, loath to leave this paradise to start their new life. Sometimes Dev would travel to one of the villages and buy food for them, such necessities as they could not get along without. He bought grain for the horses, to supplement the lush grazing beneath the hornbeams and oaks—and once a new chemise for Constance which, although she chided him for spending the money, knowing how slim his purse must be growing, she viewed with delight.

"It is very elegant!" she declared, turning round and round so that the light skirt swirled out and showed her pretty legs.

"Not fine enough for you," he said sturdily. "You deserve the best."

"Ah, but I do not need the best, Dev." She sank down beside him in the grass. "I do not need *things* at all. All I need is you."

"Do you, Constance?" She thought his voice sounded

wistful and he toyed with her breasts idly, studying them as if he wanted to avoid her gaze. "Is that really enough?"

"Of course!" she said lightly. "And now your shoulder's so well mended that you can do hard work, and we'll go to America and no one there will ever know you were on the road at all."

"Is that so important?" he asked gravely.

"It is important to your safety," she said, frowning as she drew away and shrugging off his roving fingers from her breasts, for they threatened to silence her logic and melt away her reason. "You must know that."

"I know I love you," he said simply. "And that I want to make you happy. But there isn't enough money to take us both to America, Constance."

"You can have my dowry," she told him, laughing. "For I've still got it."

"Not even then." He shook his head wearily. "We've enough passage for one—no more."

"Oh, Dev! You wouldn't go without me?" she asked fearfully.

" 'Tis a raw new country. We can't land there penniless—at least you can't. Better I go and feel out the land, better I make a place for you—and then send for you to come."

All her arguments would not shake him. They could not stay forever in this forest, he told her firmly. And three days later she found herself settled in a tiny farmlet with a comfortable couple who understood this young scribe's passion to be off to America and promised to care for his bride until he sent for her.

It had all happened so fast, Constance felt dizzy. It seemed that one moment she had ridden with Dev into Hatfield Forest, a bride, and the next moment she had ridden out and Dev was making plans to leave her.

But his jaw was set and she knew he would brook no interference.

"At least let me go with you to the ship," she pleaded. "Let me wave good-by to you from the shore." *In case I never see you again . . . in case you die on that wild treacherous sea.*

"No, for it is always possible that I'll be recognized and I've no mind to drag you down with me if that should happen."

She shivered. *The price of life on the road. . . .*

"You'll write to me?" she whispered.

A pattern of mixed emotions played across his young face. "I'll write," he finally conceded.

Feeling her world had collapsed, Constance watched him go. He had almost disappeared from view down the country lane when he turned and brandished his pistol. Then—as if the sight of her down the road had made him waver in his purpose—he bent low over his horse's neck and charged away at full gallop.

A sob caught in Constance's throat. And suddenly she remembered that far out behind the barn the road twisted back on itself and forded a little brook. Dev had not gone that way because it was treacherous for a horse's hooves but—she could make it if she ran like the wind! She could catch up with him and tell him good-by all over again!

With a sense of panic giving wings to her feet, Constance fled downhill over the uneven ground and plunged into the woods which concealed the little brook that he must ford.

She was panting and disheveled and winded when she arrived at last at the little ford, her feet making no noise on the spongy ground. But she was too late—Dev had already forded the stream. Just as she was about to call out to him she saw that he was not alone.

Riding beside him, with that unmistakable slouch that made his figure distinctive in the saddle, was Gibb.

And riding just ahead in a flaunting yellow dress with her orange head flung back, was Nan. Flashing bright as a lighted candle against the old green trees, and laughing as she called something to them over her shoulder.

All at once, Constance's bright world was ripped apart, and

she fell back against a tree bole as if all the wind had been knocked out of her sails.

There was no ship, no voyage to America, no new life beckoning. There was only the old life—the forays upon the highway, the wild rides through the night, the "safe" inns and taverns, the terrible expense of everything, the ever-present danger.

Dev had left her where she would be safe—left her with a lie.

And gone on the road with Nan! Nan, who suited a highwayman's life-style! Dev—and Nan.

At Starbuck's Nan had thrown a knife through the crown of her hat. And now that knife had pierced her heart.

Thoughts rang through her head discordantly, like clashing cymbals. She had been wrong about Dev, her own love for him had blinded her to reality. Dev had never intended to give up his reckless way of life. He had married her because she had wanted him to—but nothing had changed him. He had seen in her eyes that she was thinking of leaving and so he had placated her—with a lie.

And gone back to Nan....

For now she had no illusions at all about where he had learnt his finesse as a lover: *in Nan's arms.*

Constance made no attempt to follow, or to hail them. She turned blindly and crashed into a tree and then she began to weep in earnest. She wept for her own folly, and for the life she had thought she saw stretching before her, and for Dev's unfaith.

And then as she trudged back and the breeze that had come up dried the tears on her cheeks, she came to a great decision there under the cloudless skies of Essex: She was leaving. Wife or no, she would not wait for him here—if indeed he chose to return! Perhaps he had just shucked her off, intending to forget her. Her knuckles clenched white, and her expression was wild. *Even if he did return, she would not take him back!* Nor would he find her here!

Hawley Grange, Somerset,
Christmas Eve 1684

CHAPTER 15

"I think the Worst Thing," said Pamela earnestly, leaning over to pat Angel's silky mane as she rode, "would be to get an Unfeeling Husband, don't you? I mean someone who felt that women were like—like cattle, to be well treated but—but their opinions not *considered* if you know what I mean."

"Indeed I do know what you mean," sighed Constance, glancing down nervously as her mount slipped on an icy rut. *Dev,* she thought bitterly, *had only pretended to consider her opinions, and then, covered by a mask of lies, he had done just what he wanted to do. As men usually did.*

"Tom isn't at all like that," said Pamela.

Constance gave her a fond look. "Of course he isn't," she agreed, for she was used to conceding that Tom Thornton had all the virtues. Poor Pamela was so deep in love with him that half her conversation was about Tom.

"And I'm sure Captain Warburton isn't," added Pamela with a sideways look at the dark-haired girl riding beside her.

"Perhaps." Constance's tone was noncommittal. She didn't

want to think about Tony Warburton right now. Thinking about him made her heart pound and brought hot color to her face. *He is all that Dev was not,* she told herself. *A man who walks in the light. But even he was not faithful. Neither of them were that.*

"I don't know why you insisted on riding over to call on the Hawley girls today." Plaintively, Pamela cut into her thoughts. "And on Christmas Eve too, when we've so much to do." She glanced down at the sprig of holly which decorated her red riding cloak, and then at the similar sprig which decorated Constance's plum one. "Especially when you know I don't care for the Hawleys!"

But you did until Tom Thornton paired off with Melissa. . . .

"Why not?" said Constance reasonably. "You said yourself it's a beautiful day and the snow on the roads is hard-packed."

Pamela sighed. She was thinking of the snow fort she and Tom had never really finished, for Ned had flung out of the maze and Tom, riddled with curiosity as was she, had ridden away with him. She was dying to ask Tom what had happened between Ned and Constance in the maze, for Constance had been very brusque with her about it and left her curiosity unsatisfied. It would have been much more fun to have ridden over to Huntlands today on some excuse and talked to Tom!

"Besides," added Constance, "Helena Hawley has promised to give me her recipe for tansies." It was untrue but she dared not tell talkative Pamela that there was a meeting being held this day at Hawley Grange—a meeting carefully held under cover of Christmas Eve festivities when gatherings would pass unnoticed—of the young men who espoused the Duke of Monmouth's cause—and *she* intended to be there! Her voice turned bantering. "And I intend to win Helena's recipe away from her before you say something disastrous about Melissa's mad pursuit of Tom that sets the whole Hawley family against us!"

Pamela chose to ignore that last dig. "Tansies!" she cried scornfully, for she prided herself on being possessed of

235

housewifely talents. "Why, I could give you a *much* better recipe for tansies than Helena Hawley can! You use pure cream when you scramble the eggs, and wheat blade juice, and you must *not* forget the strawberry and violet leaves."

"*Or* the spinach. *Or* the walnut tree buds. Or the salt or the nutmeg or the cinnamon!" sighed Constance, who had been listening to this same lecture all morning and could now recite it like a litany.

"You have left out the grated bread," said Pamela stiffly. "And you must remember to sprinkle it well with sugar when you serve it."

"I think Helena mentioned something about adding tansy." Constance was deliberately vague.

"Walnut buds are much better," snapped Pamela. "Helena Hawley just adds anything available to her dishes. She will probably poison her husband if she ever gets one!"

"Oh, she'll get one," murmured Constance, thinking of Helena's statuesque beauty and straw-colored hair. All the Hawley sisters were fair. As she spoke, she was vainly attempting to keep her horse from stopping to graze by the roadside on some tall bunched grass that stuck up above the snow. It was a losing battle. The horse had a mind of its own and Constance was no hand on the reins.

"Really, Constance, can't you keep that poor beast on the road?" demanded Pamela. "Why, who is that riding toward us?" she interrupted herself.

Constance peered ahead at the man who was riding toward them with his cloak whipping in the wind. "I don't know him," she decided.

"Neither do I. But he looks to be a gentleman. I mean, his cloak is of a fashionable length and looks to be of velvet."

"How can you tell at this distance?" laughed Constance.

"And he seems to be wearing a great periwig," said Pamela as a clincher. For surely none but a gentleman would be sporting an expensive full-bottomed periwig which rose monstrously around the head and descended like a cowl about the shoulders. She giggled. "Can you imagine going to bed with a man who took off his hair and put it on a wig stand before he climbed in with you—shaved head and all?"

Constance could not. "They wear nightcaps to keep their heads warm," she murmured, remembering the tasseled nightcap and brocaded robe in which Sir John Dacey had stalked about Claxton House. She wondered who the stranger was. He must have just come from Hawley Grange, for they were fast approaching the entrance, so overgrown that it was nearly hidden from view.

"Maybe that's why he's wearing it now—to keep his head warm," giggled Pamela. "Maybe he has a perfectly good head of hair under it!"

Constance eyed the approaching stranger rather more sharply. With the riders who were galloping all across England these days carrying frenzied messages about the Cause, it was entirely possible that that wig was clapped on over a real head of hair. This fellow riding toward them could even have suffered the fate of a famous spy who had sought to dye his bright red hair a more inconspicuous color and had used a metallic dye to turn it black; instead it had given him England's most conspicuous head of hair, for tufts of it had turned every color of the rainbow.

As they were about to pass, the rider, whom they now saw was young and dandified and had beneath his large periwig the innocent face of a cherub with slightly puffy cheeks, reined up and swept them as low a bow as being mounted would permit.

"Ladies," he said. "I must admit me that I am lost. Could ye point out the way to Hawley Grange?"

"You have just passed the entrance," said Constance. " 'Tis just behind you on the left."

The traveler looked nonplussed but his hazel eyes focused on Constance with vast approval. "I do not see how I missed it," he muttered.

"You missed it because you were looking at us!" declared

Pamela blithely. "No matter, we'll take you there for that's where we're going. Are you expected?"

"Indeed I am—at least I hope so. Chesney Pell, at your service, ma'am." He swept them both another low bow. "I am here visiting the Rawlings in Bridgwater. Cart Rawlings rode on ahead, for he was eager to see a certain young lady at Hawley Grange."

"I am Pamela Archer and this is my father's ward, Constance Dacey," said Pamela, who enjoyed meeting new people even if they *did* wear detestable periwigs. She brought her horse up even with his as he turned around and rode beside him down a road that was barely more than a cowpath, for the Hawleys did not much believe in keeping up their roads either. The Squire often called it the "worst spot on the way to Bridgwater."

Constance rode slightly behind, studying Chesney Pell's rather narrow back, with its bottle green velvet cloak that kept whipping about revealing his fashionably wide-cuffed sleeves, deep-reversed and sporting a wealth of brown braid. The cut of that sleeve was very smart. She doubted it had been made here in the West Country. Which made an interesting question: Whence had the gentleman come? And what was his purpose in seeking out Hawley Grange on this of all days? If he was a courier come to bring them a message from some other part of the country, he could not be such a good choice. Unobservant. For he had managed to miss the tall chimney stacks that rose over Hawley Grange, which were visible if one looked up above the hedgerows along the road.

Such thoughts occupied her mind as Pamela, chatting with their chance-met companion, turned her horse through the overgrown entrance. Riding single file through the encroaching underbrush that threatened to choke the driveway, they wove their way through with Pamela at the lead, and emerged at last from what was almost a solid thicket to find the great mass of Hawley Grange spread out before them. Despite the chimney stacks and windows that had been added, it still looked to be what it once had been—a monastic tithe barn where the tithes from the tenants of the far-flung church lands, be it grain or whatever, was stored.

Pamela sprang down without help and stood viewing the house as Chesney assisted Constance to alight. It had an imposing bulk, this "house of sirens" as Tom had once roguishly called it, but for her it had little charm. Very plain, built of random limestone with ashlar dressings and ten bays long, to her it was still less house than barn. The walls at the gable ends rose some forty-two feet high, and the queen-post timbering supported an enormous stone roof. But Nathaniel Hawley had scrimped on the remodeling. He had not cut enough windows, so the rooms were dark. Although the seven-foot stone bases on which rested the tall oaken posts that supported the stone roof were impressive, he had added no carving or refinements such as gave charm to Axeleigh or Huntlands—nothing but the plainest of painted pine paneling and a most unimpressive staircase that wound its way awkwardly up between partition walls. Although large reception rooms had been left at the front, the rear had been cut into numerous small rooms to suit his wife's whims. The place was a veritable Mecca for the young folk who lived in the Valley for they loved to dance on winter evenings in the vast hall, cold and uncomfortable as it was, for its single stone fireplace did little to heat it. But life at the Hawleys was on the slipshod side, and nobody noticed if a couple disappeared from among the dancers and returned looking rumpled and happy.

For convenience's sake, the gabled porches on either side, which had originally been constructed to admit carts, were now used as the entrances, and Pamela had to admit that in summer when the vast doors were thrown open those rooms did have an airy lightness. But whenever the weather turned cold it became a place of gloom—unless lit up by candles for a party.

The vast "cart doors," as the Hawleys cheerfully called their converted barn entrance, were flung open even before they could reach the knocker and two of the Hawley daughters, dressed extraordinarily well for a morning at home, greeted them warmly.

They must have seen them coming down that overgrown drive, thought Pamela, casting a look upward at the small chamber above her which had once housed the grangerius, the bailiff in charge who checked and received the tithes as they were carted in by the church tenants. It was called a tallet loft and was but one of the curious features of the Hawleys' household.

"Pamela! Constance! Do come in. And you'll be—?" Pretty, flaxen-haired Dorothea Hawley was looking earnestly at the newcomer.

"Chesney Pell, at your service." Another deep bow.

"Oh, yes, Father's expecting you." Before he could even be introduced to her sister, flaxen-haired Dorothea, just turned fifteen, was marching Chesney Pell away, to disappear down a yawning hallway into the rabbit warren of rooms where, presumably, her father was waiting.

"Pamela—and Constance. How nice to see you!" Helena Hawley, half a head taller than either girl and supporting an enormous mound of straw-colored hair, was greeting them calmly.

"I came to collect your recipe for tansies before you forgot those special ingredients you were going to tell me about," explained Constance, hoping Helena would not look too surprised.

"Yes, *I* would like to hear about those special ingredients too," said Pamela with lifted brows. "No, I think I'll just keep my cloak about me for the moment, Helena—" as Helena moved to take it. "There's a biting wind out there and I'm quite frozen. I'm sure Constance is too." Her gaze was checking the Christmas decorations as she spoke—not half so pretty as those at Axeleigh but with an alarming amount of mistletoe strung about everywhere. Plainly the exuberant Hawley girls meant to have no lack of excuses for kissing their gentleman callers. And Tom Thornton would be one of those callers! Pamela simmered.

Helena Hawley, not one to be caught off guard easily, gave both her guests a vague smile and led them toward a roaring fire that did little to take the chill off the great yawning room. Behind her placid features, her wits worked as well as another's. That remark about the tansies told her that Constance had not—thank heaven!—taken Pamela into her confidence about the meeting here today. For talkative Pamela would certainly tell the Squire and no one knew yet where he stood.

"Why don't you go and ask Dorothea about them?" she suggested. "She's the one who puts in the special ingredients." She gave Constance a meaningful glance. "I'm sure you can find her."

"Yes, I'm sure I can—I'll be right back, Pamela."

Left alone with her imposing hostess, Pamela thought how perfectly right Helena looked in this background. Plain and oversized. Looking about her, she could not but compare Hawley Grange's rude interior to that of a church nave under construction. It was sparsely furnished, all the benches and cupboards—even the long refectory table—having been made by local craftsmen. For the senior Hawleys were both of a penurious frame of mind, as was reflected by the rushes that were spread over the floor in place of carpets such as Axeleigh boasted.

Nevertheless, the Hawleys were delighted with their home, which was the scene of much rude revelry, just as they were delighted with their brood of flirtatious, big-boned, deep-chested progeny.

"We're giving our usual Twelfth Night Masque," she told Helena politely. "I do hope all of you can come."

If the hope was insincere, at least Helena did not notice it. She smiled benignly on her dainty guest. "Oh, we wouldn't miss it," she said. "Some of my sisters are already at work on their costumes."

Melissa probably, thought Pamela. *It was Melissa who always sought to outdo people!*

"Where is Melissa?" she wondered.

Again Helena was vague. "I think she's out in the kitchen just now—"

"Making tansies?" Pamela's laughter pealed. "Constance will be furious if she's using secret ingredients. I never saw anyone so set on learning every least little item of a recipe!"

Helena's answering smile was rather strained. She well knew the energy of her exuberant guest and she must avoid at all costs a search of the house for the missing Constance. She hoped Constance would pass on quickly to the meeting whatever messages she had received and return—for while Axeleigh Hall with its many servants and not the slightest taint of Monmouth leanings in its owners was a convenient place for messages to be left, Pamela's presence today was a distinct embarrassment. "What do you think *I* should wear to the Masque?" she asked Pamela earnestly, hoping to divert her.

Pamela was indeed diverted. "I think you should go as Juno, the Roman goddess," she said promptly, picturing in her mind how impressive Helena would look. "Just gild a garland for your hair, tie a drapery cord around your waist and drape yourself in bed sheets!"

Helena looked a little daunted. "I thought perhaps I'd come gowned as the Old Queen and wear a wheel farthingale," she said unhappily.

"You'll never get through the door in it!" predicted Pamela, envisioning the huge reed cage that would hold out a skirt over those majestic hips. "Not unless you go in sideways and that's hardly a dazzling entrance. And if you try to sit down your skirts will fly up and show your chemise."

"Oh, dear," said Helena with a helpless look at her caller. "I suppose it's a good thing farthingales went out of style before we came along!"

"Indeed it is." Pamela cast a look about, and seeing that there were no prying eyes in any direction, backed up to the fire and eased her skirts up. The glow of the blaze felt winningly warm on her chilled bottom. "Whatever can be taking Constance so long?" she wondered. "She's had enough

242

time to memorize a whole list of secret ingredients for tansies!''

Constance was not having much success in her venture. Having found Dorothea returning to join them, she had been left by the girl (who did not approve any more than her sisters did of the Cause having a female courier) before a door with the admonition, "Knock before you enter. They warned me that any who didn't might get his head blown off."

Constance sniffed. "They were being melodramatic," she told Dorothea. "That fellow who came in with us, is he at the meeting?"

"Yes. He's down from Oxford with Cart Rawlings. I just said Father was waiting for him in his study because Pamela was there."

Study . . . *that* was a new affectation. It had been a farm office the last time she had been here. Constance guessed the Hawley girls would soon be demanding that this great barn of a place be redecorated and overrun with linen drapers and painters.

Dorothea left and Constance took a deep breath, knocked once, softly, and flung open the door. All heads turned to view her.

There were about a dozen young men in the room. They were drinking metheglin and every pair of eyes looked up alertly at her entrance. Constance readily identified them all. Tony Warburton was conspicuous by his absence, but it was well known that the gallant captain had announced contemptuously—and to the accompaniment of quickly indrawn breaths at his temerity—that he detested *all* of the Stuart kings and would be no party to bringing another one to the throne, whether it be James or this headstrong duke!

Nathaniel Hawley, the girls' father, was not there either although his son Brad was. But Constance had not expected to see the elder Hawley here, for this was a gathering of the young bloods, the ones for whom Constance served as a go-between, receiving messages at Axeleigh Hall and dutifully passing them along to Tom Thornton at Huntlands.

And there, looking golden and relaxed, was Tom Thornton himself, regarding her keenly for he knew she had not been invited to this meeting. And Brad Hawley, giving her an uneasy glance, for he shared his sisters' distrust of a female courier. There was Ned Warburton, whose gray eyes shone as she entered—she wondered if Tony and Ned ever had words over Ned's participation in these meetings about which he probably knew. There was Jim Stafford, solid and calm, who hailed from Bridgwater and headed the group—his big head swung round to survey her. There was Cart Rawlings, down from Oxford. And a number of other young bucks from Bridgwater and its surrounds.

And there was one new face, beside Cart Rawlings's, that looked startled indeed to see her—the face of the newcomer, Chesney Pell, who blew out his apple cheeks and gave his blank face more than ever the look of a fat cherub. Constance understood now why Chesney had been riding alone. Cart Rawlings had ridden on ahead to make sure his Oxford friend would have a welcome.

Constance, uncomfortable before so many hard stares, avoided Ned's adoring gaze and came right to the point. "I have not much time," she said crisply. "But I have a request to make."

"Speak," directed Jim Stafford's slow deep voice.

"I do not have any messages today—none have been passed to me, although I expect Galsworthy to come by momentarily, perhaps today, perhaps tomorrow."

"Then why are you not at Axeleigh waiting for him?" wondered Stafford.

Constance's color rose a bit. "I request that I be sent to some other part of the country—perhaps to London, where I am sure I can be of much use to the Cause."

"For what reason?" asked Stafford, who was never one to mince words.

"For—personal reasons."

Significant glances were exchanged. Stafford's face was wooden.

"I know the city well," insisted Constance. "And I could carry messages by coach—"

"Request denied," interrupted Stafford.

"Will you not even put it to a vote?" demanded Constance, a note of rebellion in her voice.

"Very well, I will put it to a vote. Are there any gentlemen here who approve this singular request?"

Not a hand was raised.

"You see?" said Stafford. "We are all of one mind. Go back to Axeleigh, Mistress Constance, and await Galsworthy's coming."

"Galsworthy could as easily stop at Huntlands," put in Tom. "If Mistress Constance would prefer that?"

"No, I do not prefer it," said Constance hastily. "I will be glad to receive Galsworthy and to convey his message to Huntlands."

"Nor do we prefer it," said Stafford heavily. "For your views are well known, Tom, and Huntlands may be watched. Better you receive such messages on the road or by other methods than to have a London agent arriving at your house."

"I'll contact you," Tom told Constance briefly and she stumbled out, hot with fury.

If she had been a man, she told herself, *they would not have dealt with her request so cursorily!* And yet there *was* a woman courier who carried messages for the Cause all about England—they called her The Masked Lady. Everyone had heard of her and speculated as to who she was. So why should *she* not do the same?

To her dismay, Ned Warburton followed her out and caught her by the arm. "Are you mad, Constance? They would never send a woman on such a venture! You would be risking your neck."

"It is, after all, *my* neck," Constance reminded him shakily. She had made this request in a desperate effort to get away from the Warburton brothers—Ned who besieged her, and Tony who did not. And it had failed. "Let me go, Ned."

"Not until you tell me what madness has come over you.

Are you so eager to leave the Valley that you would risk your life to do it?''

"I risk my life *here*," she said quietly. "We all do, you know that." She wrenched away and fled down the corridor.

"Did Mistress Constance tell you why she wanted to go to London?" asked Stafford, when Ned reentered.

"Missishness," said Ned in a hoarse voice. He stalked back to his seat and sat down. "Pure damned missishness!"

Meanwhile Constance, hurrying back to the great hall, found Pamela drinking tea with Helena and Dorothea.

"Ah, green tea?" she said in a quick attempt to divert their attention from what had taken her so long.

"No, bohea," said her hostess, offering her some of the fashionable drink.

"We are lucky to be living in England, where tea is drunk," laughed Pamela, reporting something she had heard from Tom. "For I'm told that in the Colonies they know not what to do with it and throw the liquid away and eat the tea leaves! And in Salem—which is said to be somewhere near Boston—they butter and salt the leaves to make them tastier!"

Helena gave her slow majestic smile but young Dorothea almost choked on her tea as she collapsed with laughter. "In Boston, Father tells me, they eat the coffee beans as well!"

Fresh from her recent rebuff, Constance sat silent and sipped her bohea. Dev had once told her that since tea was so expensive, the smugglers often added foreign matter such as floor sweepings to it, but she would not tell her hostess that. For a treacherous moment she thought of her old lost dreams, of how she and Dev had planned to be off aboard ship to America—and perhaps, she thought whimsically, to eat coffee beans in Boston!

"Thank you, Dorothea, for telling me what should go into a tansy," she remembered to say.

"Yes, I too would very much like to know." Pamela inclined her head forward. "You were both gone long enough to make one and here you come back separately!"

"Oh, I stopped to speak to Melissa," improvised Constance

easily and Dorothea gave her a wondering look. Constance's aplomb was a matter of frequent and violent discussion among the Hawley sisters, all of whom resented the fact that she could go into that closed-door meeting, while *they* could not.

They chatted some more and then Pamela rose. "I am sure I smelled snow in the air as we rode over," she said. " 'Tis time we were getting back."

They said their good-bys and left on horses that were miraculously already waiting. Constance guessed that someone in the tallet loft upstairs was not only watching but listening and then signalling to a boy outside.

Pamela was so incensed that she entirely missed the remarkable appearance of horses no one seemed to have called for.

"Can you imagine Melissa not even coming in to greet me?" she demanded hotly. "Even though I was there to invite them all to our Twelfth Night Ball!"

"Oh, did you invite them?" asked Constance indifferently. "I thought you'd threatened not to?"

"Of course I invited them. They're my neighbors!" Pamela looked scandalized. "Whose horse is that being led out by a groom?" she asked suddenly, craning her neck the better to see. "Why, it's Satan! Tom must have been there all the time. *That* was why Melissa didn't come out—she was too busy talking to Tom! And there's Ned's horse too and—why, there are more of them! That last horse—is that Captain Warburton's big stallion Cinder?"

The big horse belonged to Jim Stafford of Bridgwater but Constance didn't want talkative Pamela to know that.

"Come away," she urged. "If the Hawley girls are keeping their lovers under wraps, let them!"

The word *lovers,* she realized instantly, had been an unfortunate choice, for Pamela turned on her, crystal blue eyes blazing.

"Tom is *not* Melissa Hawley's lover!" she cried passionately. "And don't you *dare* say he is!" She gave Angel such a nudge with her knee as to send the startled mare off at a gallop. They were out of sight of Hawley Grange before Constance could catch up.

"Pamela," she cried in real consternation, "I'm sorry. I didn't mean—"

"Oh, yes, you did!" snapped Pamela. "Do not try to cozen me. You are always making little digs about Tom. 'Tis Ned you should be worrying about." Her voice rose indignantly. "Couldn't you see he's calling on Helena Hawley behind your back, and Tom is only taking him where he wants to go as a good host should!"

So that was how Pamela had rationalized her discovery that Tom and Ned were callers at Hawley Grange. Perhaps it was for the best. "Ned means nothing to me," she told Pamela tranquilly.

But Pamela wasn't listening. Her voice stormed on. "And all that talk about tansies and people running in and out and Melissa never coming out at all—I never saw such a house of secrets in my life!"

Constance had known one:

Tattersall.

BOOK IV
The Masked Lady

The broken dreams, the shattered hopes, the loves
  that did not last,
The ruins of a lifetime shine from her looking glass,
And she remembers how it was when life and love
  were new,
And sighs because, through all of it, her heart was
  ever true....

PART ONE
The Gallant Lie

Upon her breast, she wore a golden locket,
She wore it to remind her she had once been loved
* by him*
And come what may, she'll always wear that locket
To sear her heart with memories of all that once had
* been!*

The Road to Devon,
Autumn 1683

CHAPTER 16

Constance would never forget her introduction to Tattersall House in Devon.

To London she had gone by coach and it had not seemed at all the fairy-tale town of her childhood. The streets had not changed much, but the faces were different. Strange, unfriendly. And at her inn there she coughed from the smoke of the sea coal, for only the rich could afford to burn wood these days. Constance did not care—her whole world was smoky with her loss, for with Dev gone her life seemed cast into darkness. She thought of him bitterly—and she thought of him all the time. She was thinking of him, hating him, when at dawn she took a westbound coach.

And far to the north, just rising at a "safe" inn outside Peterborough, the man the road called "Gentleman Johnny" rose from his bed and stared yearningly out the window toward the south where he believed Constance lay in slumber. In the next room Gibb and his new light-of-love, Nan, lay sleeping. For Candless had been hanged for murder a month ago and Nan had passed on to other hands. Dev was glad for Gibb, knowing he had always fancied her. And Nan was a loyal-enough wench—she had tried to be loyal to *him*, but he had rejected her loyalty. For, fight it as he would, he knew now that his heart had never wavered from the velvet-eyed girl he had left at Claxton House—and now left again at a quiet little farmstead in Essex.

It hurt his heart to think that he had lied to her, but had he told her the truth she would either have left him or demanded that he take her with him—and that would have exposed her to all the dangers of the road. And Dev, a man of wit and imagination, was not insensible to those perils. It had made cold sweat break out on his forehead to think that he and Gibb might be shot down and Constance seized by the nearest ruffian for his plaything. Or that she might be seized and mocked and hanged beside him. These were for him recurrent nightmares.

Now he could devote himself single-mindedly to his "profession"—a profession at which the best shot in the North Country had a certain talent. He would come back to her with the spring, he promised himself. He would manage to put money away, no matter how difficult it was. He would garner enough to give them a real start in America. Together. And Constance would have all of her three wishes—a home, children, a husband who would be there when she waked.

This, he swore to himself as the sun rose over England, would be his last season on the road.

He could not know that Constance had seen him ride away with Nan and Gibb and put the wrong construction on it.

Of such small things are disasters made. . . .

For unknown to him, Constance had already left her safe resting place. She was off with tax collector's gold to launch herself on a journey that would take her as near to hell as she could ever imagine. . . .

Back in Essex, indeed she had frantically counted that gold as she tried to make coherent plans. She would go to America! No, she did not have enough money for that. She would go seek out Aunt Margaret in Devon—she had enough money to go *there*. Perhaps Aunt Margaret had not received her letter, or perhaps she had and her answering letter had gone astray. Yes, that was where she would go—Devon!

Through a bitter sleepless night in Essex she had made her plans, and left—over the protests of the kindly farm couple with whom Dev had left her—by dawn's first light.

From London her stagecoach wended its way through Surrey and Hampshire, into Dorset and finally into Devon. They spent a night in storied Winchester where, six hundred years before, the Conqueror's son had ridden for the Treasury— and claimed a kingdom. They tarried briefly in Southampton where tall ships took eager-looking settlers to America, and in Dorchester, with its great Roman amphitheater rising from the chalk. They crossed the Avon and the Stour and the Frome. They came within sight of the dark escarpment of the Blackdown Hills and crossed the River Exe at the great cathedral city of Exeter. Constance was impressed by the gardenlike beauty of the Devon countryside where late summer lingered into autumn, lush and pleasant and green.

" 'Twill change—the look o' things,'' one of her companions on the stagecoach, a rotund linen draper, warned when she exclaimed on the sleek fat cattle and smiling country girls they passed. "For you tell us you're headed for Dartmoor and that's a different kettle of fish altogether!''

And different it was. She could feel that difference as well as see it when—in a hired cart, for which she had bargained sharply now her money was running low—they climbed by stages to the great plateau, some fifteen hundred feet high, that formed the wild interior of southwest Devonshire. The wind seemed to catch them as they came into the bleak wild country, and it whipped her cloak about her and seemed about to tip the cart over. Here in Dartmoor were sudden morasses and dangerous swamps, from the reeds of which great flocks of wild birds flew up in alarm at their passing. Twice in the distance she saw thundering herds of wild ponies that disappeared over the horizon. Her driver, Will Hedge, had had good directions to Tattersall House at the last inn and he bore toward it steadily, winding between the high tors, those sloping heights that rose about them crested fearsomely with huge boulders, great granite masses, broken and strange, that loomed fiercely against the sky. Once, when fording one of the many streams that seemed to be everywhere about, Constance looked up and shivered. For looming a thousand feet above her atop the great granite tor to her left was a gigantic pile of stones that resembled nothing so much as a craggy Stone Age giant staring out sightlessly forever toward the far-off broken coastline with its rugged cliffs and sandy beaches. Although she did not know it, she was riding along the easternmost heights of a broken chain of granite heights that extended south to the Scilly Isles and there sank into the sea. From this fantastic moorland spilled all of Devon's major rivers—the Dart and the Teign and the Plym flowing southward into the English Channel, but the Taw and the Torridge winding north to empty into the storm-lashed North Atlantic.

A sudden red sunset glowed across the moors as they neared their destination, turning the morass nearby the color of blood. Night fell over them suddenly and the man riding beside her muttered beneath his breath for he had thought to find shelter sooner than this and not flounder by night over this difficult and dangerous terrain.

"We'll have to stop," he sighed, reining up. "At least until the moon is bright. The horses can't see where to put their feet and they could step into quicksand or a pothole casy as not. A body could be lost here and never found."

"But look," cried Constance. "Isn't that a light?"

"Where?"

"Over there. See? In the shadow of that great tor—don't you see it?"

"It do be a light," agreed her companion, squinting. "And most likely 'tis our destination for there's nothing else but Tattersall House on these moors for miles around, I'm told. But we'll wait a bit till the moon is brighter nonetheless.

Better to arrive late than not to arrive at all. Ye did say ye were expected, didn't ye?''

Constance nodded. She was afraid to tell Will Hedge that they had trekked all this bumpy way on a wild chance. If he discovered she was not expected he might refuse to go farther, and turn back. Or become angry and leave her here.

"Then," he grunted, "Mistress Perdant won't mind rising up from her bed to greet ye."

Perdant, thought Constance. *She must be Margaret's housekeeper. Yes, of course that would be it.*

The moors suddenly looked very dark.

Beside her Will Hedge was rambling on about the days when he had been pressed into the navy and flogged for not saying "sir." Constance hardly heard him. He was still grumbling about it when they started up again and made their way over a moor silvered by moonlight toward that distant flickering light.

Constance kept hoping it would not flicker out. Her raveled nerves were not up to keeping up this desultory conversation about matters nautical.

Her tension increased as the light grew closer and steadier, beckoning to them like a beacon across the infinity of moorland that stretched ever away.

She half expected a castle, strange and tall like the massed rocks atop the high tors, pointing like accusing fingers at the sky—but such was not the case.

Tattersall House was a weatherbeaten, half-timbered building, two stories in height with a thatched roof. It clung to the moorland as if it had taken root in the reddish soil and might sprout yet another story in the next growing season. The windows were small with heavy wooden shutters and the door on which they pounded with an iron knocker that echoed hollowly was strong and weathered. A low stone wall ran from the building like a windbreak down to a couple of outbuildings.

There was a barrenness to the place as if nobody lived there.

Constance, exhausted by her jolting journey, leaned against the door and prayed in her heart that Margaret Archer was still there and that she had not forgotten the letter she had written to Sir John. Or at least that this Perdant woman would know where to find her.

She gave a start at the creaking sound of a bolt being shot on the other side of the door. It creaked inward into darkness for there was no light at all in the hall. It had been suddenly extinguished.

Then she felt Will Hedge, who was almost touching her, give a start as well and realized that the dull gleam she could see in the reflected moonlight from outside came from the barrel of a large pistol pointed directly at them.

"What do you seek at Tattersall by night?" inquired a calm voice. A woman's voice. It had a purring lilt to it but there was a grim note that gave it force.

Constance saw that Will Hedge was taken aback by this reception. "Why—I'm here to deliver this young lady who's expected," he blustered.

"Are there others with you?"

"Only the two of us. Speak up, girl." Will gave Constance a rough nudge with his elbow.

Constance found her voice. "I'm Constance Dacey, Margaret Archer's niece. She wrote to Claxton House about me. I have her letter . . ." Her voice dwindled away as the cold blue barrel of the pistol remained unwaveringly fixed on them.

There was a moment of silence. Then the gun barrel swung down. "Clytie," called that calm voice. "Come down here and bring a light. We know the way but these strangers could break their necks in this dark hall blundering about."

So they were to be allowed in, at least! Constance felt almost dizzy from relief. She still could not see the face of the woman who had held the gun on them so steadily, only a tall dim shape as her eyes grew accustomed to the dimness.

Now a light was flickering down the stairway at the far end of the hall and Constance could see as the light approached that a scared-looking servant girl was holding a guttering candle in a round dishlike holder. Even that gave them no chance to view their hostess for she had already brushed past Clytie.

"Are—are you Mistress Perdant?" asked Constance in a strained voice.

"Yes, I am." And, still over her shoulder, "Bar the door, Clytie, and then bring some brandy. Our guests look as if they could use it."

Constance wondered if Mistress Perdant had eyes like a cat and could see in the dark, as Clytie led them toward benches that flanked an oaken table in the center of the room. The long wavering shadows cast by the single candle gave the whole scene an eerie look. Mistress Perdant was just disappearing up the wide Jacobean stairway at the back, down which Clytie had come. Her back was slender and lithe and above it was a great deal of hair piled up in helter-skelter fashion. She moved with a girl's light step. From the dark above, her voice floated down to them. "Clytie, take their things and bring our guests something to eat. I'll see if I can rouse Lys."

Constance found herself seated in a big, squarish, stone-floored room with exposed crossbeams on the low ceiling above her. To the left of the entrance yawned a huge fireplace with a long plain mantel on which reposed a row of polished pewter plates. There was a heavy paneled door which she guessed must lead to the parlour, another that must lead to the kitchen for Clytie had disappeared through it, and at the far end past the stairway was a door with heavy iron studding which must lead outside. Two small deep-silled windows looked out over the moon-silvered moors.

Apart from the table and the long wooden benches on which she and Will Hedge sat facing each other, a massive armchair at the head of the table, another at the foot, a large plain wooden sideboard that supported two branched candlesticks and a huge painted cupboard in one corner completed the furnishings of the sparsely furnished room.

Will had not much to say. He sat with his shoulders hunched, staring fixedly at the candle Clytie had left sitting on the table. They could hear her stirring around in the next room where the moonlight was apparently strong enough not to require a light.

Constance was silent too—and depressed, for her hopes of finding Margaret Archer were fast fading. She sat with her hands clutched together in her lap and watched as Will fell with gusto on the ham and coarse brown bread and tall tankards of cider that were brought. His eyes gleamed as Clytie brought in a bottle of brandy and set it down upon the sideboard.

Stiff with tension, Constance was able to swallow hardly a mouthful. She kept wondering when her hostess was coming back. Apparently never. They finished and Clytie, who had stood staring curiously at them as they ate, turned as a disembodied voice from the dark stair landing above said, "Pour out a goblet for me and another for the girl and give the bottle to the cart driver. He can take it with him to the loft over the barn. 'Tis the only extra room we have. Show the girl to the room above this one."

"D'ye want me to make it up for her?" asked Clytie.

"No. Lys and I have already done that."

Will rose. He did not look at all perturbed at being relegated to the barn to spend the night. In a household that seemed to be entirely female, he took it for granted that a male stranger would not be bedded down in the main house. With a nod to Constance, he went out and Clytie threw the bolt behind him, picked up both goblets and beckoned to Constance.

They went up the stoutly built Jacobean staircase into a second floor with low sloping ceilings. Constance had to duck as she followed short stout Clytie into what was to be her bedchamber.

Clytie, who had the goblets in one hand and the candle in the other, opened the door with her foot and set both goblets and candle down in the deep sill of the room's one small window. She departed without comment and Constance walked to the bed. She was desperately tired.

"Pick up the candle and let me see you," commanded a voice from the door and Constance realized with a start that her hostess had come in cat-footed and was standing in the doorway behind her.

Obedient to that command, Constance picked up the candle and turned, holding it so that the light played over her face.

It played over her hostess's face too as she advanced and Constance almost missed a step.

In the flickering light, she found herself looking into a pair of beautiful green eyes that regarded her steadily from beneath an alabaster forehead and a great mass of flame-colored hair. A generous flexible mouth and a strong jawline rose above a pale column of throat and a dazzling white bosom against which gleamed a golden locket suspended by a delicate gold chain. But across her cheekbones were deep scars—a single flaw upon an otherwise devastating beauty.

She could not have been past her early twenties—Constance guessed her to be twenty-two. And her umber-hued gown of heavy French pile velvet, its bodice worked with a filigree of silver threads, while worn, was so fashionable that it astonished Constance to see it here on these barren moors. She moved with complete self-confidence and her regal bearing would have become a queen.

"Do not look so startled," said Mistress Perdant dryly. " 'Tis only the remnants of the smallpox you see upon my features." Her voice was bitter. "I would rather the Black Death had claimed me instead and been done with it—'twould have been better than this. Had I been a Catholic born, I would have shut me in a convent to live out my years, but since I am not, I have found me a prison of my own making here on this desolate moor."

"I—I was not startled," faltered Constance, not knowing whether she should look at those scarred cheeks. The sight of those scars in the moonlight had been a shock in a face otherwise so beautiful.

"Nonsense, of course you were," said the tall woman

briskly. "Mine is a face that takes getting used to—but you will come to disregard it in time."

"In . . . time, Mistress Perdant?" Constance was bewildered, for why should this stranger take her in?

"Yes. 'Perdant' is the name I took to cloak my identity when I left Somerset." Her voice had a bitter edge to it. "*Perdant* is a French word. It seemed appropriate. I am Margaret Archer."

Constance felt her breath leave her. Margaret—at last! But Margaret Archer had taken another name for herself and Constance knew enough French to know what that name was. She called herself Margaret Perdant now—*Margaret the Lost*.

"You have a beautiful face," mused Margaret. "And you say you are my brother Brandon's child?"

"No—*you* said it. I have your letter." She held it out.

"Here, give me the candle." Margaret glanced at the letter. "Yes, I wrote this." She surveyed Constance up and down. "You do not look like my brother," she said at last. "Indeed you resemble your mother. I liked her."

Constance would have spoken but her throat closed up. It was the first kind word she had heard spoken about her mother since her father's death. Her tear-filled eyes spoke her gratitude.

"You look tired," observed Margaret. "We will talk tomorrow. Meantime you'd best get some sleep. We rise early here on the moors." She set the candle down and swept out, calling a good-night over her shoulder.

But for all her jauntiness as she closed the door behind her, when Margaret reached the dark hallway where she could not be observed, she reeled for a moment against the plastered wall and fought back a dry sob. She had been her usual calm, collected self while she was talking to this violet-eyed stranger who looked so crushed by life—but she had fled the room because her eyes were wet.

After a moment during which she steadied herself, she hurried to her own bedchamber and crossed to the window. And then, with both hands pressed to her mouth, she stared out across the moonlit moors and caught herself just in time. For she had almost given thanks to a God she no longer believed in for sending her this troubled child of destiny—for sending her someone to love. Almost—but not quite.

Tattersall House, Dartmoor,
Devonshire, England,
Autumn 1683

CHAPTER 17

In the days that followed, Constance was to find herself in a house without mirrors and to learn that Margaret Archer never walked outside on rainy days when she might glimpse a reflection of her scars in the puddles, and that the inside shutters were always closed before night turned the windows into dark mirrors to mock her. And that no one outside Tattersall House had ever seen her face, for when she went abroad—even to the nearest village—she wore a riding mask.

A woman less lustrous might have reconciled herself to those scars, but Margaret, who had got them at the height of her blazing beauty, could not.

" 'Tis a strange name—Tattersall," Constance ventured.

Those brilliant emerald eyes considered her mockingly. "An appropriate name, for all in tatters was the way I found it. Rags of curtains blowing behind broken panes, shutters banging on broken hinges, doors that were stuck either permanently shut or permanently open, latches that would not latch, filth everywhere. I have made some changes," she added dryly.

Constance gave an awed look around her, for although Tattersall had about it a spartan barrenness, it gave little evidence that it had ever fallen upon hard times. Spotlessly clean it was, from its well-scrubbed floors with their carpet of fresh sweet-smelling rushes—the kind used even in palaces in the Old Queen's time—to the shining pewter platters and tankards winking from the big plain cupboard.

As time went by, Constance came to see Margaret more clearly. There was a small chest of gold coins beneath her mattress—Constance had stumbled on it when she was making the bed. Wealth . . . but Margaret the Lost chose not to use it, nor to wear any of the fine clothes that were packed away in lavender in the great chests. In the days when she had been beautiful Margaret Archer who swept everything before her, Constance knew Margaret had worn those clothes. Although some of them, Clytie whispered, had never been worn at all: they were for her trousseau.

Once a year, Clytie told her, that trousseau was taken out and shaken and aired and packed away again in lavender— along with Margaret's lost dreams.

"Do you never go anywhere?" she once asked Margaret. She was studying as she spoke the well-worn riding boots, the handsome velvet and broadcloth riding habits and— surprisingly—the amber silk ball gown that hung in Margaret's press. These clothes seemed different somehow from the treasured trousseau in the big chests. They were handled casually and, obviously, worn.

The amber silk ball gown especially had made her wonder.

Margaret gave her a shadowed green look. "On occasion," she said vaguely. "In summer."

Clytie had told her that Margaret was often gone for long periods in summer. Constance could not help asking, "Do you go back to Somerset?" For she had a terrible vision that must be brushed away—a vision of Margaret, masked, prowling the countryside, finding masqued balls where she could slip in and dance a measure and then go her lonely way, remembering. . . .

Margaret shook her head. "Never. For I've no wish to be reminded of the old life. I've given up my heritage and chosen to live here at the end of the world. Such"—her voice hardened—"was the will of God."

"Does no one come here?"

"Seldom."

"Don't you even go to church?"

Margaret's face hardened. "I have forsaken God. No"— she gave a short laugh—"that is not quite true. *He* has forsaken *me*."

"But surely—"

The flame-haired woman held up an imperious silencing hand. "If you would live here," she said, "you must not try to change me. I walk a precipice and just beyond is the abyss. Life is not easy for me."

But in a way Tattersall's odd life-style was strangely comforting, for it kept Constance's mind off Dev and all that she had lost.

Only at night did memories really plague her. For the white moon that shone down on the wastes of Dartmoor was the same white moon that had followed her down the Great North Road, the same white moon that had cast soft rays through the branches of the Old Doodle Oak in Hatfield Forest.

Somewhere that moon was shining down on Dev—and Nan. Always Nan.

That was what hurt most. It was bad enough that Dev had lied to her, pretended to be leaving for America when in truth he was taking to the road again—*but to have done it with a woman! And that woman Nan!* Hot tears stung her lashes at the thought of him and she waked panting from dreams in which he held her in his arms and ran his hands along her naked body and stirred her to passion. She would lie there in her bed and let the hurt seep through her whole body and turn her face into her pillow to stifle the sobs.

They rose early at Tattersall and when the weather was fair

often roamed the moors on foot. Margaret could identify every wild flower, every weed, every herb. There were two milk cows which the servants—plump Clytie and tall reedy Lys—milked, and a sow with a brace of pigs. Staples arrived in a cart. And once a month a letter was brought by a rider across the moors and Margaret locked herself in her room to read it and stayed there for hours and hours.

They never went to church. As far as Margaret was concerned, God's domain did not include Dartmoor.

Constance felt a deep sympathy for Margaret and a very real bond grew up between them. She told Margaret how Hugh had threatened to take her by force and Henriette had helped her to escape in a wicker trunk.

"And you came directly here?"

Constance hesitated. She could not bring herself to speak about Dev—the wound was still too fresh. Someday perhaps, but not yet. "Yes," she said steadily. "I came directly here."

"And a blessing to me you have been," smiled Margaret. "For you accept me for what I am—not for how I look."

Constance had grown used to Margaret's scars by now; they did not trouble her. "Can you be so sure the world would not?" she challenged.

"Yes," sighed Margaret. "I am very sure. The world would not."

Constance's young heart went out to her.

As she spoke, Margaret's tall beautiful form stood in the center of the room washed by the light of Dartmoor—a fitful light for a storm was coming. She spoke quietly as if she were recounting something that had happened to somebody else. "They told me I was lucky the disease had not cost me my sight," she remembered. "Lucky it was not the 'black pox,' which would have carried me away in a day or two, but instead the 'discrete' type which left so many areas of my skin free from eruptions. And how fortunate that the outbreak in Bath had been one of the mildest known, and how providential that my doctor, before the marks could spread below my cheeks, found red stained glass and put it in all the

267

windows and hung red drapes about, which, he insisted, kept the rest of me from being permanently scarred. *Lucky!* What was I supposed to do? Greet my lover like poor Queen Elizabeth greeted *her* suitors, with half an inch of permanent makeup plastered on my face?'' Her veil of reserve had been ripped away and Constance stared at her, spellbound. "At last I knew what I must do. I must arrange to 'die' and yet not die. My fate would be ever to hover beyond the range of vision of those I loved—always outside the windows looking in. And so it has been since.''

Constance's violet eyes were wet. She was glad that Margaret had turned to the window, to study the wild sky and the distant moors across which lay Somerset and all that she had loved. . . .

The servants, Constance had learned, were both unfortunates that Margaret had taken in. Clytie had been a battered teenager, indentured to what she fiercely termed "a monster.'' Margaret had made her acquaintance when Clytie had been knocked into the street in front of Margaret's horse. Margaret had climbed down and picked up the weeping Clytie—and promptly bought her articles of indenture. Clytie would have a home at Tattersall House as long as she cared to stay.

Reed-thin Lys, with her perpetually frightened face, had an even more bizarre story. With a rope around her neck, she had been led into the local cattle market by her disgusted husband, who complained that she was too thin and always weeping, and auctioned off to the highest bidder. Lys was not the first to be so auctioned nor would she be the last—it was a custom that had often amazed European travelers. But this day Margaret was present and startled everyone by bidding Lys in. Lys had fallen to the ground in relief and embraced Margaret's knees, for she had been terrified of the coarse men who were bidding on her. Lys too had found a refuge in a spacious room in the big attic which she shared with Clytie.

"Marry again, if you choose," Margaret sometimes told

Lys. "What you had was no marriage, no matter what the law says!"

But Lys, like Clytie, clung to the only real home, the only real kindliness, she had ever known.

Remembering all that, Constance dabbed swiftly at her eyes lest Margaret turn and see her crying. As she did, something rubbed against her ankles and she looked down at "Tiger," the big purring tiger-striped cat who, Clytie had told her, had come to them out of a storm last winter "with his paws in bad shape and his tail near froze." He was fat and sleek now, but his checkered career was revealed by his nicked ears and his scars and his stubby tail that looked as if it might have been shortened by an enemy's teeth. She reached down and gently stroked his soft fur.

Margaret Archer, she thought, had found an outlet for her generous nature here on remote Dartmoor—she collected strays, the unwanted.

Of which, Constance supposed, she herself was one.

Constance did not learn about Tony Warburton until one day when they took a long walk together on the moors. The day was sunny, the autumn air was fresh and bracing with a tang to it that made the spirits soar. Around them the dwarf oaks and clumps of ash and willow, all that remained of a long-ago forest, assumed a wild beauty of their own.

Margaret had been telling her that these slopes, where tin and copper and even silver and gold had been mined in centuries past, would become a carpet of wild flowers come spring. She had just guided her around a low-lying green bog when Constance interrupted excitedly.

"Look, isn't that celery?" she cried, staring in surprise at a tall branched plant with many striated stems, growing at the edge of a marshy strip of water. She bent down and pulled off a stalk, would have bitten into it experimentally but that Margaret dashed it away.

"That's cowbane," explained Margaret. "Here." She bent over and pulled up one of the three-foot-tall plants, showing a cluster of fleshy roots. "Observe it well and remember it, for had you eaten it, you would surely die. Another name for it is poison hemlock."

"But you told me cattle graze here in summer!"

"And some die from eating it. But they are probably newcomers, imported from other sections of the country that are unfamiliar with it. Those who graze here avoid it or they do not last long." She was tearing up the clump with her hands and tossing it away to dry and die in the sun as she spoke. She bent and rinsed her hands in the marsh water and gave Constance a meditative glance. "I think the calves learn by watching the mother cow and having her nudge their heads away from things that are bad for them, even as a human mother would." She beckoned. "But up ahead is what I brought you to see."

They walked on, feeling the damp under their shoes, and then as they crested a low rise, Margaret waved her arm to indicate a circle of standing stones, looking strange and Druidical in this desolate place. "Men once lived here, worked here, loved here—and had bad kings, even as we do now. The ruins of their camps and hill forts are all about. I suppose we shall never know who they were."

She sank down gracefully on a large stone and Constance sat down across from her. And as the shadows lengthened across the lonely moor Margaret told her about Tony Warburton, ending with, "I knew I did not want Tony to see me like this. Ever. So with my brother Clifford's help I contrived my own 'death.' Clifford came to Bath and carried back a closed coffin that contained stones and blocks of wood. I followed, draped in mourning black, in a coach with my old nurse who pretended I was her sister who had 'helped nurse poor Margaret during her illness.'" She gave Constance a mocking look. "I attended my own funeral."

"You didn't?" breathed Constance.

"I did indeed. Clifford, as usual, was against it, but I wanted to see who took my death badly—and who did not." There was a look of suffering on her face as she spoke and Constance guessed that Tony Warburton had taken it badly and that Margaret had been hard put not to throw aside her disguise and run to him. "Then I took my faithful nurse with me and together we found this place—at the world's end."

Above them a narrow slice of moon, so white it appeared almost green against the lavender of dusk, rode the sky. The moors had changed their character now as the creatures of the night replaced the creatures of the day.

"Where is she now? Your old nurse?" wondered Constance.

"She died three years ago this Michaelmas. I miss her."

But you miss Tony Warburton more. . . .

"Did you never see Tony Warburton again?" she asked with a catch in her voice.

"Oh, yes." Margaret turned to Constance with a mocking look in her emerald eyes. "I attended his wedding. To Lucy Weatherby."

"What?" cried Constance. "Do you mean to tell me that he married *someone else*?" For somehow she had imagined an eternally grieving Tony Warburton, endlessly alone, refusing to be comforted.

Margaret gave her a grim smile. "Indeed he did! A short two months after my 'death.' Oh, it hurt me at first but—I forgave him after a while. I attended the service in widow's weeds, so draped in black veiling that none could tell who I was. And it took all my powers of restraint, I can tell you, not to stand up in the church and shout *'This man is mine. That woman cannot have him!'* And afterward I left and went on my search for a place that would be eons away."

"I am surprised you did not leave the country," gasped Constance. *I would have wanted to put a thousand leagues between myself and the man who could forget me so easily!*

Margaret gave her a crooked smile. "But you see I wanted news of Tony . . . Clifford writes me once a month and tells me how Tony fares and how things go in the Valley of the Axe. And occasionally parcels come, for he procures for me things I find difficult to buy here—nice lengths of cloth, for example. I will look among those he has sent and see if there is something from which to fashion a dress for you. Remind me when we get back to the house."

But Margaret needed no reminding. In her bedchamber she sorted through a chest full of unused lengths of material, but found none to suit her. "They are all bronzes and orange-golds and rusty colors that become a woman whose hair is flaming red," she complained. "But your coloring, Constance, is as different from mine as the mists that rise over these moors are different from the bright sparkle of the Axe as it knifes through the Valley. Tomorrow I will take you to Totnes and we will see if we cannot find some suitable fabric there."

Constance was amazed for she had somehow imagined that Margaret never ventured out except to buy staples for the larder. But the next day, with Constance riding the gentlest of the two horses Margaret kept in her small stone stable, they set out.

"You ride very poorly," Margaret observed, watching Constance mount awkwardly and jog along.

If you think this is bad, thought Constance, *you should have seen me tearing through the night, more off my horse than on, clinging to the saddle and praying I would not be thrown! With armed men somewhere in pursuit!* Aloud she said, "I was not allowed to ride at Claxton House—they thought it above my station."

Margaret's frown behind her mask was almost a palpable thing. "I will purchase you a gentler beast in Totnes—mine are too spirited."

Over heathery upland, in the shadow of the high tors, they rode toward Totnes, that ancient cloth town at the head of the Dart estuary that lay at the foot of lonely Dartmoor. Stone Age peoples had used these vast and remote granitic uplands as a summer pasturage, and later farmed here. Near Totnes they passed by the remains of an old "blowing house" where tin had been smelted in the twelfth century. Once Margaret detoured so that Constance might view the ruins of a deserted medieval village, abandoned at the time of the Black Death. In the bracing wind they stared out across the mouldering granite stones and Constance felt as if those stones were speaking to her, telling their tale of tragedy as the Black Death walked across England. She cast a sudden stricken look at Margaret in her black velvet riding mask, sitting her horse and staring so stoically at the ruins, and thought, *The Red Death walked here too and brushed by Margaret, mocking her by letting her live.*

Constance was enchanted by Totnes with its steep, narrow, winding streets and overhanging Elizabethan houses. The remains of its wandering walls reminded her of a romantic past, for in medieval days Totnes had been a walled town covering some ten acres and much of that wall still remained, while looming above all was the keep and bailey of a ruined Norman castle. And never once while there did Margaret remove her riding mask—except to sleep.

In the market place they bought fresh fruits and vegetables and packed them home on the back of the fractious horse Constance had ridden in. The beast, she thought whimsically, looked affronted at being used as a pack animal. But it was a relief to Constance to ride back on the horse Margaret purchased for her in Totnes—a gentle gray mare with soft eyes and a winning nature.

And they brought back with them several lengths of French gray linen and some mauve linsey-woolsey and lavender homespun wool.

But even that was not enough for energetic Margaret. She wrote to her brother and the next letter that came was accompanied by a man with two laden packhorses behind him. And what they revealed set Constance's violet eyes aflame with amethyst sparks:

"Fashion dolls!" she breathed, when the first parcel was unpacked and she saw the stiff little figures with their billowing skirts and careful coiffures, all clothed in the latest fashions from Paris. For Spain no longer led the fashion world and it was French fashions that were now universally copied.

"Clifford has done well," murmured Margaret as the next package spilled out a long length of lavender sarsenet silk and one of rippling violet velvet. She held the material up critically and turned to survey Constance. "He has followed my instructions—indeed this velvet matches your eyes."

Other packages revealed plum plush, rich purple wool so soft and pliable it seemed like silk itself, gleaming silver tissue, heavy Flanders point lace and spider-delicate French lace, sheer organzine silk of a misty pink-toned gray, an enormous amount of lawn and finest cambric for chemises, stiff mauve plush and amethyst satin for petticoats and silver lace, quantities of the popular narrow braid known as galloon and silk embroidery thread to decorate them and—Constance gasped at this—several pairs of silk stockings with fancy clocks, and red-heeled shoes and tall pattens and some satin slippers just made for dancing and riding boots all in her size, plus a wide-brimmed hat afloat with lavender plumes held in place by brilliants, a pair of handsomely embroidered leather riding gloves and several pairs of beaded silk ones.

"I can't believe it!" gasped Constance as a silken shawl and a sweeping purple velvet cloak with a lavishly fur-trimmed hood spilled out of the baggage that had been hauled to them across the moors.

"Had my brother Brandon lived," said Margaret crisply, sorting out a selection of ribands and pins and thread and needles, "you would have had even more. So don't protest or try to prevent Clifford and me from doing these little things for you."

Overwhelmed, Constance fell silent. And for the first time since her childhood felt cherished.

"We'll make changes in the designs," was Margaret's decision as she studied the fashion dolls. "Most of these are too fussy. We must make the most of your long clean lines, your elusive slenderness. And we'll do it with the sweep of a skirt, with careful draping, with a minimum of ornamentation."

Constance looked at Margaret in awe. Not even her mother, dainty and fashionable though she had been to the last, had considered making sweeping changes in the fashion dolls. They were from *Paris,* they were to be followed slavishly.

But independent Margaret had other ideas. Not for nothing had she been called the most elegantly dressed young lady in Somerset! She would make a bird of paradise out of a charming meadowlark!

With characteristic energy, she set about it—and lost herself in creating new designs that were even smarter than the dainty fashion dolls. She worked endless hours, stitching, fitting, pressing seams herself with heavy irons, tossing back an unruly lock of her flaming red hair that stuck damply to her forehead as she perspired by the hearth that kept the irons hot.

She would allow no one else to touch these garments and Constance was a pliable model, willing to stand till she was stiff while Margaret pinned and pinned.

In a way, that interest in clothes was what kept them going that winter. For as winter closed in and fierce Atlantic storms swept in from the sea across the forbidding moors, as sleet and stinging rain pounded alike the stunted trees and lost bogs and weathered rocks, as freezing gale winds screamed across the granite tors and threatened to knock down the chimneys of Tattersall House and tear off the roof thatch, Constance came to know a loneliness of the spirit such as she had not known before. A cut-off feeling as if the rest of the world had disappeared, been swallowed up somewhere, and she and Margaret and the two servants were alone and drifting in an endless desolate landscape.

These wintry days when it was too cold to go out except for necessity, when fingers were frostbitten and milk froze in the pail and they worried about the warmth of the farm animals and piled their straw bedding high to keep them warm, she and Margaret huddled about the fire wearing blankets for shawls. They listened to the wind, howling like a lost soul across the moors. And they ate potatoes baked in the hot ashes, hot apple fritters, and batter pudding with thick, yellow-crusted, Devonshire cream so stiff it could hold a spoon upright—cream that came from the red Devon cows who lowed in the small stone barn. After supper they sometimes played whist. Margaret was an expert player. Constance thought wistfully that Margaret was an expert in all things worldly—she rode well, she played cards well, and with her strength and grace she would certainly dance well. What a daunting beauty she must have been with that sudden flashing smile that showed a row of perfect white teeth, and her brilliant emerald eyes! And then she would go back to shivering and hoping the fire would not go out.

Christmas was the worst. They roasted a goose and from somewhere Margaret produced some sprigs of holly. Lys managed a plum pudding and they all drank hot buttered rum and sang Yuletide songs around the hearth—but every face was wistful, remembering loved ones, better days, forgotten dreams.

Not till after she had gone to bed did Constance face the kind of Christmas she had confidently envisioned last summer—a Christmas of dancing and kisses beneath the mistletoe and then of cuddling down into a deep feather bed in the firelight and making love. A Christmas with Dev.

Alone in her bed beneath the cold moon of Dartmoor, Constance wept.

It would have stunned her to know that in York, Dev—broke and cold and in hiding—was spending a Christmas as bitter as she.

Somehow the Twelve Days of Christmas were got through and it was January—a freezing January with the wind whining through the eaves and howling down the chimneys. And it was followed by a February that dumped wet heavy snow upon them and made the world a white wasteland, stretching ever away beneath a leaden sky.

In January Margaret's politics had been made clear to Constance when they learned that Sidney and Russell and Essex, arrested for complicity in the Rye House Plot, had been executed in early December on Tower Hill.

"Judge Jeffreys accepted faulty evidence! He has legally

murdered them!" Margaret hurled a pewter charger across the room so hard it dented the cupboard.

"I am surprised you remain hidden away on these moors—feeling as strongly as you do," ventured Constance.

Margaret whirled about. It was on the tip of her tongue to say angrily that she did *not* remain hidden away, that every summer she rode out carrying messages for the Cause of the Duke of Monmouth, that all of England knew her as The Masked Lady. But she stopped just in time. No need to involve Constance in her own dangerous games. Constance had much to live for—*she* had not.

"I but speak my mind!" she said and went back to her sewing. And as she sewed, she told Constance about life at Axeleigh. And about Constance's real father—Brandon Archer. Deeply in love with Anne Cheltenham, he had been riding to London to marry the pregnant Anne when a blizzard had swept down from the north, he had missed his way and frozen to death.

Constance swallowed. She had a sudden vision of that dark windswept figure resolutely bearing toward London where his Anne awaited and realizing in his last bitter moments that he wasn't going to make it—that he was never going to see his Anne again.

"How terrible," she said softly, "that he didn't get to say good-by to her."

"He did—in a way. For he had scratched in the snow the letters A-n-n-e. It must have been the last thing he saw in life—her name."

Constance closed her eyes and felt hot tears burn her eyelids. But the sob that caught in her throat was for Dev too. Someday they would catch Dev and hang him—and would she even know it? Or would he shimmer forever just beyond her vision the way the trees and the coarse grass of Dartmoor shimmered beyond the mists that rose on winter nights?

Margaret was wistful too. For speaking of Brandon's tragedy had brought the Valley of the Axe back to her and she was seeing through the walls and across the moors and over the Blackdown Hills, across time and space—to a lover.

And a night of love when, brimming with the overconfidence of youth, she had lured Tony Warburton away from the dancing and into the vast shadowy attics of the Hamiltons' massive black-and-white Tudor mansion. The music had drifted up to them, dim and far away like something half remembered. She had stood in a pool of moonlight shining in through one of the great dormers of the big half-timbered structure—stood there the better to see the complicated system of hooks she was unfastening. Because they must hurry. A late supper would soon be served and if they were not among the throng below they would be missed, tongues would wag and perhaps Clifford Archer would hear of it—and demand his reckless sister settle down and agree to a crying of the banns.

"We could be making love at our leisure in our own bed tonight," Tony had sighed, regarding her with rueful though kindling eyes.

"Ah, but isn't this more fun?" She had flashed a gamin smile at him and his hard face had relaxed.

"Margaret, Margaret," he had murmured. "When will you grow up?"

"Never!" she had promised lightly, holding out her white arms to him and letting her gown of amber velvet, darkly spangled with gold and brilliants, glide down her lithe body to the floor. And then, tauntingly, with a wicked little upward smile at him, her chemise.

As always, Tony Warburton had been rocked by the sight of her proud, naked loveliness. "You cast two shadows," he had muttered, for the moonlight coming in through the leaf pattern of the trees struck against the window glass and rendered a lighter and a darker shadow for each of them. "Yet you seem to shine with your own light. . . ."

Margaret, so sure of herself, had laughed contentedly and thrilled as he took her—almost reverently—into his strong arms.

"So I am two women—a light and a dark." She lifted her

head, swanlike, for his kiss. "It is a portent, Tony." Teasingly. "The moon shadows say you will have two women in your life!"

Tony Warburton never answered. His lips had found hers and the wildfire passion that always surged tinderlike between them worked again its old magic. His only answer was a soft sound deep in his throat, and Margaret's own sigh matched his as she melded her body against him.

It was the last time they had ever made love. The next week had found them quarreling, with Tony impatient to wed. And then had come that terrible afternoon at Huntlands when Ralph Pembroke had fought Tony for her and lost. No—*she* had lost. She had lost Tony, and then her beauty.

She had lost everything.

The moon shadows had been right. They had predicted two women in his life.

She wrenched herself back to the present. "Here, try this on." She held out a garment to Constance, watched as she struggled into it.

"This is beautiful," sighed Constance, looking down at the partially constructed velvet bodice, of a rich lustrous purple just now being overlaid with silver braid. She kicked out the flowing trained skirt that matched the bodice and swept out behind her elegantly.

"Yes, it does move well," said Margaret with just a hint of shakiness in her voice. "And with a silver-mauve petticoat— of thin satin, I think, it should do very well on a dance floor."

That was the first word that Constance had had that Margaret envisioned a future for her that included dancing. She was almost afraid to ask where she would be dancing.

In the spring she found out.

"There is nothing for you here on these lonely moors," Margaret told her in an almost offhand manner. "You are going north. To Somerset, to your Uncle Clifford at Axeleigh Hall. I have already written to him and he has arranged everything. And you will need these clothes, for life is very festive there."

279

Constance felt her breath leave her. In these lovely ball gowns she would dance at Axeleigh Hall, home of the father she could never claim! Margaret had arranged it all. She was going north, north to her heritage!

Resolutely she put from her the thought of Dev. He had left her, run away with Nan. She would take this sudden bounty that life offered, seize it with both hands, cling to it! She would forget him!

Her world would have rocked beneath her had she known the bitter truth—that Dev, ambushed on the Great North Road in early spring, had taken a slash from a saber and had lain, more dead than alive, in a hut outside Lincoln while Nan nursed him.

"Go south and bring Constance to me," he had asked Gibb weakly. "For we've such a haul of gold as will take us to America—and to her heart's desire."

And Gibb, fearing this was a last request, had ridden south. And returned with the news that Constance was gone.

Dev's face turned gray when he heard it, and he rolled over on his side and would not speak. Nan and Gibb tiptoed out and left him alone with his sorrow and his grief.

But when he mended at last—and he seemed now uncaring whether he mended or not and took a long time healing—it was a new and harder "Gentleman Johnny" who harried the highways. He was not so "dainty in those he robbed" now. Although he passed by the feeble and the elderly and never robbed a child, Gibb had seen him seize a necklace from around the neck of a beautiful woman so hard that the pearls cascaded like frozen tears as he ripped it off. A slender dark-haired woman. It was the memory of Constance that drove him.

He had become bolder too, now that Constance was not there to plead with him to "have a care for his life." Now he brazenly harried the shipping. Careless how his gold slipped through his fingers, hardly a cottager along the road but had known his largess. It bought him places to hide, allowed him to slip out like a shadow to pounce upon an unfortunate dray or wagon and demand "toll" to pass safe through his territory. And safe he kept them. Safe from other marauding highwaymen. He shot two ruffians who interfered with him and had a celebrated swordfight with another. When ambush was attempted, he and Gibb came out the victors, triumphing over their kind and leaving them dead behind them, their bodies fallen to the great slabs of Roman stones that made up the Great North Road.

"Gentleman Johnny" had forgotten he was ever Deverell Westmorland, grandson of an earl. He had become a dangerous man, "king" of the Great North Road.

Mistresses he had many and they meant little to him, passing through his hands like the gold and as soon forgotten. Not one of them ever reached his ice-bound heart.

Constance had done that to him—Constance who had loved him. And if she had been aware of it, it would have broken her heart.

Now with spring blanketing the moors with wild flowers and softening with blowing grasses the shapes of the far high tors, Margaret began constructing a dress for herself. A dress of shimmering bronze silk and copper lace—a dress of dreams.

"Oh, Margaret," whispered Constance, staring down at the lovely dress. *"You're going with me!"*

And Margaret lifted her head from her careful stitching and gave Constance a radiant look. "There is a masked ball held every year at Huntlands. Even though his father is dead, I understand Tom Thornton still keeps to the old custom. We will attend this ball—you and I. And there I will deliver you into the hands of my brother—and return at once to Dartmoor." She held up a silencing hand as Constance started to protest. "The world believes me dead and I wish them to go on believing it."

You wish Tony Warburton to believe it, and to you he is all that matters, thought Constance, and the knowledge hurt her—like the deep probing of an old wound.

But her heart would have beat faster if she had known the wild dream that was forming in Margaret's flame-red head.

She was going back to the Valley of the Axe. Back to the Midsummer Masque at Huntlands, back where she had once been a beauty and a belle.

She was going to dance with Tony Warburton.

One last time.

PART TWO
Midsummer Madness

Now she feels she has in vain crossed a bleak and
*   endless plain,*
Where God was not, where good and evil blend,
And she knows she stands at last at a crossroads
*   with her past,*
A place where truth must out and lies must end!

Torquay, South Devon,
Early Summer 1684

CHAPTER 18

The worst thing that happened to delay their going was the matter of the boots. The heel came off one of Margaret's riding boots and she frowned down at it. "I am sure it can be pounded back on," she muttered. "But who's to say it will not come off again? And these boots have grown shabby and scuffed with all this walking across the rough ground of the moors. I really need a new pair. . . ." Her face brightened. "You were saying only yesterday that if we are to attend a ball you wished you could practice your dance steps. We will *both* practice our dance steps! We'll run down to Torquay, where I've no doubt I can purchase a very good pair of boots. And we'll stay at the inn and dine in the common room and snare us some fellow to dance with!"

Constance looked up in excitement. Not only to Somerset, but to Torquay as well—she could hardly credit it!

Morning found them on their way to Torquay, for once Margaret had set her mind to do a thing she moved on it immediately.

They came riding down out of the bracing winds of the moors into the balmy breezes of Torquay and Constance saw for the first time the rugged red cliffs and sandy beaches that overlooked Tor Bay and the English Channel. Little more than a village built on steplike terraces that rose from the beach, with flowers spilling over the low stone walls. Small though it was, there was nevertheless a good bootmaker here and Margaret quickly took herself to his shop, leaving Constance to prowl about the ruins of ancient Tor Abbey with its lovely pointed arch portal. South of the gateway she found the thirteenth-century building they called the "Spanish Barn" because four hundred Spanish prisoners—survivors of Spain's ill-fated Armada—had once been crammed into it.

Bursting with lore, and with an armload of yellow flowers she had purchased from a vendor, Constance climbed the steep terraced hillside to the inn where they would stay the night. Margaret was waiting for her, pacing about outside in her riding clothes and riding mask, tapping with her whip on her new boots.

"I'm trying out my new boots," she called blithely to Constance, as she pushed back her red hair, which was blowing in the salt breeze. "Now's the time to find out if they rub!"

Constance had expected this expedition to be like the one to Totnes—having Margaret, despite her brave talk, retreat to her room and have her meals sent up. But it was not. Still clad in their riding clothes and riding boots—and with Margaret's black velvet riding mask firmly in place—they took a position at the long board in the inn's common room to await their dinner.

They were awaiting something else too, Constance guessed, and she was proved right when into the common room walked a well-dressed though dusty traveler—who stopped at sight of them and stared.

"It would seem we're making an impression," murmured Margaret, whose slow smile below her mask showed her even white teeth. "Yes, I think the gentleman dances. Observe the swinging way he walks, Constance, the fine cut of his clothes. Let me do the talking," she added hastily as the stranger approached and found a seat across from them at the common board, for there was only one long table on either side of it were wooden benches for the guests.

"A mild climate this," he greeted them with a smile. "But perhaps you ladies are no stranger to it?"

"No, this is our first time here," admitted Margaret, giving him a languorous look. "We are from Wiltshire."

Encouraged, the gentleman introduced himself to Mistress Perdant and Mistress Dacey as Owen Carey of Wales, traveling "for his health." Constance, who knew something of Dissenter politics, judged him to be one of the itinerant couriers who were marching all across England to drum up interest in Monmouth's cause. She yearned to ask him about it, but was discouraged the moment she mentioned politics by a kick beneath the table from Margaret. After that she kept her eyes cast down upon her trencher.

If that annoyed the dark young Welshman, he did not show it. Faced with two beautiful women, he ignored the shy one and conversed with the worldly Mistress Perdant.

Carey had, it seemed, been recently across the ocean. *Holland,* thought Constance, *where the Duke fled after discovery of the Rye House Plot.* But she kept silent. And under Margaret's adroit questioning as they consumed their pilchard and wine, the Welshman admitted—indeed bragged—that he knew all the new dance steps.

"But you must show us!" cried Margaret. "As you can see, we are all alone here." And indeed they were for the moment the only guests in the common room. "The floor is spacious and if music could be brought, we could dance a measure!"

Not one to overlook an opportunity to dance with so lustrous a lady, Owen Carey beckoned the landlord who promptly brought out a battered *viola da gamba* and launched into a fair rendition of "Greensleeves." Soon he was playing what Owen wanted him to and Owen himself had thrown a leg over the bench and was nimbly demonstrating his steps upon the floor.

"Now is our chance, Constance," murmured Margaret. "Observe well, for you may yet be dancing these steps in Somerset!"

But demonstration was not enough. Owen Carey, with a flourish, insisted Margaret join him on the floor. Although she laughed that she would cut a poor figure in her riding boots, she held up her skirts with one hand to keep her spurs from catching in her petticoat and moved about, as light-footedly as did he.

Constance watched raptly, memorizing the steps for later practice.

And then it happened.

Owen Carey, who had been heavily fortifying himself with the landlord's smuggled wine, cried, "I must see the face of this lady who has stolen my heart!" And with the words, snatched away Margaret's mask.

The result was immediate and electric.

Margaret's arm flashed back and she delivered a stinging slap to the Welshman's face at this impertinence. Margaret was a strong woman and her blows were not to be taken lightly. Caught off balance, Owen Carey was knocked backward. But her striking hand did not register on Carey with half the force of her scars. He slipped and fell to one knee, skittering across the floor. Still staring, he scrambled up and ran outside just as the music of the *viola* came to a sudden discordant halt.

Constance could cheerfully have killed the Welshman. She was terrified lest he had not only ruined their venture into Somerset but sent poor Margaret into perpetual solitude.

She watched in an agony of doubt as Margaret bent down and retrieved her mask from the floor. Margaret's green eyes were calm as she rose, her expression as impassive as if nothing untoward had happened. Only her hands betrayed her. They shook a little as she smoothed back her flame-red hair and fastened the mask on once again.

"Never mind," she reassured a white-faced Constance. "This has happened to me before. Give the landlord a coin, will you, Constance? For he has contributed mightily to our merriment this night."

With regal aplomb she strolled toward the stairs, her handsome skirts swishing about her new riding boots.

Constance felt her throat close up. She was vastly proud of Margaret as she gave the uneasily smiling landlord a coin and followed her up the rude wooden stairway that led up to their bedchamber.

They left early in the morning, leaving behind them the flower-choked stone walls and the wheeling seabirds, the puffins and the kittiwakes and gulls, and heading back toward the high tors with their blowing grasses, their soaring buzzards and falcons. They did not see the Welshman again.

At first Margaret thought to wear a black wig for their journey north, but just before leaving the moors she discarded that idea. "I do not like wigs," she confessed. "I feel a deal more comfortable wearing my own hair."

"But suppose Tony Warburton recognizes you?" faltered Constance. "What then?"

Margaret shrugged her elegant shoulders fatalistically: what would be would be.

Only later did Constance, heartsick, come to realize that Margaret *wanted* Tony to recognize her, to single her out from the crowd—whatever the cost.

Margaret instructed her as they rode north.

"From talking to you, I've learnt of your strong Dissenter views," she told Constance. "Be not so frank with them when you reach Axeleigh. My brother Clifford is an easy-going man. His wife was a lightskirt and flighty but Clifford staunchly believes that everything will work out if one only gives it time."

Constance gave her an uneasy look. "And what of Claxton House? What shall I say about my life there?"

"With all but Clifford avoid the subject," counseled Margaret. "Yorkshire is far away and Clifford will claim you as a distant cousin."

"But legally I am still Hugh's ward. If he were to find out where I am, so vengeful is he that he might come to Somerset to claim me!"

"If he were to be so foolish," Margaret's voice was dry, "Clifford would deal with him. And if Clifford were ill or away, a word to Tony would be sufficient!"

Pride rang in her voice and a picture sprang up before Constance of Tony Warburton—the picture the locket showed. For once when they were caught on the moors in a drenching rain they had come running in to tear off their cloaks and shake them and stand before the welcome fire to warm themselves. And Margaret, pulling off her wet cloak, had torn free the locket, which had somehow become entangled in the collar of her cloak.

Constance saw it fall—and snap open as it landed. She bent to pick it up and the firelight revealed a face to stop the heart. So *this* was Tony Warburton! A pair of cold gray eyes looked back at her from a strong sardonic face with clean-cut features, a face that looked as if laughter would light it with a wicked grin. His dark hair was silky and thick, cascading to his shoulders, his brows straight and dark, his jawline strong and clean-shaven. Margaret had not exaggerated when she had said he appealed to women! Constance hated him for being so handsome—and so faithless.

She had snapped the locket shut and in silence handed it to Margaret. The next day she noted that Margaret was again wearing it around her neck but on a different and slightly stronger golden chain.

Yes, thought Constance, remembering that strong face as they headed their horses toward Somerset . . . Tony Warburton was the kind of man who would indeed spring to a woman's rescue. Yet still she hated him—for so quickly forgetting Margaret.

They had crossed the Exe and were riding through the Blackdown Hills as they spoke. Soon they would be in the vicinity of Taunton. And now Constance stubbornly brought up again a subject that was worrying her.

"But suppose Tony Warburton does recognize you?"

"Then he'll believe he's dreaming—so long as he does not unmask me. But if by chance he tears off my mask . . ." Margaret gave Constance a steady look and pulled out a little vial from her saddlebag. "Then I'll use this."

Her voice had a harsh finality that made Constance ask fearfully, "What is in it?"

"Hemlock," said Margaret, her mouth a straight line and her jaw very square. "I could not survive the next day and the day after, knowing Tony had seen me like this, knowing his revulsion—no matter how cloaked—would be like the Welshman's."

The words, *Oh, you wouldn't!* rushed to Constance's lips but were never spoken.

She knew with inner certainty that Margaret would.

So it was imperative that Tony Warburton not recognize Margaret. That single consideration outweighed everything else, for Constance had only just realized how she felt about Margaret. This strong, dominant, tragic woman had somehow taken the place of the frail, valiant mother who had died along with her childhood, taken the place of the older sister she had never had. She felt for Margaret a real blood tie—she would have died for her.

And instinctively she knew that Margaret felt the same way about her.

Wearing light cloaks and riding masks, they rode into the Valley of the Axe beneath a white moon—for on this leg of the journey Margaret had insisted on riding by night, and avoiding towns, highwaymen or no. She had kept her large pistol ready at hand lest a dark shape spring from the bushes crying "Stand and deliver!" But none had challenged their passage, the road had been a ribbon of moonlight before them. And riding the gentle gray beside Margaret's fractious roan, Constance had thrilled to the sight of the silvery river where her father must have fished as a boy.

In their avoidance of towns, Margaret's expert knowledge of these barely discernible country trails had led them out of the way, and suddenly in the moonlight over the treetops the square tower and chimney stacks of a great house appeared. Margaret halted her roan and pointed. "Warwood," she told Constance quietly.

And Constance, looking at that moon-washed square tower and soaring chimney stacks, knew that they had ridden out of the way for a purpose: for Warwood was the lair of the elusive Captain Warburton, and Margaret must be thinking, *This could have been mine. I could have been mistress here.*

They were silent after that, riding along slowly. And Margaret was watchful for this was a part of the Valley where she was well known—and must not be challenged.

True to his word, the Squire had made arrangements for them. A tiny hut, some distance from the road by a winding path that led through the trees, awaited them. Constance, thinking that Margaret must have eyes like a cat to lead the way so unerringly, was startled when they came to a little clearing and the moonlight showed them a cottage roofed in thatch.

Margaret approached it warily, kicking open the door with her riding boot, pistol at the ready. But the moonlight showed it empty and when they went inside and lit the candles that were stacked neatly to hand, they saw that the place had been scrubbed spotless and that fresh linens had been spread on the two cots and food and drink had been set out upon the rude table.

"But your brother's servants must have done this—how could he explain it?" exclaimed Constance.

Margaret shrugged and threw off her cloak. "His servants will have scrubbed the place down and piled wood in that fireplace so we can heat water for our baths, but I'll warrant that Clifford himself brought the food and wine and linens and made these beds, for he's a careful man.''

Exhausted from her long ride, Constance flung herself stiffly upon the nearest cot. ''I'm too tired to eat,'' she told Margaret.

And Margaret was too excited to eat. She walked out of the hut and stood looking about her. Just over that rise lay Axeleigh Hall, where she had been born and spent her early childhood. It seemed eons away, unreachable, part of some other life. She could not believe that she had really done this, come all this way back into her past, driven by the fiercely burning star that for her was Tony Warburton.

Like the North Star, she supposed, she revolved around his fixed radiance, which had reached her even on the faraway sightless moors to pull her back into orbit. Now she stood beside the old stone well in the tiny clearing and wondered what tomorrow would bring. She told herself she was a fool to have made this journey, to flirt with discovery like this. That it was six years since gallant Captain Warburton had ridden out of her life. He had forgotten her by now, she told herself firmly. He would not even notice her in the crowd. Perhaps he would even dance with her and never know—of course it *must* be that way, she reminded herself, for to have him discover her, looking as she now did, would be more than she could bear.

Still she stood for a long time shivering in the moonlight of the warm summer night and every tremor that went through her reminded her of Tony's kisses, of the richness of his laughter, of the glow that lit up his eyes when he looked at her. She was lost on a sea of memories and it was with a sigh that she told herself she must get some sleep and went back inside the hut where Constance, fully dressed, lay across the cot where she had flung herself in exhaustion.

Margaret smiled at her tenderly. She had plans for Constance, great plans. . . .

But Constance, tired as she was, was only feigning sleep. After Margaret went to bed and Constance knew from her rhythmic even breathing that she was asleep, she stole stiffly from her cot and very carefully rummaged in Margaret's saddlebag until she found the little vial of poison hemlock. She tiptoed outside and emptied its contents on the ground. Then she washed and rinsed the vial with water from the wooden bucket at the well and refilled it with water—the vial was opaque, Margaret would notice no difference in the color.

When Constance woke it was well past noon. Margaret, she discovered, had already unpacked their ball gowns and indeed had shaken them out and hung them up outside in the damp air of early morning to get the wrinkles out. They had dried in the sun and with a touch-up from an iron would look as crisp as those of any of the ladies who had jolted to Huntlands in coaches, crushing their skirts as they went, or come down the dusty road in carriages.

"Bring us some more water," said Margaret, who was already busying herself heating water for their baths. "I am sure you will have no trouble finding the bucket."

Neither were hungry, but as the water heated they ate some of the ham and bread and cheddar cheese the Squire had left for them, and washed it all down with apple cider. As they ate, Margaret calmly told her how the cheese was made—the curd mats were stacked, or "cheddared," to expel whey. It was aging that set the flavor—a few months for mild cheese, but years for sharp cheese such as this. Constance, tense and excited, hardly tasted her food and wondered how Margaret could be so calm.

They took their baths in the metal tub the Squire had left for them. And then as the shadows deepened they dressed by candlelight for a night they both desired—and dreaded. And mounted their horses, riding carefully not to disturb their elegant ball gowns, and set out through the trees for Huntlands.

They had not been riding long when Margaret signalled to Constance to stop and they dismounted, and tethered their horses to a tree.

"We will walk from here," she said, lifting her skirts in her hands, and moving forward. Constance followed.

They were very near to Huntlands now. They could hear music and distant laughter, when Constance came to a sudden halt.

"What did you mean this afternoon by saying 'I am sure you will have no trouble finding the bucket'?" she demanded.

Margaret turned to regard her. The rising moon had cast a shadow over her face in its black velvet, lace-trimmed mask, and only her green eyes flashed with a haunting gleam.

"Because I saw you out by the well last night. You had forgotten perhaps how lightly I sleep. When your hand rattled the latch I came awake and saw you, vial in hand, stealing out to the well. I guessed what you were doing and this morning when I sniffed the vial it no longer had that peculiar mouselike odor—it smelled clean and fresh."

"Oh, Margaret, I did it for you," cried Constance in consternation. "I want you to live, whatever happens!"

"Well, now at least I will not die by poison," sighed Margaret with sad irony, for the moment was at hand and her own nerves too were rubbed raw. "Instead, should Tony recognize me and rip the mask from my face, I will simply leap on a horse and ride for the Cheddar Gorge."

And hurl yourself over! thought Constance in dismay. Oh, she had achieved nothing, nothing by emptying out the vial! Margaret had a will to self-destruction, she would bring death crashing down on her in a moment if the evening went wrong! For the first time, Constance wished they were back on the moors—safe.

Huntlands, Somerset,
Midsummer 1684

CHAPTER 19

The annual Midsummer Masque at Huntlands was in full swing when Constance and Margaret arrived, running with their full skirts held up across the side lawns and managing to slip unobserved through a side entrance. Constance had an impression of a long E-shaped stone house glimpsed through the trees as she ran, a house with rather simple rectangular chimneys rising tall above its steeply pitched roofs, and beautifully scalloped gables and enormous windows. Through a dark corridor they hurried toward the sound of music and seemed to burst through all at once into the great hall with its high medallioned ceiling, its strapwork, its scrolled overmantel held up by caryatids. On this warm summer night all the doors and windows stood open to let the breezes blow through and cool the dancers as they whirled about the floor, and moonlight, coming in through an enormous mullioned and transomed bay window of no less than twenty-four lights, mingled with the candlelight from the vast central chandelier.

"Remember, we are not together," muttered Margaret. "If

I can find Clifford, I will bring him to you—but if anyone asks, you do not know me."

Constance nodded, a little taken aback by the sheer size of Huntlands and by the number of masquers whirling about in full costume. She cast a look toward the screened passage and saw above it a little gallery with a row of recessed arches where the musicians as they played could look down upon the dancers.

As I looked down through the bannisters at Claxton House as a child, she remembered with a little pang.

Beside her she felt Margaret stiffen convulsively and followed her gaze. She had a flashing glimpse of a tall dark man dressed in black and gold before the crowd moved between them. His black mask was so tiny it made no effort to conceal his features—the features of the face in Margaret's locket! Constance felt a sudden leaping anger at this tall fellow who could so swiftly have forgotten a woman as true as Margaret. But wait—she had had a swift impression of a long scar on his face. This could not be Tony Warburton. The painted likeness in Margaret's locket bore no scar.

Beside her Margaret had forgotten the dancers, forgotten the world, forgotten Constance standing beside her. It was her first glimpse of Tony Warburton in six long years and she knew it might have to last her a lifetime—but it was heady wine. She moved her head and managed to find him again through a break in the crowd. He was bending gracefully over a lady's gloved hand and as he lifted his head his sardonic features came once again into view.

"There he is, Constance," she murmured.

"But the man in the locket—" began Constance, confused.

"Bore no scar?" Margaret drew a deep shuddering breath that came from the depths of her. She felt herself responsible for gashing that scar into Tony's lean amused face. "No, because the portrait in the locket was painted before Ralph Pembroke gave Tony that wound."

A sudden vision of Tony's wedding—that darkest day in her life—rose up to haunt her. She had stood there in the crowd, black-veiled and silent, knowing she should hurry away lest she be recognized, yet loath to leave the sight of him, for this time it would be forever. And beside her Annabelle Hamilton, who had once competed with her for Tony's favor, had said with a light laugh, "Tony Warburton took his wound and left the country—and now he has come back with a scar across his face that lends itself to sinister imaginings! Do you think he could have invited that wound to make himself even more glamorous in our eyes?"

She had wanted to strike Annabelle. Instead she had turned and fled—to Devon.

The truth about the scar was that Tony Warburton had paid less attention to the dagger cut than he should, so wrought up was he about other things, and the wound had healed rough so that it left a jagged white line extending from the corner of his left eye down to his sardonic mouth. Men thought it made him look keen-honed and battle-edged; women thought it made him look romantic, heroic, dangerous. Tony Warburton couldn't have cared less what any of them thought. His face—other than keeping it shaved and presentable—was of little concern to him.

"Tony wears that scar because of me," Margaret told Constance huskily.

Tony looked older, she thought, less lighthearted, more thoughtful. And her heart went out to him now more strongly than ever, seeing his—to her—grave new demeanor.

"Tony has—changed," she murmured, and was unaware that she had spoken that opinion aloud. The words drifted to Constance on a sigh.

Constance, terrified by what might happen tonight when these two came face to face at last, said nervously, "How do you mean, *changed*?"

There's less of the boy in him, more of the man, thought Margaret. But she didn't tell Constance that. Instead she shrugged. "Older," she said, moving around to get a better view of Tony. She couldn't get enough of the sight of him. All these years apart and now suddenly to see him again, not in her broken dreams, not in her wild imaginings, but here in vivid masculine flesh, strong, alive, desirable!

And once he had been hers.

With mingled pain and joy she saw him turn and look in their direction. She trembled. Did he see her? No, he did not. Wait—he was smiling at someone. Who? She turned and saw that it was on Constance that his gaze was fixed. On Constance, standing there clothed in all the radiance of her dark young beauty.

Jealousy sprang up in Margaret. Wild, unreasoning. Beautiful Constance . . . *oh, once she could have matched her, once. . . .*

And then she realized, dizzily, that Captain Warburton was striding through the throng toward them. For a moment as he approached, tall and straight as a rapier in his black and gold, with that narrow black mask only half shielding his keen gray eyes, her knees beneath her bronze silk skirts threatened to buckle. She felt faint. In a burst of panic she almost turned and ran but Constance's quick frightened gasp stopped her. In a defiant rush, her courage—and she had much of it—returned. Tony, she told herself, was undoubtedly approaching to ask beautiful Constance, so showy in her violet silks, to dance. He would ignore the tense woman over whose white bosom the copper lace rose and fell.

She waited bravely for what would come.

The music struck up just then and it was at that moment that Tony saw her, for up to then the crowd had obstructed his view. Arrested in mid-stride, a kind of shocked stillness spread over his features, to be instantly replaced by his usual cool sardonic expression, perhaps a trifle more pensive than was his wont. Through the dancers he moved toward Margaret almost without volition, as if there was no one else in the room—and paused before her with a slight bow.

It was as if Margaret had willed him to do it, thought Constance, thrilled.

Tony Warburton did not even glance at the long-stemmed

beauty in violet silks. He presented himself squarely to the woman in bronze.

"Will you do me the honor?" he asked Margaret gravely. And Margaret, struck speechless by this glorious crown to all her hopes, was silent as he led her out on to the floor.

"I know we must wait for the unmasking but—could it be that you're a stranger here?" he asked her, puzzled.

Margaret, well knowing how distinctive her voice was, dared not reply. The musical raw-silk rustle of her voice would tell him what he dared not ask. Silently, she shook her head.

"So you think I might know your voice?" he chuckled, whirling her about so that her bronze silk skirts floated out around her and then drawing her back toward him in a lithe gesture that brought those skirts swaying round his boots.

Margaret shrugged—a delightful shrug that set in shimmering motion her gleaming flame-colored curls and called attention to her magnificent white shoulders and the snowy expanse of bosom above her flawless bustline.

Behind the mask the gray eyes narrowed. "You remind me . . ." he murmured. "I am wondering if you could be a relative—" He broke off, shaking his head suddenly as if to clear it. "So you are no stranger to this valley. Then let me ask you this: Are you married to one of my friends perhaps? A wife I have not yet had the pleasure of meeting?"

She could shake her head with perfect truth to that.

"Nor am I married—any longer," he said softly. "Tell me—*were* you married? Are you perhaps a widow?"

Not a widow of the body, she thought. *A widow of the heart.* And again she shook her head.

So rapt were they, this pair, that neither took their eyes from the other's face. The music had stopped but neither had noticed. They continued to whirl to an inner music they both heard in unison—a love song of the spirit that had begun its melody the moment their fingers had touched.

Heads turned interestedly to watch them, as they glided like swans across the floor.

Abruptly Captain Warburton became aware of that attention. ''The music has stopped,'' he said with a flashing grin.

Margaret looked about her with a pounding heart. They were all watching—all the elite of the countryside. Just as they had so often stood back to watch Margaret Archer dance. She gave the crowd a graceful curtsy and took the arm the gallant captain offered.

And then as they strolled away from the center of the floor the music started up again and once more he swept her into the rhythm of the dance.

To Margaret it was a kind of heaven, newly gained, but one that—like other earthly treasures—could not last. But she would play out these minutes one by one, drawing them into a skein of memory to knit and purl on lonely nights when the wind sang its lonely song across the moors.

How she yearned to say, *Oh, Tony, I have come back. . . .* And watch his strong face light up with wonder and with joy.

For now she no longer had any doubt that he still loved her. At least, he loved the woman she once had been . . . *and was no longer!*

That last thought came crashing in upon her senses even as those senses reeled beneath the pressure of his masculinity, the deep physical attraction he had always had for her, the longing for his arms that had been with her so long. She remembered moonlit nights when she had lain beneath him sighing, she remembered the sound of straw crunching beneath their lithe straining bodies as they held lovers' rendezvous in some barn, she remembered the scratching sound of silver and gold embroidery threads in fancy coverlets in one of the hastily found and as swiftly latched guest bedrooms in other people's houses where they had slipped away from the merriment for a brief and lovely rapture of their own. She remembered so much—and it must all end. Before tonight's unmasking.

With her hands clasped tightly together, her fingers twisting spasmodically in her delicate gloves, Constance watched the little tableau from the sidelines. Her teeth had nearly bitten into her soft lower lip and she was straining forward, *willing* everything to be all right.

She gave a guilty start as she realized that someone was asking her to dance. She never knew later who it was that led her out, so rapt was she in keeping her head turned to contemplate the tall distinguished man in black and gold and the tall graceful lady in bronze silk and copper lace who swayed with him to the music as if she were part of him.

Margaret was looking up into her lover's face now boldly, realizing with confidence that the lace-edged black velvet mask she wore hid all her scars from view, that all of her that Tony could see was beautiful. For her throat and bosom were flawless and unmarked and they flashed snowy white as she whirled confidently in the measures of the dance, her shadowed emerald eyes glorious and glowing.

There was no handsomer couple on the floor than the tall captain and the lady in bronze silks that nobody knew.

Nobody except Constance. And Clifford Archer, if he were here.

Constance's dancing partner brought her back to the place where she had been standing and someone interposed himself between them and breathed into her ear, "Margaret looks well tonight. I had not hoped to see her looking so fine."

Constance stiffened. She whirled in consternation and found herself looking into a face that—despite its skimpy mask— somehow reminded her of Margaret's. Except that it was broader and less symmetrical and behind the mask those eyes flashed blue instead of green and the luxuriant hair that crowned it was gold instead of flaming red.

"I was watching for you and I saw you come in together," he murmured. "Margaret had written to me what you both would be wearing."

This gentleman in amber satin had to be Clifford Archer. Her uncle. So much older than Margaret, who seemed a teenager herself as she was whirled about the floor by the dashing Captain Warburton.

Constance cast a swift look around. Her partner had departed and they were standing for the moment a little apart from the others. "Yes, she does," she said quietly. "But I am afraid for her all the same."

"So am I," agreed the amber gentleman with a sigh. And then, hastily, "We will find an opportunity to talk later—perhaps in the solar upstairs. It would seem someone wants to meet you."

Constance was abruptly aware of a tall young man who had approached as they were talking and was now standing before her. He was dressed dramatically in a scarlet-lined short cloak—miserably hot for this warm summer night but it gave his black suit with its red revers a certain dash. She was taken aback, for even with a mask obscuring his features she could see that he looked strikingly like a younger version of Captain Warburton.

"Ned," said her uncle, cheerfully recognizing Ned despite his red satin mask, "you shall be the first to meet my ward, Mistress Constance Dacey. Constance, this startlingly garbed fellow is Ned Warburton."

It took Constance by surprise to be introduced to Tony Warburton's brother as Clifford Archer's ward. She cast a sudden grateful look at her uncle, who was claiming her as best he could—and then drew slightly away from Ned Warburton. For she felt toward him an instant aversion—*he looked too much like his brother.* Just as she had felt an instant and violent aversion to Captain Warburton, no matter how striking a figure he cut out there on the floor! He had brought Margaret sorrow and now, if things went wrong, he could bring her death!

"Mistress Constance." Gallantly, Ned bent over her hand, then turned to include Clifford Archer in his next remark. "This night is full of surprises," he declared humorously. "First Tony, who has not danced two consecutive dances with any woman since his wife died, seems unwilling to leave the

303

floor—faith he dances with his newfound lady even after the music has stopped!'' He nodded toward his brother and Margaret, still moving in perfect unison across the floor. ''And now *you* astonish me, sir, by producing a ward from a hat as it were. Tell me, Lady of Mystery, where has the Squire been hiding you?''

Constance forced to her face a quick mechanical smile. ''I have been tucked away in boarding school in London ever since my parents died,'' she told Ned glibly. ''Indeed, this is my first ball and I am afraid my dancing is sadly at fault.'' *Perhaps that would discourage this younger version of the dangerous gentleman so masterfully sweeping Margaret across the dance floor!*

But Ned was not to be discouraged so easily.

''Faith, I cannot think it,'' he declared gaily. ''Come out upon the floor with me and we will gauge the mettle of your dancing!''

''I may step upon your feet,'' Constance warned him in a cool distant voice.

''You may stamp upon my boots and welcome, if only you will keep smiling at me like that,'' Ned assured her and confidently whirled her out upon the floor where her swirling lavender silk skirts almost brushed Margaret's bronze ones. Then they were swept apart by the other dancers.

But in that brief close look, Constance had thought, *I have never seen Margaret look so happy. Dear God, don't let anything spoil this night for her. It is all she has—perhaps it is all she will ever have of her brave Captain Warburton— who rushed into marriage with another woman a short two months after she left the scene!*

Constance's anger at the Captain rubbed off on Ned. She kept her face averted from him, refusing to meet his gaze as they danced. Instead her violet eyes followed the progress of Margaret and her sometime lover as they whirled about the floor.

That anger made her response insolent when Ned with a faint chuckle said, ''I see you are eyeing my older brother,

Tony, but I feel I must warn you that he is seldom home. Let Tony get wind of a war somewhere and he's off like a shot!'' (For Captain Warburton had chosen to keep from his younger brother all knowledge of his secret intelligence activities on the Continent—lest reckless Ned try to emulate him and get himself killed!)

The violet eyes that turned toward Ned lacked their usual deep velvet radiance. They had instead a hard amethyst gleam. ''You say you have a brother?'' she asked with a faint hauteur. ''And which one might he be, in this gathering?''

Ned was a little taken aback. ''Why, he's the tall fellow in black and gold dancing with the beautiful red-haired lady.''

''Really?'' said Constance in a bored voice, not deigning now to cast so much as a glance at Tony Warburton. ''I had not noticed him. But then I do not care for black garments— even those trimmed in red or bright colors. So somber.'' Her gaze passed distastefully over his own scarlet revers to frown at his costume, which was mainly black.

Ned flushed. He cast a quick glance over the dark sheen of her hair to ponder the resplendent colors that most of the young gentlemen at the ball were sporting—shades of gold and green and orange and puce and blue. He made an instant resolve to visit his tailor on the morrow and order himself a suit that would be of a color more pleasing to the Squire's fastidious ward. Green, perhaps. For he had never been more taken with a girl in his life and her bland disregard puzzled him. It was as though all her being was concentrated elsewhere.

As indeed it was. Fear prickled through her veins—fear for Margaret. And she would have been doubly terrified could she have heard what the lean Captain was saying to Margaret now.

''I find it hard to wait for the unmasking.'' Tony smiled down at his lustrous lady in her whirling bronze silks. ''Even though 'tis only minutes away.''

Only minutes away, thought Margaret dreamily, and in the distance a great bell seemed to toll. But it was still far away and somehow every moment now seemed forever. . . .

The Captain leaned closer. " 'Tis all I can do to hold back from snatching the mask from your face here and now, so curious am I to learn who you are. You cannot be who I think you are, for heaven is not that kind to mortals. And yet—" He was smiling down at her now most tenderly. "Whoever you are, you fill these arms as no one has for years."

Tears glimmered in the brilliant emerald eyes that looked back at him. *Well spoke, Tony,* she thought proudly. *For we were true lovers once . . . we loved as no others have loved before or since our time. And somehow even through my mask you seem to know me.* That distant warning bell seemed muted now and hushed. Her treacherous heart was responding to him, beat by beat. That heartbeat thundered in her ears, deafeningly, and her fast-drawn breathing threatened to suffocate her.

Captain Warburton was having the same difficulty. He felt as if an old forgotten song was thrumming once again in his ears and he was seeing for the first time wild young Margaret Archer come bursting into the drawing room at Axeleigh. A vision of her flame-red hair haunted him—and it was *this* hair. And those emerald eyes he could but glimpse through the narrow slits in the enveloping mask that hid the whole top part of her face, those eyes even in this deceptive candlelight were Margaret's well-remembered color. And that generous winsome smile, the perfect white teeth, the soft mouth glimpsed through the gathered black lace that edged her black velvet mask—*that was Margaret's smile.* The firm but delicate jawline, the white column of her proud throat with the little pulsing area in a hollow just above her snowy bosom, her entire magnificent figure—*even the way she fit into his arms, the way she moved with him*—was Margaret to the life.

Was it possible that through time and space, defying death, Margaret had somehow come back to him?

He must know!

Of a sudden he whirled her through the dancers and out of the great candlelit hall, into the dimness of the screened area that led from the great hall to the kitchen, the buttery, the servants' dining hall.

Margaret knew what he was going to do, but she had no will to resist. Too long had she waited for this moment.

Tenderly his mouth closed down on hers and she kissed him—through the lace of her mask. All of her heart was in that kiss, all of her vanished dreams. Her body yearned toward him in a sweet irrevocable sway. He could feel the tremulous response in her, the wild sweet madness that sent the blood racing through her veins.

And Tony Warburton felt as if a distant cannon had boomed. For the touch of those lips was *Margaret's.* Unforgettable. The tingling passion that he felt in this woman, so wild and sweet, so well remembered, was *Margaret's.*

So rapt were they in the thunderous response of their own bodies that neither of them heard the thunder of hooves outside.

"Who are you?" he demanded hoarsely.

And just as she had known he would, in all her terrible fatalistic daydreams, he snatched at her mask, tearing the lace as he ripped it away from her features.

CHAPTER 20

But even while Captain Warburton, in that dim screened corridor, was in the very act of snatching off Margaret's mask, behind them in the candlelit great hall a dramatic sequence of events that capped anything a Huntlands' Midsummer Masque had ever seen was taking place.

Constance, being whirled about the floor by Ned Warburton, was suddenly anxiously aware that Margaret and her tall captain had disappeared. Even as she quaked with that realization, there came from outside, pounding down the drive, the thunder of hooves, hoarse cries and a couple of wild shots, one of which came through the open casements of the hall's enormous bay window and cut the rope that held the vast chandelier above the dancers.

The music came to a shrieking halt as the astonished musicians peered down in fright from their little gallery above. Women screamed and the crowd scattered as the heavy iron mass of the great central chandelier suspended above them crashed to the polished floor, sending fifty lighted candles flying. And from outside came simultaneously another shot and a hoarse prolonged cry that ended in a rending moan.

Someone had been hit.

Around Constance now men were running toward the front door from whence the shots had come—with Tom Thornton at their head. Boots were stamping in a desperate effort to stamp out the candle flames before they ignited fragile chemise ruffles or dainty silken skirts. Frightened servants had poured in from the rear and were scurrying about with snuffers, collecting the fallen candles. At least two satin-clad ladies had fainted and were being borne away. Beside her Ned Warburton gave a low curse and would have put her from him but that she would not let him, her fingers closed convulsively over his arm.

For in the midst of that wild scene, Constance was aware of only one thing:

Tony Warburton was back. Constance saw him spring into the room with his right hand on his sword hilt, his long strides carrying him straight for the front door and whatever trouble awaited outside.

In horror Constance swayed against Ned. For in Tony Warburton's left hand, as if forgotten, he carried a lady's lace-trimmed black velvet mask—*Margaret's!*

And Margaret herself was nowhere in sight.

A kind of blackness came over Constance. She felt she might be sick or that she might faint. As she fought to overcome it, Ned leaned over her in concern.

"Are you ill?" he asked anxiously, for megrims and migraines and fainting fits were common in a day when women wore tightly laced corsets ribbed with bone or steel.

"No," gasped Constance, her world reeling. "I need air." She clutched at his cloak to steady herself.

Nothing she could have said could have pleased Ned more, for it was her light weight sagging against him that was preventing him from doing the one thing he longed to do—to make his way to the door and find out what was happening outside.

"This excitement has been too much for you," he told her masterfully as with an arm supporting her body he made swiftly for the door. "Howls and shots and chandeliers falling! Damned disgrace, that's what it is!"

He was still blustering as they reached the comparative coolness of the air outside.

There against the statuesque backdrop of the moon-washed old trees, a strange pageant was being played out.

Muttering masked guests in their finery clustered in little groups staring down at a fallen man whose black hat had come off and whose gaudy green cloak failed to cover the gaping hole in his chest. Beside him danced a nervous horse, and someone had grasped the reins to keep the horse from running off. And behind him were ranged a troop of the King's men, in uniform.

As Constance and Ned came through the door, the leader of that troop, a rather dashing major, was finishing what must have been a dramatic challenge:

"—And will anyone tell me why this man should choose to leave the road and dash in here under pursuit?"

The masks may have concealed perfectly innocent faces, but confronted by the King's men, ranged about, nobody cared to answer that question.

"Then perhaps," he taunted, "someone among ye would care to claim the body?"

Nobody cared to claim the body either.

The major laughed and gave them all a scathing look that condemned them as rebels. "Cart this carrion away," he commanded, nudging the fallen man with the toe of a shiny boot. "Since no one cares to claim the body."

But the Squire of Axeleigh, rushing through the oaken door—a little late for he had been occupied with stamping out the flames from a screaming lady's skirts that had been set alight by the candles of the fallen chandelier—was ready enough to do so.

"Hold there!" he cried truculently. "What the devil do you think you're doing?"

The major brightened. "Do you know this man?" he drawled.

"Certainly," snapped the Squire. "He's Nick Netherbury and he's one of my tenants."

The major thrust out his jaw. "Netherbury he may be to you, but he's Jack Drubbs to us and he's been spreading rebellion here in the West Country."

The Squire, who had torn off his mask as he came through the door, regarded the major with a look of pure amazement. "Impossible," he said flatly.

The major was nettled. "We had word he was out to collect some money for Monmouth and we set a trap for him. When we ordered him to halt he fled before us—*and turned in here.*" He cast a significant look around him at the company.

Tom Thornton, who had been looking puzzled, now shouldered his way forward. "That man is indeed Nick Netherbury," he corroborated the Squire quietly. "None of us knows about any Drubbs."

"Nick's cottage is far from here," interrupted the Squire. "If Nick turned in here, it was because he hoped you'd not see the gates in your rush forward and he could hide in the bushes until you had passed and then find his way home. For it must have been as obvious to Nick as it is to me that you'd mistaken him for somebody else."

The major gave them both a suspicious look. "I can see that ye stick together here in the West Country," he sneered. "But that green cloak belongs to Drubbs—of that I'm certain."

"I know naught of the cloak," said the Squire. "But the body inside it is certainly Nick Netherbury's. He's worked on my estate since before I was born and he's never been known to dabble in politics." (Leanings Nick might have, but take action? Never!) "Ask anyone—they'll bear me out."

The major cast an uncertain look down at the dead man. It

was beginning to seem that he had captured a cloak while his real quarry had eluded him.

"I'm here on commission from Judge Jeffreys himself in pursuit of this traitor Drubbs and his ilk," he blustered. "And if there are any more of his kind hereabout ye'd be well advised to hand them over now."

"Rest assured there are none," said Tom, meeting the major's gaze squarely. "I'll vouch for my guests—and my servants."

"I cannot believe that poor Nick was ever involved in anything," murmured the Squire, shaking his head. "Nick minded his own business."

Into his remark intruded the voice of a soldier who was even now searching the body. "The fellow had this on him," he called out, and tossed a small leathern purse to the major.

Nobody was looking at Clifford Archer just then or they would have seen him change color. *He knew that purse! He had left it in a hollow tree at the behest of a blackmailer earlier this evening!* He watched in fascination as the major untied the leather thong that held the purse and with slow deliberation counted out ten gold guineas.

"A large sum, wouldn't you say, for a farm tenant to be carrying about?" the major shot sardonically at the Squire.

The Squire's face had hardened perceptibly. "I would say so," he agreed coldly. "And you may well be right. It would seem I did not know Nick Netherbury as well as I thought."

The major appeared somewhat mollified, but Tom Thornton's blue eyes mirrored astonishment at Clifford Archer's sudden renunciation of his lifelong tenant.

But Constance missed that. She was watching Captain Warburton who, now that the crisis outside was over, was hurrying back into the hall.

"I want to go back inside," she told Ned, and fled after the Captain.

Perplexed, but satisfied that he had seen all there was of interest outside, Ned followed her in.

Across the dance floor, littered still with candles and fans and a satin slipper or two and the ominous bulk of the massive iron chandelier with its heavy length of rope, she saw the Captain stride. Back into the screened-off corridor that led to the buttery and the kitchen.

Before she was more than halfway across the floor she saw him come out again. He caught sight of Constance and moved swiftly toward her.

"There was a lady here just now dressed in bronze silk," he said tersely. "She was standing beside you when I asked her to dance. Have you any idea where she went?"

So Margaret had escaped him!

"I do not remember such a lady," Constance heard herself say. "But then there were so many . . ."

For a moment his hard gaze said he did not believe her. Then he turned on his heel and left them, heading again for the front door. She guessed he was going to search the grounds.

Captain Warburton was more determined and a deal more thorough than she had expected him to be. He enlisted the aid of his host, Tom Thornton, explained tersely that one of his guests seemed to have come up missing. Tom was instantly alarmed for with a strange troop of King's men roving about looking for trouble, a lone lady might well be mistook for a conspirator on such a night.

Someone mentioned "The Masked Lady" and Constance pricked up her ears. "Who is that?" she whispered to Ned.

"She's a famous agent of the Duke of Monmouth," he told her. " 'Tis said she carries messages for him—and could do so beneath the nose of the King himself."

"Why—why do they call her that?" she asked breathlessly.

"Because none have ever seen her face," Ned shrugged. "She rides like a shadow along the summer roads and no one knows where she goes to winter."

But I do, thought Constance with a sudden pang. *She goes back to the lonely moors of Devon where she shelters outcasts like herself. . . .*

313

And suddenly she remembered a night last winter on those same cold moors.

She had been fast asleep, dreaming of Dev and the way it had been in Hatfield Forest last summer. In her dream they had just eaten a simple meal of bread and cheese and wine, and now the moon had come up and was making magic of its own through the spreading branches of the Old Doodle Oak and Dev was lying back relaxed upon the grass. *How vulnerable he looks,* she had thought suddenly. *And how dear to me* . . . And she had loosened the laces of her bodice and let her breasts ride free, and hovered over him, tempting him by brushing the crests of her nipples against his cheeks. Dev had laughed and drawn her to him and her young body had descended on his own as lightly as a feather, and she had felt his warm lips burrow in her throat, in the hollow between her breasts, and slide down, down—and felt a wild sweet passion envelop her.

And then from somewhere had come a loud noise and Constance had awakened from reliving in dreams what once she had lived in reality. Confused for a moment, she had looked up at the moon shining hazily in through her window. Not the warm melon moon that had shown down on Hatfield but the cold white moon of wintry Dartmoor.

From somewhere a shutter was banging. That must be what had awakened her. But even as she turned over to go back to sleep, she heard a horse neighing outside—a horse neighing where no horse should be. Fearful lest the closed stable door had blown open and the horses gone a-roaming on this bitter night, she jumped up. Shivering in her wrapper, she ran to the window.

It had begun to snow and against the rugged backdrop of the granite-topped tors, softened by moonlight, she saw a man alighting from an exhausted horse. And as she watched, she saw Margaret come from the house and lead the horse toward the stable while the rider disappeared inside.

Constance had stood there, puzzled. For all that Margaret was so brave and so competent, she nevertheless reigned over a household of women and even her large pistol would perhaps be no match against a roving brigand. Constance waited a bit, then quietly let herself into the hall. Below her the man, whose white face she could glimpse but dimly in the light of a single candle below, was speaking. She caught only the end of his remark "—to have a care for yourself," before Margaret said sharply, "But you're ill. Here, Gates, let me bring you some spirits."

"I'm well enough, just cold," mumbled Gates. " 'Tis yourself must watch out."

"Nonsense. Who'd look for me here? Off with your boots, Gates, and dry your feet by the fire. Hot broth and hot rum will bring you round!"

This, plainly, was no brigand but someone Margaret knew. Someone she called *Gates*. Feeling she had intruded on something she was not meant to hear, perhaps some tie with that past Margaret both cherished and dreaded, Constance beat a hasty and silent retreat.

The next morning the door to the bedchamber across from hers which had heretofore stood open was closed. When Constance tried it, she found it locked.

And so was the stable.

"Where is our guest?" she asked Margaret casually at breakfast when the servants were out of earshot.

"Guest?" Margaret looked surprised.

"Yes. I heard a horse neigh last night and looked out to see you letting him into the house."

"Oh, that fellow. He brought a letter from my brother at Axeleigh. He breakfasted early and went on his way."

"The door across the hall from my bedchamber is locked," remarked Constance. She looked up to see Margaret regarding her with a bland steady gaze.

"A bird flew into it and broke the glass. I have locked the door so that it will not blow open and chill the house before I can get it fixed."

That window, Constance knew, was above an overhang and difficult to see from ground level.

"Cook says the stable door is locked too."

Margaret shrugged. "It occurred to me that if there were strangers about, one of them might steal the horses. I've locked the stable for the time."

She does not wish me to see Gates, Constance had thought at the time. *Or perhaps she does not wish Gates to see me.* And she had let it pass, listening as Margaret told her things her brother had written about Axeleigh and the winter balls that enlivened life there.

The next morning the stable door was again unlocked and the bedchamber door stood open as always. When Constance remarked that the window had been fixed, Margaret said casually that she had some skill as a glazier. Constance had prowled around the house but there was no sign of the stranger or his horse. Even the hoofprints a departing horse would have left had disappeared under a fresh fall of snow.

Now she realized that some desperate message must have been borne by the lone rider across the winter moorlands—borne to The Masked Lady. How coolly Margaret had carried it off! Even *she* had not really suspected anything except that possibly Margaret did not wish her brother in Somerset to know that Constance was her houseguest.

She felt suddenly hurt that Margaret had not told her about this wild other aspect of her life—her dangerous work as a courier for the Duke of Monmouth. Perhaps Margaret had not wished to involve her in it.

But what Ned had told her kindled a newfound admiration for Margaret—cool, resourceful Margaret pounding the summer roads on behalf of a Cause she believed in. She wished Margaret had confided in her, so she could have helped her.

During the search, with everyone out of the house, the Squire found time to have a word with Constance in a corner of the deserted hall.

"It has occurred to me—too late, after I had already introduced you to Ned as Constance Dacey—that you might have preferred to use your mother's maiden name of Cheltenham here. If that is your desire, we could still—"

"No," Constance interrupted. Her delicate jaw was set and

316

the gaze she turned on the Squire was a stubborn one. "Hammond Dacey might not have been there at my conception, but he was there at my birth. He saved my mother from shame, he cared for me as his own, he was the father I knew in my childhood. To me he was a true father and I'll keep his name." *And wear it proudly,* proclaimed those deep and steady violet eyes.

Clifford Archer felt respect for his newfound ward growing in him. "And if Hugh Dacey finds you and makes public the facts?" he asked bluntly, for Margaret had written about Constance's fear of Hugh.

"Then if you feel shamed by my presence, I'll disappear— as I did from Claxton House," she told him defiantly.

He admired her now. She must have taken after her mother, he decided, for his brother Brandon had had none of her fire. Lethargic was the word he would have used to describe Brandon, who was slow to start, but once started refused to be stopped—a trait that had led him to his death.

"I wish I had known your mother," the Squire murmured. "I think we would have been good friends. But it was Margaret who knew Anne, not myself."

"Indeed you would have been good friends," said Constance warmly. "For my mother was brave and beautiful." *And frightened of the blows the world might deal her small daughter. . . .*

"We should not linger in here," the Squire told her. "We should go out and join the search party. I take it you have disclaimed knowing the lady in the bronze dress?"

Constance gave an emphatic nod. "I hope she is—all right," she said haltingly, and for a moment her bleak expression betrayed how heartsick she was over Margaret's plight.

"I hope so too," sighed the Squire. "Come, we must hope for the best."

Together they went outside.

The search party found a torn snatch of bronze silk trimmed in copper lace caught on the branches between Huntlands and

Axeleigh. They found a bronze satin dancing slipper lost among the tree trunks. And on one outthrusting twig a tangle of flame-red hair that Tony Warburton, who found it, touched with gentle fingers.

But they did not find the wearer.

By now—with everyone having disclaimed any knowledge of the vanished lady—there was considerable interested muttering about The Masked Lady, whose name was a legend along the English highroads. *Could it really have been she?* people asked each other excitedly. *After all she had arrived from nowhere—masked—and disappeared as mysteriously as she had come!*

They came to the conclusion, the perplexed men who put their heads together and tried to piece it all out, that unknown to all of them Nick Netherbury had been carrying the golden guineas to Huntlands for a purpose—to place them in the hands of the radiant masked beauty who would spirit those coins elsewhere for the Cause. And that The Masked Lady, realizing Netherbury was dead and the gold confiscated, had either escaped or been carried off by those who wished her harm.

Only Constance and the Squire knew better.

The practical realization that it was already too late, that whatever was done was done and Margaret—whatever her destination—was already far beyond their reach, did not influence Constance in the least. All her being urged her to rush to Captain Warburton, whom Margaret loved so much, and blurt out that even now his lost love might be dashing to the Cheddar Gorge to hurl herself over.

But something even stronger than her fear for Margaret deterred Constance. It was a bond forged between the two women during the long months they had spent together, a bond both lasting and deep. Its links were forged of respect and admiration and something else that went deep—comradeship, the lonely times they had shared together on the forbidding moors of southwest England.

She would not betray Margaret. She could not. Not even though Margaret died of it.

For Constance that was an evening of nightmarish speculations. She envisioned with a caught breath a Margaret in flight, bright hair flying, catching on twigs and jerking her head back, a Margaret who scattered bits of torn lace as she ran, leaving them behind her in the summer woods along with her hopes and dreams. In her mind she saw Margaret trip over a root, lose a slipper and run on in her silk-stockinged feet.

And she saw her—and as she envisioned this, Constance's eyes were closed and her head bent—brokenhearted, leaping onto her horse and heading for the Cheddar Gorge and oblivion.

Her Uncle Clifford was not of that opinion.

"Unless Tony got a look at her face, I don't think she'd throw away her life," he mused. "For Margaret's a strong woman, she's got a firm grip on the world, she has. And I don't think Tony saw her face. Do you? Look at him over there with the others."

Constance turned toward Captain Warburton, frowning down at the lock of hair and the bit of bronze silk and copper lace in his hands. He looked bemused, worried—but not shocked. As he surely would have looked had he stripped the mask from Margaret's face and realized she was here—and alive.

Constance drew a deep shuddering breath and turned away. "I hope you are right," she told her uncle fervently. "And if you *are* right, then I should leave immediately, for I might be able to catch up with Margaret on the road."

"No, you are not to follow her. She would not wish it." His voice was very firm and he took possession of her hand as if he felt she too might bolt. "Margaret brought you north to me and here you will remain." He held up his hand when she would have spoken, but he kept his voice low lest the others, clustered around the piece of cloth and the slipper, hear him. "Come away," he urged. "I will take you home to Axeleigh and we will talk more about it. It may be some time

319

before Pamela returns—she is off searching the woods with Tom Thornton.''

And even as they spoke, a sobbing Margaret, her world snatched back so briefly and now lost again forever, was digging her heels into the flanks of her horse and riding hard for Dartmoor. And as she rode, the events of the night wheeled around and around in her mind as the planets circle the sun—ever spinning by.

She had danced again with Tony—all her life she would have that to look back upon. She had seen admiration in his gray eyes and kindling desire and she had felt her woman's body melting under his hot gaze. She had felt his warm breath upon her cheek, she had felt his demanding mouth upon her own—and even through the lace of her velvet mask, it had been all that she would ever ask of heaven.

And then he had snatched at the mask and simultaneously all hell had broken loose behind them in the great hall. But even as his fingers closed upon the black velvet and lace of the mask, Margaret had made her move. As she had so often rehearsed it in her mind on the long ride up from Devon, her gesture was as swift and as instinctive as his own and matched it by a fraction of a second. Even as the mask cleared her face, her arm was thrown across it, shielding it as had the black velvet.

And Tony Warburton—who might in that moment have swept her shielding arm away and seen her face at last—had harkened to the screams and crashing and shots from behind the screen wall. And he had done automatically what natural gallantry and a life of danger had trained him to do. He had whirled, pushing the lady with the shielded face behind him toward safety, and with a muttered ''Stay here,'' had bolted toward the trouble in the hall.

Margaret had turned and run in the other direction, and found her way outside by the same door through which she had entered Huntlands. She told herself she was glad, *glad* he had not seen her face. For if he had, he would have felt

constrained to follow, *constrained by guilt and not by love*—
and she could not have borne that.

She ran half blinded by tears, and hoped that her directions, so carefully given, had been followed.

But the Squire of Axeleigh, so reliable in all things, had
followed Margaret's instructions not only as to the manner of
her arrival but as to the manner of her leaving.

A saddled horse with Margaret's saddlebags already packed
and a heavy black veil and widows' weeds flung over the
saddle awaited her in the shadows. She ran like a wraith
across the lawn beneath the trees and sprang to the horse's
back. A moment later she was thundering away, the hoofbeats
of her departure cloaked by the pandemonium that had broken
loose inside the hall.

Hot tears coursed unchecked down her beautiful scarred
face, to be dried by the winds of Somerset. In a quiet glade
she stopped, and while the horse drank gratefully from a little
spring, she slipped the loose-fitting widows' weeds over her
elegant ball gown, took from her saddlebag a riding mask of
dull black fabric and fitted over her head the flowing black
veil that Clifford Archer had provided.

And then she was mounted again, and flying through the
night on the dark lanes back toward Devon.

It had been a night to treasure in her memory, but it had
also been a very narrow escape. She would never dare risk it
again.

The road ahead had never looked so bleak as she brought
the galloping horse down to a steady pace and sought the
back roads she knew so well. They would not find her, no
matter how they looked, for she had a head start and was
heading south—away from everything she loved.

And now, from her broken heart, she bade her lover a last
good-by. For she knew she would not seek him out again.

Back at Huntlands, the Squire brushed aside Ned's eager
offer and took Constance home himself. Tom would bring
Pamela, he assured her easily.

They were silent as they rode toward Axeleigh beneath

321

oaks her father had known as a lad. Halfway there, Constance put the question she felt she had to know.

"That talk I heard about The Masked Lady?" she asked. "Is there anything to it?"

He shrugged. "I doubt it. Oh, there may be a woman somewhere who rides about masked carrying messages for Monmouth, but my guess is the whole story is vastly overblown—and nothing to do with Margaret, of course."

"Do you happen to know anyone called Gates?" she shot at him, remembering that night on Dartmoor and the stranger who had been gone like the mist—that stranger Margaret had claimed was the Squire's messenger.

"No," he said and turned to her, mildly curious. "Am I supposed to know a Gates?"

"Oh, no," she said hastily. "I just thought you might."

So Margaret had not taken her brother into her confidence. . . . Perhaps she had not wished to involve him in the dangerous game she played.

Again they fell silent, riding along together until the long bulk of Axeleigh Hall reared up before them and they dismounted. After the grooms had taken their horses, the Squire led her toward the front door.

There he paused. "The world as we know it is wrong, Constance," he sighed. "Yet the plain truth is that in the times we live in, it would bring shame on you to admit your true father. Would that it were otherwise and that I could openly claim you as my niece."

She nodded, from a full heart.

In the moonlight the Squire studied the upturned face of his ward. There was little of his unruly brother to be found in that lovely face, he thought. Indeed, she must have taken after her mother's side—that willowy grace, that cloud of dark hair, shining and fine, those enormous purple eyes, dark-fringed. Only her skin bespoke her blond father, for her complexion had the ethereal fairness of a true blonde. With her dark hair and enormous violet eyes the effect was startling.

"Had my brother lived, he would have been master here,"

he told her slowly. "The estate is not an entail and my father loved Brandon best—he would surely have left this manor to him, and at his death, had he no other offspring, it would have been yours. But Brandon died and my father left Axeleigh to me—and it will pass from me to my only child, Pamela."

For a moment Constance's violet eyes had widened. Had matters fallen slightly differently, *she* not Pamela would have been mistress here! Somehow she had not thought of it that way.

She waited, silent. On the decision of this rugged new-met uncle of hers would rest her future.

"The world being what it is, 'tis best none but you and I know you to be Brandon's daughter."

"Not even Pamela?"

"Most especially not Pamela. For Pamela has a loyal heart but a wayward tongue. I have warned her to curb it but she does not listen. But as you cross my threshold I want you to know that since you are Brandon's daughter, you shall be a daughter to me also and reside here at Axeleigh until you marry. I will in all ways treat you as my own and when you wed I will give you a dowry."

"I do not know how to thank you, sir." Constance's voice was husky.

"No need to thank me. Were it not for your own sake, I'd insist you call me uncle." Abruptly he blew his nose. For there had been something in her wistful smile just then that had reminded him of the older brother he had in all ways copied as a lad.

With a courtly gesture, he swung wide the door and Constance stepped inside.

"Well," he said, as light laughter drifted to them from the drawing room, "it would seem that Pamela has preceded us."

Constance, her mind awhirl, gave him back an uncertain smile.

And went in to greet the lightskirt's daughter.

BOOK V
The Conspirators

A wicked love lights up her day,
Intrigue lights up her night,
And now the devil's come to play
Games when the moon is bright!

PART ONE
The Tangled Web

*Such times are these! Men go about pursuing empty
    schemes
Of setting dukes on princely thrones and such
    unlikely dreams!
One dream alone have I—and that is you one day
    to wed
And bring you willing, smiling, thrilling to my bed!*

Axeleigh Hall, Somerset,
December 1684

CHAPTER 21

Summer had faded into fall and now in the Valley of the Axe it was winter again with snow whitening the landscape and gray skies reflecting their gunmetal vastness down into the silver river.

The Squire of Axeleigh had received another letter from Margaret and he braced himself to read it—for if it was like the other two, it was like to break his heart.

Within the month after she had left the Midsummer Masque at Huntlands so abruptly he had heard from her. The letter came, he noted with a sigh of relief, from Tattersall in Devon and it was written in Margaret's own easily identifiable scrawl. He had torn it open with shaking fingers, afraid of what might spill out.

Even so, its contents rocked him.

It was foolish of me to come back. I know that now, the letter read. *But at least I am back at Tattersall where I belong. I miss Constance, but of course I had expected to miss Constance.* The Squire's face relaxed into a smile.

How like Margaret! He would show Constance the letter and she would be pleased that Margaret had mentioned missing her, for the Squire had come to realize how close the two women were. He began to read again. *Seeing Tony again has made me realize how empty his life must be with his wife gone. I hope that he will take an interest in Constance and perhaps offer for her. She is the finest girl I know and he is the finest man. I feel they would be right for each other. See if you cannot arrange a match between them.*

The Squire had let the letter fall to the table. He sat stunned. Margaret, who loved Tony Warburton more than she loved her life, was actually asking him to arrange a match between Tony and Constance? He was appalled by the very thought.

That evening he told Constance that he had heard from Margaret and that she was well and back in Dartmoor. Constance's face brightened and she asked if she could see the letter. The Squire told her cheerfully that he had lost it, but was sure he would find it again and he would save it for her.

She had to be content with that, although it *did* seem awfully careless of him.

The Squire's lips had tightened as he walked away from her. That was certainly one letter the girl would never see. He had tossed it into the fireplace personally and watched it burn.

I cannot believe you mean what you say, he had written back. *Do not urge me to do something which you will immediately regret.*

He had hoped that such a sensible response would put a stop to Margaret's wild suggestions. How could he know that in Devon she was remembering a double shadow in the moonpath and how she had once in the Hamiltons' attic told Tony Warburton fancifully that he was seeing two women. . . . Or that she had fatalistically decided that her words had been prophetic; there were indeed to be two women in Tony Warburton's life—but one of them was not the sad little Weatherby girl, sped almost before she was wed. The other woman in his life would be Constance. So now she had written to the Squire again and in the snows of December he had received it.

Tony has not forgotten me, she wrote frankly. *I knew that when I saw him at the Masque last summer. And I will not have him grieving for me, Clifford. With Constance he would be able to forget me, once and for all—and that is what I desire, that he forget me.* And again she urged him to make the match.

Reading those words, the Squire felt unaccustomed tears sting his eyelids. Valiant, foolish, stubborn, gallant Margaret . . . his heart went out to her and he sat for a time with his head in his hands, wondering what to do.

It hurt him in his heart to think of Margaret, wasting her life away on those barren moors. Many times he had debated telling Tony Warburton that she still lived. But always he had thought better of it just before he spoke—for he knew Margaret only too well, knew her determination and her courage. He would not put it past Margaret to drink a draft of hemlock or throw herself from the rooftop if Tony Warburton came calling—for she who had once been the beauty of the county could not brook the thought of being less.

It shook him now that he had actually suggested that Tony ask for Constance himself. What would have happened if Tony had latched on to his suggestion? Would Margaret, draped in black, have come north to attend the wedding as she had done, against his remonstrances, when Tony had married the little Weatherby girl?

If so, it well might be a very different story. For Tony, while kind, had not seemed wildly infatuated with the little Weatherby girl. But with Constance as a bride swaying beside him, who knew what the effect on Margaret would be?

He had a sudden nightmarish vision of Margaret sitting

quietly through the ceremony and then, unable to bear the thought of Tony's wedding night, riding off hell-bent for the Cheddar Gorge and oblivion.

Although he did not know it, the real world was about to deal him a blow harsh enough to blend in with his dark imaginings. Even now Fate was riding toward him through the snow in the person of one Jack Drubbs, who had last summer escaped the trap the King's men had laid for him and was now coming back to the Valley of the Axe.

It had been a bad year for Jack Drubbs. April had found him summarily dismissed from his job as male nurse in London, his patient's wife shrilly declaring him both neglectful and lazy. Drubbs, who was both, had smouldered for a time at his sister's cottage near Richmond and then gone out on a quest.

Never overly brave, Drubbs had gone about his mission cautiously for it was of a new sort for him. In his time he had pilfered rings and crosses from the dead, spirited away cadavers to sell to the medical profession, and even on occasion, at the insistent (and well-paid) urgings of relatives anxious to inherit, assisted—with the aid of a smothering pillow—an elderly patient or two into the next life. But he had never openly tried blackmail.

This chance, however, was too good to miss. For hadn't the patient babbled endlessly in his delirium about a certain squire in Somerset who had done his best to kill him, indeed who even now doubtless believed him walled up as dead in the foundations of his house? Hadn't Drubbs, shut in with a patient deemed contagious, had to listen hour after hour to the wild tale of his escape—without hat or cloak or boots or doublet, on foot into the Mendip Hills where he had stolen some clothes from a clothes line and hailed a dray and somehow—for the Squire had not taken his purse—made it back to London? Never too quick-witted, it had taken Drubbs a long time to figure how this knowledge could best serve him.

Finally he had set out, but being ever cautious, he had

set up for himself an identity as a "Monmouth man," one of those roving Dissenters who roamed the English roads, preaching Dissent to all who would listen. It had given him some good contacts as he crossed England toward the West Country and had led him eventually, in the common room of an inn in Bridgwater, to a man who was ideally suited for the use to which Drubbs wished to put him: For Nick Netherbury was not only a staunch Monmouth supporter, like so many West Countrymen, but he had the virtues of being both extremely gullible and of working for the very Squire of Axeleigh that Drubbs meant to blackmail.

It was Nick who innocently pointed out the Squire, riding by on his way to make a deal on some sheep, and it was an easy thing for Jack Drubbs, unobserved, to slip a blackmail note into the Squire's saddlebag as he bargained near the bridge across the River Parrett for the flock.

The note had dropped like a shot from a catapult upon Axeleigh's squire, who had thought that business of Virginia's dead lover over long ago. But the amount demanded was not large. He was to leave a purse containing ten gold guineas—or an equivalent amount in pounds or florins—on Midsummer's Eve in the rotted hollow of the big fallen oak on the road midway between Axeleigh and Huntlands. That was the price of silence.

The note had been unsigned.

Midsummer's Eve had been chosen with intent, for on that night so many masques were held all over England that a man might wander the roads costumed and masked and little notice be taken of it.

But Drubbs's plan went further. It had occurred to him that anyone who had "murdered" a man and walled up his body might be a difficult subject for blackmail. Such a "victim" might arrive with pistols blazing. So Drubbs again enlisted innocent Nick in his designs.

Some money for the Cause, he told Nick, was to be left in a certain hollow tree; *he* could not pick it up as he had business elsewhere. Would Nick do him this favor and pick up the purse, which he would collect from Nick later? Oh, and one more thing—he'd best wear Drubbs's distinctive green cloak and tall black hat when he did it, for those who left the money might be watching and they'd believe that Drubbs himself had picked it up.

Flattered by the smooth-talking Drubbs and feeling himself a party to Great Events, gullible Nick readily agreed. And Drubbs, unbeknown to Nick, had ridden on ahead, carefully avoiding the hollow tree—for who knew, instead of gold it might contain a bell to give warning or even a poisonous snake—had passed by the tree and settled himself behind a nearby bush to observe events.

They had not been long in coming. Several horsemen had ridden up, dismounted, and hidden their mounts and themselves in the trees. Drubbs, sweating profusely, had been afraid to move. He cursed himself for his foolishness in attempting to blackmail this terrible squire.

Shortly thereafter Nick Netherbury, wearing Drubbs's distinctive green cloak and black hat, had arrived and taken up the purse.

At that point not only had the men leaped from their hiding places but another contingent had thundered down the road, their uniformed leader crying out, "Stop, Jack Drubbs! Stop in the name of the King!"

Nick, in confusion, had leaped to his mount and departed in a hail of bullets.

They had all missed poor Nick—but one had found its mark. A stray bullet had caught Drubbs in the left shoulder and he had staggered out of the bushes after the King's men and Nick had taken their quarrel elsewhere and somehow climbed upon his horse and ridden away. He had stuck it out grimly and made it all the way to his sister's cottage near Richmond before his festered wound laid him low.

And there he had lain, recuperating, for months.

It had taken those months for Drubbs to realize that he had been too brash in his talk of rebellion out there in the West

Country. The West Country was known to be partisan to the Duke of Monmouth, but this was the King's land still. It was not for blackmailing some local squire that he had been sought by a company of armed men—it was for treason. Drubbs had even guessed who had betrayed him to the King's men—that servingmaid at the inn, that Mollie! Ah, he should not have trusted her, boasting that he'd be back that night with gold to buy her a new petticoat! It angered him how she had wormed out of him where he was going. Intoxicated by the pliable female warmth of her body as they dallied through the warm afternoon atop the coverlet of his bed, he had whispered that he would find her a new petticoat in a hollow tree! Mollie had giggled and raked his back delightfully with her plump fingers—and he had told her more. He had told her the location of the hollow tree and how he'd be back that night with enough gold to take her to the fair in Taunton.

Mollie obviously had preferred to attend the fair with somebody else. She had reported Jack Drubbs to the authorities and near got him killed. Trollop! His teeth ground as he thought of her, for he had counted on Mollie being a West Country girl and a supporter of the Duke of Monmouth like the rest of them. Now when it was too late he remembered that as he tasted the wine of her kisses, he'd learnt that she was from Ipswich in Suffolk and had reached the West Country via a lover who'd left her at Bristol and taken ship for the Colonies. Mollie had drifted to Bridgwater. And had only pretended to be a Monmouth supporter to fool him. She'd betrayed him to the King's men and they had ambushed him!

Well, he'd be more careful this time!

Slowly, carefully, he made his plans—for if things went well, he could bleed this West Country squire of funds forever and never have to do another lick of work in his life. Since he'd attracted the attention of the King's men by being a too-enthusiastic Dissenter, he now took the other tack and grew a mustache and a tiny clipped beard and borrowed money from his sister to secure a second-hand puce suit and a disreputable puce-plumed hat that made him look *almost* like a gentleman down on his luck. Using the name "John Hodge," which he thought had a fine steady ring to it, he made his way toward the West Country just as winter was closing down.

To his relief, he found Mollie long since gone, run off with a sailor from Bristol. No one else associated last summer's ranting, sober-garbed Jack Drubbs, whose only truly distinctive features had been his tall black hat and green cloak, with this quiet, plume-hatted gentleman in a once-elegant puce suit, who quirked his little finger when he took his snuff, walked mincingly and spoke in an affected manner. Having secured a room at the Rose and Thistle in Bridgwater, Drubbs—more careful now—managed to make the acquaintance of the married (but flirtatious) daughter of the cook at Axeleigh. Drubbs plied her with ale in the common room, learnt from her own lips that she'd been born and bred in Bridgwater, and then with studied casualness mentioned that he'd heard the gentry at Axeleigh were all opposed to the Duke of Monmouth.

"Not Mistress Constance!" exclaimed the girl, shocked—and then covered her mouth with her hand at what she'd said.

Drubbs chuckled conspiratorially. "Neither am I," he said, and winked. The girl sighed with relief. This gentleman was one of their own—supporters of the Duke! "And neither will the Squire be when he gets a note which was entrusted to me by a friend of his," Drubbs assured her. "Do you think you could slip that note to the Squire for me without his knowing where it came from?"

"I could give it to Mistress Constance," ventured the cook's daughter.

"But she's not to know where it came from—just that it's for the Squire."

Flushed with unaccustomed drink, the cook's daughter bobbed her tow head earnestly. She was delighted to run "John Hodge's" errand for him—especially since he gave her a pair of red garters for doing it! She visited cook at Axeleigh slightly tipsy and laid the note in Constance's own hand and hiccupped that 'twas for the Squire but she'd not say where it came from.

Constance had assumed it was a letter from Margaret dropped off by one of the Squire's messengers, and had scrawled the Squire's name on it before putting it on the hall table. Her mind had been diverted by other things and it was something of a shock to see it delivered by Stebbins at dinner and observe the Squire's morose demeanor as he read it. Could something be wrong in Devon?

After supper, she had sought him out. "I thought the note might be from Margaret. Is she all right?"

Clifford Archer had turned to her with a frown. "No, it was a receipt as I told you. I have not heard from Margaret recently."

Both statements were lies. He could not allow Constance to read Margaret's most recent letter, urging him to betroth the girl to Tony Warburton!

But Constance, although puzzled, accepted his words. After all, it made sense—cook's blowzy daughter had been imbibing ale somewhere and had been entrusted to deliver this receipt. In her befuddlement, she had given the impression that the Squire was not to know where it came from, when actually she'd wanted to keep where she'd been and who she'd been with from cook, who frowned on her daughter's wandering ways!

So Constance reasoned—plausibly and wrongly.

CHAPTER 22

The Twelve Days of Christmas, with all its festivities and merrymaking, had its jovial grip on the Valley of the Axe. It had snowed heavily late Christmas Eve and all of Christmas Day, keeping all but the bravest at home. Axeleigh's squire had decreed that the ladies of the house were not to brave the tempest. Presiding in regal splendor at the head of his holiday-decked table, he had carved up the traditional Christmas goose, stuffed with chestnuts and oysters. And as they ate their steaming plum pudding—feeling as stuffed as Christmas geese themselves—from the servants' hall came the strains of the Christmas carol "Our Joyful'st Feast," popular since Cromwell's time. The Squire's household was loosely run. He only smiled as the cook's cracked voice, dominating the others in song, drifted in through the dining room door exhorting everyone to drown their sorrows in wine and be merry!

Pamela kept wondering aloud all through dinner how things were at Huntlands, but the Squire refused to take the hint.

"I'm sure they're well enough," he told his daughter calmly. "Tom Thornton's a good hand on the reins—for all he has no wife to guide him!" He laughed and quaffed his wine.

A shadow of a frown passed over Pamela's pretty face. *She thought that Tom was probably out on horseback, jogging through the snow right now*—and probably in the direction of Hawley Grange! She sighed.

Constance looked up at the frosted panes. *Another Christmas,* she was thinking, *with sleet scratching at the windowpanes and the wind howling outside.* The weather had turned truly bitter and cold was creeping in around the panes and chilling her ankles—indeed she might have been in Yorkshire, not Somerset! But here, regardless of the weather, there'd be frolics and merriment all during the Twelve Days of Christmas and she'd be expected to join in, no matter how she felt.

Like the planned sleighride to Warwood later this week, picking up other sleighs on the way and making an overnight party of it. . . . She was supposed to go with Ned. How she wished she could bow out of that one!

Not only did the snow fall heavily through the night but it hardened on the ground and its surface was such that when it stopped snowing the day after Christmas, sleds were soon flying about merrily and horses, their ankles carefully wrapped against ice cuts, pulled sleighs tinkling with bells and alive with merrymakers from house to house, fording small frozen streams along the way.

Pamela and Constance spent that day dashing about the country in the Squire's sleigh, with the Squire driving, making hasty calls on the neighbors and bringing with them gifts of big plum cakes and chestnut cookies thickly iced.

The next day found them at home receiving scads of callers, and serving great quantities of wine and accepting with thanks dozens of other plum cakes and baskets of Christmas cookies and other goodies. Everyone remarked on the beauty of Axeleigh's festive decorations and both girls were hard put to avoid the young bucks who kept maneuvering them beneath the mistletoe hung on the hall chandelier. The Squire was a jovial host and had they not had so many other places to go, his guests would have lingered, lounging about Axeleigh's flaming hearth.

Constance was glad to hear the rafters of Axeleigh ring with merriment, glad to be talking first to this one and then to that one. It kept her mind off her inner loneliness and her shame that she found herself turning sharply every time the front door opened to see if Captain Warburton might not be one of the arriving guests.

It was Dev's fault, she thought angrily, when the day was done at last, the festive callers all gone home, a late supper hastily got through and all of Axeleigh gone to bed.

Constance stood huddled in a violet woolen wrapper staring out of her bedroom window at the white and silver world the moonlight had created out of the snowy landscape. Across her line of vision a red fox trotted, leaving dainty little tracks in the snow, and disappeared into a dark line of trees. He was headed toward Warwood, she thought with a pang, and if he made tracks long enough he might even reach there tonight and perhaps find his ladylove. . . .

She brought herself up short and again thought hotly, *This is all Dev's fault! Everything that has happened to me!* For hers was a warm, impulsive nature. She was not made of stone. She could not be expected never to look at another man while she pondered whether her young highwayman husband was alive or dead! If Dev had proved true, she would never have sought out Margaret in Devon, never met Tony Warburton, never fallen in love with him against her will.

If only. . . . But it had all happened and now she was doubly miserable. This was her second Christmas without Dev—one in Devon, one in Somerset. For a wild spiteful moment she wished him dead and then she burst into tears and leaned against the cold windowpane and listened to the little clink of icicles dropping off and tinkling as they fell.

It would have driven her mad to know that in Lincoln Dev was thinking of her. He'd made a rich haul this week—a fat tax collector had dared to use the Great North Road and been lighter in the purse for it—so Dev was in funds. With a girl on each arm, he strode into a "safe" inn where the landlord winked at such as he so long as they paid in yellow gold. Prepared for a wild Christmas season, was Dev.

And then across the room, the tavern maid, with her long dark hair and her willowy body, reminded him suddenly of Constance, and the holiday revelry turned to ashes in his mouth. He rose and told the landlord in a taciturn voice to give the girls all the ale they wanted and then trudged out for a long lonely walk in the snow. After which he proceeded to get very drunk. He woke with a terrible hangover and told himself firmly that one wench was as good as another.

But he couldn't make himself believe it. Constance, he knew, had been different.

Leaning miserably against the windowpanes at Axeleigh, Constance would have been gratified to know it. As it was, she presumed the worst of him and let her hot, reckless thoughts drift toward Tony Warburton.

By the Fourth Day of Christmas, Constance had had time to think over the day she and Pamela had ridden to Hawley Grange and she had made her disconcerting request to become a traveling courier for the group of Monmouth supporters. If she had hoped they would reconsider, she was doomed to disappointment, for although they had held a brief and unsatisfying discussion of her after she had left, they were of one mind when it came to letting her out of their sight.

In truth the group did not trust her. Had she not stumbled upon Galsworthy trying to deliver a message to cook one dusk and discovered from cook—who had stepped on a thorn and could hardly walk—that the message was for Tom Thornton at Huntlands, had Tom not chanced by at almost the same time and Constance, seeing him, dashed out to deliver the message, she would never have carried messages for them at all.

"She appeared the same night the King's men pursued poor Netherbury to his death, the same night that masked woman disappeared,'' Brad Hawley, the only son among all those daughters at Hawley Grange, had objected after Constance had stalked out of the group on Christmas Eve.

"I'll hear no word spoken against Mistress Constance!" Ned Warburton jumped up threateningly.

"Easy, Ned." Beside him Tom Thornton laid a detaining hand on Ned's arm. "Let me handle this. 'Twas only because the Squire wished to introduce his ward to the county at the Midsummer Masque that she was there at all. A coincidence, that's all."

"And then she turns up delivering Galsworthy's message to you. It's too pat, Tom. Too pat indeed."

Tom sighed. Even as he leant forward he was urging Ned back into his seat. "Again that was mere happenstance, Brad. Mistress Constance had come into the kitchen as Galsworthy was delivering the note. The cook at Axeleigh had hurt her foot, Constance offered to take the note—"

"That cook is a blundering fool," grumbled Brad Hawley. "She could get us all killed."

"I agree," said Tom coolly. "And I'd far rather Galsworthy delivered his messages to Mistress Constance than to the cook. Besides, as the Squire's ward and a newcomer to boot, who'd suspect her?"

"I do," said Brad Hawley in a gloomy voice.

Stafford's big head had sunk into his shoulders. Now he straightened up and gave the contenders a hard look. "We've discussed this before," he said. "No use going over plowed ground. It was agreed we'd watch her." Across the room Ned flushed but Stafford's glance silenced him. "We've let her deliver Galsworthy's messages to Tom—but that's all. And that's all it will be unless we've some desperate need of her. We've found no reason to distrust her. In fact, cook reports that every word she's said to the servants reveals her to be an ardent supporter of the Cause. Still we'll take no unnecessary risks. But Hawley here is right to make us consider, for you'll all agree, even though Tom—perhaps rightly—considers it happenstance that Mistress Constance arrived the very night poor Netherbury was killed and a woman disappeared from Huntlands—''

''We had the famous Masked Lady in our midst and had not the wit to realize it,'' protested Tom. ''She left lest they take her.''

Stafford frowned at this interruption. ''And now the Squire's ward grows restless and asks us to support her in some far place. On the road, roaming about in coaches carrying messages. What d'ye think the Squire would say to that, Tom?''

Tom shrugged. ''I doubt she gave much thought to what the Squire would think about it. She hasn't thought it through. Once she has, she'll realize her folly and abandon the idea herself.''

''I'll vouch for her!'' cried Ned in fury.

''We don't need advice from the love-besotted!'' muttered Hawley.

''That you vouch for her is not the problem, Ned.'' Stafford waved Hawley to silence and turned his attention now in Ned Warburton's direction. ''The problem, Ned, is whether we can trust her. We're all of us risking our necks in this thing, and with the King's men roaming about the countryside we can't afford to take chances.'' He brought his hand down hard upon his thigh. ''We'll table the matter of Mistress Constance,'' he said harshly. ''It can be brought up again if new information surfaces.''

The subject of all this discussion would have been indignant to discover that they did not trust her. For was she not risking her neck like the rest, receiving Galsworthy's messages and passing them on to Tom? Who knew, the King's men might be following Galsworthy any day and catch her in their net?

But it was not a danger she gave much thought to. The emotional turmoil into which she had spun at Axeleigh occupied her thoughts far more.

Now on this Fourth Day of Christmas she was standing by the window in Pamela's bedchamber, watching occasional light snowflakes drift lazily down. Behind her Pamela, dressed in tailored indigo blue wool for the outdoors, was letting Dick Peacham, who had arrived all the way from Taunton by sleigh, cool his heels downstairs while she burrowed through her belongings in an attempt to find a favorite fan (for it was fashionable to carry fans even in winter!). As usual she was talking a blue streak. She was reminiscing as she tossed things about helter-skelter.

"That was a terrible summer for us here," Pamela recalled, her voice slightly muffled by a large gray veil which she had unearthed and which her energetic rummaging had caused to float up, almost covering her mouth.

"Was it?" murmured Constance. She was worlds away, her thoughts flying down the highroad with a wild young highwayman.

"Yes." Pamela pushed aside the veil and with it a couple of pinners. "Oh, dear, I don't seem to be able to find *anything*! Yes—first Mother died and then before Father got over the shock of *that*, Aunt Margaret died in Bath."

"What was she doing in Bath?" asked Constance idly, wondering if the rider she could see at the far end of the driveway could be Tom. If so, Dick Peacham would find himself left out in the cold!

"Well, to tell you the truth"—Pamela began scattering gloves and laces and whisks about the floor as she rummaged—"I don't think she wanted to wear mourning for my mother. They didn't like each other very much and I remember Aunt Margaret left the house wearing an orange dress."

How like Margaret! thought Constance. *Displaying her disapproval for all the world to see!*

"That must have annoyed your father," she said.

"Oh, he said he was used to Margaret's 'ways' and expected no better," said Pamela ruefully. "Where *is* that fan?"

"Perhaps it's in that chest over there?" suggested Constance.

"Yes, you might be right." Pamela scrambled up, strewing collars and tie-on sleeves and striped clocked stockings as she went. "Anyway, Father went around looking like a ghost. I was only ten at the time and at first he wasn't going to take me with him, but then he did. . . .''

"Take you where?" asked Constance absently, watching the snowflakes fall.

"To Aunt Margaret's funeral—oh, here's my fan! Imagine finding it stuffed in among these gloves! Now if I can just find my fur muff!''

"You went to Bath for the funeral? But I thought—"

"Oh, no, they brought her body back here—all that way. I remember the closed coffin—that was because she was so beautiful and her dying words, Father said, were to keep the lid shut and let people remember her as she had been in all her beauty.''

Constance's eyes smarted. She closed them for a moment and then opened them again. The snow was still falling. "Is that how it was?" she asked softly.

"Yes." Pamela's head was ducked down and she was rummaging again. "Everybody was crying and Captain Warburton was just *ashen* at the funeral and everybody expected him to kill himself with drink, but he didn't. He got married instead *right away* and you should have seen my father's face when he heard about that! He turned pale and just sort of rocked on his feet and then he shut himself in his study and I could hear him crying. Imagine! He didn't cry when Aunt Margaret died but he cried when Captain Warburton married another girl after she died! I could never understand it.''

Constance could.

"*Everything* went wrong that summer," sighed Pamela. "Oh, here's my muff!" She twirled it. "That summer my favorite colt died, and Tom nearly drowned when he fell into the river and his coat caught on a floating tree branch—he was showing off for me at the time, and people were afraid Father had brought the smallpox back with him from Bath and nobody came to visit us that whole summer.''

"Except Tom," supplied Constance, who had by now decided the rider was someone else. His head looked unduly large. Why, it was that fellow they'd met outside Hawley Grange—Chesney Pell.

"Except Tom, of course." Pamela looked proud and flirted her fan, dimpling. "Tom wouldn't let the threat of smallpox keep *him* away." Puss came into the room swishing his tail and suddenly her mercurial spirits changed. "Do you think I could train Puss to eat at table?" she demanded. "Margie Hamilton told me about a cat in Brighton that sits at table and eats *every* course—even bits of sallet!"

Constance joined in her merry peal of laughter, but her own laugh was strained. She was thinking of Margaret, with her scarred face and her memories, out there on the lonely moors. . . . She turned away from the window. "You're keeping Dick Peacham waiting an unconscionably long time," she reminded Pamela.

"Oh, he'll wait," said Pamela airily. "Who is that riding down the drive?" She craned her neck to see.

"Chesney Pell. You can recognize him by his periwig!"

"Oh, then you'd better take off that wrapper and dress to receive callers! For he's surely come to see you—I saw the way he looked at you at Hawley Grange!" Pamela was off on a merry peal of laughter, almost tripping over Puss, who leaped to safety upon the bed.

Constance was dressing in leisurely fashion when Tabby came running upstairs to tell her she had a gentleman caller, a Mr. Pell. By now it had occurred to Constance that Pell might have something to tell her concerning the Cause. At least she could talk to him about it.

Quiet and composed, she went downstairs, moving easily in her plum velvet gown with its big puffed sleeves caught up by amethyst satin ribands. She floated into the drawing room. Chesney Pell scrambled to his feet as she entered and almost lost his periwig to the depth of his bow. Behind him through the window she could see a playful Pamela overwhelming Dick Peacham with a flurry of snowballs.

"Mistress Constance!" Chesney straightened up and his cherubic face broke into a wide smile, for she was even lovelier than he remembered. "Oh, it *is* good of you to let me call upon you like this!"

Constance acknowledged his greeting coolly. She saw that Pamela on her way out had already seen to their guest, for he had set down a wineglass as she entered. "I thought perhaps you might have some message for me from the group?"

"Ah—no. I am afraid they did not reconsider." Chesney leant forward, caught by the spell of her femininity. "Had *I* had the arranging of it, Mistress Constance, you should have had your wish!"

"But when you had the opportunity, you did not vote for it," she reminded him grimly.

"Ah, but that was because I am new to this group and could not be so bold as to vote one way or the other. But we've a group in Lyme Regis on the South coast that could use you as a courier, were you there! I've great influence with *them*!" He tried to look important and only managed to look beatific.

"I'm sure that would be nice," sighed Constance. For she knew that to attempt such a thing would be out of the question. Tom and these other lads who knew the Squire might be able to hoodwink him into letting her go, but never a stranger.

"Lyme Regis," she murmured. "That's on the Channel, isn't it?"

"The English Channel." He bobbed his head and beamed at her.

"I thought you were visiting Cart Rawlings in Bridgwater. Isn't he with you?"

"No, Cart stopped off at Hawley Grange, but he gave me the sleigh and bade me Godspeed!"

And so he had come calling. She sighed inwardly, and invited him to tell her about life at Oxford. She smiled sympathetically and let her thoughts wander while Chesney Pell told her more than she wished to know about life in the great university town where he was a student.

" . . . and the Great Tom Bell tolls every night precisely at—" he was saying when there was the sound of a door opening, a slight scuffle in the hall, a sharp "Absolutely no!" from Pamela and the sound of a slap.

Chesney Pell broke off. He looked alarmed and started to rise but Constance waved him back to his seat. She managed to control her mirth when Pamela and Dick Peacham burst into the room, their color rather high and Dick rubbing his cheek ruefully. Pamela's crystal blue eyes were snapping as she pulled off her gloves, and her glance at Constance told her that Peacham had taken liberties and been brought to heel for it!

"Ned is here," she told Constance crisply. "We came in to tell you he's riding down the drive." She cast a speculative look at Pell.

Ned here again to prod her about marriage! Constance sat up straighter. Well, she would show Ned how little interested she was in his suit for her hand! When Ned came through the door she was fairly hanging on Chesney Pell's words and he was so flattered that his thin voice was turning falsetto and trembling as he spoke. He gazed at her adoringly, enraptured by all this sudden interest.

Pamela watched, bright-eyed, as Ned surveyed the two of them with a frown. Barely hiding her amusement, she led Peacham back outside.

"Mistress Constance." Ned bowed crisply.

"Oh—Ned." Constance acknowledged his presence languidly. "Chesney here has just been telling me the most *fascinating* things about Oxford. Oh, do go on, Chesney. Ned will want to hear too."

Overjoyed both by the way she leant eagerly toward him and by her sudden surprising use of his given name, Chesney Pell waxed voluble on the subject of Oxford, and hardly stopped talking until a frowning Ned, fidgeting as he sat there watching, finally rose, bowed to Constance, and took himself off.

"Why, where is he going?" wondered Chesney, surprised.

"Warwood, undoubtedly," said Constance in a cold carrying voice. "The Warburtons, I'm told, go out in any weather."

Ned's shoulders jerked slightly. He turned in the doorway. "I'll be back tomorrow to take you in my sleigh to Warwood, Constance," he said, reminding her of the planned sleighing party.

Constance's vague indifferent smile passed over him and settled again on Chesney. Ned could not tell whether she had heard him or not. His lips compressed into a straight line and they heard the front door close rather hard as he left.

"Well, I must be leaving too, I suppose," said Chesney. He peered at the window. "It's snowing harder now." He gave her a hopeful look.

Doubtless he was angling for an invitation to stay the night! "Yes, it *is* beginning to snow harder," said Constance, looking critically at the few flakes dusting down. Now that Ned had left, her sudden interest in her periwigged guest had evaporated. "You had best get started—you wouldn't want to miss the entrance to Hawley Grange again!"

Chesney rose obediently. Constance guessed he was used to taking orders from women. It did nothing to recommend him to her.

As he opened the door to depart, Pamela almost fell through it and began brushing snow from her red cloak. "I was walking under a branch and suddenly this great pile of snow fell down my neck," she gasped. "I left Dick admiring the maze. Good-by, Chesney—oh, Constance, do get it out! It's freezing my back!"

Hastily Constance shut the door on Chesney's eager "I'll be back tomorrow to take you on the sleighride!" and while Pamela shook out her cloak, she dug the snow from her shivering friend's collar.

"You can't go in Chesney's sleigh," Pamela told Constance, giving a little screech as melted snow ran down her back. "You're going with Ned, remember?"

"I am trying to show Ned that I do not love him," said Constance calmly. "And if seeming to be interested in Chesney Pell can do that—"

"I doubt that will hold Ned back!"

"No," said Constance through her teeth, for it had been very tiresome playing up to Chesney. "For Ned tells me the Warburtons are a determined lot! I don't see how you can *abide* Peacham," she added.

Pamela shrugged. "Oh, he's a trifle pompous perhaps, but"—her crystal blue eyes sparkled—"an awfully good object lesson for Tom, don't you think? Hearing how Dick Peacham dogs my footsteps?"

"You're playing with fire," warned Constance. "Tom may surprise you!"

But it was the Squire who would have surprised them both had they known that he was now measuring up every male caller at Axeleigh as potential husbands for his daughter or his ward—even Peacham and Pell!

CHAPTER 23

Since receiving the blackmail note that had jolted him from his calm sense of security, Clifford Archer had had time to think. The sum demanded was not so large, but it angered him to pay a blackmailer. He was half tempted to ride out and meet the fellow with pistols blazing. Still . . . there was his daughter to think about. And Constance. Pamela did not deserve to have it flung at her that her father was a murderer, and even though indeed he was not, how could he ever prove it? The only eyewitness, his faithless wife, Virginia, was no longer alive—and was not the telltale body buried in his cellar? Hardly the action of an innocent man, a court would say! That he had only been trying to protect his womenfolk would be doubted.

He was in real trouble and he could see no way out of it. He could pay the blackmailer this time, but there would be another time, and another. And he knew his temper—eventually he would be driven to remove the blackmailer from the face of the earth. He would become what he was not now—a murderer.

These dark thoughts had plagued him through the night and were still with him the next day as he stood pensively by an upstairs window thinking. If only the girls were settled. . . .

Peacham was even now strolling through the snowy maze with Pamela. The Squire could occasionally see the scarlet plumes of Peacham's hat rising above a low place in the maze.

Ned had gone flinging out and now there was Chesney leaving. The Squire, who had assumed that Constance harbored a secret fancy for Ned, but was too "missish" to say so, had regarded Chesney Pell thoughtfully.

Pell was eligible enough, of course. Cart Rawlings's father had told him that Pell, who had come home from Oxford with his son Cart for the Christmas holidays, was the son of a wealthy linen draper in Lyme Regis, who would come into money as soon as his widowed mother let go of the apron strings. At the same time the elder Rawlings had bewailed his own son's refusal to go back to Oxford. Love, it seemed, had the boy by the throat. He feared to leave lest Melissa Hawley be bespoken by somebody else!

The Squire had given his friend back a placid look. To have Cart Rawlings ardently courting Melissa Hawley suited him perfectly, since he'd always had an eye on Tom for Pamela and Tom had been spending too much time at Hawley Grange of late.

What Pamela saw in Peacham the Squire could not imagine. He would never understand women, he realized grimly. He had not understood his young wife and although he had thought he understood Pamela, believing her to be anxiously waiting for Tom Thornton to settle down and ask for her, now—after her calm assertion in Tom's presence that she might accept Peacham—he was not so sure that he would ever understand her or any other woman. In any event he had asked Dick Peacham to spend the night, and Peacham had accepted with alacrity.

Below him now Pamela and Dick Peacham were just strolling out of the maze, Pamela in her indigo wool with her red cloak flying in the wind, and young Peacham in his fashionable scarlet cloak enriched with gold braid hovering over her. The Squire had never seen cuffs so wide, nor quite so many gold buttons. He snorted. A popinjay the lad was—his tomboyish daughter would surely never choose a fellow who thought more of the cut of his trousers than how neatly they would swing over a saddle!

His mind came to a full stop. Down there in the snow a remarkable thing was happening. Pamela, who had seemed to give a swift covert glance in a direction past the Squire's line of vision, through the trees, had suddenly lifted her head. Archly. Smiling lips parted in a gesture of invitation. Her red woolen hood had fallen back and her golden curls spilled out fetchingly, and Peacham, apparently driven mad at the sight, had seized her *and was kissing her*! The Squire held his breath, waiting for Pamela to wriggle free and give Peacham such a slap as would rock his teeth. He had seen her in action before! To his utter astonishment, Pamela seemed to be wriggling closer and her arms had stolen up around Peacham's neck. Unbelievable! The Squire passed a hand before his eyes to clear them and turned away, telling himself sternly he would not spy on lovers.

He was not to know that Pamela had spied out of the corner of her eye Tom Thornton strolling down the snowy drive, walking his horse which was limping badly. Guessing that he would not know she had glimpsed him, she had recklessly invited Dick Peacham to kiss her *and kiss her he had*! His ardent lips had done their best to ravage her mouth, but even as her body stiffened in rejection, she had been mindful to let her arms slip around his neck, *for Tom was watching*. She was going to pay him back for thinking that Dick Peacham had come to call on Constance! Let Tom see plainly that Dick was here to court *her*!

As she pulled away, she had a strong desire to slap

Peacham, for he had attempted to take liberties with his tongue, probing hungrily at her suddenly closed mouth.

"You assume too much!" she muttered, and then suddenly seeming to become aware of Tom's presence—for indeed he stood at gaze, watching them from the driveway—she ducked her head as if in sudden embarrassment and jumped quickly away from Dick Peacham. "We're being observed, Dick," she cried merrily and, seizing him by the hand, began to thread her way across the snow toward Tom. "What brings you here, Tom?" she hailed him.

"A lame horse," replied Tom, who looked like a golden Viking in a suit the color of his saddle, and a serviceable cloak. "Didn't want to walk Satan all the way back to Huntlands on that leg, thought to rest him in your stable for a couple of days. Well, Dick, I see you're back again," he added in a bluff voice.

Dick Peacham acknowledged Tom's greeting irritably. He was confused over Pamela's response. First she had seemed to invite his kiss, then she struggled under it even while her arms wrapped round his neck, then she pulled away and bluntly told him he assumed too much! And now here was this cursed Thornton fellow again! He always seemed to be underfoot and it was hard enough to get Pamela alone without these constant neighborly visits from Thornton!

"Of course, we'll be glad to welcome Satan to our stable," said Pamela warmly, for she was almost as fond of Tom's big black stallion as she was of Angel, her own dainty mare. "Come, we'll walk you to the stable, won't we, Dick?"

Dick looked glumly at Tom. Was he never to be free of Thornton to pursue his courtship? he wondered.

A few minutes later the Squire saw Captain Warburton ride up the drive. He was surprised to see him, so soon after Ned's abrupt departure. A groom promptly appeared to take the big charcoal stallion with the white star on his forehead away to the stables—for the Squire had instructed them that in this rush of suitors coming and going, they'd best keep an eye on the driveway from dawn to dusk—and the Squire soon heard the Captain's spurs ring on the stone flooring of the hall below. An affectation, those spurs, he thought, smiling, as he went down to greet his guest, for Tony never used them. Cinder, his big stallion, he treated with affection, and the horse was so well trained to his hand that a mere nudge of the knee would send him into a gallop, a muttered word from the Captain and Cinder would gallantly take any fence!

Captain Warburton cast a quick look around the hall as he entered. For although he might tell himself that he had come here again on behalf of Ned, he knew in his heart that he had come here in hopes of seeing Constance again, of hearing the raw silk rustle of her voice that dragged across his emotions like a warm bedsheet carrying him back to other days, other times, when his world had stretched out bright before him.

There was no sign of Constance in the hall, nor did her silken skirts appear, even though the Captain spoke in a hearty carrying voice to Stebbins, who let him in and took his cloak.

"Tony!" The Squire reached the foot of the stairway and strode forward to greet him. "Ye'll sup with us, of course?"

"I'd be happy to, Clifford." Captain Warburton smiled at his old friend.

"And stay the night as well, I hope?"

The Captain hesitated. It was tempting to spend a night under the same roof as Constance, to know that she was there perhaps just on the other side of a wall, that her silky feminine skirts might swish down the hall past his door. "I may take you up on that, Clifford, for it looks to snow in earnest."

"Good," said the Squire heartily, escorting his friend into the drawing room and reaching for a bottle of port. "Pamela will have a room readied for you when she comes in. She's out by the maze leading young Peacham a chase. It seems she fancies him."

"Oh?" Captain Warburton's straight dark brows elevated as he accepted a goblet of the rich red wine. "I'd thought it was Thornton she fancied."

355

Clifford Archer sighed. "So did I, but it seems I'm often mistaken in these matters. Though what she sees in young Peacham, I wouldn't be knowing."

She sees in him a title and a chance to live in Taunton and walk on cobblestones, away from the mud and quagmires of the country, thought Tony Warburton cynically. *He had seen it on the Continent, many a time. A pretty girl, besieged by suitors, suddenly accepting the most distant one—just to get away from her own surroundings!* He didn't tell his friend that, of course. "I hear he's a head for business," he said hopefully—indeed it was the only good thing he could think of about young Peacham.

"Yes, that's in his favor," agreed the Squire gloomily. He lifted his head and fixed the Captain with an unsmiling glance, for when he had heard the determined clatter of Tony Warburton's boots in the hall just now, he had come of a sudden to a decision. One he would not be swayed from, he told himself.

"I've thought about your offer, Tony," he said frankly.

"Oh, you mean Ned's offer?" The Captain toyed with his goblet, half afraid of what was coming.

"Don't quibble, Tony." Impatiently. "I mean, of course, Ned's offer for Constance."

"Yes?" asked the Captain softly. His gray eyes were very steady, studying his wine.

"I've decided you were right. 'Tis time she stops all this missishness and settles down. Ned shall have her!" *And then even if I lose my temper and kill this blackmailer, she'll have found safe harbor.*

The gray eyes continued steady. Captain Warburton had taken blows before. "Ned will be overjoyed," he said pleasantly, and took another sip of wine. He shot a look at Clifford. "Have you told her yet?"

The Squire shook his head. "Not yet, but as my ward she'll do as I say."

"But if she doesn't know . . ." demurred the Captain.

" 'Twill all be settled by Twelfth Night, I promise you. I give you my word on it, Tony. You may consider it done."

They shook hands upon it and Captain Warburton, draining another glass, told himself it was what he wanted: happiness—for Ned and Constance. But the wine that had gone down so smoothly a moment before had now a bitter taste and he cursed himself for having advanced his brother's suit and not his own.

He could speak up, of course. He could say, *I've been thinking over what you said to me, Clifford, that you wished I'd ask for the girl myself. I've decided to do it.*

He could do it, Ned be damned. *No, he could not.* All his life the boy had looked up to him, idolized him. And Ned's affections were locked in as firmly as his own, the Captain thought grimly. He could not break the boy's heart.

"I'll honor my promise on Warwood," he heard himself say. "Ned shall have Warwood when I die. I'll write it down for you."

"I know you will, Tony." The Squire inclined his head. "No need to write anything down, your word is good enough. And besides," he added on a jovial note, "they'll both be living at Warwood to remind you!"

That brought the Captain up short. *Living at Warwood . . . Constance would be living at Warwood.* Every day he would see her, every day he would want her. Her beauty would tear at him, he would feel cursed by it as he yearned to tear her from Ned's arms.

"They'll have the place to themselves most of the time," he heard himself say. "For I don't doubt I'll be away to the wars soon enough."

"No need to die on some foreign field, Tony," the Squire told him bluntly. "From things I'm hearing, blood may run in the West Country when Charles dies and James comes to the throne."

Captain Warburton shrugged his broad shoulders. At the moment politics and the death of kings or their successors could not move him. His mind was fixed on a certain pair of haunting violet eyes, a certain winsome smile. "Charles may survive us both, Clifford," he said pensively.

"Aye, there's that possibility," agreed the Squire. "But if he does not . . ."

"If he does not, we'll meet it then." His guest could be equally blunt.

The Captain downed the rest of his wine without tasting it and silently held out his goblet to be refilled. "Yes," he repeated. "Ned will be overjoyed." He turned as Constance came into the room.

"Oh, I didn't know you had company," she said in confusion. She swept the tall Captain a deep curtsy.

The Squire flashed his friend a warning look that said he and he alone must break the news to Constance. If he noticed that Constance had gone rather pale, he put it down to a very natural excitement over what must be the Captain's mission here—to arrange a match between her and Ned.

"Mistress Constance, you look lovely today." Captain Warburton made a graceful leg to the lady. "But then you always do. . . ."

A slight flush spread over Constance's pale cheeks. Her eyes were deep and dark, violet, velvety. She felt pinned by that steady gray gaze. Oh, what was he thinking behind that calm mask of a face? Could he see through her to her wildly beating heart? Could he guess how the blood was rushing to her head, making her dizzy at the very sight of him?

She turned to the Squire. "I came down to see you, sir," she began—and of a sudden realized that she had forgotten entirely why she had come. Inspiration seized her—a way to strike back at the calm pressure of that gaze that made her feel as if her head might melt. "I wondered if Chesney Pell might spend the night with us," she said, lifting her chin at Captain Warburton. "After all, it's snowing, he is a stranger and does not know the roads hereabout. Indeed he missed the entrance to Hawley Grange the other day."

"Any man who can miss the entrance to Hawley Grange

should certainly not be out on the roads," murmured the Captain ironically.

Constance flung him an irritable look. "And I am sure Cart Rawlings would welcome the opportunity to spend the night at Hawley Grange—which he will assuredly do if Chesney does not return with the sleigh!"

"I thought Pell left some time ago," protested the Squire.

"I think I can still catch him." Constance flashed a smile of disarming sweetness at Tony Warburton.

There was something going on between these two, thought the Squire uneasily. *Some sharpening of swords.* "Pell is more than welcome to stay," he assured Constance.

Constance knew there was no chance of catching Chesney Pell—indeed she did not even intend to try. She was simply pointing out her preference for Chesney over Ned, whom she had *not* asked to stay, to Tony Warburton. "I take it we are to have another guest for dinner?" She cast an inquiring look at the Captain.

The Squire nodded. "And to spend the night as well," And as his tall guest, who had taken Constance's words to heart, started to demur, "Come now, Tony, if you're to lead a pack of sleighs to Warwood tomorrow, ye may as well start from here. 'Twill save ye a long tiresome ride. Besides Ned can marshal the servants and take care of the readying up for your party tomorrow night. It will be good practice for him."

The Captain shrugged and gave Constance a sardonic look. "I see I am overpowered," he murmured.

Constance frowned at him. "I must try to catch Chesney!" she said and hurried out.

Both men watched her swaying progress into the hall. But only one of them felt her light slippers had walked across his heart and left footprints there. . . .

Supper that night was agonizing for Constance, who felt the Captain's light gaze upon her all through the meal—felt it as if his fingers were delicately touching her face, caressing her slender throat, trailing fierily down across her bosom. She answered in monosyllables and poured out her heart in song after supper, leaning against the delicate rosewood harpsichord and letting her dusky voice wail out all the sorrows of the world.

The room was silent for a few moments after her song had ended, for there were tears in her own eyes and every note had gone right through her audience. Those notes had torn Tony Warburton's heart asunder and it was all he could do to keep from advancing upon the girl in purple velvet, seize her around her supple waist, pull out his sword and, daring anyone to stop him, carry her away!

Suffering, he watched as Constance sighed deeply and acknowledged their tribute with a small curtsy.

Pamela, excruciatingly attired in mountains of rose pink taffeta that totally disguised her lovely figure, her golden curls bouncing as she brought her fingers down upon the ivory keyboard in a last chord, studied Constance with perplexity. She should be happy, for Captain Warburton was here—and had not once taken his eyes from her lovely face! It was difficult to understand Constance, she thought. Here was a complex nature.

For herself the whole day had been irritating—save for that one moment of triumph when she had seen shock in Tom Thornton's eyes when he had caught her kissing Dick Peacham. Still brimming with malice, she had managed to seem to lean languorously against Dick in the big warm stables after Tom had brought the limping stallion in. But Tom had seemed not to notice, all his attention was fixed upon the horse. Grooms had leaped forward but he had insisted on tending Satan's injured leg himself, testing it carefully, bathing it, rubbing it with unguents. Pamela would have done as much for Angel had she hurt *her* leg, but somehow to be so totally ignored infuriated her. Normally she would have knelt down to assist Tom, but now she did not, instead she engaged Dick Peacham in a barrage of bright conversation, hardly giving him time to answer her sallies—and leaning so close to him that she could see his cheeks begin to redden.

Dick's arm had begun to steal around her when Tom suddenly looked up.

"I'll just borrow a horse if I may and be on my way," he said, a trifle grimly, observing Pamela to be almost in Peacham's arms again. "I'll be over tomorrow to see how Satan fares."

"Oh, Satan can stay here as long as he likes," said Pamela blithely. *For that would mean that Tom, who was so fond of the big black beast, would be over every day to see him!* It annoyed her that Tom should be leaving so fast. "Won't you stay to supper?" she asked. "You could ride back by moonlight."

Tom was well aware that he could ride back by moonlight. Faith, he did not need moonlight, he could find his way to Huntlands in the dark! But he was damned if he was going to watch Pamela flirt in the sunlight and continue flirting by candlelight with that fool of a Peacham. It would be a miracle if the fellow didn't trip over his own feet, getting back to the house! He rose lithely to his feet and gave Pamela a grim look.

"Thanks, but I've things to do." He swung up on the saddled brown horse that a groom had just fetched and rode away with a curt bow.

Pamela's lovely white teeth ground slightly.

"Why don't we go back to the house?" she suggested, pulling abruptly away from Peacham.

Dick Peacham blinked. All the way to the house she kept her distance. From having been almost leaning against him in the stable, she now jumped away if her skirts so much as grazed his boots!

Women, he thought gloomily, *were a fickle lot. From moment to moment you never knew how you stood with them!*

His depression persisted all through dinner as Pamela neglected him while she chatted with anyone else who would listen. The Squire put Peacham's sulky demeanor down to the desperate yearning of a youth to consummate what he had already started. His daughter certainly seemed happy enough, laughing gaily and a shade too loud and on occasion flirting unmercifully with Peacham, who would rouse himself for a second and then sink back, telling himself that she was waxing hot only so she could wax cold again!

Watching, the Squire felt regretfully certain that his daughter fancied the fellow—especially when he saw her seize Peacham's hand to hold him back as they went into the drawing room. Pamela was but trying to give Constance a chance to walk in beside Captain Warburton because she sensed how matters stood between them, but the Squire did not know that and assigned another reason to his daughter's behavior.

And after Constance had poured out her heart in song and brought tears to eyes that were unaccustomed to tears, Pamela promptly leaped up from the stool before the harpsichord and sought out Peacham, bringing him over to her father and engaging him in bright conversation. This too was to give Constance, at the end of her heartbreaking song, a chance to have a few words in private with Captain Warburton, but the Squire took it as an indication that his daughter wished him to get to know Peacham better, and earnestly endeavored to sound the lad out.

Still caught by the spell of Constance's heartrending song, Tony Warburton spirited her into the hall on the pretext of asking her if one of the family portraits had not really been painted against a backdrop of the old ash trees at Warwood and not here among the oaks of Axeleigh. It was a discussion they had been having desultorily all through dinner, the Captain maintaining that the artist must have been staying at Warwood and had his subject come to him, the Squire good-naturedly insisting that no such thing had happened, the artist had come to Axeleigh and painted everyone there while he was in residence and then moved on.

"Of course, you could both be right, you know," mused Constance, looking up at the great gilt-framed portrait in the hall. "The artist could have seen the trees at Warwood and remembered them—and painted them from memory into this portrait." She was uncomfortably aware of the Captain's tall presence as he crowded beside her, viewing the portrait near the stairs.

"I think you may have the answer," his rich voice answered her. "And since 'tis Christmas, a kiss beneath the mistletoe!"

Abruptly his long arm shot out, encircled her velvet waist, and even as she drew back, swooped her irresistibly beneath the mistletoe that hung suspended from the hall's central chandelier. She flung back her head to protest but before she could speak she was in his arms, his whipcord-lean body was crushing her soft breasts and hips, his mouth was feverishly exploring her startled parted lips.

And Constance—woman of tinder that she was—found it all too much. She melted against him with a sobbing breath and let her warm yielding lips and her lissome body in its sinuous velvet express all that was in her heart. It was a long, long kiss and Constance was almost swooning when the Captain let her go.

Margaret, was her first stabbing thought as she fell dizzily away from him. *Oh, Margaret, I have betrayed you!*

He was standing before her now, the tall Captain. He was looking intently down into her face and studying her.

"Constance," he murmured gravely. "What are we to do? About us?"

I dare not love him, she thought over the triphammer beating of her heart. *It would kill Margaret. And anyway, he was false to Margaret—he would be false to me too!*

And now that he was at arm's length, now that his compelling presence was not so breathlessly close that she trembled, now that the pressure of his demanding lips no longer stopped her heart, Constance knew what to do. She had thought about it so long that her reaction was automatic—and immediate.

"Do?" she demanded on a note of contempt. "About a kiss beneath the mistletoe?" Her face was pale but somehow she kept it calm, betraying no sign of the raging turmoil within her. "Why, you know what we are to do, Captain Warburton! We are to forget this ever happened!"

"Yes," he said pensively, thinking of Ned. "For a moment there I had forgot. . . ."

"Indeed you had," she told him sharply and swept on past him into the drawing room, leaving just a hint of the scent of violets behind her. The Squire had not even noticed her departure.

Tony Warburton stood staring after her departing form hungrily with a kind of desperation beading droplets of perspiration upon his forehead, although the hall was cold. She was right, of course, he told himself dully. He had indeed forgotten something when he had taken Ned's intended into his arms. *He had forgot his honor.*

He would not do so again.

Quietly he followed Constance in and joined the company around the fire. But he was very silent through the remainder of the evening.

"Well," Pamela asked brightly, when they were at last upstairs and she had dragged Constance into her bedchamber where Tabitha was helping her out of the elaborate rose pink taffeta creation with which she had stunned everyone at dinner. "What happened? I saw you go into the hall with Captain Warburton! Did he kiss you under the mistletoe?"

"Nothing happened," said Constance in a dull voice. She felt as if her life had ended.

"You mean he didn't declare himself? Oh, do get out from underfoot, Puss," she cried at the cat. "I almost stepped on your paw! Tabby, what's wrong with that hook? Why won't it come undone?"

Tabitha's fingers fluttered back to the hook. They had been stilled for a moment at Pamela's words, for she was very interested in all the affairs of the manor and particularly Constance's and Pamela's involvements of the heart!

"Of course he did not declare himself!" cried Constance. "How can you suggest that he would? Good night!" She stormed out of the bedchamber, afraid that if she stayed she would burst into tears.

And Pamela, still half-hooked and trying not to crush

Puss's paws as she moved, turned to look in amazement at Tabby. "Whatever do you think brought that on?" she wondered. "She sounded so furious!"

"She's in love," said Tabby indifferently. "People act like that when they're in love—demented, sort of." She gave her young mistress a wicked smile, for she too, from one of the windows, had been witness to the charade that Pamela had played out today for Tom's benefit. "She's not the only one who's in love," she added slyly.

"No, of course she isn't," mused Pamela, taking that to mean not herself but the tall Captain. "There's Captain Warburton to consider too. . . ."

Tabby barely managed to control a snort. "Get out of the way, Puss," she said, nudging the cat aside with her foot as she pulled Pamela's rustling gown over her head. "Or else you'll have to fight your way out of ten yards of taffety!"

The cat, handsomely displaying the black furry backs of his striped legs, beat a hasty retreat and with a spring plumped himself into the middle of the big feather bed.

Where they'd all like to be! thought Tabby derisively. *Only they won't admit who with!*

The Cheddar Gorge, Somerset,
The Fifth Day of Christmas 1684

CHAPTER 24

The young crowd who arrived at Axeleigh next day for the sleighride to Warwood thought the Squire looked excessively grim. Indeed he had not slept much the night before. He had left the blackmail money in the same hollow tree as before and sincerely hoped that it would be the last he'd ever hear of the blackmailer. A future spent filling hollow trees with gold coins did not appear very inviting. Neither did the prospect of having Dick Peacham for a son-in-law.

In fact, of all the suitors for either Pamela's or Constance's hand, he liked Pell and Peacham least. They would both, he thought unhappily, prove themselves inept in time of crisis— and before the morning was out Chesney at least had proved his point.

It seemed at first glance that half the young people of the county had descended on Axeleigh for the sleighing party— and more sleighs would be picked up on the way. Bells tinkled and horses blew clouds of steam into the cold air and there were happy shrieks as flannel-or fur-cloaked girls waved muffs at one another and tried to keep their hair tucked into fur-trimmed hoods or their wide-brimmed plumed hats from blowing off across the snow.

Ned Warburton had arrived in a small sleigh, a two-seater, expecting Constance to go with him, but she gave him a wave and a bright smile and quickly slipped in beside Chesney, whose pleased expression puffed out his red cheeks until he looked for all the world like Santa Claus—junior grade.

Tony Warburton, a striking figure in black and gold with his dark cloak streaming out behind him in the wind, had elected not to man a sleigh, but to lead the way on Cinder, his big charcoal stallion. He had done this in order to give Ned a better chance with Constance, and he frowned as he saw Ned's face darken at this slight. Ned gave his sleigh a vicious turn and promptly invited Margie Hamilton to ride with him. Delighted to be noticed by so dashing a young buck as Ned Warburton, Margie promptly leaped in beside him with a flurry of saffron wool skirts.

Cart Rawlings had Melissa in tow, in a two-seater he had borrowed from the Hawleys. Tom squired a triumphant Pamela for the occasion. And half a dozen other sleighs, some with four horses to draw them and carrying as many as six or eight merrymakers, glided on greased metal runners through the gates of Axeleigh and were off on the long tinkling ride to Warwood, where they would spend the night.

Almost at once a fallen tree circumvented them. Its massive bulk blocked the road and after a hurried conference it was decided not to waste time trying to move it, but to take a detour down a country lane which would lead them to the main road again.

Once again they were foiled. Another tree had fallen across the lane and resisted all efforts to remove it. Now the only way around was by a path hardly wide enough for the sleighs beneath low-lying branches that whipped unpleasantly into the passengers' faces, causing them to duck or be frosted with snow as they passed under.

"Bad planning," Chesney assured Constance loftily. He

gazed sourly at the broad back of Captain Warburton whose big stallion was breaking trail just ahead, for with the various turnabouts they had made due to the blocked roads they were now the lead sleigh. "Captain Warburton should have checked the roads before he invited us to Warwood!"

Constance was nettled. "He didn't know about it!" She clenched her hands in her muff. "The tree fell *after* he came through."

"But look at all this mess! Watch out! That branch has enough snow on it to bury us!"

Constance ducked, her fur-trimmed hood fell over her eyes and she fell against Chesney.

"*I* would have arranged it all much better," he told her confidently as she righted herself.

"No doubt," said Constance with dry irony, brushing snow from her purple velvet cloak with her gloves. "Possibly you would even have arranged for the trees not to fall on these unused back roads?"

That cherubic red-cheeked face gave her an uncertain look. Could she be laughing at him? His mother never laughed at him. True, she drove off any girl who showed even the remotest interest in him and she selected his clothes and his food and his companions and she kept a tight rein on his money—but she *never* laughed at him. It occurred to him suddenly that to Mistress Constance he might appear just as one of the pack and not as the Leader of Men his mother in her gentler moments was always telling him he was. Well, he'd just demonstrate his leadership right now! For up ahead Captain Warburton was electing to plunge through a narrow spot between some low-hanging branches while to their left the woods opened suddenly into a wide aperture and there was a smooth snowy rise just beyond.

"We'll take *this* way," he cried. "And save you being drenched with snow from those branches!" He sawed on the horse's mouth (he had a notoriously heavy hand on the reins) causing the animal to swing sharply to the left and through the aperture.

Behind them there was a shout and out of the corner of her eye Constance saw Captain Warburton wheel his mount around and gallop toward them waving his hat.

"I think we're going the wrong way," she said nervously.

"Nonsense!" cried her masterful companion. "See how smooth the runners glide over this? We'll find the road shortly, and—"

They were just mounting the rise and now Captain Warburton had come alongside. His face was full of fury and alarm. "Pull up!" he roared. "Pull up!" And when Chesney only laughed, Captain Warburton dashed forward and seized the reins and turned the horse's head by main force to the right while behind them someone screamed and a furious Chesney half rose in his seat and howled, "Let go, are ye mad?" and brandished his whip at the Captain.

Chesney was thrown back in his seat by the sudden swerve of the sleigh as Captain Warburton brought the horse around, and snow flew in the wake of the runners as the sleigh slithered to a halt.

"Whatever is wrong?" gasped Constance.

"This fool beside you near cost you your life!" ground out the Captain.

Chesney, standing up bewildered with the reins slack in his hand, cried, "Are ye mad? There's no danger here—only a guide who chooses to run us through the forest where the branches beat at us—"

"I invite ye to view it!" thundered Captain Warburton, and of a sudden he was off his horse and seizing Chesney Pell by the shoulder, dragging him off his sleigh. While the rest watched, he dragged Chesney forward until they stood silhouetted against a gray winter sky at the top of the rise and Constance saw Chesney suddenly cringe back. He broke free of the Captain's grasp and floundered back to the sleigh while Captain Warburton sauntered along behind him.

"Oh, Mistress Constance," wailed Chesney, eagerly confessing his fault as he had to his mother for so many

369

years. "There's a sheer drop past the rise. It must be hundreds of feet down!"

"Ye exaggerate. A mere hundred and fifty," came Tony Warburton's sardonic voice. "This lad near carried ye over the brink of the Cheddar Gorge. And while the horse might have seen the danger and balked or turned, the sleigh could have upset and its momentum could well have carried it over anyway."

Constance, to whom their bewildering turns and changes of direction in this alien snowy landscape had rendered everything unfamiliar, blanched. She had seen the mile-long Cheddar Gorge but once and that was in summer and from below. Above her the great monolithic stones had seemed to rise upward like the heavy slanted foundations of some ancient giant's keep, now overgrown with greenery. And this smooth white surface with only sky beyond was the top of those massive cliffs! She saw suddenly that Chesney looked about to cry.

"You couldn't know that, Chesney," she said rapidly to comfort him. "It looked perfectly safe to me."

Captain Warburton snorted and remounted his horse. But Chesney's woebegone face brightened—as it always did when his mother forgave him his blunders. "Then ye aren't angry?" he marveled.

"No," sighed Constance. "Chesney, your boots are filled with snow. You'll have to shake them out or your feet will freeze on the way to Warwood."

As he followed her instructions, Chesney glowed. Back home he had never had a sweetheart. In Oxford, girls had not taken him seriously. Now at last he had found a lady who was not only beautiful and sought after and aristocratic and wealthy—she understood his perfectly natural mistakes! He had found the perfect Woman! His cherubic face beamed on Constance with such adoration that even Captain Warburton's grim, "Ye'll follow where I lead this time or I'll take over your reins myself and let ye follow along behind!" did not shake him.

The rest of the journey to Warwood was uneventful. And in the lead sleigh that followed Captain Warburton astride Cinder, mainly silent.

Constance was thinking how wonderful it would be if all of her past could be magically erased and she could start out fresh and new, if the man beside her could miraculously change places with Tony Warburton and she and Tony could glide off together into some happy future. Or alternatively if things could have worked out with Dev. . . .

Beside her Chesney Pell thought she looked adorably pensive with her purple velvet eyes looking out into the white distance.

They made their approach to Warwood down a stately drive lined with great ash trees and Constance thought how the last time she had seen those trees they had been festooned with leaves and now they were festooned with snow. Somehow Warwood's approach always seemed decked out for a holiday. . . . And now above the snowy branches of the big trees rose up the huge square tower.

"Is it a castle?" wondered Chesney, impressed.

"No, it was once an abbey," said Constance. "But it does look like a castle from here."

And then the massive bulk of the big stone house was spread out before them with its gothic tracery above the mullioned windows and its snow-covered ivy and its look of having been there forever.

"A large house for—did you say two unmarried brothers?"

Constance nodded. "One is a widower," she said.

And then Captain Warburton himself was ushering them into the echoing great hall. The servants had brought in enormous amounts of holly and Christmas greenery, and as they stood on the magnificent Aubusson carpet and admired the decorations, Chesney whispered with a chuckle, "I see there's plenty of mistletoe."

Constance made a little dismissing gesture with her shoulders as if to shake him off. And then their cloaks were being whisked away and the ladies were repairing to the upper regions of the house to shed their riding masks—Constance and Pamela had disdained to wear theirs—and to comb their windblown curls and to dab at their faces with face powder. Some of them were using the dangerous ceruse based in white lead but most, like Constance and Pamela, were using powder made from ground alabaster—although Pamela whispered to Constance that she thought the Hawley girls were using cheaper powder made from perfumed laundry starch. Constance put this down to Pamela's jealousy of Melissa, and asked if she had enjoyed her sleighride with Tom.

"It wasn't so exciting as yours," laughed Pamela. "At least Tom didn't try to carry me over the Cheddar Gorge!" And as Constance's brows shot up ruefully, "But perhaps you talked about more interesting subjects! Tom talked about politics the whole way—he told me Dick Peacham wasn't 'sound'!" She giggled. "He kept lecturing me. Going on and on about Judge Jeffreys and his 'judicial murders' at the time of the Rye House Plot."

"Tom's right—he *is* a terrible man," murmured Constance, studying her reflection and deciding that she was pale enough—she needed no crushed alabaster.

"Oh, of course Judge Jeffreys is a terrible man," said Pamela impatiently. "And James if he succeeds to the throne will subordinate England to Ireland! And it would be awful to have the burnings of Smithfield all over again! But for myself, I don't see how we can possibly get a good king out of all this mess, for as Captain Warburton says, he will still be a Stuart and probably a bad king! But why ruin a perfectly good sleighride talking about it?"

Constance cast a nervous glance about her. The room was alive with chatter and swishing skirts as the girls, gathered together now and not yet assigned the rooms they would have later on, tore off wet-hemmed petticoats and gowns and hastily repaired rips and spatters with the assistance of all the female servants who could be spared. Since this was a sleighing party and no one had wanted to overburden their sleighs with maidservants, this gathering them all together in one room was Captain Warburton's device for seeing that every lady in the party had some assistance. No one seemed to be paying any attention to them—indeed most were occupied with watching Melissa Hawley wire up her taffy curls and apply Spanish paper to rouge her cheeks. Or with helping each other apply black patches to contrast with alabaster skin. But still Constance wished that Pamela would not express her views so freely. She wondered if Pamela knew that the Duke of Monmouth had visited England in November. She had heard that he had been denied an audience with the King. She considered warning Tom not to be so free in his talk with Pamela but decided against it—surely it would seem treacherous when Pamela, for all her shortcomings, loved him so much.

"At least *you* do not need the aid of Spanish paper," she told her flushed companion.

"No, I never do!" laughed Pamela, struggling with the help of a maid into her favorite stiff pink damask gown. She was glad to be rid of the subject of politics. "The trouble is this cold weather makes my nose red too!"

"Some alabaster powder will change that!" Constance rose and accepted assistance from one of the maids in changing her own costume.

When she was gowned at last, when Pamela had breathed, "Oh, I do love your gown, Constance—it's prettier than *any* of the fashion dolls!" when several ladies who considered themselves leaders of fashion had cast her covert envious looks, Constance stared into the mirror with a flash of defiance. Trying to be mousy and understated and casting down her eyes shyly had not worked with Ned—he had pursued her anyway. So tonight she would be flamboyant and flaunt her interest in other men and discourage him *that* way!

To that end she had chosen a rich rustling rose-violet taffeta that brought out ruby-flecked lights in her violet eyes. It had a tightly fitted bodice that tapered to a tiny waist and enormous billowing three-quarter sleeves that spilled out an extravagance of white point lace over her slender forearms. Deep

purple velvet ribands were tied into bows at the elbow of each
sleeve and similar velvet bows held back the overskirt above a
swaying petticoat of rippling amethyst silk. The gown was
daringly low-cut and showed her snowy bosom to great
advantage, for she had recklessly scorned to wear a pinner—
one of those concealing scraps of lace or semisheer material
pinned or sewn into the décolletage for modesty's sake.
Lavender silk stockings and violet satin slippers completed
her costume.

She had combed the windblown tangles from her rich dark
hair, scented it with violets, brushed it until it shone, swept it
into great bewitching curls at the sides that dangled fetchingly
and swayed whenever she turned her head—no wired-up
frizzy curls for her! At the back she wore her thick hair in a
great bun and she had set an alexandrite ornament sparkling
with brilliants near her right ear where it would flash as she
moved.

But despite Pamela's open admiration, she now regarded
her handsome reflection in the mirror with some trepidation
for it had belatedly occurred to her that she was also flaunting
herself before Captain Warburton. Well, that could not be
helped!

With flashing eyes, she joined the ladies in their elegant
trek down Warwood's wide main stairway. And had the
satisfaction of seeing the eyes of the gentlemen below light up
at the inspiring sight of her!

"You're *dazzling* Captain Warburton!" murmured Pamela
mischievously and Constance bit her lip.

"I have no desire to dazzle him!" she muttered.

But Pamela had already forgotten her. Her searching crystal
blue eyes had sought for—and found—Tom among the crowd
of gentlemen below. His golden head shone in the candlelight
and his smiling roguish face was upturned, looking at her—or
was he looking at Melissa Hawley who was mincing down
the steps right behind her? Pamela left Constance's side,
lifted her heavy pink damask skirts and darted around the
leisurely lady posing just ahead. There would be no doubt as

to who Tom would take in to dinner tonight! *She* meant to reach him first!

From the stairs Constance too had caught Captain Warburton's cool gray gaze, looking up. He stood below her, a dominating figure in elegant black and silver. His sardonic face was calm beneath the heavy gleaming hair that swung to his broad shoulders. A jewel of price sparkled from the snowy burst of Mechlin at his throat. Not by so much as the quiver of a muscle did he display what he must be feeling. Not by so much as the flicker of an eyelash did Constance acknowledge that penetrating look. Her gaze negligently passed on to Ned, lingered there without recognition—and she could see him flush. His face was angry, for this morning's slight when Constance had chosen to ride with Chesney instead of with him still rankled. She let her gaze drift past him, found Chesney in the crowd, and broke into a dazzling smile.

Pamela, had she been watching, would have been amazed.

Thus encouraged, Chesney charged forward and met Constance amid the hubbub of descending perfumed ladies at the foot of the stairs. Constance smiled indifferently at Ned, who had rushed forward too, and took Chesney's arm with determination. She rustled past both a fuming Ned in a new green satin suit he had bought expressly to please her and an unsmiling Captain Warburton whose thoughtful gaze followed her progress before he gallantly offered his arm to the nearest lady.

For the most part that evening Constance adroitly managed to avoid both the Warburton brothers—mainly by flirting madly with Chesney Pell. Ned did arrange to seat himself beside her at dinner, where she answered his remarks with monosyllables and mainly favored him with a view of her rose-violet taffeta back. Ned retaliated by deserting her after dinner and devoting himself to Margie Hamilton, who laughed and dimpled and displayed her white teeth and flirted with him for all she was worth.

Weary of Chesney's dancing attendance—for somehow his puce satin form always inserted itself between her and anyone who desired so much as two words with her—Constance managed at last to escape while Chesney and Cart Rawlings, both of them overheated by wine, were occupied with a bitter denunciation of Judge Jeffreys, a matter about which they were in complete agreement. Midway in Cart's indignant "Ye'll remember that four years ago the court had to replace Jeffreys as recorder—caught him trying to intimidate the men who controlled the City of London!" Constance made her escape. She detached herself from the merrymakers and strolled alone through the vast echoing rooms until she came at last to the armory and stood looking about her in wonder, for this was a place she had not seen on her brief call last summer.

Garnishing the walls and ceiling of the cathedral-like room were the implements of personal warfare as men of England had fought it since the time of the Norman Conquest. Pikes bristled from the walls along with ancient chain mail, bucklers, breast plates, visored helmets, spiked maces, halberds, metal gauntlets—and there were shields and lances which Warburton men must have used in long-ago jousts. Dented armor proved these contests had been no laughing matter. And some of those dents, she thought with some trepidation, looked as if they might have been made by musket balls. There was a bewildering assortment of longbows and hunting crossbows, of javelins and spears. She stared in awe at a mighty two-handed sword. It would take a giant to wield it! And there were modern weapons as well: Stacked in a corner were a number of long matchlock muskets so heavy they had to be rested to take proper aim, and in another corner were stacked iron-hilted "mortuary" swords, some of them gilded and pierced and chiseled, wicked-looking daggers from Elizabethan days, handsome chiseled cup-hilted rapiers and brass basket-hilted rapiers of the kind the Warburtons settled their differences with now.

"There is a small cannon in the courtyard if your taste runs to more massive weapons," observed a humorous voice from behind her. "Or if you take a daintier view, there are flintlock pistols and matched dueling pistols in the library."

Constance gave an involuntary start. She turned and found herself looking into Tony Warburton's amused gunmetal eyes.

"That item you were just considering with such interest is a Spanish hunting sword," he remarked.

Constance gave the wicked broad blade and heavy hilt a look and a shiver. "It does not interest me," she protested.

"Margaret loved this room," said Tony Warburton with a sigh.

"Hers was doubtless a more militaristic nature," said Constance.

"Doubtless," he agreed. "But it's cold in here. Unless you choose to don your pattens and go outside and view the cannon, let me suggest we try the dueling pistols in the library. You could enlarge your skill by taking a shot at me," he added humorously.

Constance sniffed and turned to go.

He asked himself, as he followed her, why he had mentioned Margaret's name. And decided it was purely defensive. Here in this room bristling with the implements of battle, he was fighting a last skirmish with himself against trying to claim this dark-haired velvet-eyed creature as his own. And losing the battle. The vision of Ned which he had held up to himself so firmly was fading fast away.

"You should not let that fool Pell take you home," he warned her as he fell into step beside her. "He's a bad hand on the reins and no judgment at all of what a horse can or can't do on ice and snow. On the way here, I kept expecting him to overset the sleigh."

"Perhaps Chesney is better with such things as—dueling pistols," said Constance wanly, for hearing Margaret's name had brought back to her a number of sickening truths, one of which was that she must ward off her feelings for this tall fellow in black and silver. At any cost.

"If you continue to encourage him, he may well get his chance to prove that," said the Captain shortly.

"Why?" She gave a faint smile. "Will *you* challenge him?"

"No, I will not—although I will admit that I yearned to throttle him today when he near carried you over the brink of the Cheddar Gorge. But Ned has not such a tight grip on his temper—he is young and hasty."

"Ned has no reason to call Chesney out. I do not belong to Ned!" said Constance with asperity.

It was on the tip of the Captain's tongue to tell her that indeed she did belong to Ned—or would as soon as the Squire made that clear to her. And that he would free her from that entanglement if she but gave him the word. But he checked himself grimly. He was as much to blame for the situation as any, he reminded himself. For had he not shaken hands with Clifford over the betrothal only yesterday? And now he was half a mind to sweep up the girl and carry her away himself! He wondered, shocked at the violence of his own turbulent emotions, whatever had happened to his honor.

"I think the countryside would like to know where you stand on the succession," said Constance in an effort to divert him from this talk of Ned.

Captain Warburton gave a short laugh. "The countryside well knows where I stand. I'm against all Stuarts," he added recklessly.

"That's a dangerous thing to say," she warned him. "For whatever the rest of England may do, the West Country is lining up behind Monmouth."

He shrugged. He could have told her a deal about the Stuarts, including her precious duke, whom he personally considered a heedless fool. About Charles, he was thoroughly disillusioned. As for James, his information had it that if James succeeded to the throne he would end up making England subservient to Ireland—so much for James. "Personally I think I'd prefer a non-Stuart on the throne—Mary Stuart's husband, William of Orange," he laughed.

Constance gave him a reproving frown for she was in deadly earnest about the Cause.

They had by now reached one of the great reception rooms where guests were milling about. She could see Chesney looking about, undoubtedly searching for her. With a cool bow to Captain Warburton, she made straight for Chesney and stuck by him for the rest of the evening.

"Wherever did you disappear to?" wondered Pamela when the two girls were alone together that night in the handsome high-ceilinged bedchamber that had been assigned to them. "I saw you come back with Captain Warburton. Ned looked annoyed—I don't doubt they had words about it later."

"Ned doesn't own me!" flashed Constance.

"Well, I'd say you proved *that* by spending the whole of the evening with Chesney Pell! He's quite bowled over by you, you know! I hear he's quite rich if his mamma ever lets go of the purse strings—she was left in charge of his property until such time as she finds him fit to take over, can you imagine that? I say that time will be when she's buried in the churchyard!" Pamela's laughter pealed.

Constance was hardly listening. She was looking out from their lofty third-floor bedchamber through the mullioned window at the parklike view, the snow-covered gardens, that spread out before her. "It's very beautiful here," she murmured.

"A bit grim for me," shrugged Pamela. "Granted the house is very grand but it lacks those little touches a woman would give it—it's been bachelor quarters for too long! It's so"—she searched for a word—"baronial, I suppose. Feudal. Aunt Margaret loved it."

Margaret again! "Huntlands lacks those little touches too," Constance pointed out.

"Yes, but I plan to give Huntlands those touches," said Pamela, and then flushed.

"So you and Tom are getting on rather well, I take it?"

"Well—I'm not sure," admitted Pamela frankly. "But at least he squired me over here and *that's* an improvement. Oh, I *do* love him so, Constance."

"I know," said Constance softly. She refrained from adding, *Everybody knows!*

"And now that Melissa Hawley is spending all her time

379

with Cart Rawlings—I caught them kissing behind the drapes in the library—I'm sure Tom will lose interest in her."

Or perhaps gain interest now that he has competition! thought Constance uneasily. 'So, perhaps,'' she said on a lighter note, "you'll be redecorating Huntlands come summer!''

And neither of them could foretell there in that peaceful bedchamber that next summer redecorating would be the last thing on anybody's mind, that before that terrible summer was over, ball and shot would have whistled through English gardens like the one below them and the West Country would run red with English blood.

Warwood, Somerset,
The Sixth Day of Christmas 1684

CHAPTER 25

A message had come for Tom that his prize mare was foaling and he left Warwood early the next morning before the guests were up. Miffed that he had not waked her and taken her along, Pamela promptly climbed into Dick Peacham's sleigh for the ride home. She waved her muff gaily at Constance who, against all advice, was riding back with Chesney—and hoping he would not overturn the sleigh.

Chesney departed Axeleigh almost on arrival and set out for Hawley Grange to join Cart Rawlings. But Dick Peacham, who slipped on the ice when he got out of the sleigh and claimed he had turned his ankle, was left over.

Pamela had an answer for *that*. She propped Peacham's leg up on a pillow, told him sweetly that she had dozens of things to see to—and left him immobilized by his own lies. After dinner she pleaded exhaustion and left the bewildered Squire to entertain young Peacham, who discovered suddenly that his ankle was making a fast recovery and made it up the stairs under his own power.

Now another morning at Axeleigh had come and gone and taken with it—at different times and in different directions—both a frowning Tom Thornton and an exuberant Dick Peacham. For just as Pamela was seeing Peacham to the door she glimpsed through the window Tom Thornton riding down toward their stables, bringing with him on a lead the horse he had borrowed. Why, he had passed by the house without stopping to say hello! She flung open the door to glare at him and at the sound of the door opening, Tom looked back and waved a gauntlet glove at her. Instantly Pamela abandoned her plans to bid Dick Peacham a bored good-by and to Peacham's amazed delight she threw her arms about him and gave him a warm good-by kiss. Let Tom view *that*!

And again the Squire, just rounding the corner of the house, stopped short and took note of her surprising behavior.

Tom Thornton took note of it too. If only Pamela had not had her face pressed so closely against Dick Peacham's florid one, she would have seen the sudden angry ripple of Tom's shoulder muscles that strained against the woolen material of his scarlet coat. But he did not turn his course from the stables. *Damme, Pamela was too good for Peacham!* he was thinking hotly. Of course, if Pamela was determined to make a fool of herself, he supposed he could not stop her—short of calling Peacham out, which he would have been ashamed to do, for Peacham was no shot at all and was known to be the poorest sword arm in the county! He was unaware that it was a good-by kiss, for Peacham's horse had not yet been brought round.

Pamela, having pushed Peacham away to see how Tom was taking this, was disappointed to find only his broad back in view. She bade Peacham a swift good-by, announced that she was cold and had forgot her shawl and went quickly back inside, shutting the door rather hard behind her.

She would have been delighted had she been able to observe Tom's entry into the big stone stable. Full of impotent fury, he flung himself off his horse in the wide doorway, tossed the reins to the nearest groom and stomped to the spacious stall where, the stable boys assured him, Satan had passed a comfortable night. Tom felt the big horse's leg gingerly. Much better. Indeed he could probably ride Satan home right now. *But that of course would give him no very good excuse to stop by tomorrow and see how matters were proceeding between Pamela and that bumbling Peacham fellow.* For Tom had no way of knowing that Peacham had already departed.

Not admitting to himself why he did it, Tom rose.

"Best I leave Satan here another day," he said. "I'll look in on him tomorrow." He vaulted back into the saddle and took a shortcut back to Axeleigh that was perilously deep in snow, rather than cantering back down the driveway to the road. He told himself he was being civil, not exposing Pamela and her new lover to his curious gaze—even though a quick glance had assured him they were not in sight. But he swore at every tree limb that whipped his face along the shortcut, and when he lost his hat to one he dismounted and seized it with such force that he crushed the brim.

Afternoon came to Axeleigh. The peacocks strutted across the snow uttering their demonic screams. Cook swore at Tabby, who had run by chasing Puss and overturned a whole crock of cream upon the stone-flagged flooring. Constance huddled in a window seat and read. Pamela, with loyal Tabitha at her side, checked out the cellars to be sure they'd have enough food for the upcoming Twelfth Night Ball, and came up to scold Constance for reading when they had so much to do.

With a sigh, Constance put down her book and helped Pamela supervise the counting of the linens to make sure they would have enough of everything for it was so cold outside that laundry would freeze on the lines. When Tabby suggested they could hang the laundry in the chilly attics to dry, Pamela shook her head.

"All those wet linens would make the air so damp," she

explained. "And the servants sleep in that warren of rooms up there. I wouldn't want any of them to catch cold."

Constance thought of Claxton House, where the servants' health was never given a thought, and smiled at Pamela. She would make a wonderful wife for Tom—if only he had the sense to see it!

Tom came over and got Satan the next day. Having asked one of the grooms casually if "that Peacham fellow" was still in residence and been assured he was gone, he left contentedly, riding Satan jauntily down the drive. Pamela, who was busy supervising the airing of the beds, was furious when she learnt she had missed him.

"We can find some excuse to ride over to Huntlands," suggested Constance, amused.

"No, there really isn't time. There's an awful lot left to do because so many guests will be staying over, and they'll bring their maids, and their coachmen must be seen to—oh, it will be a terrible crush, I promise you!"

The Squire, passing by, heard that and smiled. He had not yet told Constance of his decision to betroth her to Ned. Indeed he could not bring himself to do so for she seemed so downcast, flitting by him with her dark head slightly bowed— as if life was raining blows upon her!

Well, he would tell her and make the announcement all in one evening at the Twelfth Night Ball. Such an occasion of merriment would buck up her spirits and she would realize what was best for her. But as Twelfth Night approached, he found that he was not looking forward to it. Indeed he felt old these days. He had a harem-scarem daughter who seemed intent on marrying the wrong man, a ward who seemed intent on becoming an old maid, a sister in hiding and believed dead by all, and now a blackmailer had dredged up the only disreputable thing he had ever done in his life—he was not up to these intrigues!

He sighed and wished fervently that the Twelfth Night Ball was over.

It was on him soon enough.

For the occasion his daughter had chosen a stiff olive plush petticoat and an overgown of heavy buttercup yellow satin with an enormous flaring skirt. Almost every inch of the satin was so heavily embroidered with olive silk thread that the entire garment could have stood alone. Her big puffed sleeves were lined with matching olive plush and decorated with myriad yellow rosettes to complement the yellow rosettes scattered on skirt and bodice. To Constance she gave the impression of a face with a head of golden hair rising out of a flowering bush.

She herself was wearing a very plain rosy-amethyst changeable silk over a sinuous purple velvet petticoat latticed in silver threads. She had chosen it because it moved gracefully and because its neckline was shockingly low. For her mood tonight was rebellious.

The Squire, watching the two girls drift down the stairs to greet their guests, was proud of them both. With approval he noted Constance's high color—indeed her purple velvet eyes seemed to be throwing off amethyst sparks—and determined to tell her about her betrothal the first chance he got.

But the sparks he saw in her eyes were the sparks of rebellion. For Constance was feeling angry and bitter. She had been thinking of Dev who had so lightly taken her and so lightly left her. And now as she came downstairs she was thinking, *I should get out of all this! I should forget Dev and accept the first man who offers to take me far away from here! Away from Tony Warburton and Ned and this constant bringing up of Margaret's name to make me feel even worse than I do!*

The Squire was smiling at her approvingly. She greeted a group of arriving guests and flashed him back a smile, dangerously bright.

She looked up in time to see Dick Peacham make his entrance. Gaudy in peach silks, he all but danced in and hovered over Pamela.

Cart Rawlings, with a resplendent scarlet-clad Melissa on his arm, was arriving too—and with them Chesney Pell, who bent down to whisper, "Cart stayed so long at Hawley Grange on the way here I was afraid I'd be too late to lead you out in the first dance!"

"Well, you aren't too late," smiled Constance, thinking how that would annoy both Ned and Tony, who had arrived earlier.

Now all but a couple of late-arriving guests had come, and the musicians, hidden behind a screen, were striking up.

"My daughter and my ward shall both lead off the dance!" called out the Squire jovially.

"The Daffodil and the Iris!" cried someone and there was a scattering of friendly laughter and applause as Dick Peacham escorted Pamela, frowning because Tom was so late, to the floor and Ned, suddenly stepping in front of Chesney, led out Constance.

The satin-and-beribboned company, the ladies with their artful black face patches and cunning coiffures, the gentlemen garbed like peacocks with lace at throat and cuffs, watched as the handsome foursome swirled into the dance. Only Chesney stood open-mouthed and furious that his lady had been snatched from his arms and without so much as a by-your-leave!

"I had promised the first dance to Chesney." Constance gave Ned a look.

Ned's answering look was just as level for the Squire had assured him he would make the announcement tonight. So whatever game Constance was playing, whether she wished merely to make him jealous or whether she really had a passing interest in this fellow from Lyme, all would be resolved tonight. Once publicly betrothed, if Chesney Pell tried to come between them, he'd call him out, damme, he would!

"I did not hear ye do so," he said pleasantly.

"You didn't ask! You just seized my hand and plunged forward!"

"Perhaps that is what you need," he smiled. "A forceful hand on the reins."

Constance gasped. "Don't speak of me as if I were a horse!"

"Why not?" he said imperturbably. "You're fractious, you insist on taking the bit between your teeth—and you bolt!"

Constance's teeth ground. "I had thought you would be dancing the first dance with Margie Hamilton!" she snapped.

So she had noticed all the attention he had paid to Margie Hamilton at Warwood. Ned favored her with a benevolent smile. "The Hamiltons are our neighbors. It is incumbent upon me to be nice to their daughter."

"Don't be stuffy!" cried Constance. "You spent the whole evening with her at Warwood! Why aren't you with her now?"

"Because I prefer you. Sometimes I wonder why, but I do."

Constance was trembling with rage when Captain Warburton, neatly stepping before Chesney—in fact, nearly treading upon the toe of Chesney's boot, which was pulled nimbly out of the way just in time—claimed Constance for the next dance.

"You have an infuriating brother!" she cried. "He treats me as if he owns me!"

So Clifford had not told her yet.... Tony Warburton gave her a sardonic smile. "Ned is in love with you, Constance."

"Ha! He acts as if he's gone mad!"

"Love is an emotion that drives men mad—hadn't you heard?"

"It didn't drive *you* mad," she said—and immediately wished she hadn't said that.

"Oh, it did—once. I have better control of myself now, I hope." He leaned forward, speaking in a richer tone. "If I declared for you now, would you accept me, Constance?"

"No!" She would have wrenched away from him but his hold was too tight.

He laughed to cover the hurt he felt. "Ah, but then I have not declared for you, have I?"

She gave him an enraged look. And was still trembling when Chesney claimed her for the next dance.

"Have those Warburton fellows said something to offend you?" he cried. "If so, tell me, and I'll call them out!"

"*Both* of them?" Constance was fascinated by such temerity.

"Both!" he declared staunchly.

The idea of Chesney pitting himself against Ned—much less against the dangerous Captain Warburton—was so ludicrous that it put her in a better humor. She was about to tell him she had given better than she got, when the dance ended and she was swept away by Ned, and before Chesney could reclaim her the Squire said, "Could I see you in the library, Constance?"

Ned's eyes gleamed. At last! Very readily he relinquished her and went off to find himself a drink. A few minutes from now he'd be a betrothed man and everyone would be congratulating him—including his brother, who'd been acting morose lately. Probably restive at so much inaction and anxious to get away. Ned felt suddenly very excited. It had been hard on him, knowing the Squire had accepted his offer and not letting on that he knew. Well, the playacting would soon be over! He flashed a grin at Tony who gave him back a grim measuring smile.

In the library the Squire was preparing Constance for what was to come. "You are in all ways a tractable niece—and I hope you will be so now."

Constance gave him a bewildered look.

Clifford Archer squared his shoulders. "I have betrothed ye to Ned Warburton, Constance. I've given my word on it."

Fear shot through Constance. Once he had set a course, the Squire—like her dead father who had plowed doggedly through a blizzard to his death—would stick to it.

"I—I would not be betrothed to Ned, sir," she gasped.

"Ye do not choose Ned?" He brooded upon her. "Well, no matter," he sighed. "Ned is a good man and ye will come to realize it once ye are wed."

Constance found herself trembling. Her mind flitted about

388

like a hummingbird, sampling what to say. If she told the truth, if she said, *I was the fifteen-year-old bride of a highwayman who left me for another woman,* she would not be believed. It was too bizarre. If she said simply, *I am already wed,* she would not be believed either—for she had given no inkling of that to anyone, not to Margaret, not to Pamela. Not even the marriage records of Essex would back her up for they had been married under assumed names! She must think of something else—and quickly. Something that *would* be believed.

"I *cannot* marry Ned," she appealed. And that was true enough! "I cannot in honor marry him," she added huskily, suddenly drooping her head so that she was studying the carpet.

"And why not?" Clifford Archer was eyeing her in some alarm.

"Because—" Constance cast about. "Because I am already betrothed. To someone else."

"Who?" Inexorably.

Constance felt suffocated. "It—it is a private matter between him and me!" she cried, bringing up a pair of violet eyes with a wild appeal sending amethyst sparks toward him.

"A private matter no longer," said the Squire grimly. He thought for a moment. "Are you saying"—his voice was reluctant, as if the words could scarce pass his lips—"that you have gone too far with this fellow, that you cannot draw back?"

Constance nodded miserably.

There was doubt in his eyes.

"I—I have slept with him," she admitted. And then in a wisp of a voice, barely above a whisper. "I fear I may be pregnant by him."

A long deep sigh escaped the Squire. "Ah-h-h," he said softly. "That makes a difference." He chewed at his lip. "Is this true?" he demanded sternly. "Or is it a fabrication to postpone your betrothal to Ned Warburton?"

"It is true," she whispered, hating herself for lying to him.

"Then"—the Squire passed a hand across his face as if to brush away cobwebs—"Who is this fellow? Bring him to me that I may deal with him."

"I—I will not bring him to you," she said shakily. "He does not deserve your wrath." She drew a deep breath. "*I* chose him and *I* trapped him!"

Clifford Archer gave her a look of wonder, almost of awe. "I see you are of the new breed of woman," he muttered. "More like Margaret than my brother Brandon!"

Margaret would have understood my falling in love with a highwayman, thought Constance rebelliously. *Had it been Margaret standing here instead of you, I would have told the truth!*

She turned to go.

"Not so fast," said the Squire, who had recovered himself sufficiently to deal with this new problem. "Before you bring dishonor upon us, we must get you wed."

Constance stiffened. "I will not tell you his name!" she cried indignantly. "For I know what you would do!"

The Squire sighed. "Very well. Make your own arrangements. Perhaps it is best that I not know his name at this moment for indeed I would be tempted to send his teeth crashing down his throat!" A visage she had not known could be so cold now confronted her. "But be quick about it," he commanded. "Bring him to me before the evening is over and we will announce your betrothal for all to hear." He leant forward menacingly. "I take it he is *here*?"

Barely controlling a shiver, Constance turned and fled.

Immediately the Squire sought out Tabitha. "Let me know at once if Mistress Constance tries to leave this house," he instructed. "And prevent her even if you have to throw yourself upon her and bear her to the ground."

"I'll watch her, sir," Tabby gulped.

"See that you do." He went back to the festivities and found Pamela, who was standing for the moment alone, sadly watching Tom whirl round the floor—with someone else. Dick Peacham would have partnered her, but he had gone for refreshments. He would be back presently with a couple of piled-up plates and would try to lure her into some corner and propose marriage again. She started as her father's voice broke into her reverie.

"Have you seen Constance?" he asked. "She cannot have come into this room more than a minute ago."

Pamela gave a confused look about her. She had been so wrapped up in her own affairs that she would not have noticed if the King himself had passed by! "I could look for her," she volunteered.

"Never mind. Has she told you she is secretly bethrothed?"

Pamela gasped. "No, she has not!"

There could be no doubt of the truth of that remark, thought the Squire. Pamela's pretty mouth had dropped open and her eyes widened to saucers at the very thought.

"Is there some special lad she favors?"

"I—" Pamela was recovering herself. In a vague way she felt that in matters of the heart, friends must stick together. "You will have to give me time to sort this out," she said weakly.

"So you do not know of some special lad, then?"

"I know that she sometimes weeps in her room," said Pamela carefully. "And sometimes when one is talking to her, she becomes still and silent and looks out into the distance as if she is in some other place."

Weeps in her room . . . looks out into the distance. The Squire gnawed that over. It would fit her situation all too well if the lass thought herself pregnant by some young buck who had not openly declared for her!

"Do not worry about it, Pamela," he told his troubled daughter. "All will be well."

Pamela found neither his stern look nor his grim tone reassuring. She turned as Peacham found her and almost blundered into the plate of little cakes he held out. Impatiently she took it, her blue eyes scanning the room, her mind tallying swiftly over the list of young bucks who danced attendance on beautiful Constance. There was Ned Warburton, dancing with Margie Hamilton. Captain Warburton was talking to Nathaniel Hawley. Who then was missing?

Chesney Pell was absent.

"Have you seen Chesney?" she asked Peacham.

"Yes. He was asking where Mistress Constance was, since he was leaving early with Cart Rawlings. Someone told him she'd gone upstairs."

Constance had indeed gone upstairs. To change to boots and riding habit and somehow reach the stables. She intended to run away—tonight!

The Squire had already guessed her intention. He bounded up the stairs, threw open her door and saw the riding habit thrown upon the bed. Constance backed away but he pounced on her. "So this is your answer!" He glared at the telltale riding habit.

Constance blanched.

The Squire stared down at her. Her face was very pale. He did not want to precipitate her into doing anything foolish— like running away in that thin ball gown on this bitter night. She might freeze to death as her father had!

"I promise that I will let you speak to the lad before I do," he said in an altered voice. *"But I will have his name.* You are not to play games with me!"

"I will die before I will tell you his name!" gasped Constance.

The Squire's face darkened. In rage he took her by the shoulders and began to shake her. Before his frustrated fury, Constance felt her very bones were being shaken loose.

"Sir!" cried an indignant male voice from the doorway. "Sir, what are you doing to Mistress Constance?"

The Squire's grip loosened—but not enough that Constance could wriggle free. Dazed by the sudden appearance of someone else in their small violent world of question and answer, they turned to find themselves looking into the anxious round face of Chesney Pell. A very pale face as he quailed before the Squire. "I must protest!" he cried weakly.

"Mistress Constance is a frail flower. You will hurt her if you persist in shaking her like that!"

A frail flower! This violet-eyed wench who was defying him! The Squire ground his teeth. And of a sudden, he saw this fellow who was seeking his ward among the bedchambers in a different light. *This* was the fellow who had haunted his house of late, languishing after Constance. *This* was the fellow into whose sleigh she had leaped, when she was supposed to go with Ned. And they had spent the night at Warwood—*together.* Light broke over him suddenly.

"It was *you!*" he thundered, turning so fierce a countenance on Chesney that the Oxford student took an involuntary step backward.

"*I?*" he faltered. "What have *I* done to merit your displeasure?"

But Clifford Archer now had his quarry in view. He flung Constance aside and his chest seemed to puff out and his shoulders widen as he advanced upon Chesney. If he could not wring the truth from the wench, he would have it from the lad if he had to throttle it out of him!

Constance saw Chesney's danger better than he did. In another moment the Squire would be upon him, vengeful and dangerous. She flung herself upon the Squire, wrapping her arms around his sleeve. "Run, Chesney!" she cried. 'Run!"

Bewildered by events he had no knowledge of, Chesney was already backing nimbly away. Now at the flaring alarm in Constance's voice, he turned and broke into a run.

With a roar the Squire took off after him, stumbling as his spurs—for every fashionable gentleman wore his spurs indoors, even in the West Country—caught in Constance's velvet petticoat and threatened to trip him. Angrily he shook her off and she wavered, righted herself, and watched his enraged progress down the hall.

Chesney, unfamiliar with the house, had already turned in panic up a stairway that would lead him into the attics. The Squire went thundering after.

There was another stair leading up, at the other end of the

house. Guessing that Chesney would shortly be dashing the length of those attics with the Squire in hot pursuit, Constance kicked off her high-heeled dancing slippers and raced toward that other stairway, meaning to intercept Chesney before the Squire caught up. As she reached the confusing warren of rooms that comprised the attics, she could hear Chesney crashing about in the darkness and behind him somewhere the Squire—for neither had paused to light candles. All the servants were downstairs attending to the guests and so were not party to the mind-boggling events taking place in their quarters.

Constance found Chesney before the Squire did.

"Over here," she hissed and almost lost her breath as he promptly collided with her.

"What the devil is the matter?" he whispered in a shaken voice. "Has the Squire lost his mind? He was going to attack me!"

She shuddered as some distance away she heard a crash— the Squire had collided with a washbowl and pitcher. "Take off your boots," she muttered. "And don't ask questions."

Used to being controlled by women, Chesney meekly set himself to removing his boots. He required help in getting them off and his spurs ripped her dress. But get them off they did at last and, boots in hand, she led him on tiptoe through the maze of rooms and finally down into her bedchamber where she closed the door behind them.

"Here, put your boots on." She tossed them to him. "You must leave here at once—and don't come back. Go directly to Oxford—or better still, Lyme. Do you have relatives somewhere that you could visit?"

Chesney, his head whirling, made no move toward his boots. "What is happening?" he wailed. "What have I done?"

"The Squire thinks—" she hesitated. "Oh, never mind what he thinks. Just get you gone!"

"He thinks I have offered you some offense?" A little light

was filtering into Chesney's thick skull. "That I have taken liberties with you?"

"Worse," said Constance grimly.

"But all I have done is asked for your hand in marriage," gasped Chesney. *"And you refused me!"* He picked up the boots.

In the back of Constance's mind was nourishing the thought that if Chesney fled, the Squire would undoubtedly pursue him—and that would give her time to get away. She would try to reach Margaret in Devon. She would tell her everything—well, not quite everything, she would not tell her that she had fallen in love with Tony Warburton! But she would fling herself on Margaret's mercy and—

"What does the Squire think I have done?" An anxious Chesney was interrupting her thoughts.

Constance took a deep shaky breath. What she had to say would rid of her Chesney in an instant!

"He thinks," she said, "that I am pregnant by you."

Nerveless fingers let the boots go thudding to the floor, spurs jingling. Chesney sat down upon the bed as if his legs would no longer support him. "How could he think that?" he croaked.

"Because," sighed Constance, "when he tried to betroth me to someone I did not wish to wed, I told him I was pregnant."

"It is a lie, of course?" bleated Chesney.

"Of course. And when I refused to name the man, he tried to shake the name out of me."

And he had blundered into that! It came to Chesney suddenly that they were alone together in a bedchamber—alone at last. And that Constance looked very beautiful as she stood there defying the world, defying the Squire who had sought to make her wed some other man. *Wed some other man!* Chesney's hackles rose at that. True, he had accepted the turndown she had given *him* with good grace, not really expecting to snare so lustrous a wench. But—suddenly he saw the Perfect Solution to all this, shining before him. He opened his mouth to tell Constance about it and at that moment the door to the bedchamber burst open and the Squire came through it.

"So?" he cried. "First you run away and now I find you in my ward's bedchamber, sitting on her bed *without your boots*! What have you to say to that, sirrah?"

Chesney cast a mild look down at the offending boots. He curled his toes in his socks, cocked his head and gave the Squire a cherubic look. "I have nothing to say about it," he sighed. "You are well aware of my feelings for Mistress Constance. Indeed I sought your permission to pay court to her—"

"But not to bed her without first wedding her!" cried the Squire, fixing Chesney with a baleful glare.

Chesney hung his head. No more eloquent admission of guilt could be had.

Constance gasped.

The Squire turned to her. "So now we have the fellow's name," he said heavily. "*And it will be your name too, mistress, as soon as the banns can be cried!* Repair that rip in your dress, Constance—and you, Pell, put on your boots. I will expect you downstairs in ten minutes when I will announce your betrothal." His menacing gaze turned on Chesney.

Chesney quailed before that look, but only a little. He was to have Constance! Forgotten were his studies at Oxford—that could all go away once he was a married man. Forgotten was his doting mother in Lyme Regis—she would *not* go away, and to date she had made his every decision. Forgotten was the advice of Cart Rawlings, who had muttered that it might not be wise to dangle too close after Mistress Constance, she might yet be proved a King's agent. Forgotten were all of these things. He was going to have Constance!

"Oh, Chesney, you must be mad!" In consternation, Constance sank down beside him after the Squire stomped out. "But there is still time for you to get away. Put on your boots, you must hurry! I will find some way to detain the Squire while you make your escape."

"How will you detain him?" asked Chesney curiously.

"Why—I will lock the door after you are gone and pretend to him that you are still here, that—that we are making love and do not wish to be disturbed."

"Very well, let's do that," said Chesney enthusiastically, throwing his arms about her. "We will lock the door now!"

Constance, who had been about to add "Eventually the Squire will break the door down but by then you will be far from here—" paused with her mouth open and at that moment Chesney's eager mouth closed down over hers in an enthusiastic if not very expert kiss. She felt his lips, his eager tongue, as she tried to push him away.

"I will have no dowry!" she flung at him, thinking to rid herself of him that way.

"No dowry?" He drew back. "But I thought Cart said—"

"No matter what Cart said, I will not *accept* a dowry from—" in her excitement she had almost said "my uncle" —"from the Squire under these circumstances!"

Chesney's head bobbed in agreement—it was a head much used to bobbing in agreement. He had been agreeing with his mother ever since he was born. *Perhaps she will change her mind,* he thought. *Cart had said Constance would have a dowry almost as large as Pamela's. A girl would not be such a fool as to turn that down! Not when she'd had time to think about it.* In any event, his mother had lots of money.

"You are a fool!" cried Constance desperately.

"Not such a fool," corrected Chesney with indisputable logic. "For have I not just won *you*?"

Those simple words set her blinking. And suddenly she realized this was the easy way—to become betrothed to Chesney.

It would buy her time. Time to make her plans. Time to run.

PART TWO
The Strange Wedding

He's relatively sure that she's relatively pure
(At least he hopes so in his nervous heart!)
And he never even dreams that she isn't what she
  seems
And is marrying him to leave here, for a start!

The Twelfth Night Ball,
Axeleigh Hall, Somerset,
January 6, 1685

CHAPTER 26

Professing a calm he did not feel, the Squire led the pair of them—a beaming Chesney with his boots restored to him, and a Constance who was at least pale and steady and whose ripped gown had been hastily pinned together—into the center of the floor of his festive drawing room. Questions, explanations, could be satisfied afterward, the important thing was to make it all official!

The musicians were taking a break and everyone turned around to watch as the Squire cleared his throat portentously.

"I would announce to this company the betrothal of my ward, Constance," he told them in a clear ringing voice, "to a gentleman from Dorset whom you've all met—Chesney Pell."

His announcement had the effect of breaking up the party. Although most guests flocked around, offering their surprised congratulations, some did not:

Across the room Ned Warburton turned ashen. He glared at Constance, who lifted her chin defiantly and looked away from him. With a muttered curse he flung out and they could hear him crash into the front door as he attempted to barge through it.

Tony Warburton's thunderstruck gaze swung from the Squire to Constance. For a bitter moment he held his ground, then strode after his brother. Constance, feeling she was dreaming all this rather than living it, could see through the window Ned's figure racing across the drive in the moonlight with Tony in hot pursuit, headed for the stables.

Margie Hamilton, who had had her eye on Ned from the first, found her father and gave his arm a tug. "I have a terrible headache," she complained. "I think I'm coming down with something. Couldn't we go home?" *If they hurried,* she was thinking, *they might even catch up with the Warburton brothers on the road, walking their horses and talking it over. And they could ask them in for a hot drink, for the Hamiltons' residence was next door to Warwood.* (Margie could have walked to Warwood, had she chosen, rather than go there by sleigh the other day.) *And over a hot drink, who knew what a young man on the rebound might do?*

The Hamiltons soon departed.

"Oh, Tom, go after them," urged Pamela under her breath, as soon as she could break away from the well-wishers and find him. "I'm sure Constance would rather marry Ned than that—that inane Chesney Pell!"

Tom was equally certain. He departed, shaking his head.

But whatever passed between the Warburton brothers—and Tom did not catch up with them and neither did the Hamiltons—Ned was back at Axeleigh the next day.

A very determined Ned who insisted upon seeing Mistress Constance even though she sent down word that she was indisposed.

"Tell her I'll break down her door if I have to," he warned Pamela.

Pamela, sparkling-eyed, laughed. "I don't think it will come to that," she said. "Here she comes now."

And Ned looked up to see a very composed Constance

descending the stairs. His hot gaze took in every inch of her, the soft slither of her wine velvet skirts as she moved toward him, the glorious dark cloud of her hair, the enticing feminine aura of her, the drifting scent of violets. The cold eyes that considered him.

"I guessed you would not take no for an answer," she told Ned quietly, for she had overheard his last comment to Pamela.

"I'll leave you two alone to talk it out," said Pamela hastily. "Chesney is sleeping late," she added. This was to inform Ned that Chesney was here but would not be interrupting whatever he had to say to Constance. For after the ball the Squire had firmly escorted Chesney to a spare bedchamber and informed him that he would occupy it until the banns were cried and he and Constance were safely wed.

He had done more than that, had the Squire, but Pamela did not know it. He had told Tabitha she was to sleep on a cot in Constance's room—and to guard her well. He had told her that if Constance ran away or if she told Pamela what he had said, he would dismiss her.

"No need for you to leave, Pamela," said Constance briskly. "I think Ned here is about to ask me why I chose Chesney over him. Is that not so?"

Ned, who had not expected this frontal attack, reddened. "That is so indeed," he muttered. "I would hear it from your own lips."

"Very well, I *wish* to marry Chesney and live in Lyme Regis. Is that enough for you?"

"No, it is not," cried Ned, thrusting out his jaw. "What is this attraction Pell has for you? Is it Lyme Regis? Is that it? Do you wish to go away from here so much that you would even *marry* to leave?"

Constance paled for his chance thrust had struck home, and Pamela, who had turned about, looked bewildered.

"It is the Squire's desire that I marry," she told Ned in as calm a voice as she could manage just then. "I have made my choice. Can you not accept it?"

Ned's baffled look said that he could not. "I'll call Pell out," he muttered. "I'll rid the world of him!"

"If you do that," Constance's voice rang out contemptuously, "I will publicly declare you a coward and a bully for calling out a man you know you can best—and never speak to you again as long as you live!"

For a long moment they stared at each other and Pamela watched, fascinated, this battle of wills.

Then, "Good day to you, Ned," said Constance composedly. "I see no reason to prolong this conversation." She started up the stairs and turned halfway up. "I think you might stop by the Hamiltons on your way back to Warwood," she called down. "Margie Hamilton would be glad to see you!"

Grinding his teeth, Ned flung out. He almost crashed into Pamela with the force of his departure.

Pamela fled up the stairs after Constance. "You wouldn't talk to me last night," she cried. "Although I was dying to know! Whatever made you decide to marry Chesney? I couldn't believe it when Father made the announcement!" Having caught up with Constance, she ran along beside her. "Oh, do tell me," she pleaded. "Or I shall surely die of curiosity!"

Constance turned on her. "Your father will tell you that I have been to bed with Chesney and that that is a good reason for marriage!"

That brought Pamela to a full stop. "And have you?" she gasped.

Constance sighed. "No. But your father will have me marry him anyway." She threw open the door to her bed-chamber and beckoned Pamela inside. She was about to tell her the truth, but looking into that avid pink and white face, those fascinated crystal blue eyes, she knew she could not. Exuberant Pamela would never be able to keep it to herself! "For reasons that I cannot tell you," she said, "I am not a virgin as Ned—indeed as all the world—thought me to be."

Thrilled, Pamela waited for further revelations.

"And your father is determined that I shall wed *someone*.

He got it into his head that it was Chesney who had seduced me—''

"And it was not?"

"No, it was not."

"Who was it?" breathed Pamela. "Captain Warburton?"

Constance's body gave a great jerk. "What makes you ask that?" she cried wildly.

"Well, anyone could see from the way you look at each other—anyone except Ned, who has eyes only for you," she added hastily. "I mean—well, when the announcement was made last night I was looking right into Captain Warburton's face and for a moment I thought he might walk over and strike Father down! And then he took off after Ned—''

Constance turned away. When she spoke she had got control of herself. "No, it was not Captain Warburton. *Nor anyone you know.*"

That was a great disappointment to Pamela, who had been hoping for Captain Warburton.

"You aren't going to tell me who it was," she accused in a complaining voice.

"No, I am not." Sharply. "And do not ask. I have already confided in you more than I should."

"Well, *I* certainly wouldn't tell anybody." Pamela bridled resentfully.

"Not even Tom?" Constance shot at her. "For he is sure to ask you—on Ned's behalf!"

Pamela caught her breath and her eyes widened.

Constance studied her for a long moment. Then abruptly she flung her arms around her and began to cry. "Oh, Pam," she wept, "I am in such a terrible mess and no one—*no one* can get me out of it!" She dabbed at her eyes. "Your father has Tabitha *guarding* me," she said shakily. "I'm being watched lest I escape!"

"Of course you're not being watched!" cried Pamela warmly. "Tabby only moved in with you because your room is warmer and her bones have been hurting her these last days."

"Ask her to move into your room and sleep by the hearth and see what happens," cried Constance scornfully.

Pamela did. Tabitha declined, insisting Constance's room was much the warmer.

That made Pamela very thoughtful. She wished Constance had confided in her who it was who had seduced her. It might have helped, she thought.

It might indeed, but in no way that she was likely to guess.

The morning had brought Ned but the afternoon brought a more formidable visitor from Warwood—Captain Warburton. A very determined Captain Warburton indeed, who tossed his reins to a groom and strode inside without being announced.

From the window of Constance's bedchamber Pamela saw him arrive and turned to report excitedly, "Captain Warburton just rode up."

"I have been expecting him," said Constance grimly. And waited for Tabitha or Stebbins to knock on the door and announce that the Captain was here to see her.

"Well," said Pamela in some surprise as the moments dragged on. "It would seem the Captain is not here to see you."

"Then he will be interviewing the Squire," said Constance wearily.

That interview was not going well. Tony Warburton had swept in unannounced and caught the Squire seated at his desk in the library at work on his estate accounts. The Squire looked up as he entered.

"I've been expecting you, Tony," he said.

"I little doubt it." The Captain's lean visage looked exceedingly grim. He was peeling off his gauntleted riding gloves as he spoke and now he tossed them onto the desk. "I feel you owe me an explanation, Clifford. You promised the girl to Ned. We shook hands on it. You said you would announce it at the ball. Yet when you made the announcement it was to betroth her to someone else. Ned is sore aggrieved over it, for he feels there's something strange going on. He cannot believe that Constance is attracted to this fellow from Lyme—nor can I!"

"Have a drink, Tony," sighed the Squire, reaching for a pair of goblets and a bottle of Canary. "You're going to need it."

Calmly his guest sat down and took the proffered goblet. The Squire had time to think that Tony Warburton had always had a very steady pair of eyes—never steadier than today when they looked across the desk with a cold uncompromising gleam.

Clifford Archer came directly to the point. "I told Constance that I was betrothing her to Ned," he said bluntly. "And she objected. She told me that she was already secretly betrothed and had gone too far with the fellow."

Captain Warburton was looking at him in some amazement. "Surely not *Pell*?" he murmured.

The Squire nodded vigorously. "She said she feared she was pregnant by him." His next words were got out with difficulty. "I know I gave you my word, Tony, and 'tis God's truth I meant to honor it. But I couldn't cheat Ned by giving him damaged goods."

Across from him the lean Captain's gaze had gone thoughtful. He twirled his goblet, looking into the brilliant wine without seeing it. What he had just heard seemed to him incredible. Constance, he knew instinctively, was a woman of tinder—but that she should submit to Chesney Pell? Never! He knew his woman better than that.

"So I take it ye spoke to Pell about it?" His gaze upon his friend was bland.

"Aye, I caught them together and he admitted it! He's staying with us now," he added grimly. "And will be until the banns are cried and they are safely wed."

"Ye—caught them together?" The Captain's look was keener now.

"Aye. I was trying to shake the truth out of her and Pell came up and interfered. I pursued him to the attics and when

I caught up with him he was in her bedchamber *with his boots off!*''

He had probably tugged them off to flee without a clatter, thought the Captain sardonically.

"And what did he say then?"

"The fellow admitted it! Damme if he didn't!" The surprise he still felt was mirrored in the crystal blue gaze Axeleigh's squire turned on the Captain.

Surprise was mirrored too in the gray eyes that met his— and disbelief.

"And what did Mistress Constance have to say?" he wondered.

"Oh, I listened not to the wench. She was tugging at one or t'other of us at the time, I believe. But I told him he *would* marry her—and he seemed pleased."

"Which is not too surprising," murmured the Captain. "He's been dangling after Constance ever since he got here."

"Aye, he had asked me if he could court her," agreed the Squire wearily. "But then so many others have asked that I'm deadened to it by now."

Across from him Tony Warburton nodded sympathetically. "I can see your problem, Clifford."

"Ye can see that I had no choice, Tony?" demanded the Squire eagerly. "The fellow admitted he'd debauched her and they were already secretly betrothed without my knowledge. That was the way of it, Tony. Ye'll not hold it against me? For we've been friends a long time. I could have sent Pell packing and forced it the other way—but 'twould have been a shabby trick on Ned."

Captain Warburton nodded. To his friend's mystification he was looking almost happy. He was thinking, *This clears the way for me with Constance. Ned is out of it now—and not by my doing. He'll not hold it against me now if I take her for myself!* In fact, hadn't Ned said vengefully this morning at breakfast that he was going to squire Margie Hamilton everywhere, right under Constance's fickle nose? As for Pell, he'd simply brush him aside! He rose. "I thank you, Clifford, for being so frank. I'll be going now—but I think I'll just offer Mistress Constance my felicitations first."

In puzzlement the Squire rose also. "It's very decent of you, Tony, to take this attitude. You'd have been within your rights to have called me out!"

Tony Warburton laughed. It was a lighthearted laugh—as lighthearted as a boy's. "Oh, I'm a civilized man, Clifford. I'd not be calling ye out for making a decision any man of honor would have made." His big hand clapped the Squire warmly on the shoulder. "Well, good luck to ye, Clifford—whoever your ward's husband turns out to be."

He left the Squire puzzling over that remark and went off in search of Constance.

And found her just descending the stairs. She paled at sight of him.

"I thought you'd gone," she said.

"Or else you wouldn't have come down," he said ironically, and swept her a mocking bow.

"That's right." She was nettled by his tone. "I suppose the Squire has told you all about it?"

"He has."

"Well, then?" Those purple velvet eyes challenged him. *What do you want of me?* they asked. That soft voice, like the whisper of the wind through the rushes, raked raw across his alert senses—that voice that seemed to him an echo from the past. *Why do you stay?* it seemed to be saying.

"I came of course on Ned's behalf," he said carelessly, watching her.

She tossed her dark head. "Ned is no longer to be considered. I am betrothed to another now."

"So I have been told. *And* the circumstances."

She flushed. "I will bid you good day, Captain Warburton."

"Constance—" he hesitated. "Are you sure you have not something to tell me?"

"I don't know what you mean."

"Well," he said humorously, "it seems a bit soon to

decide yourself pregnant by someone you have known scarce a fortnight!"

Constance draw herself up to her full height. "That is not your affair, Captain Warburton. I have known him long enough!"

"Granted." He smiled down at her speculatively. "But you could have known him for years and I'd never believe that you'd go to bed with him."

Her face was crimson. "*Good day* to you, Captain Warburton!"

"Good day to you, Mistress Constance." Again the tall Captain favored her with an ironic bow.

She stood very still on the stairway as he swept out and rode away.

He was riding away to Warwood, and her heart rode with him.

Axeleigh Hall, Somerset,
February 2, 1685

CHAPTER 27

In the Valley of the Axe no snow had fallen since the Christmas season but Constance's wedding day dawned bright and cold and before breakfast was over a leaden sky had settled overhead and there were occasional flakes of snow flying. Before the morning was half gone it was snowing hard and the Squire frowned as he looked up at the sky.

"We'll be lucky if we don't get another blizzard," he muttered.

Constance stared out at a world gone white and hoped silently that the roads would be blocked, the preacher unable to get there, and the wedding perforce delayed.

But of course she would not be that lucky! She left Chesney chatting with the Squire and went up to her bedchamber.

A terrible lethargy had come over her since her enforced betrothal to Chesney Pell, a fatalism. She felt as if she were being swept along by great forces and was powerless to resist. Now she walked about wringing her hands. She had been watched every moment, even the stables were guarded—it was obvious this wedding was going to happen.

An hour or two passed and then Pamela stuck her head in—a very fashionable head, every golden curl done up in the latest style, pomaded and adorned with ribands. An adoring Tabitha had slaved over it since breakfast.

"There's someone waiting in the side corridor by the garden door who says he must see you," she told Constance.

Constance, who was just listlessly holding up a brilliant to her hair, swung her head around. "Who is it?" she asked—but Pamela was gone, dashing on to the "housewifely duties" her tomboy soul seemed to enjoy so much.

Pamela was enjoying this wedding far more than she was, thought Constance. She rose with a swish of amethyst satin skirts and hurried down to the little corridor that let out onto the garden—although unused in weather like this. Could it be Galsworthy with some message for the Cause? she wondered as she rounded the back-stair landing and clattered down the last flight on her high heels into the dark little vestibule where her caller must be waiting. If so, he had certainly picked a bad day for it!

It was certainly no one for the Cause. Her breath caught as she recognized the tall figure of Tony Warburton, lounging against the doorjamb. He had not removed his heavy woolen cloak and his hands were still encased in wide-gauntleted riding gloves. He strode forward with a jingle of spurs as she came to an uncertain halt, not sure what to expect.

"I have come for you," he said briefly. "I cannot think that you mean to marry this fool, but Ned thinks you will and Clifford means to see that you do."

Escape! He was offering her escape!

"I thank you for this, Captain Warburton," she said shakily, her eyes large and luminous—and very grateful.

His smile gleamed down at her. "Change to your riding clothes," he directed. "I will wait for you here. I have a horse for you saddled and waiting by the gate."

"I think I should warn you I am a very poor rider—in case there is pursuit," she told him doubtfully.

"I have already observed your riding." There was a note of gentle triumph in his laughter. "But no matter. Your horse is gentle, and if need be, mine can carry double."

"Were you seen coming here?" she asked fearfully.

"Certainly," he said in an easy voice. "But 'tis believed I am an early guest, here to attend the wedding—not to abduct the bride!"

Abduct the bride! Her heart was beating hard enough to smother her. "What shall I pack?" she asked helplessly, for she had so many clothes and how much could a horse carry?

"No need to pack anything. We will buy what we need on the way."

His calm control of the situation held her fascinated. "Where are we going?" she asked in a small voice.

"We will ride for London," he told her. "Where a quick marriage ceremony can be readily had. And then if need be we will come back and have the banns cried here and I'll marry you again before all of Somerset!"

They would ride for London—*and on the way she would escape him and find her way to Margaret in Devon*. She looked away.

"They may—follow us," she said in an uneven voice.

"Pell is a fool," he said softly. "We will lose him handily. And Clifford will head for Warwood to confront me, believing I would take you to my stronghold to defy the world—he will be too late to catch up with us. They will both abandon the search, for they are not like me—I would follow you to hell!"

And then his strong arms were around her, drawing her to him. His lips were upon hers, warm, seductive. Her every sense tingled rapturously—and then stilled.

I would follow you to hell, he had said. *And he meant it!* That meant, if she ran away, that he would follow her to Tattersall—and Margaret. And he would see Margaret without her mask and Margaret would drain a vial of hemlock.

She would be responsible for Margaret's death! And even if she did *not* go to Tattersall, if she followed her heart and ran away with Tony, Margaret would hear of it and the result would be the same.

A cold numbing stillness stole over her. She seemed to wilt in his arms.

Mystified, he let her go, looked down at her in puzzlement. "What is wrong, Constance?"

She cast about in her mind for some way to push this man she loved so much away from her. "Have you thought of Ned?" she whispered. "How *he* would take the news that we have run away together?"

His jaw hardened. "Ned is young. He will get over it."

"But he may not!"

The gray eyes that looked into hers were very steady. "Ned is my brother and I love him well," he said. "But it is I and not Ned who stand here ready to rescue you from an abominable marriage."

"How do you know it is so abominable?" she muttered.

"Because you cannot see yourself bound to a fool!" he burst out. "Of that I am certain. Just as I am certain that you told Clifford a lie to rid yourself of Ned and somehow got caught up in it!"

She flashed him a startled look.

"So I was right," he said, and gave a low laugh. "Pell did not bed you. I'll wager you are still a virgin."

All her senses urged her to go to him, hold him, never let him go. But for Margaret's sake, she had to fend him off. To Dev she owed nothing—he did not love her, had left her for another woman. But she could imagine in terror how Margaret would feel if she heard that Constance—the girl she had entrusted with her innermost thoughts—had run away with Tony Warburton. Putting herself in Margaret's place, it made her feel sick to think about it. She took a step backward and her face was very pale. "You are wrong about me. I am not a virgin."

He caught his breath. "No matter," he said briskly. "I care not what went before. We will start afresh, you and I."

If only she could!

"We cannot—start afresh, Tony."

"And why not?" He seized her by the wrist even as she cringed away from him. "Little fool, I will take you away from here by force! I will not stand by and see you marry an insipid boy!"

"I cannot go with you, Tony," she said hopelessly.

"Why not?"

"Because"—it was hard to get the words out—"I have made a bargain and I must honor it."

"Are you saying you love Pell?" he demanded.

Her eyes fell away from him. "No. But I mean to marry him."

He looked amazed. "Why this changeabout? A moment ago you were hot to escape him!" His voice harshened. "Is it Ned's tender feelings you fear for? Let me handle Ned!"

"No—it is not Ned." She took a deep breath. "I want to marry Chesney," she said stubbornly.

"I'll not believe it! You want to marry him?" He sounded incredulous.

"Yes, I do." And suddenly she did—for it would solve everything so neatly. She could not go to Margaret, and if she ran away from Chesney now, Tony would surely follow. And she had no money, no other place to go. Chesney offered safe haven, far away in Lyme Regis. She would go with him to Lyme and there she would release him from this "fake" marriage, she would admit herself a bigamist! But first she would go with him to Lyme! And put long miles between herself and this masterful captain who threatened to drown her resolve with his vibrant presence! "I will admit that you attract me, Tony," she added shakily. "But I intend to marry Chesney." And as his jaw hardened, "No one is forcing me; it is my own desire."

She heard his sharp intake of breath. He took her lightly by the shoulders, touching her as if she were delicate and precious, and she stirred beneath his touch. He looked down keenly, searching her face.

With the greatest effort of her life, she managed to keep every feature immobile and looked back at him with big unfathomable velvet eyes.

"Then this marriage is on your own head!" he said abruptly, and his hands left her shoulders.

She closed her eyes—and heard the door slam.

At that moment she felt all her resolve leave her. She sank to the floor in a satin heap and wept. Wept for the old love that had proved false, wept for the new love she could not have. Wept for herself, and for the life that stretched out desolate before her.

It was Tabitha who found her.

"Here, get you up!" cried the serving girl, scandalized. "What will people think if they find you crying, with the wedding guests already arriving!"

"Yes, they must not see me like this." Constance dashed the tears from her lashes as sturdy Tabitha tugged at her.

Pamela, who had been watching from the windows, expecting to see at any moment Captain Warburton gallop away with Constance and make a sensation in the county by abducting Axeleigh's bride, could control her curiosity no longer. She arrived just as Tabitha got Constance to her feet.

"You didn't go with him?" she gasped.

"No," sighed Constance. "I didn't go with him."

"Then you're really going through with it?" marveled Pamela.

Constance nodded.

"I don't understand you!" cried Pamela, exasperated.

Neither did the Captain. Although he flung out of the house at Axeleigh in a rage, before he was a mile from the gates his temper had cooled. There was something here he did not understand but his instinct for the woman had been sure. Constance desired *him*—and not Chesney Pell. He had felt her tremble in his arms, felt her heart race—and he had seen the patient boredom with which she looked at Chesney.

Thoughtful now, he brought Cinder to a stop and then turned the big charcoal stallion's head around and arrived, covered with snow, back at Axeleigh's front door. He would attend the wedding. All was not lost until the final vows were spoken!

Captain Warburton was but the first guest to arrive. Others straggled in all day, half-frozen. They shook off the snow from their cloaks and stamped their numbed feet to restore the circulation before the great hearths that were piled with fragrant woods, apple and hickory, in honor of the occasion. It was a strange time for a wedding, most of the guests agreed—most brides sensibly chose to wait for May or June, when people did not have to struggle over icy roads to attend the ceremony! But they whispered their criticism behind their hands, for the Squire of Axeleigh was a generous host and well liked across the county, and if he chose to hold the wedding of his ward in such weather, that was of course his privilege—he was paying for it.

"Maybe there's need for hurry, could be there's an heir on the way," whispered a gossipy lady in saffron plush, just being revived from her cold journey by a glass of wine.

"Nonsense, the girl is marrying him for his money," reproved a lady who was just coming unwrapped from the wet shawl and cloak she had worn through the driving snow.

Pamela, threading her way through the arriving guests, heard both comments and frowned. Better to have had the wedding in June, she was thinking unhappily. Without all this haste. In June (if the wedding was still on) Chesney could have given his bride a proper nosegay instead of that dried gilded bouquet. And the couple could have thrown open their bridal casements on their wedding night and breathed deep of the garden's perfumed air, and the next day beneath blue skies they could have ridden off through summer meadows fresh with dew. They could have crossed the silver ribbon of the Axe on their way down into Dorset to the seaport town of Lyme.

All the way to Lyme . . . it wasn't as if Constance would be living nearby—at Warwood, for example, where they could see each other often. Oh, dear, she was going to miss Constance most awfully! She cast an angry look at Captain Warburton, urbane as ever, who leaned against the mantel with one booted foot resting on the heavy brass fender. Before the evening was over Constance would be a married woman. Married to the wrong man. *Why didn't Captain Warburton do something? It was unthinkable that he would just stand by and let this happen!*

Someone remarked that the wedding couple would be lucky if they could get through the gates tomorrow at all, the way it was snowing, and someone else laughed and said, "We'll all be here for a week, the way it looks—let's hope the Squire's wine cellar holds out!"

Pamela's eyes automatically sought the windows and she saw that the snow that had been falling throughout the day was indeed coming down heavier now. It formed a curtain of white outside, gradually turning blue in the early winter dusk.

She sighed as Constance, pursued happily by Chesney, moved into her line of vision.

To Constance the whole day had had a nightmarish quality— surely it must be a bad dream from which she would soon wake. None of it seemed real to her: Not the richly garbed wedding guests thawing out in the drawing room or clustered around the Squire. Not the wedding gifts. Not the impressive display of refreshments in the dining room, where two great swans in full feather and stuffed with chestnuts flanked a suckling pig with an apple in its mouth. All three reposed on large silver chargers in the center of a long board piled high with delicious Cheddar cheeses, pigeon pies, oysters, plum cakes and dainties of every description.

The sight of Pamela looking as if the enormity of her costume might overset her brought a wan smile to Constance's lips. Dear Pam! She had fussed and fumed over every detail of this wedding about which she herself couldn't care less, and there Pam was—her maid of honor—bravely gowned in blue and silver. Pamela's gown was of stiffest sky blue damask. Its full bell-like sleeves and enormous overskirt were lost under a forest of blue satin rosettes, her sky blue plush petticoat so heavily encrusted in silver it crunched as it moved. For a moment affection for generous, warm-hearted Pamela overwhelmed Constance and her eyes smarted.

A trifle pale, the dark beauty stood calmly receiving guests in a violet-hued gown of deep supple French pile velvet darkly spangled with silver. Its dramatic effect was only slightly marred by the bewildering profusion of riband rosettes which, according to custom, had been lightly stitched to the gown and would be snipped off and carried away by the guests as "favors." Beneath her petticoat she wore a pair of ornate beribboned bridal garters which would be ceremoniously—and boisterously—snatched off later by members of the company. She stood very straight and proud, her lovely face was very set. A gilded wedding circlet gleamed from her cloud of dark hair and a necklace of small pearls—gift of the groom, who had sent for them from Bristol—encircled her white throat. Her deep purple eyes had never looked so velvety—or so lost.

It was all that Captain Warburton could do to restrain himself from seizing her on the instant and carrying her away.

Beside her, Chesney, her flushed-faced groom, seemed to need to restrain himself from kicking up his heels. A look of childish triumph was spread across his cherubic face and his weak chin was obscured by the goblet that he raised repeatedly to his lips. He was beginning to stagger a bit and Pamela wondered if he would be able to stay on his feet through the ceremony.

Ned Warburton was conspicuous by his absence but Margie Hamilton was there, pouting, in the company of her parents.

Melissa Hawley was there too, in a crimson dress edged with black braid. She was hanging on to Cart Rawlings's arm and she giggled as she looked at Chesney.

"Chesney is probably drinking because he is afraid of how his mother will take this," she told Pamela.

Pamela was startled. "Afraid?" she echoed. "Why should he be afraid?"

"She believes him to be still at Oxford," Melissa laughed. "Indeed he has written to her as if he *were* still at Oxford—"

"Come along, Melissa," interrupted Cart, giving her arm a tug. He was red with embarrassment that Melissa should divulge what Chesney had told him in confidence.

"Wait," cried Pamela. "I am sure Constance thought—do you mean his mother actually knows nothing about this marriage?"

"Nothing at all," purred Melissa. "Constance is to be a surprise to her." Cart wrenched her away before she could say anything more.

All the wedding guests who were expected in such weather had arrived by now and Pamela drew Constance aside and repeated what Melissa had told her. "Did Chesney tell you this?" she demanded. "For he told Father that his mother was ill in Dorset and that was why she would be unable to attend!"

Earlier that day Constance had suffered an attack of remorse. It had seemed to her that she was playing a very shabby trick on Chesney—after all, she had no intention of staying with him past their arrival in Lyme! She had drawn him aside.

"You do not have to go through with this marriage, Chesney," she had told him soberly. "We can escape together. Pamela will help us. And I will go with you as far as Lyme."

Chesney had bethought him of his mother and how she had always shooed away any girl in whom he took the slightest interest. But this time would be different—this time he'd present her with a Fact Accomplished!

"If ye mean to escape"—he had wagged a mocking finger at her—"then perhaps I'd best tell the Squire to put a guard on you! For I mean to go through with this marriage!"

Constance had come away, telling herself it was all predestined. She was not meant for happiness. Or anything she wanted. She was meant to go through with this sham of a marriage.

And now Pamela was telling her that Chesney's mother was ignorant of the whole affair.

Suddenly that too seemed foreordained.

"No, he did not tell me," she said, amazing Pamela by her calm acceptance of the situation.

"But this is terrible!" cried Pamela in real concern. "She will cast you out!"

There was a look of desperation in Constance's violet eyes. "I do not think so," she mumbled. "But in any event I must take that chance." *For how could she tell Pamela that this marriage was but a device to take her to Dorset, and that she would break the news to Chesney and flee to Devon as soon as she got there?*

"But Father won't force you to—"

"It's too late." Constance laid a quieting hand on her arm. "The ceremony is about to begin."

The sonorous words fell dizzily about her. *Cherish . . . honor . . . obey . . .* words which had taken on such a glorious meaning to her in Essex when she had looked deep into Dev's smiling green eyes and plighted forever her troth. Now they fell upon her like hailstones upon a roof—meaningless, nothing but sound and fury. *If God struck down liars with lightning bolts, I would be the first to go,* she thought with a shiver as she said, "I do."

She tried not to look ahead. Soon the guests would be boisterously snatching away her bride's garters.

And then—!

Then she would be alone with Chesney. Alone in a big canopied bed.

Shakily she accepted the wine goblet Chesney offered. His hand was so unsteady he nearly spilled it on her dress. Everybody was now toasting the bride, they were clapping Chesney on the back, offering him congratulations, they were kissing her upon the cheek.

Someone said roguishly, "Are you ready for bed, Chesney

lad?'' and Constance's cheeks burned. She must somehow keep Chesney downstairs drinking, get him so drunk that he would tumble into bed and pass out. And then tomorrow morning—oh, if only it would stop snowing, for tomorrow they must leave for Dorset!—tomorrow she would hoodwink Chesney by telling him what a magnificent lover he had been—even though he could not remember it! And she would find reasons why they could not sleep together in the inns where they stayed on the road to Dorset! Migraines, menstruation! Her mind leaped ahead, feverishly.

Captain Warburton watched her, a strange stunned expression on his face. He had never thought she would go through with it—he could not believe it even now.

The riband ''favors'' were being snipped from her gown amid much laughter. People were eating and now toasts were being drunk at random to the ladies' eyelashes and eyebrows, although wicked glances were being cast at other parts of the female anatomy even as the glasses were lifted high. Constance felt suffocated. Chesney kept on drinking.

And then she could postpone the moment no longer. Chesney was still on his feet, for with a frown the Squire had firmly taken his last glass from him and muttered something about ''consideration for the bride.'' Chesney had bobbed his head drunkenly.

The very force of the crowd around her bore Constance upstairs. Leading the pack, she saw Pamela in her enormous blue and silver gown cast a worried look back, and gave her a brave answering smile. Whatever happened now, she told herself she would somehow go through with it—so that she might leave forever behind her the sight of Tony Warburton, scowling from below, and seek refuge in Devon.

Tony Warburton was not among that tipsy crowd of well-wishers who, amid shrieks of laughter and merry shouts, snatched off one of the bride's beribboned garters. It was of violet satin a-sparkle with brilliants and Constance had insisted those garters be tied well below her knees lest impudent questing hands be tempted to reach above and wander along an elegant naked thigh.

But custom was custom and must be followed. One of her stockings was now sliding down but Constance tried to keep her full skirts from being tossed up as eager hands sought her other garter beneath her swirling petticoat and chemise.

In the midst of all this, the party about the bride became suddenly aware of a loud commotion downstairs. *Late wedding guests,* thought Pamela. *And no wonder, people are crying out—with the snow as deep as it is, the miracle is that they ever got here at all!* And then—just as Constance was being backed amid a wild flurry of skirts to the wall in the contest for the garter:

"Where is Chesney?" cried a piercing female voice from the hall below. *"Where is he? Deliver him to me this minute!"*

The questing hands fell away from Constance's skirts. One and all turned agape to meet this unexpected interruption as heavy footsteps pounded up the stairs.

In the doorway of the bridal chamber where all the merriment was taking place a large figure appeared—so large indeed it seemed to block the door. The woman who stood there panting from the rapidity of her ascent up the staircase was a stranger to all of them. She had accusing black eyes and she had not bothered to remove her snow-covered outer garments but had labored up the stairs with one gloved hand still in her fur muff and the other attempting to hold up layers of woolen petticoats and a dark velvet overdress that ran rivulets of rich crewel embroidery. Her enveloping fur-lined woolen cloak brushed against the doorjambs and her large fur hood had fallen back to reveal a bejeweled coif peeking out from beneath the encircling wrapping of a red knitted scarf. "Where is Chesney?" she repeated, on a note of rising fury. *"Where is my son?* I am here to stop this farce of a wedding!"

Someone in the crowd gave Chesney a shove forward and he emerged into his mother's sight looking dejected and befuddled.

She plunged forward and seized him, shook him like a small boy. "Are you such a fool that you would attempt to marry without my consent?" Melting droplets from her clothing flew into Chesney's frightened befuddled face.

"Madam, they are already married!" The Squire, incensed, had followed her up and now he stepped forward on Constance's behalf.

"Bah!" cried his imposing new guest, focusing her fierce gaze on the Squire. "Chesney is leaving—with me!" Pamela's blue and silver form would have blocked her way but Chesney's powerful mother grasped her lurching son, who was so unsteady on his feet that he almost fell, and brushed the girl aside like a feather. Pamela ended up rather hard against the wall.

All the young people who a moment ago had surrounded the bride now streamed downstairs after Chesney and his charging mother. With a shudder, Constance followed, and leaned down over the upstairs railing, looking down into the hall below.

The big woman's charge carried her all the way to the front door. There she paused and turned majestically to fix her glittering gaze on Constance, standing above her in bridal disarray.

Chesney turned too. "Con—Constance?" he stammered.

"There will be no room for this brazen hussy in *my* coach!" cried his mother. "Married or not!" She seized her son by the ear and dragged him forward by sheer bulk.

"Constance!" wailed Chesney as if he expected the slender girl above to fend off this leviathan who had hold of him.

Cart Rawlings found his tongue. "We will lend the bridal couple our own coach," he began eagerly. "And Chesney can return it to—"

"Never!" roared Chesney's mother. "My poor deluded boy shall ride with me!"

Pamela gasped.

Cart had never felt so foolish, but he remained a friend of Chesney's to the end. "Well, then, Constance can ride after you in our coach,'' he offered hurriedly. ''And Chesney can return it later. Or if you, sir''—he turned a pleading countenance to the Squire—''would prefer to furnish Mistress Constance with a horse?''

''A horse? Are ye mad, Cart?'' The Squire surged forward in a towering passion. ''My ward will not trail after her bridegroom alone through a howling blizzard. Not in a coach and not on horseback! Good riddance to you, Madam! You can take your son to Dorset or to hell for all of me!''

With a sniff, Chesney's overpowering mother dragged her protesting son through the front door and the Squire kicked it shut behind her with a force that nearly knocked him backward off his feet.

The sound resounded through the house like an explosion. Outside in the snow there was the muffled roar of Chesney's mother's domineering voice and the sound of a whip cracking as the tired snow-covered horses were wheeled about to depart presumably for the nearest inn that would give them shelter on such a night.

Mouths gaped at this strange departure of the groom—with his mother and without the bride. But of them all no face was more amazed than Tony Warburton's as he turned to look up at what had been—so casually, it seemed to him—tossed away. She was standing very still, perhaps with shock, in her bridal gown with the riband favors all snipped loose and one of them, perhaps the one she had been about to bestow on Pamela, still in her hand. Her face too was still and almost calm—and so beautiful it hurt to look at her.

With an effort of will, Tony Warburton forced his gaze away and held in check the sinews that yearned to send him up those stairs at a bound and sweep her up and away.

Chesney Pell—under duress, of course—had allowed himself to be led away from what Tony Warburton would have chanced hell for.

Constance, gazing down at the door through which her bumbling bridegroom and his furious mother had just departed, told herself dreamily that this was her punishment for a shabby deed: limbo again. Neither heaven nor hell but a suspension in between. Once again neither wife nor widow. . . .

And now she must face all over again the soul-shattering pressures of her life along the Axe.

An embarrassing silence now fell over the hall and all eyes turned irresistibly to Constance staring down at them from above.

Pamela pitied her.

But Constance had all the aplomb of a sleepwalker who has slept through it all. She looked down upon them as if she did not see them at all, as if none of the evening's events had touched her, while humiliation seeped through into her very soul.

And then, catching up whatever shreds of dignity she still possessed, she turned and disappeared in the direction of the bridal chamber and the empty bridal bed that awaited her.

They heard a door quietly closing.

The Squire, still purple with fury, downed a goblet of wine so fast he choked and had to be thumped on the back. He had expected to cap the evening's merriment by bestowing a dowry on Constance, but the unexpected arrival of Chesney's termagant mother had set him back on his heels. He would not dower the wench now, by heaven! Not a penny of his wealth should be bestowed on a worthless pup who let his mother haul him away from his bridal bed by the scruff of the neck, without even a struggle!

Pamela disappeared upstairs in a blue and silver swish, in an attempt to comfort Constance. And found the door firmly locked against her.

"Go away," Constance called in a trembling voice. "I don't want to see anyone just now."

Pamela stole away.

Downstairs the guests, most of whom were staying the night, milled about in little groups, chattering in amazement over what had happened.

Tony Warburton, who had been grimly silent all during this macabre performance, detached himself from them. Flinging

426

on his cloak, he strode outside and took a long silent walk in the snow. He was trying to come to terms with himself and he found it no easy task. At last he gave a short contemptuous laugh, a laugh that consigned himself to the devil—fool that he was, so set on a woman who would not have him!

Ned, he thought grimly, would probably laugh on hearing what had happened. And then most likely weep.

Numbed with cold and with boots slushing with snow, Captain Warburton took himself back into the candlelit house and astonished the company by the amount of drink a man could consume and still remain grimly sober.

CHAPTER 28

Before the week was out, an event of such import occurred that it overshadowed even the delicious scandal of Axeleigh's deserted bride. On February 6, that merry monarch—dissolute Charles II—ill since February 2, succumbed to apoplexy.

News of the King's sudden death spread like wildfire across England. Charles's brother James had succeeded to the throne the same day and subtle changes in government immediately appeared, for James was a fanatic and—like the French King Louis across the Channel—believed himself possessed of a divine mission to rid his land of the Protestant faith.

News of the King's sudden death reached Margaret in Devon and sent her out upon the road, despite the winter ice and mires, to London to receive her orders. For now the Duke of Monmouth, hearing of his father's death, would be on the move. He would come from Holland with an army, he would send James packing—everywhere the mutters were the same.

And Margaret, who had just penned another letter to her

brother at Axeleigh, once again urging him to betroth Constance to Tony Warburton, missed by one day her brother's letter which would have told her of the wedding that went wrong.

The news of the King's death reached a Valley of the Axe still floundering in snow, and as the snows of February melted into a muddy March there were meetings and ridings about and much serious conjecture about the anticipated "invasion" of the Duke of Monmouth, to claim, as Charles II's firstborn son, the throne of England.

In the last years of his reign (while the Squire's pretty daughter was rejecting suitors with almost childish glee), Charles II had ruled alone, having hastily disbanded in Oxford a Parliament that was pressing to forbid his brother James to succeed him to the throne. Shaftesbury and the other Whigs could not forget that James's wife, Anne Hyde (who had married James in a midnight marriage), was daughter to the man who had pushed through Parliament the infamous "Clarendon Code" which imposed savage punishments for attending any but Church of England services, and effectively deprived Dissenters of both religious worship and education by the Five-Mile Act which forbade nonconformist ministers or teachers within five miles of any town—for Charles's successor to have such a father-in-law was unthinkable!

But at Axeleigh, there were other concerns.

Chesney had not come north for Constance. She remained at Axeleigh. He was still at his mother's house in Lyme, for that lady had refused even to let him go back to Oxford, trumpeting that he was "no better than a babe in arms" and "wattle" in any strumpet's hands!

"What does Chesney say?" Pamela asked, noting the barrage of letters that came up from Lyme.

"Nothing," said Constance, dismissing Chesney's hysterical entreaties with the one word. She felt very ashamed of herself. For now at last the appalling truth was borne in on her:

Escape had not been her only reason for marrying Chesney. She was punishing herself by this marriage—punishing her-

self for giving her heart to Dev—and losing him; punishing herself for betraying Margaret by treacherously falling in love with Tony Warburton. Now her hot face went down into her hands. *She was not only a scandal, she was a cheat! She was cheating this fool she had married!*

"I have sent him back his pearls," she muttered.

Constance must be got out of this despondency, thought Pamela. "Do you think the Duke of Monmouth will invade?" she asked, in an attempt to get Constance's mind on other things. "Father says wiser heads will hold him back."

Constance lifted her own head and gave Pamela a long level look. "He is Charles's firstborn son! Of course he will invade," she said scornfully.

"Then there will be a battle, for James will not give up the crown easily."

"Yes, there will be a battle," said Constance tersely and went back to glooming.

March slid into a rainy April and still Constance skulked about the house, remaining in her room except for meals, refusing to see visitors. Not that there were many callers for her these days, for Constance was no longer the eligible dowried young lady she had been before her disastrous marriage to Chesney. Women had always been envious of her—it was young men come a-courting who had flocked around.

The Squire too was depressed. The blackmailer had increased his demands. The last time he had put thirty guineas into the hollow tree.

Pamela, surrounded by so much gloom, did her best to keep everybody's spirits up. Dick Peacham, to her enormous relief, had been called away just after the Twelfth Night Ball to his uncle's bedside.

"Dying," he had told Pamela dramatically. "And he has promised to leave me half of what he owns!"

Pamela couldn't have cared less if Dick's uncle left him half the kingdom, but she had tried to seem interested. "Of course you must go," she had assured him. "And stay till the end!"

But the end was slow in coming. Dick Peacham found himself twiddling his thumbs at the bedside of an uncle who was gradually recovering and yet loath to let his favorite nephew out of his sight.

Peacham's absence had lightened Tom's heart. Pamela would forget the fellow now, he was sure. But he reminded himself that Peacham's departure had left Pamela without a ready escort and in April he squired her to a party at the Hamiltons'. As was usual now, Constance had refused to go. But Pamela was determined to enjoy the evening. It had been thrilling to come in on Tom's arm. Ignoring Margie Hamilton's sly little digs about Tom being interested in Dorothea Hawley (for although flirtatious Melissa had been real competition, earnest young Dorothea, Pamela felt, was not), Pamela had clung to that arm even when Tom would have shaken her off. Then she had sighted Dorothea making her entrance along with the rest of the Hawley family.

Dorothea's flaxen hair was self-consciously arranged, stiffly curled by her mother to be flat on top and to fall into corkscrew ringlets at the sides that imitated—by accident, not design—spaniel's ears. To hold them well away from Dorothea's "blooming cheeks," as her mother insisted on calling them (loudly, to call attention to her daughter), these curls were wired to stay in place.

"Be careful, Tom," whispered Pamela roguishly. "If you startle Dorothea by bending over as if to steal a kiss, she may rear up and put out your eyes with those wires that hold her side curls!"

Tom looked thoughtful for he had indeed considered planting a kiss or two on those much-vaunted "blooming cheeks"—if he could get Dorothea away from her twittering mamma long enough.

When she got back, Pamela told Constance about what she'd said, hoping to make her laugh.

"Watch out for Dorothea," warned Constance. "Melissa

was only flirting with Tom—*she* wants every man. Dorothea is going to single one out and play for keeps. And if it's Tom she's after—!'' She left the sentence unfinished.

Pamela only laughed.

But while Pamela thought about Tom and Constance thought about all her mistakes, the countryside was seething with rumors:

Monmouth had sailed from Holland with a large force. He had not. He was not coming till fall. He was already here. He had landed in Dover. He was marching on London. He had not landed at all. Argyll's forces had sailed to Scotland. They had been sunk. They had not sailed at all. Monmouth had been imprisoned by the Dutch. He had not. On and on it went.

With all the fervor of the disappointed in love, Ned flung himself into the Cause. ''Ye should join us,'' he told Tony.

''And help another Stuart gain the throne?'' The Captain quirked a sardonic eyebrow at him.

''Yes!''

Captain Warburton shrugged. He had had much experience of wars and this one was likely to be short and tragic. For he could not see the English people as stirred up enough yet to unseat James. Nor could he imagine them putting an illegitimate son on the throne of England.

He had found himself thinking often of Margaret of late.

He had loved her wild spirit, and her generous heart. He had loved her endearing ways. He had loved her courage and the way she had always tried to match him. He had loved the rustling sound of her voice and her quick wit and clever mind. Even stripped of her beauty, he knew he would still have loved her, that for him flame-haired Margaret was a woman for all times and all seasons.

Constance had so reminded him of Margaret—not in looks, but with that rich raw silk voice of hers and with some inner wildness that he sensed whenever he was near her, a breathless reaching out to life, an eagerness to be, to try, to dare. He could not understand what had driven Constance to wed so poor a stick as Chesney Pell, but marry him she had, no matter what came later.

He kept his distance from Axeleigh—as did Ned.

Meantime The Masked Lady was in great demand. Margaret, an obvious aristocrat by manner, voice and bearing, was a natural choice for messenger between aristocratic houses. A lady in a riding mask could join unnoticed large hunting parties, groups riding desultorily down country lanes, she could slip into a Masque and dance the night away, while receiving or giving information. Margaret was kept busy plying the roads with dangerous messages carried in her head or on thin parchment under her voluminous skirts. But it must have been the same whimsical fate that had caused her to leave Tattersall one day before the Squire's letter arrived that brought her in May to the Great North Road.

She was carrying a message from a peer in London to a peer in Lincoln—and neither gentleman wished to be involved if his messages should go astray, for neither had a taste for the block. So The Masked Lady was the perfect solution. She had picked up her messages at a London masque and would deliver them the same way at a masquerade ball being held in Lincoln just so she might deliver her messages, masked and anonymous.

The messages were sealed and Margaret had little doubt that they would be signed only with an initial. That what they contained was treasonable and would mean her death if caught was something to which she gave little thought. She counted her life as already ended. All that happened now was anticlimactic, a postscript written to a vanished life.

She might have chosen to ride on horseback up the Great North Road to deliver her messages but so far she had had very good luck by coach. Besides, highwaymen were not interested in letters. They would snatch the earbobs from her ears and the brooch from her shoulder and demand her velvet purse (she carried two, one containing gold coins tied beneath her skirts, the other containing silver and coppers and in plain sight). The gold chain and locket with Tony Warburton's picture (she would fight for that) was well concealed beneath her handsomely tailored traveling clothes. And unless they searched her thoroughly they would not find the small pistol or have reason to discover that Margaret was a very good shot.

When Margaret settled her bronze broadcloth skirts into the stagecoach in Peterborough, she was expecting an uneventful ride, for the driver had boasted openly that *his* coach always got there safe, for the owners paid the famous highwayman "Gentleman Johnny" a fee for safe passage. Margaret had heard that name often that spring. It was said that Gentleman Johnny "owned" the Great North Road. He was the best shot in England and could strike a thrown copper penny dead center farther than most people could see the penny.

Margaret, who had no great love for highwaymen, was for once glad to be under the protection of one. She would make her journey to Lincoln swiftly and be there in time for the masked ball, where she could deliver her messages and be gone.

But the second day troubles plagued the coach. It had a wheel that kept coming loose. The passengers were irritated as they waited in out-of-the-way places for it to be repaired.

They were a mixed bag, those passengers: a nondescript gentleman from Chichester with nothing to say, two maiden ladies journeying to join a nephew in Lincoln, and an arrogant young man with a sturdy body and a dissipated face—and when she learnt his name, Margaret forgot all about the rest of them.

"So you are Lord Dacey of Claxton House?" she murmured to the young gentleman who was staring rather pointedly at her handsome bustline. "I knew your father."

It was untrue but Hugh Dacey had no reason to know that. "Indeed?" he said in his slightly unpleasant voice. "And who may you be?"

"Lady Treymayne," said Margaret glibly. "Of the Lancashire Treymaynes. You may have heard of my brother-in-law, the Duke of Ascot?"

All eyes turned toward this titled lady, whose broadcloth gown suddenly assumed a more elegant cut and whose red hair took on a brighter flame.

"Indeed? Lady Treymayne?" Hugh's dissipated face gained the semblance of a smile. "Do you always travel in that mask?" he asked bluntly, for he now desired to see the face of this titled lady with the elegant figure. He was hoping the face matched the figure, for he was considering inviting her to Claxton House—aye, and making her welcome! He had never bedded the sister-in-law of a duke. It would be a milestone on a long career of debauchery.

"Always," said Margaret, lightly touching her mask. "One's complexion is so delicate." And indeed the smooth peachbloom skin that showed along her jawline gave evidence of that. "The road dust . . ." She gave a little expressive gesture of her beautiful shoulders.

"Ummm," said Hugh. "And where is your abigail?" he shot at her, for unlike the others his suspicious nature was not convinced that any lady traveling alone was of high degree.

"Poor thing, she came down with a cold—and so did my coachman. I left them both in Peterborough with my trunks. They can follow me to Lincoln when they are better."

Hugh's brows shot up. A coach of her own, by God! And a coachman and an abigail. It would be a pleasure to bed the lady! He could brag about it later!

"Ye are in a hurry to reach Lincoln, then?"

"Oh, yes. I am to attend a friend's wedding." She did not volunteer the name of the friend and Hugh did not ask. The coach jolted on.

"That cursed wheel is making us late," he grumbled.

"Yes," she agreed. "We lost two hours back there."

And even as she spoke, the fat coach almost went over on its side and the brakes screeched as the driver pulled the horses to a halt. He came down from his high perch.

"Trouble with the wheel again," he shouted and was rewarded by Hugh's curses, which sounded above the general grumbling of the passengers.

By now Margaret thoroughly regretted her decision to travel by coach—except for one thing: Hugh Dacey. As they disembarked and found seats on flat stones by the roadside, she queried him about life at Claxton House.

"You have a sister, I believe. Is she still unmarried?" For Constance had told her about Felicity and her lace.

"No, married and gone to live in Coventry." Hugh snorted.

"I take it you did not approve the marriage?"

"I had no chance to approve it. She ran away with a traveling seller of laces who chanced to come by the house in my absence!"

Constance will be glad to hear that Felicity has escaped you! thought Margaret, thinking to send this information to Constance via her next letter to Clifford Archer—a letter that would have to wait, for these were troubled times. Rebellion was in the air. The Duke of Monmouth might already have set sail for England.

"Felicity is well, I take it?" she asked, unperturbed.

Hugh grunted. "Well enough for a woman who has just given birth to twins," he told her morosely. "She seldom bothers to write."

Another tidbit for Constance.

"And yourself? Have you married? It is important when one has a title to pass on, you know."

He gave a short laugh. "No, I've never married. Too busy with wenching." He gave her a nasty grin.

Margaret regarded him coolly. *Everything Constance has said about him is true,* she thought. And pitied the child Constance had been—that child who had had to deal with him. "But there must be plenty of handsome dowries awaiting only your consent," she murmured ironically.

In point of fact there were none at all for Hugh Dacey's reputation was unsavory to the point where civilized folk would scarce let him in their houses, but his chest expanded. "Many," he agreed. And then, in a spirit of bravado, "If this coach breaks down again, I've a good mind to cane the driver!"

Considering the brawn of this particular driver, Margaret considered that a very risky business. But on Constance's behalf she thought it would be nice if Hugh tried it—and got his bones broken. "Exactly what I would do if I were a man," she sighed. "Ah, if only Lord Treymayne were here to do it for me!"

"And where is Lord Treymayne, may I ask?"

"Interred in a marble vault in his favorite estate. In Suffolk."

"Suffolk, you say?" Hugh Dacey had acquaintances in Suffolk. They were not, however, of the consequence of those for whom Margaret on occasion carried messages, and she stunned him with her knowledge of great houses there over whose thresholds he had never trod.

Thus amicably they passed the time, and both—when the driver gloomily asked the passengers if they cared to seek shelter at a nearby cottage or go on with a half-mended wheel in the gathering dusk to an inn down the road—voted to press on.

They had gone barely half a mile when, at a turn in the road, the horses neighed and reared up and the coach came to a sudden rocking halt.

"If it's that damned wheel again—!" Hugh Dacey had seized his cane and was half out of his seat.

"I think it is not," said Margaret calmly, for she had cast a glance outside and had seen a masked man with a gun pointed at the driver.

"Everybody out," roared the driver's voice and as they spilled out of the coach, the nondescript gentleman from Chichester suddenly pulled out a pistol and ordered the passengers to "stand steady."

"An accomplice!" raged Hugh. "A damned accomplice!" He jumped down beside her, almost oversetting her as she reached back to help the two twittering elderly ladies down.

Everybody but Margaret had their hands up. She was pretending to cower a bit, and keeping her hand near the pistol in her pocket in case of need. These highwaymen could have her earbobs, but she would fight to keep her locket.

The danger inherent in this pattern of behavior never entered her mind. She regarded her life as finished. She had already lost everything that mattered. With Death she could now afford to play games. She tensed as the masked highwayman dismounted and approached while the other one mounted a spare horse.

Gibb was watching Dev in disapproval. He had not cared for this venture from the first—although he could well understand it once Dev had acquainted him with some of the facts.

Margaret had half expected him to pause before her, to denounce her as the notorious Masked Lady and to seize her. For why should not a King's agent pose as a highwayman? Indeed it seemed to her an excellent ruse.

But to her surprise he marched straight up to young Lord Dacey and stood staring into that flushed belligerent face.

"Step forward," he ordered Hugh.

"It's too bad you don't have your cane, Lord Dacey." Margaret gave him her sunniest smile.

Hugh was too frightened to appreciate the malice in that gibe. "Y-you won't shoot me?" he worried.

"You'll have to chance it," came the ironic voice of the masked man. A pleasant voice, cultivated. Margaret, who was sensitive to voices, approved it.

Hugh took an uncertain step forward.

"Closer!" snapped the highwayman. And as Hugh wavered forward on the uneven ground, he added softly, "Can you think of any good reason why I shouldn't shoot you?"

"Oh, please!" gibbered Hugh. "I've never seen you before—I *can't* have done you an injury. Take my money— take anything! There's a titled lady here on the coach—*take her!* She can bring you a fat ransom!"

Margaret's look of cold scorn was interrupted by the highwayman's ringing laugh. "Always consistent," he said. "Courageous to the end!" He pointed the pistol at Hugh's face and Hugh backed away.

"If you move a step farther," said the highwayman in a conversational tone, "I shall put a bullet exactly between your eyes."

Hugh came to a shivering stop and stood teetering with one foot on a rock.

"Such a show of spirit!" mocked the highwayman, and of a sudden thrust his pistol into his belt. A shadow of hope flashed over Hugh's face to disappear at his tormentor's next words. "You're to take no comfort from the fact that I've put my pistol aside for the moment. That fellow up there"—he nodded at Gibb—"is nearly as good a shot as I am. He could drop you before you'd batted an eyelash. You can put your hands down now." Gingerly Hugh did so. As if to satisfy their curiosity, the sinewy fellow in the black mask addressed the passengers. "I don't usually bother with coaches carrying ordinary passengers," he explained pleasantly. "But for this particular coach I've been waiting. For it carries with it this particular gentleman from Yorkshire"—he nodded at Hugh— "and when I learned he'd gone visiting to Peterborough, I've waited these three weeks past for him to come north just so I could give him this."

And with a sudden violent gesture his right fist struck out and cracked against Hugh Dacey's jaw, delivering such a blow that launched Hugh backward with a crash against the coach.

One of the elderly ladies screamed.

"Is anything the matter, Lord Dacey?" inquired the highwayman politely. "Come, step forward again. I stand here relatively unarmed and I give you my word that my friend here will not shoot you down if you best me."

Hugh whimpered and shrank against the coach.

"What, do you hesitate?" mocked the highwayman. "I've seen you kick men half to death because they didn't polish your boots well enough." His voice harshened. *"Step forward!"*

Margaret laughed. "I think Lord Dacey is lost without his cane," she remarked. "He had promised that if the wheel broke down again he would thrash the driver with it."

The driver, his hands still lifted in the air, turned a look of enraged disbelief on Lord Dacey. "He couldn't thrash me if I had one hand tied behind my back!" he roared.

"Well spoke," approved the highwayman. "Which of us would you care to thrash just now, Hugh? The coach driver or me?"

"I think you've broken his jaw, Johnny," said Gibb calmly.

"He has another," said Margaret dispassionately.

Hugh began to gibber.

"He's lucky it wasn't his neck," said the highwayman in disgust. "But if the lady here still requires some amusement—?"

Hugh began to cry. Thinking of all that Constance had told her, Margaret savoured every tear.

"I take it Dacey has offended you in some way?" Dev asked, hoping for an excuse for some new attack on Hugh.

"Not recently," smiled Margaret. "But I think he had it in mind for later."

Dev gave her a puzzled look, but he had tarried on this dusky road long enough.

"I note your companion here called ye Johnny," bawled the stage driver as Dev mounted. "And my principals told me in Peterborough that they paid ye good money reg'lar to let our coaches through."

"You'll note also, then, that I haven't robbed your passengers," that pleasant cultivated voice reminded him. "I've just settled an old score with one. A personal matter."

Margaret's interest quickened. So this was the famous Gentleman Johnny who patrolled the Great North Road with the insolence of a feudal baron!

"I have need to go north quickly," Margaret spoke up. "And I would pay in gold for safe passage—and a horse."

"Don't do it, Johnny," said Gibb quickly.

"I'll make you a bargain," said the masked lady merrily. "We'll keep on our masks until you deliver me safe within reach of Lincoln! You'll have the gold, I'll have safe passage— and none will be the wiser."

Something in her voice stirred old memories in Dev. Her voice reminded him of another voice that had raced along his heartstrings like heavenly music. He was suddenly curious as to who she was.

"You can come," he said shortly. He reached down and swung her up in front of him. "Although you can take no baggage, my lady."

"No matter," she said carelessly.

And so it was that Margaret met Dev on the Great North Road.

Constance would have been thunderstruck, as her hopeless violet gaze scanned the skies over Somerset, to know that Margaret was riding—as she herself had once ridden—mounted up before Deverell, racing through the night up the Great North Road.

"It would seem," Margaret said humorously, "that you've had some previous falling out with Hugh Dacey."

"Over a woman he tried to order to his bed, and who fled him in a basket atop a coach!"

Margaret's heartbeat seemed to slow down. *Surely there could not be two such?*

"And this lady meant something to you?" she surmised.

"I married her."

Margaret felt fatalistically as if she had known it all along. *This* was what Constance had not told her. "So it was *you* who made Constance so unhappy," she murmured.

The caught breath of the young highwayman came as no surprise. He reined up so suddenly that Gibb nearly plowed into him from the rear.

"Who are you?" he asked thickly, and snatched away her mask.

A beautiful face, scarred across the cheekbones, considered him. "I am Margaret Archer."

"Of Tattersall House, Devon," he murmured.

"I see you have heard of me."

"So it was to *you* Constance fled the day she left me!" He looked down fiercely into her face. *"Where is she now?"*

441

Margaret considered him. She had all the courage in the world. It would not have daunted her in the least to have refused him this information. But now she remembered how dejected Constance had often seemed that winter in Devon, how she had secretly wondered if the girl had not fallen in love in York. *So she had been married to this young highwayman!* Constance had kept her secret well. Margaret, who kept so many secrets, could admire that. She considered him soberly. "I think you broke her heart, Johnny."

"Dev," he corrected her. "Only Constance and Gibb here know my real name. On the road I'm Johnny."

"Dev," she said, trying out the name.

Of a sudden she bethought her of her exhortations to her brother to get Constance married to Tony Warburton. *Suppose he was trying to make it happen? What terrible pressure might be brought on Constance to wed? And what of Tony? Was she forcing them both into a bigamous marriage by nagging at Clifford?* Worry clouded her features. *What of Tony, who might find his life smashed again?*

It occurred to Margaret that she was creating a hell on earth for those she loved best.

"Dev," she said earnestly. "I care not what you have done, nor what you yet may do. But I am confident of one thing—Constance loves you. And great pressure is being put on her to marry, for she has told no one about you. When you have left me in Lincoln, get you quickly to Somerset. You will find her living at Axeleigh Hall near Bridgwater at the home of my brother, Clifford Archer, who calls her his ward."

"She would not care to see me," said Dev bitterly.

"You are wrong. She drooped all winter in Dartmoor and showed no interest in anything. Now I know it was because of you."

From the depths of him, Dev wanted to believe every word she said. He wanted to imagine Constance grieving for him, waiting for him, wanting him back.

"It's too late," he said, and took the lady to Lincoln.

But he tarried in Lincoln only for the night. As Margaret had known he would, he was mounted next day on a fresh horse and he told Gibb, who shook his head at this dangerous nonsense, that he was bound for Somerset.

BOOK VI
Of Death and Moonlight

In the mirror of the past, now she sees herself at last,
All the heartache, all the strivings, all the lies,
And the mirror mocks her now, she who's broken every
*   vow,*
Like her heart, she cannot mend it with her sighs.

PART ONE
Midnight Silk

Now he has met her once again, who so had changed
  his life.
Abandoned highwayman was he, who took her then
  to wife!
Wide flung in welcome are her arms, her shadowed
  eyes implore...
To stay would be to love her less, to leave to love
  her more!

Axeleigh Hall, Somerset,
May 1685

CHAPTER 29

Spring had spread its glory over the Valley of the Axe. Apple blossoms that had earlier festooned the orchards had dropped their petals, little rivulets burbled down to the river, and the meadows were thick and soft and brilliant with wild flowers. Birds caroled into the clean pure air, and the shadowy fastnesses of the Mendip Hills, with their steep sides and spectacular limestone gorges, rose regally as a backdrop to the emerald countryside that edged the silver river.

The blackmailer had proved a drain on the Squire's supply of cash and the Squire was gone to Bristol to make a deal to sell a shipment of cheeses, big as millstones, for which the area around the Cheddar Gorge was famous. He would be gone for several days.

That left Pamela in charge and she had been up late, checking the door locks and the snuffing of candles. Finally deciding to undress, she was down to her chemise when she heard a piercing shriek from downstairs and dashed down in her satin mules without even donning a robe. She found a little scullery maid trembling as she stared at the kitchen window.

"There was a face there," the girl gabbled. "Looking in at me, it were!"

Pamela did not wait. She seized a pistol from the library—after all, Axeleigh had been left in *her* care—and went outside to investigate.

Her light satin mules were irrevocably stained by dew as she walked across the grass. Suddenly a horse neighed nearby and a mounted figure flashed by her. Forgetful that she was hardly dressed for riding, Pamela dashed to the pasture where in this delightful weather the horses were spending the night. She whistled for Angel and leaped aboard the pretty mare. Riding astride, she thundered off through the gates and down the road to Huntlands in pursuit of the prowler.

Around her the world was silvered by moonlight and Pamela got a fairly clear glimpse of the man she was following as he turned a bend in the road. She could see that he wore a countryman's tall hat. But that was no plow horse he was riding! Although he had a head start, fleet-footed Angel would have been able to catch up with most horses, but she could hear his hoofbeats steadily pulling away from her.

No matter, she knew these roads! There was a shortcut through a break in the hedge that she and Tom often took. She and Angel dived through and when they came out on the road again the hoofbeats were closer. Then they seemed to disappear. Pamela slowed, walking Angel as she listened.

But the slapping branches of the hedge had taken their toll. A twig had caught in the satin riband that held up her chemise. Unnoticed, it was coming undone and the whole garment was threatening at any moment to cascade down over her slender shoulders.

To her right a twig snapped and she came instantly alert. Perhaps the prowler was attempting to ambush her! Her hand tightened on the pistol, but the sound stopped. Some little night animal must have made that sound—perhaps a fox or ferret out hunting, scurrying home to its den at the sound of her horse's hooves.

What came next happened too swiftly for her to recount accurately.

There was a break in the hedgerow on her right and of a sudden a horse and rider plunged from it. Pamela brought up her pistol but a determined gauntlet-gloved hand seized her wrist and swung the barrel away from him. A strong arm encircled her waist and she found herself lifted in a single swoop from the saddle and crushed against a hard masculine chest. A face she could not see because it was shadowed by a wide-brimmed dark hat was suddenly thrust against her own and a pair of warm lips pressed down upon her sputtering mouth an impudent kiss.

Against her will she found herself yielding to that kiss, found her resilient female body instinctively fitting itself to the contours of a deep chest that was warm and delightful against her own. Soft pulsing sensations were stealing through her body and her eyelids fluttered shut of their own volition. There was a gentle pounding in her breast, a fevered feeling, that came no doubt, she was to tell herself later, from her blood being stirred up at being attacked on this country lane!

She was limp and breathless when he let her go, the gun forgotten in her grasp. Then her eyes flew open and she saw him peering down at her.

And realized that she was staring up into Tom Thornton's amazed face.

Pamela drew back with an angry gasp. To think that Tom would waylay her, pounce upon her like that! And even as she drew back, her chemise riband, which had been working its way through the eyelets as she rode, responded to that last convulsive motion by falling free, and the soft white lawn material, edged with delicate point lace, slid down across her bosom, glided below it, and bared her firm rounded young breasts to Tom's startled view.

He blinked at so rousing a sight and would have enthusiastically kissed her again but that she drew back a trembling arm and her hand cracked like a sharp report across his face.

"How dare you look at me?" she cried in a passion, snatching at her errant chemise and pulling it up to cover her breasts.

Tom was used to the violent outbursts of his lovely lady—and he felt there was some justice to the blow. Before she could strike him again, he seized her other wrist, laughing. "I knew not who you were," he protested mildly. "I thought I was being pursued down the road and I reined up in the hedge. When I saw in the moonlight a lady on a white horse, clad in a thin chemise, I but thought to pay her some tribute!"

"Ohhh!" In fury Pamela writhed in his arms and the gun she had forgotten she still held went off with a deafening roar.

Instantly, she heard quite nearby the clatter of hooves. And with that sound, her purpose in this mad chase by moonlight was recalled to her.

"After him, Tom!" she shouted. "Don't let him get away!"

She would have broken free and remounted Angel, who reared up in the road at all this excitement, but that Tom, who kept his grip on her, seemed suddenly to have trouble with Satan. The big black horse reared up, nearly toppling them both off and losing Tom his hat, and when they finally got things sorted out again and the horses quieted, there was but the faintest clip-clop in the distance and it was hard to tell from which direction.

"You were saying something?" Tom had reached over and seized Angel's reins—as if she could not control her own horse! She was hard put not to slap his hand away.

"I was saying you've lost me my prowler that I pursued almost to your gates!" cried Pamela wrathfully. "What's the matter with that mount of yours? His manners are terrible!"

"Ah, that's Satan for you—unpredictable. Here, you can't ride about the country in your underwear, Pam. Take my coat."

" 'Twill hardly hide the fact that I'm wearing my chemise," Pamela pointed out, gazing down at her bare legs. "Indeed, wearing a man's coat will call attention to the fact!"

"You're right," said Tom instantly. "Come along with me and we'll get you something to wear."

Pamela might have protested, but Tom—more masterful than ever—had a firm grip on Angel's bridle, a strong arm around her waist, and was escorting both of them firmly through the gates of Huntlands and up the drive.

She hoped sincerely that none of the servants had heard the shot and would be up to view her dishabille. Being half-dressed had seemed of no importance as she swung onto her horse to pursue the intruder but now she felt rather foolish being escorted along with a big smoking pistol dangling from her fingers and a chemise that had to be tightly clutched for with every motion it threatened to bare her firm young breasts to the world again.

Luckily for her reputation, there was no one about. The master of Huntlands came and went at all hours, she was reminded. And even if the distant report of a pistol had caused someone to peer out of the windows, it was probably nothing unusual to see him come riding in escorting some chance-met lady. The thought made her frown darkly.

Tom brought her into the great hall, set her down upon a cushioned chair before the huge fireplace, cold and empty on this warm May night, and threw his coat over her in case any of the servants should wander in. Pamela drew up her bare legs under it and waited. The moonlight coming in through the big windows made the room a magic place—but not so magical that Pamela was not deciding busily how she would redecorate the house when *she* became its mistress. She had not yet reached a decision on the draperies, whether they should be peach or gold, when Tom strode back, carrying a woman's light flowered calico dress over his arm.

"Here, this should be a near fit." He tossed it to her.

Pamela regarded the flowered dress suspiciously. "I thought this was a bachelor's establishment!"

Tom shrugged, but his blue eyes sparkled.

Pamela shrugged off the coat which had been spread over her like a coverlet and stood up, holding the dress to her to measure its size.

"Why—I know this dress!" she cried in sudden indignation. "It's the dress Dorothea Hawley wore to the picnic on Thursday when she was supposed to have fallen in the river and gotten drenched and *you* said you'd take her home!" She grasped her chemise to her and waved the dress at him. "How do you explain how it got here?"

Tom looked pained. "It will fit you—I think."

"It will not!" exploded Pamela. "Dorothea Hawley's *much* flatter and her waist is *far* thicker!"

Tom grinned and left her to dress alone. Muttering, Pamela rethreaded her chemise riband and slipped the offending dress over her head. True to her prediction, it was tight about the bust and hung loosely around her waist, the light fabric fluttering in the breeze that came in from an open casement. Her crystal blue eyes were snapping when Tom returned.

"I'll return the dress to Dorothea," she said sweetly. "So you won't have to."

His dark gold brows elevated. "No need to do that," he told her. "It was so wet, we came by here so she could take it off and change into something dry—she's very susceptible to colds, you know, can't stand a draft."

Pamela sniffed. "And I suppose she went home *naked*?"

Tom sighed. "She borrowed a kirtle and blouse from one of the servants and she's sending the kirtle and blouse back tomorrow and having this dress picked up." He grinned at her. "Shall I send her word you arrived in your chemise and were glad of the chance to wear her dress home?"

Pamela gave him a quelling look. "That won't be necessary," she said stiffly. "You can just say you've already sent it back and *I* will tell her that it was delivered to me by mistake. The Hawleys are giving a party tomorrow night. I'll deliver it to her there."

"Resourceful, aren't you?" grinned Tom. But somehow it

pleased him that Pamela should want to make sure that he didn't return the dress to Dorothea personally.

It was the first time he had been appreciative at all of her jealousy of him, which was apparent to all who knew them. He guessed it was because she had looked such a lovely sprite out there astride the white horse with her clothes falling off in the moonlight. So different from her usual high-necked sumptuous gowns that encased her in splendor but kept you from seeing that there was a real girl underneath it all.

Tonight it had been abruptly borne in on him that she was a woman grown—and a desirable one. She seemed a young peach tree in first blossom, and he had felt a sudden overwhelming desire to touch her petals—to trail his fingers through the silkiness of her hair, to trace patterns on the whiteness of her skin. His senses heated up as he remembered the deliciously yielding flesh of her slim young body. The touch of her lips had been wondrously soft, her body had smelled faintly of roses, and her hair had moved against his cheek like finest silk. It was hard to realize that nymph in the moonlight was the tomboy who only yesterday, it seemed, he had snowballed and taken fences with and taught archery and bowls.

This wild creature met by moonlight with her long golden hair floating out like a skein of silk in the wind and her light chemise riding up around her dainty thighs, this lissome silken body divorced from the yards of embroidered damasks and stiff brocades of which she was so fond, was another Pamela. Not the tomboy companion of his boyhood, not the flushed rather comical little girl who had a "schoolgirl crush" on him over which the county tittered. This dazzling being with her flashing crystal blue eyes and her skin the texture of rose petals, this brave and lovely girl who would, half-dressed and alone, recklessly pursue an intruder through the night down the dark roads of Somerset—and then for a moment melt in his arms more seductively than any girl ever had—was a new and wondrous Pamela.

And Tom, who had been seriously considering single-minded young Dorothea Hawley, now reconsidered.

He was seeing dainty Pamela in an entirely new light.

"Pam," he said in a deeper voice than she had ever heard him use. He bent over her, smiling down at her in her ill-fitting dress. His fingers toyed with her fair hair while a finger of his other hand lifted up her chin. "You've grown up to be a beauty, you know," he told her caressingly.

A lifetime she had waited for him to say those words. Pamela's heart was thumping and she was unable to speak. She could have kissed the prowler who had brought Tom to his senses at last!

"Very lovely," he said, and bent to kiss her.

It was a long exploring kiss of great tenderness and it brought her every sense alive—indeed it brought alive senses she had not known she possessed. She relaxed in his arms and leaned against him languorously.

His questing fingers slid down her throat, feeling it throb, lightly testing the texture of the skin. On down they slid over the pearly expanse of her bosom in Dorothea Hawley's low-cut, tight-bodiced dress. Those fingers were nearing her nipples. . . .

Impudent! She slapped his hand away—but it was a playful slap.

He laughed. "Funny," he said. "I never really thought of you as a girl before."

"I know," she said. Her eyes were big and luminous.

"And now"—his voice was puzzled—"I can't imagine how I missed you."

Her heart was singing.

"I don't suppose," he murmured, leaning close, "that I could tempt you to stay the night?"

At her shocked expression, he laughed. "Come along, Pamela." He pulled her to her feet. "I'll escort you home to Axeleigh!"

On the way back they reined in their mounts in the shadow of convenient patches of trees to kiss again—and yet again.

So rapt in each other were they that they might have missed the gates had not the horses turned in automatically.

"Ah, Pamela, Pamela," he sighed as he paused for a last lingering kiss at her front door. "I don't suppose you'd care to ask me in to spend the night?" he grinned.

"Get you back to Huntlands!" laughed Pamela. "If the servants are watching, we're scandal enough as it is!" But her voice was shaky with desire. She had watched Tom pursue so many girls—ah, it was wonderful to be the one pursued! Her imagination raced on. A short betrothal—and married in cloth of gold, just like she'd always planned. Her father had said he'd be back in time for the Hawleys' party; perhaps Tom would ask him for her hand *there*! The Hawleys' party! She turned in sudden consternation to Tom.

"I forgot—Dick Peacham is back and he'll be taking me to the Hawleys' party! Oh, Tom—"

"No matter, I'll see you there." Tom gave her another kiss and was gone with a wave of the hand, riding off toward Huntlands.

Pamela stood there watching until he was out of sight. And walked in on air. Tom was hers—hers at last!

That wonderful knowledge kept her awake until nearly dawn. And so she did not see Constance steal out in that dawn, expecting Galsworthy. She had been fast asleep when Galsworthy, arriving unexpectedly early, had peered through the kitchen window in hopes of signalling cook—and been scared off by Pamela brandishing a pistol.

But Galsworthy did not come. Constance told herself he would surely come tonight and determined to stay home from the Hawleys' party to wait for him.

Clifford Archer was late in getting home. He remembered that he was supposed to take his daughter to a party at Hawley Grange and supposed he'd have time only to change his travel-stained clothes before he did so.

He found instead a note:

Dick Peacham has come home and is squiring me to the party. I will see you there.
                                        Pamela

Clifford Archer sighed. So he was to be bored with Peacham's company again. Oh, well, he supposed that was a cross that fathers of marriageable daughters had to bear!

Dick Peacham was not one of Monmouth's supporters and it startled the Hawleys to see Pamela stroll in on Peacham's arm, for they had thought him safely gone. They hoped the new arrivals would not notice how predominantly female was the gathering at the moment, for most of the young bloods—Monmouth supporters all—were holding a meeting at the far end of the house. And Peacham was a King's man, they were almost certain.

Innocent of all this, Pamela, who was carrying a flowered calico dress over her arm, detached herself from Peacham and went looking for Dorothea. She found her just coming from the corridor that led to the meeting room.

"Tom asked me to return this to you, Dorothea," she said. And then—because Tom had squired Dorothea several places—she couldn't resist adding, "As you can see, I've had it washed and ironed. *And most of the grass stains on the back came out.*"

Dorothea bridled at the implication of Pamela's words. A narrow gleam came into her eyes. She had always been jealous of Pamela, next-door neighbor to Tom Thornton and—in Dorothea's view—practically a bedfellow, romping about with him on horseback through the summer meadows! It had always been her intention to snare Tom and she was not to be robbed of her chance by a golden girl who wore clothes like gilded boxes!

"How nice of you," she said sweetly, and in reaching for the dress, dropped a ring to the floor.

Pamela leaned down and picked it up—as Dorothea had meant her to do.

"Oh, you are not to see that—*not yet!*" Dorothea dimpled

458

as she snatched back the ring from Pamela's hand. But Pamela had seen what Dorothea meant her to see. It was Tom's distinctive signet ring that he always wore on his little finger.

"Where did you get that?" asked Pamela, her face blank.

"Will you promise not to tell?" Furious at Pamela's implication that she'd been lying on her back in the grass with Tom and determined to retaliate, Dorothea leant forward. "He wants no one to know about it but—we are secretly betrothed!"

Tom's ring . . . *secretly betrothed!* With those few words, Dorothea had split her world in two. She felt as if she had been all her life climbing a mountain, struggling higher, ever higher into the sunlight *so that Tom would see her, notice her, love her.* And now suddenly she had been plunged down into an abyss.

Tom did not love her, he was but toying with her—as he had toyed with so many girls. *It was Dorothea he meant to marry!* For Tom would not have parted with that ring otherwise. It had been his father's—it meant much to him. Pamela wanted to run away and hide and weep and beat her head against the wall.

But she did none of those things. She was her father's daughter, courageous to the end. And combative. Anger rose in her suddenly. She had been made a fool of last night—and she would strike back! She asked herself what would irk Tom most? Why, to have her elude his clutches, of course—and she would. She would not be one more conquest for uncaring Tom Thornton!

By heaven, she would strike him a blow! She would betroth herself to Dick Peacham!

With an airiness she did not feel she turned away from a slyly smiling Dorothea and blundered toward her father, who was just coming through the door.

"I must speak to you," she cried, tugging at his arm. And when she had got him aside, she said in a rush, "Dick Peacham has offered for me again" (as indeed he had, all the way from Axeleigh to Hawley Grange), "and I have decided to accept him. I want you to announce it. *Now.*"

The Squire stared at her, trying to collect his wits. "Are you sure it is Peacham you want?"

"Yes, I am very sure!" Pamela's voice shook. "Make the announcement *or I will!*"

"Very well," said the Squire, for in spite of the fact that he did not like Peacham very much, with the blackmailer's demands rising ever higher, he would be very glad to see his daughter settled. "But if this is some whim of yours, Pam, I warn you that I will hold you to it—and so will young Peacham." He beckoned to Peacham and took Pamela by the hand and strode to the center of the room—and lifted the glass that had been thrust upon him almost as he entered. "Ladies and gentlemen," he said. "I wish to announce the betrothal of my daughter Pamela to a gentleman who needs no introduction—Dick Peacham. A toast to the bride and to my future son-in-law!"

Dick Peacham's surprised face was suddenly radiant. He turned rapturously to look down into Pamela's upturned rebellious face. Little minx! She had given him no inkling of this on the way over. And now he was to have not only a beautiful and virtuous bride but a large dowry as well! He puffed out his chest as people crowded around his satin-clad form to offer congratulations.

But there was one who offered no congratulations.

Tom Thornton was just coming down the hall as the Squire made his ringing announcement. He stopped stock-still and for a moment his face lost all its color. Then he strode forward, brushing people aside to reach Pamela.

"What's this about a betrothal?" he growled.

"Why, didn't you know?" Pamela, who had by now got control of herself, gave him a bland smile. "I'm going to marry Dick Peacham."

So she had been but playing with him last night! Egging him on—and all the time intending to marry Peacham and gain a title!

"I wish you joy of him," said Tom bitterly and whirled about, almost crashing into Dorothea, who had glided through the crowd after him.

"Tom." Dorothea drew him aside. "I found your ring in the hall just now. You must have pulled it off when you drew off your gloves."

Men from the meeting were sauntering in now, singly and in pairs. Tom had been so eager to see Pamela that he had dashed on ahead—and for this!

"Thank you, Dorothea," muttered Tom. "I didn't realize I'd lost it."

"It's so pretty," sighed Dorothea, flashing her hand so that Pamela, who was watching them, could see. "Would you let me wear it, Tom—just for the evening?"

"Certainly," he said in a harsh voice. "You can wear it for the evening, Dorothea." He too was looking at golden-haired Pamela, meeting her gaze grimly.

But Pamela had seen enough. *Proof,* she thought sadly. She turned away—toward Peacham.

That night she told Tabitha about her betrothal and to the girl's astonishment burst into tears.

Later she would see that ring back again on Tom's finger—and be too proud to ask him how it got there.

The Rose and Thistle,
Bridgwater, Somerset,
June 5, 1685

Chapter 30

Pamela and Constance were just dismounting from their horses outside the Rose and Thistle in Bridgwater when the inn door was flung open and a booted foot propelled Jack Drubbs into the late afternoon sunlight of the innyard.

"Well!" said Pamela, stepping nimbly aside as Drubbs staggered forward to sprawl almost at her feet.

"Perhaps we shouldn't go in after all," demurred Constance with an apprehensive look at Drubbs, who had come to his feet with a snarl and was shaking his fist at someone in the dimness within but making no move to return.

"But it's so hot and dusty," protested Pamela. "And my throat is parched and yours will be too before we get to the Ellertons!" She swept her light blue linen skirts around Drubbs, who had snatched up his hat, clapped it hard on his head and was stalking away, muttering.

Today at lunch Pamela had proposed this jaunt to visit Mary Ellerton, five miles the other side of Bridgwater.

Constance had looked up in surprise. "But the Ellertons

will insist we spend the night and you'll miss Dick when he comes over tomorrow morning!''

Pamela's answering look told her that missing Dick Peacham was just what she had in mind. She had been despondent ever since her betrothal had been announced. She was trying to postpone the wedding but the banns were already being cried.

"By all means, you should both go." From the head of the table, Clifford Archer, who was usually against overnight jaunts, chimed in. Constance, aware of how badly she had disappointed him in her marriage to a runaway bridegroom, told herself there was little chance she would run into Tony Warburton on the ride, and agreed. In fact, the wave of excitement that had engulfed England these breathless days was gradually bringing her back to life; she would be glad to feel the breeze ruffle her hair as she rode down country lanes, glad to see the hospitable Ellertons, who were often guests at Axeleigh.

And now here they were, stopping by the Rose and Thistle for a tankard of cider, cooled in the springhouse, before they continued their journey.

As they came out of the sunlight into the inn's dim, low-ceilinged interior, the gentleman whose booted foot— after a few minutes of heated argument—had propelled Drubbs's body through the inn door, was sauntering back to his seat at a far corner of the common room. He was a tall gentleman with a rather rakish carriage, and he wore unremarkable clothes—a coat and trousers of russet, well-polished boots that at the moment were dusty from travel, a spotlessly clean though rather plain cravat. His sword was serviceable and he carried two pistols stuck in his belt—but that too was unremarkable in times like these of political unrest. The handful of men in the common room relaxed as the tall gentleman took his seat again for they had all been witness to the incident when Drubbs, passing by, had carelessly spilled some ale on the russet gentleman's sleeve, been insolent about it, and got himself booted out.

Pamela and Constance seated themselves near the front

door and began to fan themselves with the carved ivory fans they carried. The innkeeper's wife, seeing it was the Squire of Axeleigh's daughter and his ward who graced their establishment, bustled over with the tankards of cool cider herself and the girls surveyed the other occupants of the room.

Everyone present was looking at them, but on one they had made an indelible impression. The russet gentleman in the corner, with his plumed hat fashionably shadowing his eyes, brought that hat a little lower with his right hand and regarded them through his fingers as he bent over his ale.

Pamela's back was to him and he could not see her well. But Constance's gaze passed over him listlessly only to snap back again. And then remain. All of her being stilled suddenly.

That russet hair spilling gracefully from beneath his wide-brimmed hat, that fine hand that obscured his face, the very stance of those broad shoulders—she waited for him to move and as if she had given him a signal, he brought down his concealing hand and looked calmly into her face.

It was Dev!

Her long hours of practice in covering over plots against the Crown, her brief eventful time as a highwayman's ever-watchful bride, that day stood Constance in good stead. Nothing but her sudden pallor gave the slightest hint that anything was amiss and Pamela, turning to speak to her, thought it was the light that made Constance appear so washed-out.

"Ye go to Bristol, ye say, sir?" One of the room's other occupants, a farmer who had struck up a conversation with Dev before Drubbs had spilled the wine, now continued it.

"Aye, to Bristol," said Dev, his steady gaze still on Constance.

Attracted by his rich cultivated voice, Pamela, her face shadowed by her wide-brimmed plumed hat, glanced back at the speaker and noted that his gaze—oblivious to all else—was concentrated on Constance. But that was nothing new—Pamela was used to seeing men look at Constance as if a thunderbolt had struck them. And indeed some of them had been looking at Pamela that way lately! She did not see Constance shake her head imperceptibly.

That faint gesture was not lost however upon the young highwayman. Dev noticed suddenly the richness of her amethyst gown, for all that it was dusty, the resplendent violet plumes of her hat, the elegance of her bearing—no, she had always had that, it had just been less apparent in faded mauve linen than it was in heavy rippling silk. Giving no sign that he had dashed all the way across England to find her, he waited.

He had not long to wait.

Constance sat quietly sipping her cider. She no longer looked at Dev. Her thoughts were whirling. Dev—*here!* And no sign of Gibb or of Nan. She passed a distraught hand over her forehead.

"Pamela," she murmured. "If you are my friend, ask no questions. Tell the innkeeper I am ill and take us two rooms for the night."

Pamela gave her an astounded look. "But—" she began.

"Oh, please," murmured Constance in an anguished voice. "*Do as I ask.* And then just—just disappear for a while!"

Bewildered and more than a little irritated by Constance's mysterious manner, Pamela got up. Her back was still to Dev as she approached the innkeeper, who was now standing beside his wife at the front door, listening to her tirade about how badly the new scullery maid had washed the trenchers.

"My friend has been ill," Pamela told him. "The journey has overtaxed her strength, I fear. I think we had best lodge here for the night."

"Ye can have the room to the left of the stairs," said the innkeeper, rubbing his hands. " 'Tis my best."

"We will need two rooms, for my friend needs to rest undisturbed."

"I'm sorry, mistress, but 'tis my last room."

"No, there's the scribe's room down the hall," interrupted his wife. "He's off to Bristol and won't be coming back tonight—if ye don't mind his things being there."

"I don't mind at all," spoke up Constance's voice. She

had risen and joined them and she was clutching her head and swaying slightly. "I think I'll just go up now," she added faintly.

Mystified, her face still concealed from Dev by her wide-brimmed hat, Pamela watched Constance mount the stairs, shepherded along by the innkeeper's wife. Then she went out the front door and took a restless walk around Bridgwater. Although she was eaten up by curiosity, she lingered on the bridge across the River Parrett, skimming stones across the smooth water. Why on earth would Constance want to linger at the inn when the Ellertons' big hospitable house was only a comfortable ride away?

She turned from the bridge with a sigh and her eyes widened.

Here in the flesh was her explanation! Captain Warburton, looking very fit and with his plumed hat riding rakishly on his dark head, was sauntering on horseback down the dusty street. As she watched he turned into the innyard and dismounted, went into the inn.

That was why Constance, who had refused to leave Axeleigh all this time, had been so willing to come along today! She had never had any intention of visiting the Ellertons! The Rose and Thistle had been her destination—and a tryst with Captain Warburton!

Pamela was thrilled. Instantly she forgave Constance for her deception. Constance was probably sworn to secrecy, she told herself, and lost herself in romantic imaginings of their clandestine meeting. In order to give them more time together, she lingered by the bridge, skimming stones. It was dusk before she went back to the inn. Noting that Captain Warburton was nowhere in evidence and his horse was gone, she ignored the obvious explanation that he had but stopped by for a tankard of ale on this thirsty day and then ridden on back to Warwood. Perhaps he and Constance had run away together! If so, she would give them a chance to get far away before pursuit could be launched. She ordered her dinner sent up.

Hardly had Pamela left for her walk than Dev had finished

his ale, paid for it, and sauntered out into the deserted innyard. He had rounded a corner of the inn and seen across a low roof a window—and framed in that window Constance, beckoning to him.

In moments he was up and over the roof and dropping through the window into the scribe's small bedchamber. The cramped room was littered with the scribe's possessions—a small writing desk, inkstands, parchment, goose quills—the tools of his trade. And with his clothes and other few belongings. But Dev saw none of those. He saw only the woman for whom his heart had hungered all these long months—the woman he had thought lost to him forever.

"Constance," he said huskily—and took her in his arms.

When first she had seen him sitting there in the common room below, Constance had felt herself transported back to Hatfield Forest, to a world of young love and hope, and the breeze that rustled the leaves of the Old Doodle Oak had seemed to touch her hot face with its cool breath. There had been moonlight and magic in the sight of him, danger and gold and wild rides in the night. But now—now she had had time to consider, and other memories had come flooding back to her, bitter memories.

She pushed him away. "Where is Nan?" she asked.

"Nan?" He was startled. "In Lincoln, I suppose—with Gibb. Unless she's left him. She has a restless foot, has Nan."

She would not be beguiled. "I saw you leave with her, that day in Essex."

So that was why she'd left him! A great joy came over Dev. It explained so much!

"She and Gibb were together then," he told her. "She's been with Gibb since Candless was hanged. A woman like Nan's not one to stay long without a protector."

She did not know whether to believe him or not. "Then *you* were not her protector?" Her violet eyes searched his face.

"Not after I met you." Sincerity rang in his voice.

"But you lied to me," she said. "You did not go to America—you went back to your old life on the road."

"I had to, Constance." He was sliding his arms around her shoulders even as he spoke. "I had given the last of my money to the couple who were to care for you until I returned. I could not leave you unprotected!"

Bright shame flooded over her suddenly. She had put a wrong construction on things, fool that she was! In her jealous heart she had imagined Dev run off with Nan, spending wild nights in "safe" inns and highway taverns, when all the time—!

"Oh, Dev," she whispered, and melted against him. "I'm sorry for what I thought. I'm so sorry!" *And sorry too for all that I have done later, for taking other vows—and most of all sorry that I let my heart stray elsewhere.* She let her pliant expressive body tell him of her regret, and sagged against him softly.

The soft inert weight of her, almost feather light in his arms, set Dev's blood to racing through his veins. He had no need to tell her now how he'd managed to find her—it was enough to hold her, to love her.

It was as if they had never been apart.

They swayed together toward the scribe's lumpy bed—and never felt the lumps. Her dark hair clouded out around her face on the coverlet, and the waning sunlight glimmered into the glory of her velvet eyes. Those eyes were speaking to him, telling him what he wanted so desperately to know:

Constance still loved him. She wanted him back.

And suddenly all that had transpired in the interim seemed to her a dream. Captain Warburton, who had loomed so large on her limited horizon, was gone like a ship in the night. She was back again on the highroads, back with her dangerous lover. Forgotten was Chesney Pell and the tangle she had made of her life. Her troubles seemed suddenly whisked away by the wind. Dev had come back and all was right with her world.

She opened her mouth to tell him so and he put a finger to

468

her lips. "Don't talk," he murmured. "Just let me hold you. *Oh, God, Constance, how I've missed you!*"

Those words were to Constance the sweetest in the world.

Through the long soft summer dusk they dallied there, deeper in love than they had ever been, trying to make up for all the lost hours, all the lost nights. Dusk dragged into darkness, yet neither of them felt the need of food. Their hunger was of a deeper sort, a hunger for each other that would never be assuaged.

"How did you find me?" she wondered.

And he told her about that meeting with Hugh and Margaret on the Great North Road.

"She told me you had been living with your uncle. Have you been happy?" he asked.

Constance caught her breath. Now was the time to tell him of her farce of a marriage last February—but she could not. "Sometimes," she answered evasively. "Sometimes I have been happy." And told him a little about life at Axeleigh. "But don't talk about me," she added quickly. "Tell me about you. I want to know all that has happened since I've been gone."

"There's naught to tell," he shrugged, for he knew she would not approve his ventures, that he stormed up and down the Great North Road, giving drays and wagons and coaches safe passage for a fee—and strewing gold as if it were water and taking his fun where he found it. Oh, no, she would not approve!

And then as the moon rose they forgot to talk and they made love again, slowly, wonderfully, with pent-up passion that surpassed even the heat of the afternoon's delightful dalliance.

Constance had thought Dev's lovemaking had reached its epitome in Essex, but she had been wrong. Tonight there was a tenderness in him that even she—so thrillingly responsive to his touch—had not known before. It was as if they hovered on the brink of some great disaster and they and their world would be swept away by morning, as if these golden treasured moments were all they would ever have. As if they were making love for the last time.

But the glow that suffused her body at his touch was the old glow she had known in his arms in Essex, and as his long body pressed against hers, crushing the softness of her breasts against his beating chest, she felt her senses flare up and with a little sob that welled unbidden in her throat she flung herself against him, clasping him to her, sliding her legs along his own, turning, twisting, urging him on.

But the tall young highwayman needed no urging. His quest for her had been a quest of the heart. It had led him westward all across England to Somerset. The girl in his arms was the one radiant guiding star of his life. He had found her! At last . . . *And she was his*.

The first time he had taken her, in Yorkshire, it was a boy's lovemaking—intense, enthusiastic, inexperienced. A lovely interlude but one that had left her pensive, as if there could have been somehow—*more*. And her own responses had been a girl's responses, instinctive but unsure.

Later it had been the rash young highwayman who had held her prisoned in his arms. A vigorous lover, untamed, questing, exciting. And she, still young and untried, had responded wondrously to his touch.

Tonight was different.

Tonight it was a man's experienced arms that held her, a man's hard chest and sinewy loins that pressed against her own. In the long months that had elapsed since he had held her last, Deverell had learned much—of himself and of life. And tonight was the test of that knowledge. He held Constance to him almost reverently for in his rough life he had not thought to see her again—except perhaps someday from a tall gibbet while she stared upward in horror. For surely a forgiving God would grant such a small request.

And now, magically, she was in his arms again.

Dev buried his face in the soft hollow of her throat and counted himself the luckiest man alive.

And the lean young highwayman, who had dreamt of this

moment through a hundred tossing nights in dozens of "safe" hideout inns and remote cottages and straw-bedded stables, or lying beside cold running streams with his head pillowed on his saddle—made the most of it.

In their hurry, they had not even bothered to undress and now at last, expertly, Dev managed the hooks down the back of her dress, reaching beneath her to do so, and all the while smiling down into her eyes—big and dark and wondering that her dream too could have come true. She felt his clever fingers trace a sensuous madness down her woman's spine, for tonight she was aglow with passion. She reached up and caught him to her again with a sob of joy before he could even wrest away her bodice.

"Oh, Dev, Dev, I have missed you so. . . ."

But Dev's hungry lips as they glided over the side of her body he had managed to bare, gliding along the fair expanse of her breast and down the lovely pale valley between her rounded breasts, had encountered something else besides the maddening silkiness of her skin.

They had encountered a narrow black riband.

Constance, lost in a wild world of passion, for it had been so long, *so long*, had scarcely noticed when Dev reached up to push the riband impatiently aside. Nor when his fingers had encountered what dangled from that riband—a ring. That it was a ring she had torn from her finger in anger he had no way of knowing—or that she wore it around her neck because Pamela insisted that the Squire would think it terrible of her to leave it off entirely. And she had not returned it to Chesney when she had sent the pearl necklace back to him because she had felt in fairness that she must see him when she gave it back, tell him face to face that she was a worthless wench who did not love him, who had used him only to get away—and that she was sorry and would disappear from his life forever.

Dev knew none of this. His fingers closed around that circlet of gold and a chill went through his heart—for this must be an important ring for her to wear it secreted beneath her clothes.

Even as he covered the soft pulsing mounds of her breasts with kisses, he was fingering that ring, weighing its significance in his mind. Even as his lips caressed and teased into hardness the delicate pink crests of those round breasts, even as he savoured their response, he was thinking.

A narrow band of gold—*and he had given her none.*

Constance had married someone. This was her wedding ring! She must have stripped it from her finger at sight of him! He thought back, even as his fingers ran lightly down her spine, making her squirm and shudder against him in joy, he tried to remember whether there had been a flash of gold on her hand downstairs. No, she had been wearing riding gloves, he would not have been able to see the ring on her finger.

But that was the reason for this secrecy—not, as he had thought with warm appreciation, a shielding of his identity from the law which might have been pursuing him.

For a moment harsh jealousy stabbed at him and he felt a puzzled wonderment go through her body as his own long frame momentarily stiffened. But then he relaxed against her, forgiving her even this last crushing blow.

Constance was the love of his life and he could forgive her even this. Instantly he was making excuses for her:

Great pressure has been put on her to marry, Margaret had said. And Constance had given way to that pressure. And why not? She had thought him unfaithful and she had been lonely—as *he* had been lonely. And had he been faithful to her on the road? Not his body certainly, although he knew now that his heart had never wavered from the girl he had first taken in his arms at magical Fountains Abbey and taken as his bride in Essex, made love to in filtering moonlight beneath the storied Old Doodle Oak. Constance had had to make her way without him—and making one's way was more difficult for a lass than for a lad. Small wonder that she had seized what life offered and married some young buck who—

as he had observed downstairs—could give her the luxury to which she was entitled. He discounted her talk of Axeleigh. She would be visiting Axeleigh, he felt, but making her home in some handsome country house where a doting husband waited.

But she was still the lady of his heart and it was a rich gift she was giving him—the gift of her love, a shining thing, untrammeled by explanations or recriminations, untroubled by thoughts of the future—a future in which he would obviously not be included. Life had made Dev lawless, but he had a deep sense of justice. To the fact that Constance was legally his he paid not the least attention—to him a woman belonged in the arms she felt most comfortable in. And who could blame any lass for not choosing to ride forever beside a highwayman who might smile into her eyes on a Thursday and lie dead in his blood by the roadside on Friday? Certainly Dev could not.

But for the wonderful gift of her love, so freely given, he would be ever grateful. This night, *this night* belonged to him and he must not let her know, must not tarnish the open-hearted loveliness of what she was giving him. There in the warm intimacy of that lumpy bed, lying upon a worn coverlet in the scribe's cramped bedchamber, they were sharing again all the joys they had known. They whispered and laughed and touched and dragged their lips playfully along each other's bare skin, they swayed and moved together in an ecstasy that went deeper than any physical sensation, for it was a joining of the spirit, exalted, beautiful past anything they would ever know in other arms.

Deep in the heart of him, Dev forgave her. He ran his hands lingeringly down her body and along her smooth hips, he let his long muscular legs rasp lightly against the satin softness of her thighs, he entered her with the reverence one reserves for the most sacred of temples—and lost himself in a rush of feeling that swept over him with the stormy impetuosity of a millrace.

Tomorrow he would face the unhappy truth that she was his

no longer, tomorrow. . . . But this night, *this night* of love was his to keep.

Shaken by the glorious intensity of his lovemaking, Constance lay in thrilling wonder. She had known a moment of cold fear when Dev had touched the riband that held the ring she had torn from her finger with an angry, "And unless Chesney comes for me, I will never wear it again! Never!" (For in the excitement of finding him again, she had clean forgot she was wearing it.) But he had only groped to rid her of it, sweeping the riband with its metal object alongside her. And that moment when his body went rigid and she had felt her stomach muscles contract and her breasts shiver against his ribcage—that had been nothing. Perhaps she had inadvertently caught him with her elbow when she had sought to pull back the long tangled hair that was caught in the pillow. No, Dev had not guessed, she told herself. And whatever happened tomorrow—and she dared not face that really—*this* night, this wondrous voyage of rediscovery and of reclaiming, was theirs, *would be theirs forever.*

But to be on the safe side, she murmured, "Here—let me." And pushed him back a little, just far enough that she could struggle out of her bodice—and incidentally rid herself of ring and riband, tangling them both hopelessly in the folds of amethyst silk material and pushing the bodice with its ring secreted, careless of wrinkled fabric, beyond her pillow.

She told herself contentedly that she was safe. Safe for the moment. And never dreamt that the man into whose arms she slipped again so gloriously, and whose strong arms welcomed her without reserve, had already guessed her secret. . . .

But as he claimed her again, she blissfully forgot her worries. Her senses trembled and she found her thoughts were tumbling, flying away from her with the authority, the boundless skill, the elegance of each new thrust. And as she flung herself against him, softly, rhythmically, her heartbeat seeming to pace itself to his, she had no need to think, only to feel herself shimmering in the glow of their burning passions. It was a dramatic joining, combining a boy's impetuosity and a man's skill and sureness in holding the fever pitch of mounting, cresting passions—a wicked delightful postponing through long shuddering shimmers of ecstasy that golden moment when, together, they went over the brink and were lost in the silken vastness of their love.

But afterward conscience gnawed at her. As they lay together, bodies touching, still a-thrill in the afterglow of that wild sweet joining, she told herself it wasn't fair, she had to tell him. And then, once he knew the truth, if he wanted to leave her, to fling her away for contracting a bigamous unconsummated marriage, he could. But first she must tell him *why* she had done it. She had done it because—at this moment it was hard to remember in any logical fashion just why she had done it. Another man's strong arms had beckoned and she had felt a need to run, to escape. And that need, combined with fury at Dev for betraying her, had driven her into marriage with Chesney.

For whatever reason she had done it—and every reason seemed paltry and unworthy now—she had done Dev a great wrong. And she who had never lied to him must now tell him what she had done *and let him decide whether to forgive her or no*.

"Dev," she said in that soft languorous raw silk murmur that set men's senses wild. "Oh, Dev, I've a confession to make."

She was going to tell him about her marriage! And he didn't want her to, for it would somehow change and damage this wondrous intimacy between them.

"Confessions should be made in sunlight," he murmured. "Moonlight's for something else. Let's not waste it!"

And even as her lips parted to tell him everything, his own warm lips closed down gently upon hers and cut off the words. Then his tongue was probing intimately past, into her softly parted mouth, and she felt herself gasp again at the tingling feeling that went through her.

"Constance, my Constance," she heard him murmur, the words echoing softly against the back of her throat. Or did she only imagine she heard him say that as his warm demanding body slid against hers and her world drifted away and explanations seemed unimportant and mistakes were forgotten and all that mattered or would ever matter was right here in her arms.

She would tell him, she promised herself guiltily. She would tell him and somehow, *somehow* he would forgive her.

And then she forgot that foolish unconsummated marriage, forgot it as if it had never been, and abandoned herself to the joy of being in Dev's arms once again, those arms that for her would always be the *only* arms.

Elegantly, gently, he took her again and swept her with him on a magnificent upward march to the very peaks of passion. Had her senses been less shattered, her scattered thoughts less like butterflies that fluttered by only to flit away again, she might have asked herself—and worried—what brought this special quality to his lovemaking tonight, this feeling he communicated to her that they must wring from these moments enough sweetness to last a lifetime—a going-away feeling.

That feeling was still with her when at last, lingeringly, he let her go and cradled her warm, still-pulsating body in his arms, letting his hands run lightly over her bare skin, pausing to tempt here, to excite there, and to caress, as if he were stroking a cat's silky fur, the richly gleaming triangle of dark curly hair at the base of her hips. Constance swayed toward him again and felt her senses ripple wildly at his touch.

"Ah, it's been a long time, hasn't it?" he laughed softly, and took her again, this time in a golden glide to summer mountains far away and with a richness that surprised her even as she collapsed in shuddering ecstasy against him.

Come down at last from shattering emotions, from world-shaking heights, she found a golden sleepiness stealing over her, a rich warm feeling that relaxed her completely. Tomorrow was soon enough to talk about one's mistakes, she thought, lulled by the sleepy remembered glow of their passions. Tomorrow when the sun was up she would look into

Dev's keen laughing face and drop her eyes and try to explain what had driven her to this final madness.

Tomorrow . . .

Even as she thought it, her young exhausted body was drifting off to sleep.

Not so the young highwayman. Although a delightful lethargy had stolen over him in the wake of his dazzling performance, he would not allow himself to fall asleep. When he was certain that Constance had drifted off, he rose quietly and went to the scribe's small writing desk. Dipping quill to inkwell, he penned in the moonlight a note upon a stiff sheet of parchment.

When he had finished, he signed it with a flourish and sat considering it for a long time before he went over and laid it gently upon the pillow beside her.

Constance did not stir. She lay on her back, breathing evenly. Her arms were trustingly outflung and the dark tangle of her hair gleamed in the moonlight and haloed the pale oval of her face.

Deverell Westmorland, son of an aristocratic house, stood looking down at her and warring with his thoughts. He wanted nothing in life so much as to stay by her side. Her pale near-naked body in its light chemise that now rode around her chin tempted him, and his strong jaw worked as he traced those elegant lines and thought of the delights he had known with her. A few more hours of her company—ah, what would be the harm?

But even as his hand stretched out yearningly to touch and caress the slim white pillar of her naked thigh, he drew back. For what could he offer her? What could he *ever* offer her? The dangers of the road? The rough inns, the long hard rides, the company of cutthroats and bawds? And what if he were killed, what would happen to her then? Gibb would try to aid her, but would Gibb be able to?

She had a husband now, obvious wealth, a life of ease.

Who was he to deprive her of all that? He was a wanted man, hunted all across England, and if now he wrested her away from the only security she had ever found—and then if he were taken and hanged high on some lonely gibbet, what misery would he know in those last moments of his life, knowing what he had done to her?

Yet she was here within reach—and he desired her more than he had ever desired anything. In silent agony, he wrestled with himself.

But there was a gallantry in Dev. A gallantry that had come down to him across the years from those long-ago ancestors who had fought at Agincourt and at Crécy. A gallantry that would not *permit* him to bring ruin or shame to the woman he loved.

With an effort that cost him much, he wrenched his gaze away from the temptingly lovely sight of Constance's frail white body displayed so elegantly there upon the bed and set his clothing to rights. In haste. His belt was jerked round his waist with a punishing yank, his arms thrust violently through his coat sleeves. With unaccustomed fierceness he tugged on his boots. At last he moved softly to the open casement and climbed through it, out upon the moonlit roof.

He cast a quick look around before he dropped to the ground—and saw no one.

But the moonlight had tricked him. Mirrorlike, it shone upon a window that concealed a pair of bright eyes.

His departure from Constance's bedchamber was being observed.

Pamela, excited by her romantic imaginings about a masterful Captain Warburton carrying Constance away with him, had found it difficult to sleep. She had risen and gone to the window for a breath of fresh air, and as she looked out she saw a man just dropping over the edge of the roof. And he looked to her very much like the stranger she had seen earlier downstairs in the common room.

So swiftly did it all happen, so silently, so suddenly was the figure gone that Pamela could almost persuade herself that she had seen nothing, that her excited imagination had conjured up an illusion. Then she told herself sensibly that it was more likely some guest who had got himself drunk and been put to bed by a servant—and then waked up to discover he had drunk up the money to pay for his lodgings: some fellow who was leaving by a route that would not take him downstairs past the waiting landlord!

Presently she heard a horse's hooves leaving the vicinity of the inn and another possibility occurred to her: The innkeeper had a pretty daughter and *her* room might well lie along this roof! This fellow who had left by the roof could be her lover stealing away in the night.

Pamela sighed and gazed wistfully out at the moon. For she too had thought she had a lover—and had found him false. Would the innkeeper's pretty daughter find her lover false as well? *Like as not,* she decided. Cooled by the breezes of the summer night, Pamela leaned pensively on the sill and wondered how she could ever get out of her impending marriage to Dick Peacham.

When Constance woke, her world—so confused of late—had come back into focus. Now she knew that she did not truly love Tony Warburton—she loved Dev. She had loved him all along.

She stretched luxuriously and turned her head to smile at him.

There was no russet head upon the pillow beside her, no long muscular form lying there.

Only a note.

She snatched it up in fear. It was very brief but it rang through her head like a great gong.

I should have confessed to you last night that ours was not a legal marriage, the note read. *I bribed the "preacher," who by profession is a gunsmith. I must tell you that I have married an heiress in Bristol and am on my way to America.* Here the ink was blotted as the pen had quivered. It ended firmly, *I will always love you.* And it was signed *Dev.*

Dev had done his work well. Constance found every word believable. Dev had found her again—and stayed to enjoy her body. And then gone merrily on. And this time the liaison was not some light love like Nan that he could readily shake off. This time he was legally married. And on his way to America.

She had lost him.

She reread the note twice before she crumpled it and her world crashed in about her. And then she put her white face in her trembling hands and rocked with agony.

All men—*all men* were untrue.

Even Dev.

Tersely refusing to go on to the Ellertons', Constance rode home in a state of near collapse. All her new-made dreams lay in ruins about her and she answered Pamela's chatter in monosyllables.

Pamela could stand it no longer. She reined up. "You have quarreled with Captain Warburton?" she burst out. "Is that it?"

Constance gave her a bewildered look. "Captain Warburton?" She sounded as if she had never heard the name before.

Pamela refused to speak to her all the way home.

Axeleigh Hall, Somerset,
June 5, 1685

CHAPTER 31

Clifford Archer had been glad to see the girls go. In fact, he had encouraged them to spend a night or two at the Ellertons—it got them out of his way.

For the blackmailer had at last overplayed his hand. Egged on perhaps by a feeling that England was drifting fast into revolution, he had demanded five hundred guineas in gold— and Axeleigh's squire was of no mind to pay it.

Evening found him carefully cleaning his dueling pistols. He would have two in case one failed him. This night, he told himself grimly, he would become what he was paying hush money to keep the world from thinking he was—a murderer. Or else a dead man. In which case, he could give thanks that the banns were already being cried for Pamela and Dick Peacham.

Before he left for the hollow tree he carefully wrote out his will and signed it and left it in his writing desk—just as he would have done had it been a duel he was about to fight.

And then he rode through the gates and down the familiar road toward Huntlands, perhaps for the last time.

He was early and he secreted himself in the bushes near the hollow tree and waited—just as Jack Drubbs had once waited.

But by now a swaggering Jack Drubbs felt very sure of himself. He had no need to hide in bushes, for was not the money always waiting in the hollow tree? And tonight's piece of work would make him a rich man. In silvery moonlight he rode boldly up to the hollow tree, dismounted and reached inside.

It was a shock to come up empty—and an even greater shock to look up and see a man standing solidly between him and the waning moon.

Drubbs recognized the square body of the Squire.

"I've decided not to pay," said the Squire, and brought up his pistol.

Jack Drubbs was catlike fast. He slithered to the side, brought out his own pistol and fired at the same time as the Squire.

Tom Thornton, who had bedded a tavern maid in Bridgwater this night and was headed for home half-drunk and very late, had slowed his pace as he passed the gates of Axeleigh, for he was thinking painfully of Pamela. Now as he rode, he kept hearing hoofbeats behind him. Although he paused several times, they came no closer. Nobody passed him. Whoever it was waited patiently until he started up again. The hoofbeats were somewhat distant but it annoyed Tom to think that someone was following him. The tavern maid, he'd heard, had a jealous lover somewhere—perhaps that was who was following him. Some fellow with murder in his heart who had laid back on the first leg of the journey and was now catching up. That thought sobered Tom. As he approached Huntlands he looked for a convenient spot to leave the road and watch to see who passed by—and found it just short of the hollow tree near which the Squire waited patiently for his blackmailer.

The Squire had heard Tom's hoofbeats and presumed it was

the blackmailer. The blackmailer had presumed the rider ahead was the Squire. Maybe he had had trouble raising so much cash, and was now riding out late to deposit the money on this lonely road. For him. With that pleasant thought in mind, Drubbs waited a bit when he no longer heard Tom's horse, assuming it was taking the Squire a bit of time to place the money in the hollow tree to his satisfaction. This pause had given Tom time to walk his horse silently over the soft sod and so come up across the road, well hidden by bushes, directly across from the hollow tree.

And so he had witnessed in amazement the encounter between the Squire and the blackmailer.

Tom spurred his horse forward as both men fired. He saw both shots go wild, saw the Squire dragging out another pistol. Simultaneously he saw the blackmailer mount in a single leap and ride down the Squire, dashing into him with his horse and sending the Squire—who did not leap out of the way in time, taking aim on the blackmailer as he was—flying to the side. Drubbs would have gone after the fallen man but that Tom and Satan crashed through into the road at that moment. Drubbs wheeled his horse around and fled. And his horse was the fleetest the Squire's money had been able to buy him.

Tom, who wore—as all gentlemen of the time did—a sword at his side, but who was not carrying a gun, put Satan to the test that night. Streaking forward at a dead run, he ducked as the blackmailer turned and fired at him point-blank.

Satan fled down the road like a shadow, pursuing the fleeing Drubbs. Tom was brandishing his sword in the moonlight as he rode, leaning forward, urging the big horse on. He had almost reached Drubbs, thundering close on his heels, when Drubbs—who had been hampered by the necessity for reloading his pistol as he fled—turned and fired wildly—and this time the bullet, as he ducked, went clean through the crown of Tom's hat and creased his hair. So close were the two thundering riders now that Tom took a wicked swipe at

Drubbs, his blade flashing in the moonlight. Drubbs, who wore no sword (having no skill with one), pulled out a dagger and threw it at Tom. It whistled by, missing Tom as Drubbs's horse stumbled over a rock, and Tom, lunging forward in the saddle, drove his sword entirely through Drubbs's body.

The impact carried Drubbs off his horse and to the ground. In a moment Tom had dismounted.

"Who are you?" he demanded, but Drubbs's eyes were already glazing. His head fell to the side, limp. Tom retrieved his blade and coolly wiped it on Drubbs's cloak. He frowned down at the fallen man, remembering the Squire's, *"I've decided not to pay."* Then he bent down and went very thoroughly through Drubbs's pockets. It was clear to Tom this man must be blackmailing the Squire for such words to pass between them on the road by night, and he half expected to find incriminating papers—love letters to a married woman perhaps. Instead he found a considerable purse of gold coins, which he grimly pocketed.

Leaving Drubbs where he was, he rode back to find the Squire groaning, for although the blackmailer's shot had missed him clean, Drubbs's horse in its surge forward had sent him flying and he had twisted his back painfully as he fell.

"He'll not bother you again, whoever he was," Tom told the Squire as he helped him up. "I've done for the fellow— left him back there on the road."

"Then ye must get ye gone, Tom," gasped Clifford, ashen from pain. "I thank you for doing what I came to do, but 'tis no affair of yours and I'll not have you suffer for it."

"No one will suffer for it," shrugged Tom. "Can ye ride?"

"I don't know." Clifford Archer groaned as Tom assisted him to his horse, and lay writhing across his horse's neck as Tom led the horse through the trees and across a meadow to Huntlands.

"I'm up and about so late that none notice my comings and

goings," Tom told the Squire. "We'll say ye were visiting me and ye fell down the stairs, too much to drink—right?"

The Squire, very white about the lips from pain, nodded.

Tom got him inside, poured out brandy and gave the Squire some. Then he got him to bed.

Once his guest had been made comfortable in the big airy bedchamber, Tom tossed the purse of coins he had taken from Drubbs upon the bed. "I don't doubt these rightfully belong to you," he said. "And I don't care to know why you paid them."

The Squire spilled the coins out on the bed and counted them out. He had back now most of the gold he had given Drubbs. He looked up at Tom. "I never knew his name," he said. "But eventually he'd have broken me. He was bleeding me dry." He considered the sturdy master of Huntlands who had killed a man for him this night. A pair of calm blue eyes gazed back at him from the face of a golden Viking. "I'm beholden to you, Tom." And as Tom shrugged his broad shoulders, "I wish it had been you instead of Peacham," he said wearily.

Tom turned away with a hardening jaw.

So did he.

Deverell was not so lucky as Tom. He had left Bridgwater shortly after Tom and by the same road. Riding along pensively with his thoughts on Constance, he had heard distant shots ring out and curiosity had impelled him forward at a gallop. Normally he would not have been so careless, but tonight he was full of tolerance and kindness toward his fellow beings. Indeed he was in just the proper quixotic mood to rescue someone and the quirk of fate that had led him down this particular road at this particular moment now led him forward at a rush.

Tom had already removed the Squire from the road and the pair of them were well into the trees when Dev galloped by—he never saw either of them. What he came upon a little later was a man in a puce suit and light cloak lying on his back near a little waterfall that gushed down out of the hills. Blood stained the man's doublet and cloak and Dev could not tell whether he was alive or dead.

Swiftly he dismounted and knelt beside the fallen man. And in surprise recognized the surly fellow he had booted out of the Rose and Thistle that afternoon.

He tore apart the fellow's doublet to expose the wound and see how bad it was, staining his hands with Drubbs's blood as he did so. Useless, he saw. The man was dead. Dev sighed and would have risen but at that very moment a stout club descended on his head and he slumped senseless atop his earlier adversary.

When he woke, he was in jail with the worst headache of his life.

A laconic jailer, jangling large keys, explained the situation to him. One Alger Tupper, whose young wife had come suddenly into labor with her first child, had been last night trudging from his cottage to the home of a midwife some distance away when in the distance he had heard shots. Tupper had prudently stayed crouched where he was for a time and then had crept over a rise to see what appeared to be a gentleman kneeling over a body on the road.

A wandering brigand, Tupper had thought, and had eased his body forward over the soft ground without breaking so much as a twig.

The plash of the waterfall had concealed the sound of Tupper's footsteps, thought Dev ironically, and opened his mouth to explain that he was the would-be rescuer—not the assailant.

Tupper had struck him down and had, it seemed, draped both bodies over Dev's horse (Drubbs's horse having run away) and plodded on to the midwife's, roused her and sent her scurrying to his cottage where she had delivered Tupper's young wife of a bouncing eight-pound baby boy! Meanwhile Tupper, mindful of his duty, had tied Dev's hands and feet securely and brought both victim and presumed assailant on to the constable in Bridgwater. It was Tupper's view that the deed had not been done alone for he had heard, he thought, distant departing hoofbeats. But as Dev's hands were covered with the dead man's blood, and as the dead man's purse was missing, it seemed reasonable to accuse Deverell of the crime.

In vain Dev (whose papers identified him as one George Mayberry) told them he had spent the night at the Rose and Thistle in Bridgwater and had only just reached the scene of the trouble when an overzealous Tupper had struck him down ("But the landlord claims you took no room and departed the common room early in the evening"). In vain Dev pointed out that his sword was clean ("You wiped it clean on the deadman's cloak") and that neither of his pistols had been recently fired ("You could have carried a third and thrown it away somewhere"). In vain he protested that he had spent the night in the arms of a lady ("Who is this lady? Will she come forward?") Steadfastly Dev refused to name her, giving her reputation as the excuse (and indeed he thought he had brought enough grief on Constance without involving her in this). And when witnesses from the Rose and Thistle remembered before a hastily called court in Bridgwater that Dev had had an altercation with the dead man earlier that same evening and had indeed booted him from the inn, Dev found himself adjudged "guilty of murder on the Bridgwater Road" and sentenced to be hanged on Monday next.

It was all very cut-and-dried and logical, as British justice so often is.

And so Dev found himself facing a rope rather sooner than he expected.

At Axeleigh on their return from the inn in Bridgwater the two girls were met by an excited Tabitha, who ran out, skirts flying.

"We thought it best to send a message to you at the Ellertons'," she cried.

"A message?" Pamela frowned. "But we never reached the Ellertons', Tabby. We—"

" 'Tis about your father. He's had an accident. In his cups, he was. Fell down the stairs and twisted his back. Wait!" she wailed, for Pamela was already off her horse and running for the front door. "He's at Huntlands."

"At *Huntlands?*" Pamela swung about and gave Tabitha a blank look.

"That was where it happened," Tabitha told her importantly. "And Master Tom, he rode over and said as how 'twas best the Squire should stay there for a bit."

"Constance, you stay here—someone must be in charge." Pamela was up in the saddle again. "Find a horse, Tabby, and follow me over. I'll be sending you back for whatever we need."

She was gone before Constance could collect her wits. She watched an excited Tabitha flying down to the stables to get a horse and then went dejectedly inside. She hoped the Squire wasn't badly hurt. Meantime there was her own problem. She tossed her reins to a groom and, once inside, ascended the stairs heavily, went into her bedchamber to think.

Of a sudden her face whitened. All the way home she had been thinking of Dev, lost to her forever. But now it came to her with the force of a blow that her marriage to Chesney was no longer fraudulent. Now that she had learned that her "marriage" to Dev had no legal force, that meant she was well and truly wed to Chesney!

Her knees gave way and she sank down on the bed.

Dear God, what had she done? In her foolish perversity, she had done a disreputable thing: She had married a man for whom she cared nothing, thinking all the while in the back of her mind that she would, when she chose, undo what she had done. Indeed she had planned to do so with a few well-chosen words: *Go look at the marriage records of Essex—you will find my name there. At least you will find the name of Mistress Penelope Goode who married one John Watts. And I was that Penelope Goode.*

Only now she knew that her name would not be there—not Penelope Goode's name, not John Watts's. She had trapped herself. Silently she pulled out the black riband that was tucked into her chemise and stared in horror at the golden wedding band.

She was bound to Chesney now. Bound forever by a narrow band of gold.

It never even occurred to open-hearted Pamela that the story the two men solemnly told her at Huntlands about her father's unfortunate fall down the main staircase was other than the truth. She winged about the big airy bedchamber like a beautiful moth, making the Squire more comfortable. She sent Tabitha back with orders to assemble an enormous number of things—all of which the Squire protested he didn't need—to be brought over later. She fussed over him and gave cook endless orders—and then rode home beside Tom.

The master of Huntlands concealed his yearning well. Although it was torture for him to ride back through summer meadows beside beautiful Pamela, knowing that she was soon to wed Dick Peacham, it was a torture he could not bring himself to avoid. He was ready and waiting to take her home and watched her covertly all the way back to Axeleigh, wondering how he could ever have missed the beauty she had become, marveling at the radiant femininity of her.

"Your father will be fine," he assured her for the tenth time. "The doctor says he needs only rest."

"I'm sure of it," Pamela agreed, for riding beside the golden Viking of Huntlands had lightened her spirits—even if there was still Dick Peacham to be dealt with tomorrow and the next day and the next!

It did not escape Pamela that the ring Dorothea had waved under her nose was back again on Tom's little finger and the thought that Tom and Dorothea might have had a lovers' quarrel pleased her no end and added to her cheeriness. For although they were still wary of each other and avoided any mention of her impending marriage, the ice between her and Tom was melting.

It was with a happier heart than she had known since her

betrothal to Dick Peacham that Pamela bade Tom good-by and skipped upstairs, two treads at a time, to tell Constance that the Squire was resting nicely. Surely such good news would lighten even Constance's gloom!

At the landing she encountered a white-faced Tabitha, who was wringing her hands.

"What has happened?" demanded Pamela. And when Tabitha only gulped and choked, she began to shake her. "Has something happened to Puss?" she cried, for that was the only thing she could think of that would make Tabby act so.

And then she saw Puss, handsome and confident as always, strolling down the hall toward them.

"What has happened, Tabby?" she asked in an altered voice, and cold fear poured over her.

" 'Tis Mistress Constance," gasped Tabby. "She's gone all strange-like. She broke her looking glass and I think she was going to use the broken pieces of glass to cut her wrists—"

To slash her wrists! Pamela pushed Tabitha aside and sprinted for Constance's bedchamber. She threw open the door and skidded into the room just in time to see a disheveled Constance rising from a prone position on the bed.

"Tabby told me," gasped Pamela.

"Yes. Well, don't worry, I won't break any more mirrors," said Constance crisply. "How is your father?"

"He'll be fine. But *you,* whatever made you—"

"It just all came over me for a second and it was too much to bear."

"*What? What* was too much to bear?" Pamela ran to her friend, sat down on the bed and put a protective arm about her shoulders. "Oh, Constance, if you'd only tell me about it!"

Constance gave her a jaded look from those lovely violet eyes. *Confession,* they said, *was good for the soul.* Yet if she confessed all to Pamela, others would be hurt: Margaret. Captain Warburton. Clifford Archer.

And yet—she had to talk to someone or go mad.

"It's Chesney, isn't it?" demanded Pamela. "He's written? He's coming?" She studied Constance's face. "He isn't coming?"

Constance sighed. She patted Pamela's hand as if she were a child and looked into Pamela's earnest face, so full of anxiety now. Anxiety for *her*. Poor Pam! She deserved to know at least a little of what had happened.

"There's so much I haven't told you," she whispered. *"So much I can never tell you."*

Pamela gave her a troubled look. "Perhaps you should try anyway," she said sensibly.

Constance swallowed and twisted her fingers together. Now that she was about to begin, it was hard to find the right words to make Pamela understand.

"I was married before." She chose her words carefully.

Pamela was amazed. She had always felt that Constance and her father shared some secret, something they were keeping back from her, and now she knew what it was— Constance was a widow! And keeping it a secret because she didn't want to wear the weeds!

"When I thought he had left me for another woman, I—I ran away. And came here." No need to tell Pamela about Margaret, about Devon. "I married Chesney believing he would take me to Lyme—far away from the Warburtons and all my problems here." She looked squarely at Pamela. "I did not know if my first husband was alive or dead."

Pamela's crystal blue eyes blinked. "You mean you *married* Chesney, not knowing?"

Constance nodded. She did not explain her intricate reasoning.

"But, Constance," cried Pamela distractedly. "You cannot go about marrying people at random! At least, not without first ridding yourself of the first one! You will be declared a bigamist!"

That bent head nodded hopelessly. "I was ready to face all that. Once we arrived in Lyme, I meant to tell Chesney that ours was no legal marriage, that I was already wed. His mother certainly would have been glad to see the last of me."

She lifted her head and abject misery stared out of her velvet eyes. "But now I cannot go to Lyme at all for I have learnt that my first marriage was a sham."

"Someone wrote you about it?" gasped Pamela.

"Yes," said Constance. For surely that was the best thing, to let Pamela believe she had heard the news by letter. *And wasn't it true, after all? Dev had left her a note!*

"How *shabby!*" Indignation lit up Pamela's face.

"And that is not the worst. For if I was not legally married to Deverell, *then I am legally married to Chesney!*"

Pamela was looking at her in horror. Constance had kept all of these revelations bottled up! Now she understood all of Constance's behavior—the sighs, the inattention, the restlessness. Constance had wanted to marry Captain Warburton—but had pushed him away because of her secret marriage. And to escape him she had flown into marriage with Chesney—a marriage she meant to shake free of. And now to learn the shattering truth—that her marriage to Chesney was binding and would forever bar her from marrying Captain Warburton! *No wonder she had broken a mirror! No wonder she had been about to slash her wrists!*

"You could divorce him," whispered Pamela.

"Divorce, you know as well as I do, can only be had by Act of Parliament!"

And divorce by Act of Parliament would not be an easy thing to come by! The two girls stared at each other hopelessly. Constance was well and truly trapped—by a narrow band of gold.

In the days that followed, the Squire remained at Huntlands, and Pamela—with Tabitha in tow—rode over every day. For Constance, she insisted, was "needed to give Axeleigh proper supervision in her absence" and a young lady of quality never rode about the countryside alone. Numbed by the sequence of events, Constance was glad enough to be left alone to brood. Tabitha gave her daily reports of how things were going at Huntlands, even when Pamela was too busy to do so.

"Master Tom, he don't leave the house when Mistress Pam's there," she reported importantly. "Finds ways to be where she is. She acts like she don't notice, but"—conspiratorially—"*she does.*"

"But she's to marry Dick Peacham in a fortnight," objected Constance, for disgruntled Peacham was all but camping on Axeleigh's doorstep, although Constance (to Pamela's vast relief) had steadfastly refused to allow him to spend the night at Axeleigh since the Squire's accident. She had told him calmly that it would be most improper since, during the Squire's absence from home, they were but "two young women, alone and unprotected." Dick Peacham, always a stickler for the proprieties, had been forced to accept that.

"Mistress Pam don't seem to remember she's to marry him," said Tabitha cheerfully. "Sometimes she acts mad at Master Tom and sometimes it's like old times with them laughing and joking together."

"What does the Squire think of all this?" demanded Constance.

"Oh, his back hurts him something awful," sighed Tabitha. "He groans a lot when he thinks nobody hears. The doctor says it will take time to mend and he shouldn't be moved."

So Pamela was likely to linger at Huntlands till the very eve of her wedding! thought Constance grimly.

In the restless countryside, political events were moving ever swifter and not until Sunday afternoon did Dick Peacham arrive at Huntlands and innocently drop a thunderbolt on Tom.

As it turned out, it was Tom's second thunderbolt of the day. The first came with a discussion he was having with Pamela as they sat in a window seat on the second floor looking out over the lawns of Huntlands.

Pamela had not been able to contain herself. Swearing him not to tell the Squire, she had told Tom of Constance's predicament. Now, after rehashing it once again, she gave Tom a slanted look.

"I'm going to save Constance." She stated it coolly. "From Chesney and from that terrible old harridan, his mother."

"How?" he asked bluntly. He was thinking how pretty she looked in her daffodil yellow dress with the light shining on her hair. A bit stiff the dress might be, but *he* knew what a beauty was inside!

"I'm going down to Lyme and propose marriage to him!"

This time she had struck a nerve. A solid jar went through Tom's hard muscles and his blue eyes were filled with alarm. "You're mad, Pam. He's already married and you're betrothed to Peacham." It was the first time Peacham's name had crossed Tom's lips since the Squire's accident and it had a bitter taste.

"*Actually,*" Pamela cocked her head and her voice grew dreamy. "I suppose I'm really going to propose to his mother."

"You're going to propose—to his *mother?*" Tom felt his world, which had been so solid and firm a moment ago, as steady as the limestone hills that rose as a backdrop to the Valley of the Axe, shake and quiver beneath him.

Pamela dimpled. "Yes, I'm going to ask her for Chesney's hand in marriage."

"*Why?*" asked Tom weakly.

"Because *she* decides everything for him, she'll decide that too. She was furious when her little boy, the lad she supposed to be at Oxford getting his head stuffed full of knowledge, was actually in Somerset getting himself married to a penniless waif—for that's the way she thinks of Constance, I know that from Chesney's letters to her—she lets me read them. They'd be funny—if the whole thing weren't so sad! He keeps squeaking up about a dowry and how a large one 'might make all the difference in the world!'"

Tom snorted.

"His mother resents the fact that her darling son didn't find himself a fortune *and* a girl she could manage!"

"*You* certainly don't fill the bill," protested Tom. "*You* tried to block her from dragging Chesney out of the bridal chamber last February. She certainly won't imagine that *you're* someone she can manage!"

"I'll try to seem more biddable when I ask her for his hand," sighed Pamela. "I'll tell her I was in love with Chesney all along and that it *broke my heart* to see him marrying a conniving schemer like Constance, and I'll ask her if there isn't something we can *do*."

Tom's honest face mirrored his amazement. He hadn't believed Pamela capable of such guile.

"And I'll mention the size of my dowry and how I'm an only child with no mother to guide me." She was laughing now for all that she was dead serious. "And she'll believe me, for she thinks Chesney's *perfect* and all the girls are after him. He told Constance that in his letters! And then she'll prod Chesney into an annulment because she'll want him to marry a fortune—me!" Yes, the more she thought about it, the more reasonable it sounded. His termagant mother was the only person living who could make Chesney declare before a magistrate that he had not bedded his bride. And after all, it was *true!* But Chesney had written hysterically in his letters that he had told his mother he had had "relations" with Constance during their short betrothal—to keep his mother from trying to annul the marriage.

"Suppose she insists on a marriage contract between Chesney and you *before* she pushes him into an annulment?" Tom, ever practical, shot at her.

Pamela hadn't thought of that. "She won't," she said hastily.

"But *suppose she does?* What then?"

"Then"—she lifted her golden head—"I'll sign it!"

Tom opened his mouth and closed it again. He looked very fierce. They had both forgotten that Pamela, no matter what she signed, could not arrange for her own dowry, something the virago in Lyme would hardly fail to overlook.

Pamela noted that expression. "And then, if she tries to *enforce* it, you can challenge Chesney to a duel, and his mother—to save her darling son's life—will give me back the document and we'll all be as we were!"

They had both forgotten Peacham and the upcoming marriage. The very thought of Pamela being shackled by her own consent *by contract* to marry somebody else, even in jest, had so shaken Tom that it had rattled his brain. "And why would we do all this?" he demanded.

"So Constance can marry Captain Warburton, of course!"

Tom blinked. This was something he hadn't heard about. "Don't you mean Ned?"

"No, I do not mean Ned. I think she's in love with Captain Warburton. She loved him so much she wasn't willing to marry him bigamously and break his heart."

"But she was willing to marry Chesney bigamously?" Tom quirked a golden eyebrow at her.

"Oh, you don't understand at all," said Pamela impatiently. "She meant to let Chesney out of it, don't you see? She married him just to keep from being pushed into marriage with Ned because that would be something she couldn't back out of, and if Ned found out she'd been married before and never divorced, it would break his heart, and besides I'm sure she couldn't stand to be married to Ned and live that close to Captain Warburton whom she really loves!"

Tom looked dazed. Feminine logic escaped him completely. He thought how simple life had been before Pamela had tangled him into her affairs. And now he was secretly planning to call Dick Peacham out—if Pamela gave him the *slightest* encouragement—and end her betrothal abruptly. With a sword. And *she* was trumping up a duel for him with Chesney Pell! He wondered briefly if he would ever know serenity again.

Pamela gave him her sunny smile and threw her arms around his neck. "*We'll* save Constance!" she cried. "You and I!'' And suddenly Tom didn't care whether he had serenity or not—he had something better: a wicked golden wench to love forever.

"I'll cut him down, Pam," he promised hoarsely. "If you insist. But I still think one of the Warburtons should do it—whichever she plans to end up with, of course."

Pamela was about to say, "Oh, no, this will be *much* better," when through the window she caught a glimpse of Dick Peacham riding up the drive. "Oh, dear, it's Dick," she said. "I do hope he hasn't seen me!" And glided away from the window. "Oh, Tom, *do* get rid of him for me!"

Fired by her recent careless embrace, Tom rose to his feet. "I'll call him out, if you give me the word," he offered. "All in all, I'd much prefer it to calling out Pell!"

"Oh, don't be silly," said Pamela, giving him a little push. "I mean, get rid of him—not kill him! He'll want to nag me about making lists of wedding guests, and ask me again have I remembered to ask everyone who might die and leave either of us any money—oh, I just can't face him today!"

Only too glad to rid her of Peacham, Tom's boots briskly made it across the room. He met Peacham at the front door, opening it before Peacham could bang the iron knocker.

"Oh. Thornton. Will you tell Mistress Pamela I'm here?" Peacham's manner was formal.

"Surprised you didn't pass her on the road," said Tom blandly. "She's gone back to Axeleigh."

Peacham looked confused. "But she couldn't have! I'd have seen her."

"She probably took a shortcut through the woods," laughed Tom. "Maybe you can catch her if you go that way. How've you been, Dick?" He tried to force jocularity.

Peacham, mounting up, responded in kind. "Very well indeed. Will we be seeing you at the hanging in Bridgwater tomorrow?"

The words seemed to linger suspended in the air. Tom, who hadn't been keeping up with things, dancing attendance on Pamela as he was, seemed to feel a cold draft of air rush around him. He kept his voice light. "Didn't know there was one, Dick. Who's to hang?"

"Stranger. Name of George Mayberry. Killed a fellow on the Bridgwater Road—not far from here, I take it."

"You mean he confessed to it?" exclaimed Tom.

Dick Peacham gave him a puzzled look. "Didn't have to. He was found bending over the body with blood on his hands. Fellow named Tupper brought him in. I'd come by to ask Mistress Pamela if she'd care to attend the hanging with me tomorrow."

Tom rallied. "I doubt me she will. Pamela doesn't like hangings."

Peacham frowned. "Will I see you there?" he asked frostily.

"Oh, yes." Tom's voice was grim. "I'll be there."

From the window above, Pamela had heard their conversation. As Dick Peacham rode off, she ran to find Tabby. "Ride back to Axeleigh," she told the girl rapidly. "I want you to arrive before Dick Peacham gets there. Tell him I came home because I felt poorly, I can't see him and he's not to come over tomorrow, I intend to stay in bed all day. Hurry, now!"

Tabitha did as she was bid and managed to meet Dick Peacham on the front steps of Axeleigh.

Peacham's mouth tightened at the message Tabitha delivered. Damned cavalier treatment he was receiving from Mistress Pamela these days, and their wedding just days away! He rode off in a huff, determined that he would let the lady cool her slippers this entire week!

To Pamela the name George Mayberry had meant nothing, and she had forgotten all about the hanging when she arrived back at Axeleigh.

So Constance went to sleep that night unaware that Dev, who'd been going by the name George Mayberry, was to be hanged in Bridgwater the next day.

PART TWO
The Beautiful Liar

Truth is a beautiful shining thing
And lies are blacker than night,
Yet in love's hot arms in a glorious spring
Is a wee small lie not all right?

Bridgwater, Somerset,
June 11, 1685

CHAPTER 32

It was a glorious day for a hanging. In the sunshiny weather people had been filtering into the market town of Bridgwater since early morning and parking their wagons and carts in a circle around the hastily constructed gibbet. For a murderer named George Mayberry was to be hanged this day and hangings were great social occasions. Now as the day wore on and the moment approached, a mixed gathering jostled: rude carts containing bluff country fellows and their giggling women, satin-clad aristocrats who had disdained their enclosed coaches on such a day and made the journey on horseback, and ladies who had arrived in open carriages with big silken skirts billowing out of the sides and ruffled pastel parasols waving in the June heat.

Tom was there. He had ridden into Bridgwater to give himself up. For although he had wrestled with himself all night, by morning he knew he could not let another man hang for what he himself had done.

Not till he shouldered his way through the crowd that was

gathering around the gibbet did he hear about the wench: The condemned man, it seemed, claimed he had spent the night with a woman and refused to name her. Married beyond a doubt! There was speculation that it might be true, and if so, what a rare scandal if she spoke up to save him!

That made Tom think. If there was even the *smallest* chance this Mayberry fellow might be saved by something other than Tom's own confession, he preferred to take it.

He settled himself to wait. Time enough to speak out when Mayberry was on the scaffold!

Pamela arrived late. Indeed she would not have come at all save for something Bates, Tom's old butler, had told her when she arrived at Huntlands to see how her father fared.

"I don't know what's got into Master Tom," Bates confided to her in an aggrieved voice—for Pamela was a great favorite with Bates, who had known her since she was born. Indeed all the servants at Huntlands wished Master Tom would give up his wild ways and marry sweet Mistress Pamela.

"What's he done, Bates?"

"Locked his will and a note for you in his desk—to be delivered in case something happens to him—and galloped off to Bridgwater to attend the hanging as if the devil himself was after him!"

If something happened to him! Pamela regarded Bates with alarm, for these were uneasy times. "I'll go after him, Bates," she decided.

Bates gave her a contented look. Mistress Pamela, looking imperious today in her thin scarlet taffeta riding habit, such a departure from her usual stiff garb, would see to it that nothing happened to Master Tom! He watched as Pamela, calling Tabitha to follow her, rode off for Bridgwater with her tulip red plumes waving on her hat.

But Tom had a long head start. The prisoner was about to mount the scaffold when Pamela arrived. She hardly looked at him—it was Tom for whom her crystal blue eyes scanned the crowd.

Ah, there he was, dressed in tan broadcloth and looking remarkably glum. She waved to him but he didn't see her. Well, whatever had driven him to dash into Bridgwater, she thought, at least he was safe now—and in plain sight. And after this grisly business of hanging was got through, she would make her way to him and find out why he should gallop away after leaving such cryptic instructions for Bates.

She scanned the crowd restlessly to see who was there and who was not: The Hawleys were out in force, Dorothea craning her neck wistfully toward Tom, some distance away. The Ellertons had come over from past Bridgwater, and the Rawlings. The Hamiltons were there, but not the Warburtons. Dick Peacham, she noted with a sinking feeling, was there in gaudy satin but he had not seen her. She was trying to scrunch down in her saddle when Tabby plucked at her arm.

"There's room up there." Tabby, who enjoyed hangings and had been to three, pointed. With a sigh, Pamela, to please Tabby, edged a nervously dancing Angel up toward the front of the crowd. Peacham, she told herself, was sure to see her anyway! She tried to avert her gaze and look away from the tall russet-clad fellow just mounting the scaffold.

Suddenly her bright head swung back so that the tulip red plumes danced on her hat and she regarded the condemned man with such a lively interest that a nearby lady nudged her companion and muttered tartly that the Squire of Axeleigh's daughter seemed quite taken by the prisoner!

Indeed he was something to look upon, was the man just now mounting the scaffold. His air of command set him apart. He might have been mounting the steps of a throne, thought Pamela with a queer little tug at her heartstrings, rather than climbing toward his death at the end of a hempen rope. Sinewy lean, he moved almost contemptuously to the platform with the light-footed grace of a prowling tiger. The daunting look in the cold green eyes that raked the assembled crowd made the hangman wonder nervously if the prisoner might not try at the last moment to break free—and he felt the ropes that bound the prisoner to make sure he was securely shackled.

Pamela studied him narrowly, *for this was the man on the roof she had glimpsed that night at the inn*. Around her she could hear light conversation buzzing. Would he name the wench? Was it true? Listening, Pamela began to speculate on whether this "George Mayberry" had been calling on the landlord's daughter—or his wife! Her heart went out to his gallantry in refusing to name the lady. Also, it seemed to her unlikely that a lover, whose only apparent altercation with the victim had been an argument over some spilt ale, would be incensed enough to pursue him down the Bridgwater Road and kill him. *And had he even had time to do the deed?* She was inclined to doubt it.

Across the way Dick Peacham had discovered her. He waved his plumed hat wildly. Pamela regarded him with distaste and of a sudden she cocked her head and a new and wicked light danced in her crystal blue eyes. She could aid this gallant fellow on the scaffold and she could rid herself of Dick Peacham too—and with the same stroke!

She leaned over and spoke in a low voice to Tabby, who reared back with a shocked look. "But I couldn't"—she began to protest when Pamela's shush silenced her. Several moments of muttered discussion ending with *"Ask him*—and you shall have your choice of my petticoats if you do!" capped the matter and Tabby, looking scared, dismounted. She began to push her way through the crowd.

" 'Tis good luck to kiss a man about to be hanged!" she cried defiantly. "My gramma told me *she* kissed a highwayman on the scaffold and after that she gave birth only to boys! I want her luck!"

In the ensuing laughter, Tabby was urged forward and scampered up the steps to the platform. There—apparently enjoying the dramatic effect her interruption had caused—she clung to the prisoner, kissing him, some thought, rather more than twice. And several exuberant young girls had to be restrained from following her example as she flirted her skirts down from the gallows to the accompaniment of catcalls and a scattering of applause.

"Now there's a hot wench," someone was heard to say as Tabby, her bravado evaporated, scuttled back to Pamela and whispered something to her, ending wistfully with "Can I have the red petticoat?"

"You can. Hush now."

For the prisoner was about to launch into his parting speech before the rope claimed him.

Dev looked out over their assembled heads—that gathering of the curious who had come to see him hanged. This truly put the crown to a wasted life, he was thinking sardonically. To die for a murder he didn't commit! Fate had strange twists. If his uncle had died and his father had lived, he'd be a peer of the realm today—instead of a hunted highwayman!

At least—his face softened—he had held Constance in his arms one last time. By God's grace, he'd had that!

He cast a last thoughtful look at the blue skies over Somerset—the last blue skies he would see this side of hell. For name Constance he would not. They'd have come from all over England, he thought grimly, if they'd known they were hanging "Gentleman Johnny" of the highroads! Ah, well, he would depart this life as George Mayberry—after all, what did it matter? He gave a mental shrug. And if he felt a bitter disappointment that Constance had made no attempt to save him, he told himself it was no more than he deserved, and that probably she was far from here by now and did not even know.

At least *he* would not brand her as an unfaithful wife! He would carry her secret to his grave!

"I say again that I am innocent of this crime." His strong voice carried over the heads of the crowd and they hushed to listen. "I repeat that I spent the night in question at the Rose and Thistle in the company of a lady. And not ambushing some chance-met fellow on the Bridgwater Road! 'Twas my bad luck to find the body, and as I checked to see whether he was dead, I was hit over the head and ended up here."

"Name the lady!" bawled a raucous voice from the crowd and there was a ripple of laughter. And someone else shouted mockingly, "Speak up, lady! Save your lover!!"

In the sudden expectant hush as the condemned man looked sternly about him, Pamela rose in her stirrups.

"Very well, I *will* speak," she announced recklessly. And now her calm voice rang out across the throng. "You have been very gallant, sir, in protecting my reputation"—she gave the prisoner a sunny smile—"but I cannot let you die for it. It is true, what this gentleman says. He did indeed spend the night in question at the Rose and Thistle. With me. In my bedchamber."

Around her there were gasps. Townsfolk and countrymen alike gaped at her. Satin-clad ladies dropped their fans from nerveless fingers. Gentlemen choked on their snuff.

For the golden-haired lady who was speaking had turned up her nose at one time or another at proposals of marriage from half the eligible gentlemen here. They could not, they felt, be hearing her aright.

Pamela ignored their mutterings. "So I demand that you release him," she added, heedless that she was shredding her reputation with every word she spoke. "For I can swear that on the night in question his mind was not on murder. He was"—the slight flush on her soft cheeks deepened—"otherwise engaged. And lest you fail to believe me," she added defiantly, using the information she had got from Tabby, "I would tell you that the prisoner has a scar on his right side just below his belt."

Dick Peacham's face was contorted. He looked as if he might fall down in a fit.

From the crowd the magistrate who had condemned Dev now raised his voice. "See if there is such a scar," he commanded. Rough hands were laid upon Dev and the scar promptly located.

The deep frown of the magistrate abruptly lightened. Only this morning a woman named Mollie—just returned from Bristol and seeing the murdered man displayed in his coffin—

had identified him as one Jack Drubbs, whose treasonous activities she had reported to the King's men last summer. The magistrate, a King's man to the core, had decided that this George Mayberry had done the country a service by eradicating Drubbs, and had been looking for some excuse to let him go. Now he had found it.

"Release the prisoner," he said dryly. "It seems there has been a miscarriage of justice here."

From the scaffold Dev—who had been more astonished than anyone at this outburst from a perfect stranger—was looking down at Pamela in joy. Now he understood. Constance could not come herself—but she had sent this lustrous lady to save him!

Another face in the crowd was mirroring joy at that moment: Tom's.

How she had learnt about it, he couldn't know—unless the Squire had told her. But it was clear to him that Pamela had ridden in to save his hide! And blasted her reputation to do it! She had spoken up to keep him from confessing to killing the blackmailer in a wild duel on horseback on the Bridgwater Road! Darling girl! He turned his horse's head, jostling his way by brute force toward Pamela.

And it was at that moment that a dusty rider on a lathered horse, waving both arms and his weathered hat, galloped into the outer edges of the crowd, shouting hoarsely. And as those nearby heard what he was saying, there were exclamations and people turned to look at this new wonder, riding at them through a cloud of dust.

And now for the first time Tom—and Pamela too—could hear it clearly.

"The Duke of Monmouth has landed at Lyme! All of the West Country is flocking to him! Thousands are pouring in to Lyme!"

A thrill went through the crowd. The Duke had landed! Their soon-to-be king had landed! The West Country would rise, the whole of England would rise in rejoicing! As one, they surged toward this dusty messenger, bearing him and his horse by the sheer weight of numbers down the street.

Magically the crowd around the scaffold had cleared.

In towering fury, beribboned Dick Peacham had taken himself elsewhere, vowing he'd see himself in hell before he'd marry that wanton wench! There was no one in the immediate vicinity but Pamela—and Tabby, who skulked nearby—and Tom and Dev, the latter just rebuckling his belt and sauntering jauntily down from the gallows.

Tom, about to ride over and thank Pamela from the depths of him—checked his forward rush as he saw the tall former prisoner saunter toward Pamela and bow low. A horrible thought struck Tom at that moment—*Pamela could have been telling the truth!* Perhaps she had *not* connived with Tabby to learn about the scar! She had indeed been at the Rose and Thistle in Bridgwater that night! Had she taken this handsome stranger to her bed? The knuckles that gripped his sword hilt turned white and he sat very still in the saddle.

"My fervent thanks, my lady." Dev was saying to Pamela. "Might I know to whom I am indebted?"

Pamela, intent on Tom, who sat some distance away, steadily regarding her, barely noticed him. "It is not necessary for you to know my name," she shrugged. "I did not do it for you!"

No, he thought tenderly. *You did it for Constance.* And wondered of a sudden what quixotic reasoning had impelled this lustrous lady to lie for him.

"I understand," he said quickly. "I will get me gone." For surely this glib-tongued lady would wish to renounce her lie the moment he was out of sight! Constance could rest easy in her new-made marriage, he vowed silently as he strode away. Nightfall would find him far from here and he would keep his distance from Somerset and never trouble her again!

To Tom, whose hand had closed fiercely over the hilt of his sword, sanity returned. A little while ago he had been resigned to raising his own voice to stop the hanging. Now there would be no need to do it. He could thank Pamela for that at least! He wheeled his horse around and headed for the crowd that encircled the dusty messenger from Lyme.

Sadly Pamela watched him go. She barely inclined her head when the man she had just saved from the gibbet rode by and—full of wrong conclusions—saluted her with a last wave of his hat as he began a journey that would lead him all the way to Lincoln. She did not care what happened to him.

Tom might condemn her, she thought—but then he did not love her, so what did his condemnation matter? At least she would be free of Dick Peacham!

Huntlands, Somerset,
June 12, 1685

CHAPTER 33

Pamela had many misgivings when she told her father what had happened in Bridgwater, but he took it surprisingly well.

"So you have made yourself a scandal in order to rid yourself of your betrothal?" he mused.

"That's about it," admitted Pamela, flushing.

The Squire studied her. She was Virginia's daughter, right enough, and ripe for scandal—but she was his daughter too, charging directly where her heart led her. "Perhaps now you will follow your heart," he said cryptically, thinking of Tom. Tom, who but a short time before had gripped the Squire's hand, asked him to look after Huntlands for him, and ridden away to Lyme to join Monmouth.

"He didn't even scold me!" Pamela told Constance in wonder. "And when Dick Peacham's note arrived formally breaking our betrothal, he just snorted and tore it up! In fact, the whole thing seemed to buck him up. He had himself loaded onto a wagon and came home with me!"

Constance could see how being rid of the prospect of Dick

Peacham as a son-in-law might hearten the Squire. "But I still don't understand why you did it, Pamela," she insisted. "I mean, some stranger is being hanged and you—"

She broke off as Stebbins came in to announce Captain Warburton.

The Captain strode into the drawing room. He was almost chillingly handsome in black and silver with wide-topped boots and wide gauntleted riding gloves which he had not bothered to remove. He swept both young ladies a graceful bow with a flourish of his plumed hat.

"'Twas the Squire I came to see," he began, his gaze passing over Constance, who was regarding him uneasily. "But perhaps one of you may know. Ned has ridden off without a word, his bed's not been slept in. Do either of you know where he went?" And when they shook their heads in surprise, a deep voice from the hallway said, "He left with Tom Thornton to join the Duke in Lyme." And they all turned to see the Squire, leaning heavily upon a cane, come into the room.

"Hotheaded young fools," muttered the Captain, but Pamela swung on her father accusingly.

"You didn't tell me that! I thought Tom was just avoiding me."

"Your behavior didn't merit your being told," the Squire told her crisply. He turned to the Captain. "You've no doubt heard how my daughter distinguished herself at yesterday's 'hanging'?"

"Yes, I heard." Captain Warburton gave Pamela an amused look. "And put not much stock in it!"

There was a glint of amusement in the Squire's glance too. Then he sighed. "Tom left before he heard the straight of it."

"How did you come to select a stranger for this honor, Mistress Pamela?" wondered Captain Warburton. "I'd have thought there were easier ways to break a distasteful betrothal," he added shrewdly.

"Oh, I saw the fellow climb over the roof that night at the inn," dimpled Pamela. "And I didn't think he'd have either

511

the time or the inclination at that late hour to dash out and commit murder!''

''Over—did you say *over the roof?*'' demanded Constance, her face gone chalky.

''Yes,'' shrugged Pamela. ''And I got Tabby to ask him, there on the scaffold, if he had any scars—and he did!'' Now that the truth was out, she could laugh about it.

And Dev had a new long scar—new since Essex. This George Mayberry who had so nearly been hanged was Dev! Constance got unsteadily to her feet. ''I think I need a breath of air,'' she gasped.

Captain Warburton found her on the front lawn as he left. He gave her a puzzled look. ''We'll agree that it's no longer my affair,'' he said. ''But did you know this George Mayberry?''

Constance gave him back as steady a look as the one he gave her. ''We'll agree,'' she said distantly, ''that it's none of your affair.''

The Captain jammed on his hat and left.

Back inside, Pamela, who had by now ferreted out part of the story, grasped Constance as she came through the hall and swept her upstairs.

''The man who left over the roofs that night at the inn—he was visiting *you!*'' she accused.

Constance had been shocked to discover that Pamela had discussed her situation with Tom. Now she gave the other girl a sad look. ''I don't have your icy control, Pam. My life is like my riding—I keep careening raggedly off the track. No grip on the reins like you have.''

''Then *he* was—''

''The man I married—'' She had been about to say ''long ago''; suddenly it seemed forever, in some other life. ''Once,'' she finished.

''And to think, he might have been hanged for something he didn't do!'' gasped Pamela.

''Yes, except for you.'' *And happenstance.* There was always that.

"I never dreamed, when I saw him ride off toward the east—"

"Toward the east?" cut in Constance sharply.

"Yes."

Not toward Bristol, then . . . Dev had lied to her again.

"Tom shouldn't have left without telling me good-by," worried Pamela.

"No, he should not," sighed Constance.

"And especially since there could be a battle."

Constance gave Pamela a jaded look. "If England rises as expected, there'll be more than one battle."

As it turned out, there was only one that really counted— and it took place at Sedgemoor. But they were not to know that—not yet. What they knew was that the Duke of Monmouth was moving north, gathering supporters as he went. Mostly they were country people, ill armed, untried in battle, and filled with enthusiasm for the Duke whom they now boldly called "King Monmouth."

The Squire's frown deepened as the month of June proceeded. Monmouth had indeed gained a large following since landing at that ancient pier of unhewn stones known as the Cobb in Lyme Regis. With only eighty-two men and a drawn sword, he had plunged into the narrow blue rag-stone alleys of Lyme and been received by the villagers with a hail of flowers. Although the gentry had not flocked to join him, others had. Without difficulty he had seized Axminster. People rushed to join his banners every day, and it was with some eight thousand horse that he rode into Somerset.

"The Duke has been crowned king in Taunton!" Pamela rushed in excitedly to tell her father and Constance as they sat in the drawing room. "I just heard it by way of the Hawleys' head groom. He says he is off to join. Oh, do you not think we should go to Taunton, Father? There are bound to be all sorts of balls in celebration!"

She is thinking Tom will be there, thought Constance, and was not surprised when the Squire growled, " 'Tis a bit soon to celebrate. Wait until battle is joined—this young duke may not prevail!''

Pamela paled a bit. "You do not think that battle can be avoided, Father?" she faltered. "I had hoped that if everyone joined him—"

"Everyone will not join him," Constance reminded her. She had received word through the Hawleys that she was to remain where she was and channel messages. Galsworthy had come by only this morning and had brought gloomy news— all over England King James was having Monmouth's supporters put under "preventive arrest." He would give them no chance to lead uprisings against him! "Only in the West Country is there such optimism," she said, and the Squire gave her a brooding look. *If only my daughter had shared your view,* he was thinking, *perhaps she could have dissuaded Tom Thornton from joining this shaky Cause.* He did not know Constance as well as he thought.

"What news of Captain Warburton?" asked Pamela, with a quick look at Constance.

"No news," rumbled the Squire. "He remains at Warwood as a sensible man should in times like these!"

Pamela, whose heart was with Tom wherever he rode, made a face at them and flounced out into the garden.

But the advancing days of summer brought little cheer. There was now a price on Monmouth's head of five thousand pounds, dead or alive. Undismayed, the young duke drove through Glastonbury.

Ominously, word reached Axeleigh—even as the Duke reached Bridgwater amid much exultation—that Albemarle, at the head of the King's troops, was advancing on Bridgwater. No novice in war, Monmouth was determined to present a moving target to his enemies. He brought his troops west from Glastonbury, determined to attack Bristol but found himself checkmated—Lord Feversham had already thrown a regiment of foot-guards into Bristol. With his unseasoned troops Monmouth now turned east toward Bath but found it impregnably defended.

Hoping for better luck, he swung south—and defeated his half-brother, the Duke of Grafton, at Norton St. Philip.

And now word came that the Scots, on whom Monmouth had counted, would not be riding south to aid him. Argyll had been routed in the western Highlands—he had been captured and was as good as dead already. The Duke hastily called a council of war at his present field headquarters, a half-timbered inn known as the George at Norton St. Philip.

And it was there that Captain Warburton found him.

It was a tribute to the confusion that he was ushered in at once, and what he had to say only created further dismay.

"I bring word that the local militias are gathering against you," the Captain told him grimly. "It is not too late to flee. Under cover of darkness your men can disperse—most can make it back to their homes and wait for some more fortuitous time to place you upon the throne in Whitehall, Your Grace."

His "Your Grace" was noted with frowns by those who were now calling the Duke "Your Majesty."

"Who let this man in?" demanded Lord Grey arrogantly. "His opinion is not solicited!"

Captain Warburton turned on him a forbidding glance. "You are trapped," he warned. "Bristol and Bath have stood ye off. Even now Feversham and the Scots are headed toward Sedgemoor. More troops are joining them."

"We know that. Be on with it, man," cut in an impatient voice.

Captain Warburton favored the speaker with a cold look. His voice slowed to an insolent drawl. "I'm hearing word of 'preventive arrests' all over England. Elsewhere the revolt has been nipped in the bud. It's over. The West Country stands alone."

About him now no one was smiling. For a moment they saw their future plain: the fields littered with dead, the green untried soldiers fighting valiantly with plowshares and poles and rusty muskets against cannon and seasoned troops.

"I am come to deliver Your Grace to safety," said Captain

Warburton impressively, "if ye will have it. I know these back roads and I ask only that I be allowed to pick my own men to get ye safe away to Holland—to wait for better days." *And those men would include Ned and Tom Thornton and the other Valley lads.*

"There will come no better days!" cried someone. "We have already defeated Grafton, we must make our move now!"

The handsome young duke gave him a distracted look. "I thank you for your offer," he told Captain Warburton. "But methinks me there must be some way to win the day!"

At that point someone came in and muttered in Lord Grey's ear. He went out to find a flushed, mounted young captain, whom he recognized as Tom Thornton, and beside him on a dancing white mount the most beautiful blonde it had ever been his privilege to view. Lord Grey, who appreciated beauty, was quite bowled over.

"This young lady is a neighbor of mine," Tom told him. "She has come to see me and since I know all the rooms at the inn are taken—"

"You would wish to escort her home," Grey finished for him. "But you're needed here."

"Mistress Pamela cannot be expected to ride back alone in the dark," stated Tom. His jaw was thrust out.

Grey did not even notice that outthrust jaw. His reflective gaze was on Pamela, who watched him with sparkling crystal blue eyes. "This conferring is apt to be a long business and could well take till morning," he said. "The lady can have my room for the night."

Tom was startled. He would have protested but that Pamela, dimpling at Lord Grey, murmured, "I had heard of your courtesy, sir, but I am overwhelmed by your generosity!" She dismounted in a pretty flurry of scarlet riding skirts. "Now we can talk in private," she told Tom.

Lord Grey watched grimly as they went into the inn. It was not the first time he had stood aside for lovers, and there could be no mistaking the way this pair looked at each other.

He went back inside where Captain Warburton—unknown to Tom and Pamela—was being shouted down.

With a bow, the Captain left and went in search of Ned. Finding him was not easy, for Ned and two others were out on a reconnaissance mission. Looking around him at other young fools, so eager to fight and die in this hopeless Cause, the Captain heaved a deep sigh. Fools they might be but they were West Country fools, and he knew that when the battle was joined, he would be with them. Not to fight for any Stuart, but to fight beside his own. He settled himself in the encampment to wait for Ned.

Meanwhile, inside the inn, Tom was leading Pamela up the stairs.

"You shouldn't have come here, Pam," he remonstrated. "Is the Squire mad that he allows you to go jaunting about the countryside alone in times like these?"

"Father's abed again and could not stop me," Pamela told him as they reached the landing. "For he slipped on the stairs and fell down the entire flight and has hurt his back again— more grievously this time, I am afraid."

Tom stared at her. Himself he had invented that lie about the Squire's having fallen down the main staircase at Huntlands and now it had come true over at Axeleigh! There was Someone Up There counting the hairs on your head after all!

"But he had others to stop you," he pointed out.

"They have all run away to fight for the Duke—except Stebbins, who is too old, and I managed to elude *him*." She was walking into the room Tom indicated was Lord Grey's as she spoke and now she tossed her scarlet-plumed hat on the bed and whirled to face him. "Latch the door, Tom."

"But I'm not staying, Pam. Consider your reputation if—"

"My reputation is long gone. I scattered it to the winds at Bridgwater." She sighed and gave him a slanted look. "You see before you a scarlet woman, Tom." Her excited laughter tinkled. "The color of my riding habit is appropriate!"

"Pamela!" he protested. But he latched the door.

"And I have heard there is a great host gathering on Sedgemoor to face you." She gave him a steady look.

"That is true."

Her attack veered. "When you went to join up, why did you not tell me good-by?"

That reminded him of the scene in Bridgwater when a plumed-hatted stranger had swept her an elegant bow. And she had known the location of a scar below the stranger's belt! "You were already occupied with telling someone else good-by," he said grimly.

"Oh, Tom! You could not have thought that man mattered to me!"

His golden brows shot up. "I thought he might. Since you so candidly admitted you spent the night with him at the inn!"

She gave him a roguish look. "Surely you did not believe it?"

"I knew not what to believe. First you betrothed yourself to Peacham—"

"But that was only because Dorothea Hawley showed me the ring you had given her and told me of your secret betrothal."

"Ring?" echoed Tom. "I gave Dorothea Hawley no ring— nor is there any secret betrothal!" Suddenly he remembered the ring he had lost that Dorothea had found. "And it was because of this that you plighted your troth to Peacham?"

She nodded. "And then I wanted out of it but I knew my father would hold me to it because he had given his word, so I—"

"Invented a lover!" Tom was staring at her, near bereft of speech.

"On the spur of the moment." She gave him a demure smile. "How else was I to wait for you, Tom?"

The anger that had gnawed at him ever since that day in Bridgwater melted away in an instant. Tom had almost been hoping that he would die in battle, now that Pamela was lost to him. That she should be suddenly restored near took his breath away!

"Then you mean—"

"That man they nearly hanged was Constance's lover, not mine. He'd been in *her* room—not mine."

The joy that washed over Tom was so overwhelming that it staggered him. Almost without volition, his arms went around Pamela.

"Oh, Pam! And I thought—!"

"But you were wrong," she whispered. "I have never loved anyone but you."

They were silent for a long time, kissing, murmuring. Then Tom pushed her away from him. Firmly. "You still shouldn't have come, Pam. Harm could befall you here. Battle will be joined soon—and it is possible we will lose."

"I couldn't let you go into battle without knowing how matters stood between us," she said wistfully. "And whether you meant to return to me—or to Dorothea Hawley."

"I think you know the answer to that." Tom's voice was husky.

"Yes. I know the answer now. Oh, Tom, come home with me! Forget Monmouth, come home!"

"And leave Ned and the others?" He gave her a startled look.

"Oh, bring them too! Quick, before it is too late!"

"Pam, I can't in honor do that." He said it gravely and she felt the rebuke in his voice.

"Then take me with you into the battle, for I would die too!" She flung herself against him and began to cry.

"I'm not going to die," he told her, pushing her away a bit and smiling down into her tearstained face. "And who knows, we may win!"

"Constance doesn't think so," she whispered.

His face stilled at that. "And what does Constance say?" he asked carefully.

"That even the local militias are rising against the Duke,

that the revolt is dead except here in the West Country. Oh, Tom—''

"Hush, hush," he murmured, bearing her to the bed and setting her down upon it. "All is not lost. We've a great force here."

"Farmers against seasoned troops," she said bitterly.

"But right is on our side," he corrected her in a stern voice. He was thinking how ravishing she looked in her scarlet riding habit.

"Right?" she scoffed. " 'Tis might not right that wins battles!"

How silky her fair hair was! He found his fingers touching it, almost against his will, and then easing down to stroke her white neck—and tangle his fingers in the white froth of lace she wore like a cravat. She shivered at his touch—and stripped off her riding gloves.

"Tom." Her voice was pleading. "I know I have gone about everything all wrong. I should not even have come here—'' Even as she spoke her hands had stolen around his neck and she was bringing his face down to hers. "And yet now that I *am* here, now that we both know how we feel, now that you're going to send me back tomorrow, now that you may be killed"—her voice broke—"oh, Tom, couldn't we at least spend the night together?"

Something caught in his throat, making it difficult for him to speak. Tom Thornton—whom people had murmured was well named, for was he not a prowling tomcat where the ladies were concerned?—felt an enormous tenderness steal over him. Little Pamela, whom he had always meant to take to his bed—eventually—had actually spoken for him.

"Pam," he said huskily. "I can't let you. Suppose I'm killed?"

"Then I'd have something to remember you by," she said simply and her crystal blue gaze was the most honest he had ever known.

"Your father would never forgive me for taking advantage of you," he sighed. "He trusts me."

"And *I* will never forgive you if you don't!" she said shakily. She snuggled against him, every slight movement robbing him of his resolve. "*I* trust you too!" And when still he hesitated, "If you don't," she flared, "I promise you I'll ride home alone *tonight*—no matter how dark it is or how many cutthroats line the road!"

A chuckle gurgled in Tom's throat. His lovely girl was threatening him if he did not take her to bed at once!

He groaned for there was that about her that stirred his blood. The very touch of her silky flesh was liquid fire in his veins, and he knew that tonight he was about to break faith with an old friend—by seducing his daughter. A dishonorable thing. Yet he could not stop himself. He caught her by the shoulders in a grip that was both fierce and tender. There was a roaring in his ears as he warred with himself. He wanted this dainty golden girl as he had never wanted anyone before, and he knew instinctively he would never want anyone so much again.

"God help me, Pam," he muttered as his hands left her shoulders and his suddenly stumbling fingers loosened her bodice. "I swear to you I'll have the banns cried as soon as I get back."

But he might never come back—and they both knew it.

"Oh, bother the banns," murmured Pamela, feeling her own blood race at every touch of his fingers on her slender torso. "Just stay the night with me, Tom!" *And tomorrow somehow I'll persuade you to go home with me!* she promised herself.

She untied her big fashionably detachable sleeves and flung them from her, like scarlet flowers, to the floor. A moment later her tight bodice came free and Tom's hands slid up under it—for it was, like so many handsome garments, made separately from the full skirt—and eased it away from her body, leaving her standing in her scarlet riding skirt and delicate white chemise before him. The material of that chemise was so sheer that her pink nipples could be seen through it.

Delicately, reverently, as if he must not mar or sully this exquisite creature before him, Tom lifted her chin with one finger and lightly kissed her lips. "You're sure about this?" he said huskily. "For once done, there's no going back."

She was smiling at him. Confidently. "I care not where I go, Tom—so long as it's with you," she said softly—and for answer gave a sudden tug to the white satin riband that held up her sheer chemise and let the fragile white lawn material float softly down about her hips, a white cloud drifting over her scarlet riding skirt.

That smooth pale torso, so suddenly bared to his view, was so lovely he drew in his breath sharply. She was as beautiful in the dusk as she had been by moonlight—radiant.

With a soft sound in his throat, Tom swept her up and carried her to the bed, laid her gently upon the coverlet. Nothing would stop him now!

It was early still. Through the small window, half obscured by the black ragged pattern of the tree branches, a narrow slice of melon moon, of a brilliant whitish green, blazed against a lavender sky. Observed by neither of the lovers, who were intent on matters of the flesh, that sky shaded to mauve and then to gray gold as it neared the earth and ended in a flush of soft orange scarlet.

Tom had tugged off Pamela's boots—for her spurs were catching in the coverlet. He had let his hands glide up sensuously along her smooth firm thighs as he himself removed her stockings and her garters. And then he had risen and tugged off his own boots, divested himself of his outer clothing while Pamela watched, her eyes large and dark and glowing now, from the bed.

Those last minutes of the fading light flickered by with their pulsebeats, with the lavender deepening to dark gray blue and the orange scarlet to rose madder and then to a thin crimson line as the dying sun retreated over the western horizon. They had plighted their troth, unspoken, on the worn coverlet of that upstairs room at the George, with a military conclave going on downstairs—plighted it forever, heart to heart.

Outside, the marshes and meadows of Sedgemoor had now changed their character as the creatures of the night replaced the creatures of the day. Ferrets roamed the marshes and big-eyed owls stalked meadow mice. From somewhere came the wild cry of a nightjar.

But the lovers were oblivious to it all. Battles might rage, thrones might topple, worlds collide and they would not know it. Their dreams were as old as time—and as fresh as tomorrow. Spellbinding. This night was theirs—theirs to take, theirs to hold, theirs to cherish forever.

The hum of men's voices below was loud enough to carry to all parts of the inn, for there was much dissension, much loud wrangling over what to do—but it is doubtful if Tom or Pamela, lost in their dream of love, ever heard it.

They were more intent upon the easing down of a riding skirt over rounded hips, in the silky rustle of a chemise as it was urged down a slim body, past dainty white legs, in the soft urgency of a man's lips upon a pink female nipple. Tom, experienced lover that he was, brought to this night all the best that was in him, teasing, caressing, gently exciting her passions, building her up to that heated moment when she would change from girl to woman. Pamela, enraptured, thrilled to his touch, her eyes wide and dark with desire, her lips slightly parted, her breath gasping in her throat.

And now at last was the moment—and she met it bravely, holding back with clenched teeth the cry that threatened to break from her lips as her maidenhead was pierced. For a moment she sagged against him and he, considerate of her pain, held her comfortingly close and murmured endearments.

And then the turmoil that had engulfed them both was driving him again and he thrust once more with determination—and Pamela's soft ragged sigh told him, as her trembling body did, that he had won through. Their bodies closed, locked, threshed together upon the inn's hard mattress, and the bed that was to have known Lord Grey's more sober form this night was merrily cavorted in by two strong young lovers who for these wondrous moments had thrown away all thought of the future or what might lay in store for them.

Masterful, sure of himself, Tom led his trusting lady into lands of wild delight. His every touch was a goad to her senses. He swept her up and up, each breathless moment filled with new sensations and lovelier than the last. She felt she was floating along tall precipices, teetering on the brink of mighty chasms, a flower blown upward by the wind, fluttering toward the stars amid vast heavenly explosions that tossed her this way and that and filled a dark world with light.

She clutched him tightly, lest she lose her road and all this beautiful new world collapse about her.

And when his own passion had crested and he had brought her with him back to earth, back to this tiny room at the George, back to the worn coverlet that supported their pulsing naked bodies, Tom, lying beside Pamela, had time to think. And to thank Whoever Arranges Things for these last hours spent with his golden girl before the battle. For he had been on reconnaissance earlier in the day, even as Ned was now, and the enemy had seemed to him more numerous than the great flights of wheeling seabirds that swooped over Bristol harbor. With all his heart he wished he could go home with Pamela, this lovely child-woman who nestled beside him smiling in the moonlight, but he was committed to this Cause, just as Ned and the others were committed. This was a West Country fight and he could not shirk it. His heart would be riding home through the summer countryside with Pamela on the morrow, but his body, lean and hard and ready for this, would be lunging through the shot and saber charges of Sedgemoor. . . .

Driven by his hard thoughts, he turned to her again, caught her in his arms with all the urgency that surged through him on this, the eve of battle. And this time her response was less hesitant, more sure. She was learning the wild byways of love, and he was teaching her—just as he had once taught her to take high jumps zephyr-light atop a thunder-hooved hunter.

He was proud of her, this brave, lovely girl in his arms, who had dared the wild marauding countryside to find him and make things right between them. And his last thought, as he drifted off to sleep with Pamela cradled in the crook of his arm, was that he would survive this battle. He would let no cannon ball find him, he would outwit every saber thrust, he would win his way back to her. And love her—forever and ever. . . .

Dawn found Tom shaking her awake. "Lord Grey will want his room back, and you must get you gone before we go into battle and it's too late to get you out!"

"Oh, Tom." She flung herself against him again and another precious half hour was added to their joyful memories of each other.

But then, tenderly, he pulled her from the bed where she seemed rooted for the day—for she was determined to keep him with her.

"You must be away, Pamela," he told her, ruffling her rumpled fair hair as he spoke. And when her slim white arms would have pulled him back to bed, he resisted, shaking his head.

Annoyed that she could not keep him, she watched him dress and then flounced up herself and dressed while they talked. Tom had laid his great pistol on the windowsill, she noted, and his sword was hung over a chair. She wished wistfully that she could march him out of here at gunpoint and save him from the battle that was shaping up.

They were arguing as she dressed.

"Constance says the revolt is finished elsewhere," she was saying. "She says 'preventive arrests' have trapped the leaders all over England. I do not know how she knows, but she says it is true. She says the West Country stands alone, Tom!"

A shrug of broad shoulders was his only answer. He was standing near the door.

"Oh, why doesn't the Duke give up now?" she cried. "Why wait until you're all slaughtered? He must know it's hopeless. If he ran for it now, he could get away to Holland, the troops could disband—they could seek amnesty, they could get away, back to their homes!''

"Pam,'' he sighed. "What good is it to talk this way? Our course is set—what will be, will be.'' He turned alertly as boots marched toward the door, thinking Lord Grey might be arriving to reclaim his room, relaxed as the footsteps hurried on by.

"It's terrible,'' she said. "I won't *let* you go!'' She stamped her boot and then picked up Tom's pistol, held it up critically. "This gun needs cleaning, Tom.''

"I know,'' he muttered, turning his head again as more footsteps hurried by.

"The Duke should have had the sense to stay in Holland, waiting until the country was prepared for him,'' she burst out. Through the window she now eyed that same duke balefully, for he had come striding out of the inn and was now standing beside his horse, about to mount up. "But no, he had to come charging back before anyone was ready,'' she flung over her shoulder. "And now he's going to get you all killed!'' Of a sudden the handsome duke below seemed to her a monster.

Below her, all were concentrating on the Duke. No one was looking up.

"I hate him!'' she cried in a choked voice.

And brought up the pistol.

He was there below her in all his splendor. Handsome, commanding, acknowledged son of a king albeit on the wrong side of the blanket, claimant to the throne. About to fight the decisive battle of his career—the battle for England.

But Pamela from the window did not see the Duke as a leader of men, as a rightful king. She saw him as a good-looking fool in fine garments, deluded by his own ambition, leading everyone she loved to sure destruction.

Well, he would not live to do it!

Almost unconsciously, her finger tightened on the trigger. She did not consider the consequences, she did not think past this breathless moment when she viewed a would-be king down the shining barrel of a pistol.

For the flicker of an eyelash the fate of the West Country hung on the trigger finger of a reckless sixteen-year-old girl.

The George,
Norton St. Philip, Somerset,
July 5, 1685

CHAPTER 34

Some violent undertone in her voice made Tom turn. She had always been an easy handler of firearms—she was today. He saw the pistol being leveled at something below in the innyard—and he had a terrible sinking feeling as to what that something might be.

"Pamela!" The name was ripped from him as he sprang for her.

He saw it all in a kind of terrible slow motion. He seemed to sail through the air even as the gun went off. He was crashing into Pamela, snatching the gun from her hand, seeing her white face, hearing the sob in her throat.

Below her there was pandemonium—but no bloodshed. Fate had not yet decreed that it was time to end the Duke of Monmouth's ill-starred life. At the crucial moment, just as Pamela fired, he had bent quickly to examine what seemed to him an imperfection in the creamy lace of his boothose—and it had saved his life. The bullet had whistled safely by him to imbed itself in the hard-packed earth of the innyard.

But abovestairs, the force of Tom's impact brought Pamela's light body slamming up against the wall.

"I missed!" she whispered, stricken.

There were shouts from the courtyard now and cries, "Is His Grace all right?" by those who had forgotten for the moment that the Duke was now acknowledged by them a king. "Is King Monmouth all right?" roared someone.

Against the wall, a white-faced Pamela had now realized what her folly would cost her—Tom's life and her own. For even though she protested his innocence, who would believe her when he stood there with a smoking gun in his hand? But she had endless courage.

"Reload!" she cried. "We'll stand them off!"

But Tom was not listening. He was casting a quick look out the window. No one was looking in his direction just now; they were all clustered around the Duke or running into the inn. He dropped the smoking pistol through the window and spun around to face her.

"Oh, Tom!" she cried in despair when she saw he no longer had the gun.

"Pam, forgive me," he said rapidly. And before she knew what he was about, his fist cracked against her jaw. The blow had been timed with neat precision—and with just sufficient force for its purpose. He caught her sagging body as she fell, swept her slight weight up in his arms, and had reached the hallway before the first man—a major in the Duke's army—charged up the stairs.

"The roof!" cried Tom. "I think the fellow's up there! My betrothed here was saying good-by to me and we heard the shot and saw the pistol drop past our window! *Is the Duke all right?*"

"Aye!" The word was flung over a broad shoulder as the major charged up the attic stairs. "Surround the inn," he bellowed.

Meanwhile Tom was pushing his way down a clogged stairway with Pamela in his arms. "She saw the pistol fall past our window and fainted," he kept saying. "She needs air.'' Like an onrushing flood, men parted to let him bear his limp scarlet burden past.

Down in the courtyard he moved boldly toward the group around Monmouth and glibly repeated his story.

"We'll need ye here—ye're witnesses,'' said a harsh voice. He thought it was Grey's.

"My betrothed has a weak heart,'' protested Tom. "There's a doctor down the road. I'm afraid this has been too much for her—''

"Bear your lady away to the doctor,'' came the young Duke's rich voice, overriding his subordinate. He shouldered a frowning Grey aside and stepped forward. "Faith, she's a beauty!'' He made a languorous gesture of dismissal. "Let them go, Grey. We do not need witnesses—we'll have the fellow himself.''

The Stuarts, for all their faults—and they were many— were always capable of magnificent gestures.

Tom gazed for a fleeting moment into the Duke's eyes. Did he see perchance a twinkle there? He thought so. A broad smile lit his own strong features.

"Thank you, Your Gra—Your Majesty,'' he said. "As soon as I see to my lady, I'll be back.''

"See that you are!'' The carefree gallantry that had endeared the Stuarts to so many rang in that voice. "See that you are!''

The horses were but a short distance away. With Pamela in his arms and leading Angel, Tom was off toward Axeleigh, riding into the trees.

In his arms Pamela stirred. Her long lashes fluttered and suddenly her crystal blue eyes were fixed on him accusingly. "You struck mc!''

Tom looked down into that indignant face. Along her jawline there was an ugly red mark. It hurt him to see it there. "I saved you, Pam,'' he whispered huskily. "Those men back there would have killed you had they known you fired the shot. 'Twas the Duke himself gave me leave to go,'' he added caressingly. "I think he guessed 'twas you who fired the shot but the Stuarts have ever an eye for beauty.''

Pamela felt her jaw gingerly. "I suppose I'm glad I didn't kill him," she sighed. "It all came over me—how he's leading all of you to your death. And I lost my head."

Tom brought his horse to a halt and pressed a kiss on that wistful upturned face. "You'll be safe riding to Axeleigh alone from here," he said. "At least I hope so. Keep a sharp watch out for trouble."

"But you don't have your pistol, Tom—they'll know!"

He kissed her again. Lingeringly. "I'll tell them I gave it to you—to keep you safe on the road home."

She sighed, a long-drawn-out, fatalistic sigh. For she had known clear down to her boots that this moment of parting would come at last, no matter how desperately she tried to postpone it.

"Tom," she whispered, still clinging to him as he transferred her gently to Angel's back, handed the reins to her. "Tom—oh, Tom, don't get yourself killed!"

He grinned down at her, but there was a constriction in his throat as he answered. "I won't," he promised softly. "Wait for me at Axeleigh."

She nodded, her heart too full to speak. Bright tears spilled from her lashes and blurred her vision of him as he rode away—back toward the Duke's men, back toward the battle that was shaping up—the battle for England.

She waited until he was out of sight. Then she turned and rode home.

Pamela had reached Axeleigh—and far away Dev had reached Lincoln—before the first shot was fired in the mists at Sedgemoor.

At Axeleigh disastrous news had been filtering in all day. In a desperate move to surprise the army arrayed against him, Monmouth had decided to attack by night. Stealthily, at eleven o'clock, he had begun the dangerous trek across the marshes of Sedgemoor, honeycombed by shallow ditches called rhines. Thick fog covered their movements as the long thin columns wavered raggedly over the rough stones of a slippery causeway across the Black Ditch. Confused by the thick fog, the guide turned the wrong way, somebody stumbled, a pistol snapped—and Feversham's troops were alerted. Monmouth's cavalry blundered into the Horse Guards at a ditch known as the Bussex Rhine—and were cut down. At their backs Monmouth and his pikemen from the shires brought up against the ditch. For three hours the battle had raged—untrained shiremen gallantly standing up to the best cavalry in Europe: the Grenadier Guards, the Dumbarton Regiment of Scots, the Life Guards and the Oxford Blues from Zoyland. By dawn it was all over and cannon had triumphed over pikes and scythes.

Constance almost had to hold Pamela back bodily from dashing off to the battleground. "Wait here," she told the younger girl sternly. "There's a messenger should be by soon who will bring us tidings. His tidings are always correct."

Pamela turned a startled face toward Constance. There had been something in her voice, a ring of authority. . . . "You were with them all the time?" she murmured.

"All the time." After all, what could it matter now to admit it?

"And you never told me." Pamela sounded aggrieved.

"They didn't want me to, Pam."

"And why not? Oh, surely, they didn't think I'd *betray* them?" For Tom to have thought that of her would have broken her heart.

"No, of course not, Pam. They just thought you talked too much. That was the reason I dragged you to Hawley Grange that day. A meeting was being held there—you noticed the horses as we left."

"A meeting? Tom and all of them?"

"All but Captain Warburton." Constance sighed.

"Then the Hawley girls knew!" cried Pamela.

"Yes, they were part of it."

"And Margie Hamilton?"

"No, she wasn't part of it. Not so far as I know."

Pamela subsided. So much intrigue winging around her ears and she hadn't even been aware of it.

Constance guessed what Pamela was thinking. "Your mind was on Tom," she comforted. "It was all you could think about. But now you can serve him best by being here when he comes back—to hide him."

Pamela's crystal blue eyes widened at that. She had been thinking only of the outcome of the battle, of death and injury. It had entirely escaped her that the survivors would be hunted men!

They were standing by the gates of Axeleigh as they talked, asking news of anyone who passed.

"Garn!" cried Pamela suddenly, for she recognized the man trudging down the road toward them as being one of Warwood's tenants. He was one of Ned's men who had gone into battle armed with an old battle axe hastily snatched from the wall of Warwood's armory. Now he had no weapon at all, only a bandaged head—and he was walking heavily, leaning upon a stout stick. "Oh, Garn, what news?"

"All's lost," he told her hollowly. "And the Duke run away. 'Twas a foggy night and them marshes is treacherous. Whoever was leading us missed his way and led us into a ditch. And then they was all over us, the King's men. So much cannon and shot, no man could stand before it." He shook his head, remembering.

"Oh, God," she whispered. "But what of Tom? Tom Thornton? And Captain Warburton, was he there? And Ned and the others?"

"Master Ned's dead. Captain Warburton saw a horseman coming at Ned and he leaped forward with his sword. But a cannon ball got Ned—he went down, all bloody." Garn shivered. "And the Captain did impale the horseman with his sword, but the horseman had a pistol and it went off in the Captain's face and I heard him say 'I'm blinded' as he fell. And Master Tom was hurt—I don't know how bad—and he leaped forward and bore the Captain away, out of the trampling hooves—and someone struck me down just then and when I come to, I crawled away and someone sitting on the ground with a hurt leg bound up my head and I've been walkin' ever since. All the lads from hereabouts is dead, I think. And the main roads is lined with those as got away and was hanged by the King's men. Grinnin' down from the trees they are, just danglin' there.'' He shuddered.

Tom was hurt!

Pamela felt her senses swaying. Constance clutched at her arm and she recovered herself. Garn needed help. "Come in," she said. "We'll give you a hot meal and some fresh bandages for your wound, and we'll hide you in case the King's men come looking."

"When the King's men come lookin'—and they will, never doubt it—I want to be at Warwood," said Garn gloomily. "Cook there will swear as to how I got my head wound when I tripped over the cat and fell onto the fire tongs." He was shuffling off down the road even as he spoke.

"Well, at least let me give you a horse," she cried.

"No horse—I'd have to explain how I come by it." He was moving on, still looking watchfully to right and left.

"Pam," said Constance sharply. "Pam, hold on to yourself." *Blinded,* she thought. *Those keen eyes gone forever. . . . And poor Ned, dead in his blood.* But Pamela was looking as if she might faint.

Pamela leant against a tree trunk, pressing her hot face against the rough bark. *Oh, God, let him not be hanging from a tree!* she prayed. *Let him still be alive. Let him come back to me!*

The King's men came next day and it was Constance who faced them, not Pamela. For Constance knew Pamela was fully apt to charge at them, brandishing a pistol. Pushing Pamela firmly aside, she answered the door herself.

Her soft voice and gentle demeanor somewhat took the starch out of the major who confronted her. She made him a deep curtsy that rustled her violet silk skirts. "You have come at last!" she sighed. "We were so worried here with the Squire in bed with a bad back these past weeks and only women and servants about! We half expected the rebels to seize the house!"

The major eyed her doubtfully. He was from Surrey himself and he'd been told that all these West Country gentry were in this rebellion up to their ears. He swept her the low bow her beauty and gentility merited. "'Tis our mission to search out rebels and we've been ordered to search the houses hereabout," he told her on a note of apology.

"Oh, then come in, come in," cried Constance, peering about her fearfully. "For if there are rebels hiding about, we do want you to find them. And we'll count on you to take them away!"

"Oh, we'll do that, mistress," the major promised her grimly.

Pamela hovered in the background behind Constance as they searched the house. Her white face gave added credence to the picture Constance had painted of a household of fearful women and their servants. And the Squire's groan and his unsuccessful attempt to rise as they reached his bedchamber all contributed to the major's impression.

"A wound?" he inquired of the Squire, frowning.

"God knows, I wish it were!" gasped the Squire, writhing painfully in his bed.

"He wishes it were a wound taken in King James's service," Constance supplied instantly. "For 'twas all we could do to keep him in bed when he heard there was rebellion afoot, and as you can see, he's in no shape to fight."

The major offered his condolences and went on to Huntlands, where he arrested everybody who had not had the sense to flee.

It was the same at Warwood.

And if their owners were convicted of treason, both properties would be forfeit to the Crown.

Every day brought new horrors, new names added to the death list, new faces that had been spied hanging from roadside trees in the summary vengeance the King's troops had exacted upon the fleeing remnants of Monmouth's shattered army.

"I suppose we should count ourselves lucky that Tom and Captain Warburton are in jail in Taunton instead of hanged on some tree," sighed Pamela, for by now they had learned where both men were and that Tom's wounds were minor. She thought of how she had planned to ride to Lyme and confront Chesney Pell's mother in Constance's behalf. It seemed eons ago and unimportant.

And then word reached them that Chesney Pell was dead, hanged along some unnamed roadside in Somerset along with half a dozen others.

Pamela would have no need now to go to Lyme.

Death had annulled the marriage.

Weeks had passed. Three times the two girls had ridden into Taunton, hoping to see the prisoners. Three times they had been denied. But the fourth time, shuddering past the rotting bodies of West Countrymen strung up on the trees by the King's victorious troops, they were allowed at last to see them.

So dark were the crowded little cells that Tom—leading a blinded and hesitant Captain Warburton—blinked at the sunlight shining through the window as he was brought into the tiny room where the girls waited. "I'm not used to the light," he quipped as he entered. "For 'tis a devil's hole in there!"

Pamela would have thrown herself into Tom's arms but that the jailer held her back. "Stand back, mistress," he warned. "Stand well apart, all of you. For I'll not have any knives or pistols passed to these prisoners!"

Pamela gave Tom a wan smile. "We'll have you out soon," she told him with a cheerfulness she did not feel.

"The trial is day after tomorrow," he reminded her wistfully.

"What news?" asked Captain Warburton.

"A thousand dead, fifteen hundred taken prisoner," said Constance steadily. It tormented her that he could not see.

"And the Duke? We receive no news here."

"Taken. On the eighth, as he fled over the Mendips." Her wonderful voice reminded him of Margaret's. "I suppose he was trying to reach the New Forest and the coast."

"Where was he taken?"

"Near Ringwood in Hampshire—sheltering beneath an ash tree." She hesitated, but he would want to know. " 'Tis said his hair turned gray as he fled. And after he was taken he went on his knees to King James. He even offered to turn Catholic to save his life—but the priests declared he cared only for his life—not for his soul!"

Captain Warburton shook his dark head. So the handsome lad had broken beneath the strain.

"He was hanged on the fifteenth," finished Pamela expressionlessly.

"Then the Cause is truly lost," mused Tom.

"It was lost long ago," declared Pamela with asperity. "When the fool sailed from Holland with only eighty-two men at his back!"

Tom smiled down fondly upon his warlike lady. "Ye should have been a man, Pam—but I'm glad you're not!"

"I should have been a better shot," she said cryptically, and gave him a bright smile that said, *Have courage! All is not lost!*

Mindful of the presence of the jailer, the two couples sought opposite sides of the room. And Constance asked in a low voice, "What do the doctors say about your eyes, Tony?"

He shrugged. "They can find nothing wrong with them— save that I cannot see. 'Tis thought the bullet passing so near did it." He groped for her hand. "Lean toward me, for I've a request to make of you."

"What is it, Tony? I'll do anything."

"I ask that ye marry me, Constance."

"You can ask me that?" she cried in disbelief. "When I don't know how you can forgive me, how you can even speak to me?"

The Captain's dark brows lifted. Even though he could not

537

see her, she could see that the pain in her voice had struck through to him. "Forgive you for what?" he asked slowly.

"For Ned. I—drove him to his death," Constance faltered. "He would not have been in this thing save for me."

"You are wrong, Constance." Captain Warburton's voice had a sad ring of truth to it. "Ned was in it from the start. He told me all about it the night before the battle." He hesitated. "They never quite trusted you, Constance—Stafford and the others."

"They thought I might be a spy for the King?" whispered Constance incredulously.

"Very possibly," Captain Warburton said wearily. "After all, you had appeared very suddenly and mysteriously, you seemed to have no past. And there was a lovely lady who appeared with you and vanished—a lady selected carefully, I think, to make me believe..." He did not finish that sentence. Instead he cleared his throat and went on in a crisp low tone. "A lady who was, by a ruse, to worm secrets out of me, I think. For I was a King's agent for years, and it was thought at Whitehall that I'd gone over to the other side."

So he had thought the lady in bronze silks at the Midsummer Masque an imposter, cleverly impersonating his lost Margaret, a woman brought in to woo and win from him the secrets of the Cause!

His voice dropped a shade lower. "So I ask you to marry me, Constance. As soon as it can be arranged—tomorrow, I hope. But in the meantime, I'll bribe the jailer—he's susceptible to that—and I want you to plan to spend tomorrow night with me. Here in the jail. We'll have some privacy."

He could feel her recoil. "Here in the jail—oh, Tony!"

"The object," he said grimly, "is to get you pregnant. You're married to Chesney Pell—"

"He was caught and hanged. I'm a widow."

"Wife or widow, it makes no difference." His broad shoulders shrugged. "But if you're pregnant when you're taken—and you *will* be taken for there are too many who know of your complicity in the rebellion—you'll be condemned but you can plead your belly.''

As condemned women do at Newgate, she thought, shocked.

"It will save your life, Constance. And after I am gone—"

"Gone? Oh, Tony, you won't be gone!"

A faint bitter smile curved his strong mouth. "They're sending George Jeffreys to try us and he's a hanging judge, sent here to wreak the King's vengeance on the West Country. He'll bathe this land in blood and I'll hang with the rest.''

"Oh, Tony, no." She was sobbing now.

"And after I'm gone," he repeated steadily, "you'll have months before the baby is born for Clifford to buy your way out of prison or plan your escape. Tempers will cool. Kings always need money. A pardon can be bought. Or an escape can be contrived. Clifford Archer wasn't in the rebellion but he's a good man in a fight and a cool one—he'll find a way out for you.'' He reached toward her and, regardless of the jailer's warning, she took his hand, conveyed it to her wet cheeks where he traced a pattern lovingly with his fingers. "If we cannot arrange the wedding, you'll still be all right. None will know the child is mine save you and me. The world will think it is Chesney's. And it will be something for me to remember and think on as they lead me to the gibbet,'' he said huskily. "A night spent with you and the knowledge that I've saved you by it.''

She clung to his hand with her heart full to bursting. *So much she could not tell him, so much . . .*

"Will ye do it, Constance?" he asked softly.

"Yes,'' she choked. "I will.''

And why not? she asked herself wildly. *Dev, who had pretended to love her, had deserted her. Ned, who had truly loved her, was dead on the field at Sedgemoor. Chesney, who had loved her in his fashion, was hanging from a tree somewhere. Who was left but Tony Warburton to fill her empty world? And Margaret—wherever she was—would never know what had happened in a jail cell the night before the*

*trial. For a wedding could never be arranged this quickly—
not here in the Taunton jail!*

"But they won't hang you, Tony—they won't," she heard
herself babble.

"Jeffreys will want to make a show here," speculated
Captain Warburton thoughtfully. "He'll prefer to hang us in
bunches and make a spectacle of it, I suspect, rather than
string us up one by one. So there'll be a little time after
sentence is passed upon me." His hand gripped hers and there
was strength and comfort in that grasp. "If I'm released, I
promise that—blind or no—I'll get you out of here, Constance,
away from the threat of arrest. I'll get you away to Holland.
But if the trial goes against me, I'll arrange with the jailer, for
a price, to give us a private cell the night before I'm to be
hanged. He'll view it as a condemned man's last request and
pocket the money righteously!"

Unable to speak, she leant against him and inwardly railed
at a world that would let so gallant a man die.

"I'm sure it won't come to that," she said unsteadily, and
drew away from him as the jailer rattled his keys as a sign
that their visit was over. "But if it does, I'll be ready."

"Remember," he said softly. "Tomorrow night."

He pressed her hand again and then for a moment his lips
sought hers in a hungry lonely kiss that almost broke down
the last of her reserves. At the jailer's roar of "Here now,
none of that!" she stumbled away from him and went through
the door dabbing at her eyes. But once outside she raised her
head proudly. With an erect back and a face sternly set she
walked with Pamela past the curious who thronged the jail.

Pamela's face was flushed, her eyes snapping. "They mean
to hang Tom, Constance, *but I won't let them!*"

"Come away," murmured Constance. "We're attracting
attention." She drew the angry blonde aside. "We'll speak of
it," she said, "on the road home."

"I'm not going home! I'm going to stay in Taunton!"

"You're going home," said Constance harshly. "We have
to consult your father—make plans!"

Pamela realized the sense of that. Reluctantly she assented.

They rode home almost in silence. Pamela was occupied by imagining—and rejecting as impossible—one scheme after another to save Tom. Always in her excitement she would think up a new one.

Beside her Constance was quiet and sad. Whatever hare-brained scheme reckless Pamela had in mind, she herself could see no way out. Tom and Tony would be tried and condemned. Pamela would have to be physically restrained from assaulting judge and hangman alike. She herself would spend one unforgettable night with Tony Warburton beneath the shadow of the sword and a day would come when the two men would walk out into the sunlight and mount the tall gibbet and die with the rest while a sad, angry, frightened crowd of watchers, people who knew they might well be next, muttered below.

And it would all be over—no, not quite. Because soon an arrest order would come for her and Pam and they too would be hauled away to jail.

But for herself she had decided not to go.

She would not wait for the King's men to come for her. She would sweep up Pamela and head for Tattersall in Devon!

Axeleigh Hall, Somerset, August 1685

CHAPTER 35

A chestnut horse cantered down the driveway of Axeleigh and a woman with striking red hair, wearing a riding mask, dismounted easily, tossed her reins over the hitching post and clanged the front door knocker.

Stebbins, who let her in, fell back half a step and lost color.

"Mistress Marg—no, it can't be!" he gasped.

"I thought you might recognize me, Stebbins," said Margaret with composure. "Not a word to anyone else though. Is my brother in?"

Constance appeared on the stair landing, stopped in amazement, and then flew down the rest of the flight.

"Margaret!" she cried. "Oh, I've been so worried about you—the Squire rarely gives me any word of you."

"Doubtless because I've not written," said Margaret. "Bring my saddle bags in, will you, Stebbins?"

Stebbins, who had by now recovered himself, gave her a wide grin and hurried outside to do her bidding. Wild and beautiful Margaret Archer had always been a favorite of his, and he had grieved sincerely when he had heard of her "death."

"Before Stebbins comes back," said Constance, knowing Margaret would not wish to burst into tears before Stebbins, "there's something I must tell you. Captain Warburton has been blinded."

"I know," said Margaret, with surprising calm. "It is what brought me back."

"You—knew?" Constance could not understand how Margaret could take such bad news so well—and then she realized. Of course, now that Tony could not see her and realize she had lost her beauty, Margaret could afford to come back. "There is something else," she faltered. "Captain Warburton and Tom Thornton are both in jail in Taunton awaiting trial tomorrow."

"I knew that too." Margaret was peeling off her riding gloves as she spoke. The black velvet riding mask remained firmly in place.

"And since he feels that I am bound to be implicated sooner or later—you must have known that I was?"

"Yes, I heard of it."

"He expects to be found guilty and hanged, but—oh, my life has become very involved since I left you and—and Captain Warburton plans to bribe the jailer for us to spend a night together so he can get me pregnant, and then if I am taken I can plead my belly and gain time until the Squire can rescue me!" she blurted.

Margaret paused in removing her gloves to consider this. Then she looked directly at Constance and the green eyes behind the black mask gleamed. "How very resourceful of Tony," she murmured. "But you must let me handle it. And now take me directly to Clifford—we have much to discuss."

They found the Squire reclining against the slanted back of his brocaded "sleeping chair," which had gilded ratchets for adjusting the angle. He leaped up at sight of Margaret and fell back, wincing.

"Are you ill, Clifford?" she demanded.

"No, 'tis just that I fell—twice. And hurt my back both times. 'Twill eventually heal but—what brings you here, Margaret?"

"Tony, of course. And other things."

"I would swear Tony never conspired to bring down the King," burst out the Squire. "And if he was at Sedgemoor, then I'd believe he was there to bring Ned home!"

"Yes, but others will not believe it," said Margaret crisply. "And they're sending George Jeffreys out, and he's a hanging judge—you will remember how he executed Russell and Sidney on faulty evidence?"

"Aye," agreed the Squire soberly. "And others too."

"Yes." Margaret's lovely mouth tightened. "And was rewarded with a peerage for it! 'Tis plain to me that Tony will be found guilty—and Warwood will be forfeit to the Crown. To prevent that, I've brought papers with me, Clifford, which Tony will sign and you will keep—and show if necessary— deeding Warwood and all its goods to you. And a deed which he will keep hidden, deeding Warwood back to him."

The Squire was regarding his always surprising younger sister in open-mouthed wonder. He would have expected her to insist they gather men together and take the jail by storm and free Tony Warburton—and instead she was mouthing words about deeds and property!

"His deed to me will have to be signed—and witnessed," he heard himself say.

"Oh, we'll manage that," said Margaret coolly. "I would suggest Tom Thornton do the same thing—deed Huntlands to you, and you deed it back to him. For he's like to be hanged as well."

Pamela came into the room just then in a flurry of scarlet riding skirts, for she was planning to ride to Taunton with Constance. "Indeed he will not be hanged!" she cried. "For I shall not allow it!" She stopped with a gasp. "You're—"

"Margaret," supplied the graceful red-haired lady in bronze

silks. "Please do not raise your voice or alert the servants. I would prefer my presence here not to be known."

"But—but we thought, I mean we *all* thought—"

"No, Clifford always knew—and so did Constance."

"Margaret," said her father with a wry glance at Constance, "is here to decide all our futures for us."

"Hardly that," demurred Margaret. "Just Tony's. And mine."

She was so sure of herself. Constance, who had never been that sure in her life, envied capable Margaret—proposing, disposing, settling, all with the greatest dispatch. She was reminded in a way of Captain Warburton, who never seemed to falter or know qualms or indecision.

"Are you worried about Tom?" Margaret shot at Pamela.

"Yes," admitted Pamela.

"You are right to be," said Margaret. "But there is time yet. We will snatch him from the scaffold by force, if necessary."

Both Pamela and Constance looked at her with admiration and awe. Margaret had such aplomb. They could almost imagine her riding up, pistols blazing, and scattering the crowd before her.

"However," added Margaret with a shrug, "there are better methods and we will try them first." She turned a challenging expression on Constance. "Are you still married? For I learnt of it but lately. Clifford here did not write me of it."

"Indeed I did," protested the Squire. "The letter must have been lost."

"Anyway, word did not reach me until recently that you were wed."

"In February," supplied Pamela. "To Chesney Pell. He was hanged by the King's troops."

"I am widowed," admitted Constance.

Margaret stared at her. "And what will you do if your part in this uprising becomes known?" And at the Squire's sudden start, "What, did you not know of it, Clifford? Constance here has been a focal point for messages for the Cause in this part of Somerset."

Constance moistened her lips. "I—I had planned to come to you at Tattersall," she admitted.

"Impossible. I shall not be there."

"Well, then—" Suddenly she knew what she wanted to do. It was all blindingly clear to her. "I shall go and search for a certain highwayman," she said defiantly, "who rode off in the wrong direction. He should have taken the Bristol Road but he did not."

Only Margaret had any idea what she was talking about. "And you think you might find him on the Great North Road?" she asked softly.

It was Constance's turn to stare. "You know about Dev?" she whispered.

Margaret laughed. "Information is my stock in trade. And remember, I have roved the roads these summers past. But come now." Her voice raised. "If you should find your highwayman, do you think he would take you in?"

"I think he would protect me from all the devils of hell, could I but find him!" Constance's own voice rang out with all the surety of love.

"He is nearer than you think," said a voice from the hall, and they all spun around to see a tall russet-clad man lounging in the doorway—a man Pamela instantly recognized as the "George Mayberry" she had rescued from the gibbet in Bridgwater.

"Dev!" cried Constance, and all the gladness of spring was in her voice. "Oh, Dev, you didn't desert me after all!"

"I did, but I came back," he said, as she flung herself into his arms.

"Then there was no heiress, no ship leaving for America?"

"Plenty of ships," he shrugged, smiling fondly down into her face. "But none for me—and no heiress, unless *you've* come into a fortune!"

"I think I should introduce my—" she began.

"No, let me," interposed Deverell. "Deverell Westmorland,

Earl of Roxford.'' He swept the company a low bow. ''And this lady''—he indicated an open-mouthed Constance—''is the Countess of Roxford, as the marriage records of Essex will show—although we did a bit of fancy footwork with the names!''

Constance gasped. ''But Dev, you said—''

''I lied. I thought you had found a new life and that I could offer you nothing. But when I returned to Lincoln, Gibb told me that the Earl of Roxford and his son had been drowned at sea—'twas thought they might have been mixed up in some plot against the Crown and were escaping at the time but nothing could be proved. The earldom is mine now—and with it, Wingfield.''

Wingfield! His wonderful ancestral home in Kent!

''I can take care of you now, Constance—and I intend to. Constance Dacey may be sought for in the West Country for crimes against the Crown, but Lady Roxford of Wingfield will never be questioned!''

It was all too much for Constance. She swayed against him dizzily.

It was also too much for the Squire, who demanded explanations—and got them.

''Gibb is dead,'' Dev told her soberly. ''He rode west with us from Lincoln.''

''You mean you came together?''

''All three,'' said Margaret. ''But Gibb had a heart seizure not ten miles from here. We brought him to Axeleigh—and now we will take him on to Taunton.''

''I do not understand,'' complained Constance. ''Why—''

''You will,'' said Margaret briskly. ''Are you ready, Dev? We must ride for Taunton at once if we are to get there tonight. Clifford, we'll need fresh horses.''

The Squire was only too glad to furnish them. And anything else they needed. His exhausting younger sister was as usual sweeping all before her.

''I am surprised you kept those drapes,'' she murmured as she went out. ''In the drawing room, I mean.''

"Father kept them because you selected them," said Pamela, who insisted on riding along on the chance of seeing Tom. "He's always been very sentimental about you."

Margaret laughed. "For an unsentimental man!" she quipped. "No, you can't go, Constance. We need someone here in case things go wrong." She was striding through the front door even as she spoke, with all of them trailing in her wake.

Outside they could see Gibb's body, lying inert across the saddle.

"I forgot—we'll need something to prop him up. Wooden braces beneath his cloak will do nicely." Margaret was giving directions even as Stebbins raced to bring what she asked. "And then we'll pull his hat down over his eyes—*so*. And he will ride between us and appear merely taciturn or drunk if anybody speaks to us."

In awe Constance watched this ghoulish procession ride away. Lady Roxford! She still could not believe Dev was back—or that she had become a countess!

"Constance," called the Squire, who had hobbled out leaning on his cane. "Come in and tell me again what all this is about. I can't get the straight of it!"

Pamela learned the details of the planned operation as she rode beside Dev and Margaret, who, she felt, were remarkably cool, considering that Dev was a wanted highwayman and Margaret the famous Masked Lady they were combing England for! And they were going directly into Taunton, which was full of royalist troops! But what they were going to do nearly took her breath away.

Taunton was teeming with people. They milled about uneasily. For the demon Judge Jeffreys and his entourage had just arrived. He would begin Taunton's own Bloody Assizes tomorrow, dealing with the miscreants as speedily as he had dispatched Lady Alice Lisle and others in Winchester. Pamela was horrified to hear that poor old Lady Alice—widow of a member of Parliament in Cromwell's time—had been sentenced by Judge Jeffreys to be burned to death at the opening of the Bloody Assizes at Winchester for innocently giving shelter to two "traitors." King James had allowed beheading instead and Lady Alice had had her head chopped off in Winchester marketplace. It brought to Pamela anew the horror of their situation, with Jeffreys already in Taunton and their own Bloody Assizes about to begin.

She was still under the dread spell of Judge Jeffreys's ferocity when Dev bribed his way into the jail and, bearing Gibb's weight on one arm while Pamela propped him up on the other, with the connivance of the jailer they substituted his limp body for Captain Warburton's live one.

Margaret had remained outside.

"And you must shout out loudly that a man is dead here and, when the jailer comes, identify the body yourself and let no one else near," Pamela cautioned Tom just before they left. "For although Dev has given the jailer enough gold to make him rich, there's still the chance that if somebody saw that the body *wasn't* Captain Warburton's they might make an outcry and then we would all be lost."

"I'll do my part in it," promised Tom, looking down hungrily at Pamela. "Oh, Pam, if I had it to do over again!" he burst out.

"I know." Wistfully she put a finger to his lips. "But it's no good wishing backwards, Tom. I'll be at your trial tomorrow. I'm not going home—I'm staying in Taunton. And if worst comes to worst, we'll snatch you from the gallows!"

He gave her a sad proud smile. Dainty Pamela, so slight and yet so brave! But they both knew that talking about "gallows snatchings" was only whistling in the dark, for the gibbet would be well surrounded by the King's men and it would take a large force to dislodge them.

"Do not despair, Tom," Pamela said softly, and kissed him on the lips.

It was all Tom could do to restrain himself from trying to overpower the jailer and making a break for it there and then!

Captain Warburton was silent as, dressed in Gibb's unfamiliar clothes, which almost fit him but not quite, he was led

549

into the light. In silence the four of them left the jail—only to
meet another problem.

Pamela refused to go home, even though Captain Warburton
broke his silence to urge her in his deep rich voice to go
home first and counsel with Clifford. Surprisingly, Margaret
said nothing.

By good fortune a room was found for Pamela in short
order—no mean feat, for with a motley collection of King's
partisans and Dissenter families rubbing elbows uneasily in
common rooms all over town, the inns were crowded. But
space was made for her in the room of two weeping old ladies
who had come in to plead for the life of their nephew who
would be tried tomorrow.

Pamela bade them a swift good-by, for to linger here was
dangerous. She stood in the bright sunlight outside her inn
and watched the three of them depart: Margaret, the superb
rider, swaying like a willow reed on her chestnut mount; Dev,
giving her a lazy wave as he rode off on one of those fleet
unpretty nags he favored; and between them, tall in the
saddle, the broad-shouldered figure of Captain Warburton,
oddly dressed in the slouchy clothes Gibb had favored.
Captain Warburton's command of his horse was as sure as
ever—she supposed some things never left you no matter
what happened to you. She sighed. In the brief time she had
seen them together Margaret had not made herself known.
Perhaps she was glad just to be with him, to have him back,
any way at all.

As she would be glad to have Tom.

Even when the three had disappeared down the crowded
street, Pamela lingered outside the inn, listening in fascination to a muttered conversation between two soberly garbed
gentlemen nearby. Tomorrow's assizes would be as bloody as
the last, they gloomily predicted, with innocent and guilty
alike being hustled to the gallows.

Well, Tom would not be hustled to the gallows! she thought
hotly. Suddenly she could bear to hear no more. She turned
and went into the inn's dim low-ceilinged interior. Her

scheme for freeing Tom was a wild one. She only hoped she could pull it off!

As they rode back to Axeleigh, Dev told the Captain how they had managed to switch Gibb's body for his. He had been cautioned by Margaret not to mention her name and he did not. Constance had whispered some of Margaret's story to him before he left and he gave them both a compassionate look. Even blinded as he was, Warburton cut a handsome figure, Dev thought, watching the Captain expertly guide his horse along beside them. Odd that Constance had not fancied him—instead of, as he had been told vivaciously by Pamela, some pallid lad from Lyme who had let his mother mouse-trap him out of his wedding night! Still, he told himself he was lucky that dead lad had been his adversary and not the dashing Captain, who stared about him dull-eyed as he rode—for soft-hearted Constance would never have left him now that he was blinded! Riding along, as Margaret led them down shady unused lanes and weed-grown back roads, circling towns and hamlets where any of them might be recognized, Dev thanked God that so many bullets had missed him and that his love—in her own tumultuous way—had proved true.

They saw no one except in the far distance as they rode and Margaret never spoke once. Dev supposed the Captain thought her to be Constance, and he too fell silent, dreaming about Constance, seeing her at Wingfield, planning for the future.

There were two reunions that night at Axeleigh Hall. In Constance's large bedroom, she and Dev surveyed each other with a kind of wonderment—as if all this might suddenly be snatched away.

Then—"Oh, Dev!" Constance felt a sob rising in her throat as she clutched him to her, uncaring that his belt buckle was digging into her flesh.

"I had thought you might be dressed for bed, we got back so late," he murmured, looking down at her riding clothes.

"I suppose I am still at heart a highwayman's bride," she

murmured with a rueful laugh. "I felt I must be garbed for instant travel!"

"You'll get over that at Wingfield," he said, untying her big fashionable detachable sleeves as he spoke. "How women can wear these things, I can't understand!" He managed to wrest one of them off.

She laughed. "You do it this way, Dev." She didn't ask him if there'd been other women since she'd left him—of course there had! The important thing was that *none of them mattered!*

"Have you missed me?" she asked, as the other sleeve left her.

"Every minute," said Dev, leaning down to plant a kiss on her bare shoulder.

"And would you have come back if you *hadn't* inherited an earldom?"

He pushed her away for a moment and looked deep into her eyes. "Only if I thought you needed me."

"Oh, Dev, I'll always need you—how could you ever have thought anything else?" She blushed as he eased down her bodice and her breasts suddenly sprang free and he fondled them lazily while her trembling hands undid the hooks.

They didn't talk much after that. Their eyes were busy drinking in the glad sight of each other, their hands were busy touching, questing, their bodies were building up wild tensions that threatened to overcome them even as they moved in unison to the big square bed.

And then they were on that bed, locked together in joyous harmony, murmuring soft rash endearments and extravagant compliments—and not hearing them at all, or caring. They were together again, together!

Constance's white arms crept round his neck in a hold that she never wanted to break and Dev's long hard body was pressed against hers with such force that she gasped. They tossed and turned sinuously, driving each other's passions ever onward until, with a surging thrill that seemed to permeate every inch of her, she gave a little cry as the climax of their passions was reached and they both swept over a bright precipice into a world of showering sparks.

It was a wild young highwayman and his waif of a bride who made love that night in the big bedroom at Axeleigh—but it was the Earl of Roxford and his beautiful countess who would wake and make ready for a journey.

Meanwhile in the green room that had once been Margaret's, a dramatic scene was taking place.

Captain Warburton and Margaret had been ushered into that bedroom by a silent Constance—and left there. Alone.

Margaret closed the door.

Captain Warburton turned toward the sound. "I know that you are a woman," he said, "despite the fact that you have spoken not a word all the way from Taunton, for I can hear the silken rustle of your skirts. And every time you came close to me, the scent of lilies of the valley was wafted toward me. Constance wears the scent of violets—and Pamela roses. *Who are you?*"

For a long slow moment Margaret considered him—tall and dark and dangerous. And blind—he could not see her. Then she tossed her orange-plumed hat to a chair. "Haven't you guessed, Tony?" she asked softly, and her voice had that remembered rustle of raw silk that had always set the blood in his temples to pounding.

"Meg?" he said wonderingly. Then with an abortive gesture, "No. Margaret is dead. *I saw her buried.*"

"A casket filled with wood and stones, Tony. *I* was not in it."

He shook his dark head as if to clear it. "It can't be you—if I could see you . . . my senses are playing a trick on me."

"No trick, Tony." Margaret's green eyes were brilliant with tears. "I'm Meg and once you loved me."

"Once?" He reached out, feeling for her hand, and she gave it to him willingly. "No, *always,* Meg. Always."

She flinched. "Don't say that, Tony. You cannot see me as I am today. If you had, you'd be grateful I left."

"Never that! But what has come upon you, Meg? Why would you run away like that?"

"You fell in love with a beautiful girl, Tony," she told him in a choked voice.

"Ah, so I did." His own voice was rich-timbred and caressing. "And love her yet."

He had drawn her to him now, this woman in bronze silks, and she was shivering slightly against his travel-stained coat. "And when my face was—*disfigured*"—she was caressing his cheek with gentle fingers as she spoke and her face beneath its velvet mask was full of yearning—"I chose to let you believe me dead rather than stay and watch you flinch from me."

"I'd never have flinched from you, Meg!"

Ah, but you would, Tony, in your heart! You would!

"What manner of man you must have thought me!" he muttered. "To think I'd desert you!"

"I know you'd have married me, Tony," she said sadly. "And then you'd have found yourself stuck with me—as I am, not as the girl you fell in love with. I couldn't let you do it."

"But where have you been, Meg? How have you lived?"

"I found me a place on Dartmoor—'tis called Tattersall. Of late I've only wintered there. Summers have found me riding down the highroads as masked as any highwayman. You'll have heard of me, Tony—I'm known throughout England as The Masked Lady."

"Then it *was* you I danced with that night at Huntlands when the chandelier fell and you vanished? My heart told me it was you but my head refused to let me believe it!"

"I was bringing Constance home and I—I could not bear to leave without seeing you once again."

"And all this time you've lived on the moors and ridden the highways alone?"

"All this time, yes."

His arms had gone round her protectively and now they tightened. "I would to God I had known before," he said hoarsely. "For now a bullet has winged too close—and blinded me."

"It's *because* of that I can let you find me again, Tony," she whispered, laying her head on his shoulder so that the heavy skein of her bright hair brushed his cheek and burned fierily against his strong jawline. "Because you can't see me—as I am now."

"Yet I've yearned to see you," he murmured, and his exploratory fingers roved over her hair, caressing its gleam. "Nights I've been riding, 'twas the glow of your red hair carried me home, Meg—it lit the way for me, it did, just remembering it."

She wished she'd had time to comb it, for his fingers seemed to revel in it, brushing it gently as if it were fine silk.

"You mean you'd accept me—blinded?" he asked softly.

"If you'll accept me—scarred," she said steadily.

He held her the tighter and then his questing fingers—as she had dreaded they would—lifted her mask and roved beneath it. Lightly his fingers touched her damaged cheeks—and moved on. "The same straight little nose," he exclaimed. "The same proud chin, the same long lashes and high arching brows, the same big eyes—and, I don't doubt, the same level expression, half disapproving of my wild ways."

"No—approving always, Tony."

His fingers moved on, down her throat. "The same lovely skin," he murmured, "pulsing under my fingers, the same sweet flesh." She stirred as his fingers toyed with, then managed to unloose her bronze silk bodice, pushed aside her lacy chemise and eagerly roved over the straining breasts beneath. "As lovely as ever," she heard him breathe—and then without warning he swept her up in his arms. "You even weigh the same!" he cried jubilantly. "Ah, it's my girl I've got back—my Meg!"

She was weeping now, but she did not want him to know it. She clung to him with all her strength. *He is blind, he cannot see me,* she told herself. And for the first time in a man's presence, flung her mask away.

"You'll have to guide me, Meg. There should be a soft bed in this place, fit for my princess."

His princess . . . yes, he had called her that. "Behind you," she whispered huskily. "Just step backward one step, Tony, and you'll find it."

He stepped back with confidence, felt the bed behind his knees and thighs and went over backward, pulling her with him. They were laughing as they fell, almost smothered by the soft goose-down feather bed that closed up around them.

They never knew later how their clothing was removed. Their garments seemed to fall away from them as if they'd never have need for those clothes again. The years had fallen away and it was young Tony Warburton and lovely Margaret Archer who embraced in the big bedroom at Axeleigh. For them this night held a kind of magic, a sense of enchantment, of time forgotten and lost. They moved together with a grace and beauty that had in it strength and courage and no regrets. They were together again, these two star-crossed lovers, and all the past was swept away in an instant. For them it might have been another summer, years ago.

On that bed of ecstasy, they never even bothered to throw back the silken coverlet. In the hot August weather the breezes wafted in bringing with them the scent of flowers, and chirping whirring sounds from a leafy world.

The soft breezes ruffled Margaret's bright hair as it fell shawl-like over Tony Warburton's deep chest and broad shoulders. And her strong voluptuous figure fitted close to every cranny of his long naked body. She filled his arms as never before, and with her came all the sweetness of love, all the bittersweet pain of loss, all the triumph and rapture of being together again.

Wild pair they were and wild they would remain. But tonight they met on common ground—the wild sweet homeland of the heart. For them it was a night of sighs and caresses—and no explanations, not a one. They could accept the past, these two, accept it as tranquilly as they would meet the future.

It was enough that God had given them back each other. They would never have need for more.

"I've made arrangements, Tony," Margaret told him, even as—in their third bout of lovemaking—his kisses dragged across her trembling naked stomach, causing her body to lurch deliciously beneath his sweet assault. "With a sea captain in Bristol. We'll away to Holland, Tony, where none can touch us. Will you like that?"

Captain Warburton would have professed to like hell at that moment, if Margaret had demanded it. He mumbled something unintelligible and fitted her smooth hips more comfortably to his own, stretched a long muscular leg between her long legs and rolled her over atop him. "I never thought to hold you again, save in my dreams," he marveled. "Though I saw your face in the fire's light every night when it burned low on the hearth."

"I've seen *you*, Tony," she admitted. "And not in the firelight!" But she refused, even though tickled and coerced, to say where. For this was no night to be talking about other brides, or tears she'd shed—this was a joyous night for them alone.

"We can be married on shipboard," he suggested.

"Yes," she said, smiling. "I had already thought of that."

"But we won't have Warwood, you know. It will be confiscated by the Crown."

"I've arranged for that too. You've deeded it to Clifford—you've only to sign it to make it so. And he's already signed a deed back to you."

Captain Warburton laughed, a contented laugh, deep in his throat. She was a managing woman, his Margaret—*but such a woman*!

And under the thrall of love, he took her again.

The stars outside did not shine more brightly than the glow of the lovers inside the sturdy walls of Axeleigh.

The Bloody Assizes,
Taunton, Somerset,
August 1685

CHAPTER 36

At Taunton the Bloody Assizes were in full swing in the ancient castle built by William Giffard, Bishop of Winchester. The great hall had been commandeered for the occasion as being large enough and suitably impressive. But, for the moment, the mind of George Jeffreys, Baron of Wem, who had brought to this West Country market town his legal expertise and his infamous reputation as a "hanging judge," was not on either the town or the frightened people it was his duty to try—and then to hang. For Judge Jeffreys was under no illusions: his royal master, James II, wanted the West Country punished, and punished bloodily. Especially here in Taunton where the Duke of Monmouth had dared to assume the title of "king" last June 20.

He'd made inquiries on his arrival here yesterday—surreptitious inquiries for none were to know that he'd known a West Country woman once. Virginia Archer had been a lightskirt and their single evening together had been brief and pulsing. He'd left under startling circumstances best forgotten and never heard from her again, of course, but the silken brush of her hip against his thigh had left a memory that was never quite erased and he'd wondered countless times what had become of her.

Now he inclined his handsomely periwigged head as the man he'd sent to make the inquiries whispered into his ear. *Dead these many years,* he was told. *Survived by her husband, the Squire of Axeleigh, and by a daughter—age, oh, sixteen, seventeen.*

Judge Jeffreys frowned down his long nose. A daughter born seventeen years ago? That *could* make the child his. For a moment it frightened him, the thought that *he* might have sired one of these sulky rebels who sat before him waiting to be judged. Then his harsh nature reasserted itself. If *she* were brought before him, he'd give her an even shorter shrift than the others! But of course there were few women among the accused who stood silently before him and at the moment none of the crucial age.

He heard a case and disposed of two unfortunates—sentencing them both to the rope, and then his head came up almost in disbelief.

Pamela Archer! Had he heard aright? Could the witness just now being sworn be Virginia Archer's daughter?

Airily Pamela took the oath. She would settle up with God later—today there was Tom to be saved.

"Who are you?" demanded Judge Jeffreys, interrupting the prosecutor.

"I am Pamela Archer, Your Honor."

"No, I do not mean that. Who is your father?"

For a moment fear gathered in Pamela's heart, fear that her father might be dragged into this. "He is Clifford Archer, sir."

"The Squire of Axeleigh?"

She nodded, amazed that this notorious "hanging judge" should have heard of her father.

Judge Jeffreys paused and moistened his lips. He had a

cruel mouth, she thought, and his snake-bright eyes were fixed on her with a malevolence that made her squirm.

"How old are you?" he demanded.

"Seventeen," flashed Pamela, for was she not going on seventeen? And would not every year of age carry more weight with this fierce periwigged fellow on the bench?

Jeffreys, who had been unconsciously straining forward, sank back with a sigh. Seventeen . . . she *could* be his, then. He remembered the lightskirt well, and this girl, though she did not have Virginia's coloring, had her flavor, the same winsome smile, the same regular features, the same reckless toss of the head, the same—charm that had won him then.

Was she perhaps his daughter? he speculated. He looked on her with morbid interest, there in her scarlet riding habit with her cheeks flushed and her crystal blue eyes shining—perhaps with guile. In the back of his glance glowed a dull hatred, for he'd have naught to do, he told himself violently, with any of this treacherous scum who had dared to challenge his royal master.

But what she had to say was to set him back on his heels.

"I have ridden all this way to tell you how Tom Thornton came by his wounds—they were not wounds gained at Sedgemoor."

Judge Jeffreys looked from the golden witness to the golden accused standing in the dock. Cut from the same bolt of cloth, they looked to him. But his gaze now held a glimmer of interest. "How were they taken, then?"

Pamela leant forward. She had an audacious air this morning and she was every inch the lightskirt's daughter, smiling into the eyes of this demon judge who was sentencing men and women to death by the cartload! "You will have heard perhaps that the Duke of Monmouth was fired upon from a window of the George on the morning of the battle? Mine was the hand that held the pistol."

Jeffreys sat back and stared at her. A novel defense this.

"But you missed?" he surmised.

She nodded vigorously. "My heart was in it, but my hand

was not so steady as it should have been. And the accused, Tom Thornton, who had followed me there when he learnt my intention, did fling away the gun and carry me through the crowd of men who came storming into the building. And we would have made it safe away save that in the melee he was shot and before I could bring help the battle of Sedgemoor was raging—and poor Tom was dragging himself home when the King's men seized him.''

Jeffreys sat drumming his knuckles thoughtfully on the table. Something about the girl's ridiculous story had the ring of simple truth about it; it could not be overlooked. He who had in his life sentenced so many to death on such flimsy pretexts found himself wanting to know more.

''Why did you do it?'' he shot at her.

That at least she could answer truthfully. Pamela leant forward and her voice rang out across the hushed courtroom.

''Because I love the West Country,'' she declared passionately. ''And this mad young duke was bringing death to all of us! And it came to me that I could put an end to this slaughter that was sure to come if I but put a bullet between his ears!''

She looked so fierce and lovely standing there in the witness box with her face flushed and her blue eyes snapping that even Jeffreys was convinced. Dour man that he was, he could see the humor of this situation. An indignant daughter of the gentry suddenly firing on a pretender to the throne—he had heard about the bullet that had been fired from the George, and that it had possibly been fired by a woman. He had no doubt that the woman was standing here before him.

As his gaze passed thoughtfully over the assemblage before him in the courtroom, another face leaped out at him. A face that was etched in his memory with fingers of fire. It was the face of the Squire of Axeleigh and the last time he had seen that face it was contorted as the Squire surged toward him—and then for a long time he had known no more. He had waked to find himself in the process of being buried in the foundation of the Squire's house—with his attacker gone somewhere and a single candle burning. He would never forget his fright as he had stumbled away in his smallclothes after having tried with trembling fingers to replace the pile of clothing topped by a hat that had been piled across his body—a pitiful effort to avoid pursuit by the vengeful Squire.

And the Squire was looking at him with equal horror! Good God, the fellow recognized him—after all these years! It had been a nightmarish situation that had haunted his dreams; he had once been afraid that he had babbled about it in delirium and had been delighted when his wife had dismissed his male nurse as incompetent.

George Jeffreys, who had struck fear into so many, felt himself squirming beneath the Squire's accusing gaze. He could not know what was going on in the Squire's mind at that moment, but from his own sense of guilt he could imagine the Squire leaping up and condemning him at the very moment Jeffreys discredited a daughter that—who knew— might be his! He was a baron now! The thought of public humiliation scalded him.

He began to perspire and the stone in his body that caused him such anguish began to hurt.

"Are there other witnesses?" he demanded waspishly.

"Only those who saw us flee," meditated Pamela. "One of them, of course, was the Duke—and he is dead. I suppose the others are too."

Beneath the Squire's burning gaze, Jeffreys made up his mind quickly. He turned a glowering face to the jury, and as always they quailed before the fury in his eyes. "I hereby instruct the jury to give due consideration to this young woman's story," he said. "For I did hear something to the same effect myself, how a woman had fired on the Duke of Monmouth and been spirited away."

Triumph flared in Pamela's eyes. She had no doubt of the outcome now. That jury up there was eager to acquit. They would gladly have acquitted everybody of the charges had they not been so terrified of this implacable judge who seemed bent on offering up all of the West Country to the hangman.

Tom was the only prisoner to escape Jeffreys's wrath that day and Pamela the only lady to walk away from that grim mockery of a courtroom with a glow of happiness in her eyes. The Squire, hobbling along beside them as best he could, could have told them a deal about the reason for their good luck, but he chose not to.

Wistful eyes followed them from the courtroom for Tom was known to have been a rebel as much as the doomed men and women who glumly awaited trial—and that Pamela should have saved him with what they all believed to be such a dazzling lie somehow bucked them up and gave them courage for what was to come.

"Hurry," muttered Tom. "For anyone put on the rack, or frenzied with fear at thought of the scaffold, may denounce us—in hopes to save his own skin."

The lightskirt's daughter needed no further urging. She plunged forward through the crowd, eager to put Taunton and its "hanging judge" behind her.

And for once the Squire, having observed her performance in the courtroom, was glad that she was in some ways like Virginia. It was something she had certainly never inherited from him—the ability to carry off a lie with such aplomb!

"Stay but one more night," pleaded the Squire. "For who knows when if ever I will see you all again? And since Tom has deeded me Huntlands to save it from the Crown, and I'll now have to take care of Huntlands as well as Warwood, ye owe me that!"

"I'll only stay if—" began Pamela rebelliously.

"I know, I know." Her father held up his hand. "The banns have not been cried. But you can be married on shipboard like Margaret and Tony here—and meantime, I'll look the other way."

With a rapturous smile, Pamela embraced him. "I knew you'd understand," she said happily.

The Squire gave her a wry look. *He had always under-*

stood, that look said. *It was just that he had not always approved!*

And so Pamela and Tom spent the night—their second night together—in her big airy bedroom.

"Just think," she said, leaning back in his arms as they disported themselves, naked, on top of the dainty embroidered coverlet. "We could have been whiling away the time like this all along—but instead you chose to play the field!"

Lazily Tom traced the length of her pale torso with his questing fingers. "I was practicing up for you," he grinned.

"Nonsense!" She pulled away from him, giggling, for the slightest touch of his fingers sent shock waves rippling through her soft female body. "You loved it and you know it! And now you want me to go away with you! How do I know you won't play the field again?" she demanded roguishly.

"Because I've found something better." He pulled her back with strong fingers. "But if you draw back any farther, you'll fall out of bed, and when the Squire hears a thump like that, he'll think you booted me out of your bed and he'll come up to investigate!"

"I don't wear my boots to bed," she pouted, lifting a dainty bare foot to prove it.

"No—thank God." Tom's gaze brightened as he looked along that long shapely expanse of leg, extended for his inspection.

"I'm going to redecorate Huntlands, you know," she sighed, easing back against him.

"You can redecorate all you like—if ever we dare live there." For they both knew it was but a matter of time before new charges would be filed against him, and Tom dared not retrieve Huntlands from the Squire lest he be tried in absentia and Huntlands seized by the Crown.

"We'll live there." Pamela snuggled into a better position beneath him and her voice grew ragged and breathless as he made his first thrust within her. She lay pulsing in his arms, feeling delicious tremors course through her, feeling herself grow lazy, indolent, beneath his velvet touch—and then tense again and excited as she found herself swept fiercely along by his passion until her own tindery self, the very soul of her, careened along the very peaks of wonder. "We'll live there—" Her voice was muffled, dreamy. "Because I'm lucky, Tom. I have *you*—at last."

His strong arms tightened about her and he buried his face in the rosy scent of her hair.

He knew who was lucky—the man who held her in his arms!

And later, hours later, when Constance and Dev had stolen down to the kitchen for a snack—for all this lovemaking had made them both desperately hungry—they lifted their heads and listened, for the sound of a viola trembled down to them. And then Tony Warburton's attractive baritone voice softly singing "Greensleeves," that lovely love song a young king had once written to his lady. And after a minute his voice was replaced by another voice, infinitely sweet. It was high and lilting, a wild lovely sound, and the lovers who had just seated themselves in the big dining room to enjoy their Cheddar cheese and brown bread and cider paused to listen.

So must the mermaids have sounded, singing from the wild rocks, thought Constance suddenly, and remembered the lost wild sound of Margaret's singing on the moors. Only there was a contentment in that voice now, a deep-felt peace that had not been there before. She met Dev's green gaze and suddenly her own eyes were wet. From across the handsome table Dev placed his strong hand over hers and gripped it. And his smile cut through the raindrops of her tears.

Gallant Tony Warburton and his lady were together at last and even the gods must be smiling today.

It was time to leave now, time for the Squire to embrace his daughter and his sister and his ward and tell them all good-by, time for the new earl and countess, Dev and Constance, to ride for Kent while the rest of them rode hard for Bristol and a ship that would carry them to Amsterdam beyond the reach of a vengeful king.

But in the green room that had been hers in childhood, Margaret lingered.

"Will we ever come back, Tony?" she wondered, turning to the tall figure, already dressed, who stood by the window, silhouetted against the summer sunlight.

"Of course we will," he said decisively. "But we must hurry now, Meg. The groom has already brought up the horses and the Squire is waving me to come down."

"Waving you—!" Margaret felt her knees would melt. Her face turned white. *"You can see!"* she whispered accusingly and snatched up her mask, held it up before her face with trembling fingers.

"I got back my sight in the jail," he told her calmly. "But Tom and I thought it best for me to keep it a secret—to aid in the escape we planned had you not chosen to 'rescue' me."

"You have seen me without my mask!" The agonized words were torn from her.

He strode across the room and caught her arm, as in horror she would have whirled away from him. He spun her back to face him. It was a relentless face she saw, a face upon which mixed emotions played. For how could he tell her, how could he make this proud strong woman understand it was the wild heart of her he loved? That he loved the girl with wild hair flying who took the hurdles laughing, the reckless girl with her flair for clothes and her mad flirtatious ways, the dauntless woman who was good company for any road he'd ever care to travel. How could he make her understand that it was *her*—not just her beauty—that he loved? The words trembled in his heart but he had not the knack of saying them.

"You've tricked me, Tony!" she cried, grief-stricken—and tried to wrench her arm away.

The Captain's grip tightened. He was giving her a very steady look. "Meg," he said slowly. "If you won't have me, then I'm going to ride back to Taunton and handsomely take the blame for this entire rebellion—I'll say *I* put Monmouth up to it!''

She gave him a startled look. "Don't joke about such things, Tony," she said uneasily.

"I mean it, Meg." He gripped her arm ungently. "I'd have thrown my life away for less. Oh, Meg, you proud little fool, can't you see that to me you're *still* beautiful, that you will *always* be beautiful to me? And that I'd love you *even if you weren't?*"

Still beautiful . . . to him. Margaret's glorious green eyes misted over.

"Oh, Tony," she choked, collapsing against him. "Tony..."

And the love they had known the night before when passion's rapture held them in thrall was as nothing to what they felt at that magical moment, looking deep into each other's eyes. . . .

EPILOGUE

A toast to all rapt young lovers
'Neath the white sails of honeymoon ships
Who must hold their love fast, for the lies that have passed
Their ardent lying lips!

Another tragic hour had passed for England, but for the lovers, already setting sail across a wine-dark sea, battles were forgotten. The days were clear, the wind was brisk and fair, as if even the elements approved their voyage. And the nights, as clear as the days, were brilliant with stars—a good omen, they felt, for the future.

As the English coast faded in the distance, they tried to forget those summer days when the Great Cause had seemed—for such a little while—a certainty. They turned their faces resolutely toward the future—a future which seemed destined to be spent in Holland. Pamela and Margaret learned to love the quaint quays and steep-gabled houses of Amsterdam, the cosmopolitan gaiety and the cheerful way the City of Canals embraced traders from across the earth. But it was the glories of the English countryside that ever called to them and every summer they looked with shadowed glances into each other's eyes and saw mirrored there the silver river that wound through the Valley of the Axe in distant Somerset.

But behind them—ah, behind them was utter misery. Beaten, disinherited, those who were left behind watched helplessly as The Terror now fell upon France where, as many in the West Country had predicted, King Louis XIV—safe now, he felt, from any retribution now that a fervently Catholic James II sat upon the English throne—revoked in October the Edict of Nantes, which had protected the worship of dissenters. In the awful days that followed, whole provinces of France were almost emptied out as French Protestants, known as Huguenots, fled the country.

But the West Country rebels had been right about one thing—the temper of the English people. They had but advanced their cause too soon. For the harsh rule of James II was endured but three summers more before the bloodless Glorious Revolution of 1688 cast him out and William of Orange took the throne by invitation. With him came a Bill of Rights, Christian nonconformists were once again permitted to worship freely. Parliament repudiated Jeffreys's Bloody Assizes (Jeffreys himself tried to escape disguised as a common seaman but was caught at Wapping and died in the Tower). Many confiscated homes and lands were restored, and freer winds blew across England.

For the battered West Country, which had fought so bravely in a lost Cause, this was good news indeed—although there would ever be a sadness as West Countrymen and women thought of those they had lost to guns and hemp and slavery in the West Indies.

And in Holland, there was joy indeed. For the ''daughters of the Axe'' could return at last to Somerset.

Tom and Pamela (who were wearing wooden Dutch clogs at the time) danced uproariously like happy children when they heard the news. They threw their arms about each other and kicked off their wooden shoes while Pamela gasped with delight, "We can go back, Tom! Back to Axeleigh! You can take your scandalous bride back home!"

"Back to Huntlands," he corrected her, laughing. "And" —his merry open face hardened—"you'll be 'received' in every house in the Valley, never doubt it—and anywhere else you care to go!"

At this blunt declaration of his devotion, Pamela's crystal blue eyes misted over and sparkled with unshed tears of joy and love as she took his face between tender hands and kissed him with all the ardent warmth of her impetuous nature. And then Tom bore her away to bed, there to shed their Dutch clothes and celebrate in their own chosen way, with rapturous touching bodies and wild exuberant lovemaking, the fact that they had won through, that there was this day an extra splendor to add luster to their wondrous love for each other.

They were going home at last!

Home they sailed, with Pamela babbling happily about redecorating Huntlands and seeing her father and Angel, her dancing Arabian mare, again. Pamela was born to be a housewife and she transformed carelessly run Huntlands into a home such as Tom had not known since his mother died. She brought with her Tabitha, her bright-eyed maid, who was soon to marry Ralf, the stable master, and raise her own brood. For Ralf had fallen in love with Tabby the moment that, carrying big purring Puss in her arms, she had pushed open the huge stable door and stood silhouetted against the blazing sunlight with her rich auburn hair catching its fire and her russet skirts seeming to blaze at him invitingly. Her greatest triumph came when, in a borrowed coach and finery that would have become a duchess (both supplied by indulgent Pamela), she and Ralf went on their wedding trip to visit her parents, where she loftily described the fine cottage to which Ralf was taking her—and for the first time in her life had her family listen to her in respectful awe.

And in the big stone stables at Huntlands, Angel bore Satan handsome foals, just as in the great house—now entirely redecorated by Pamela, who still loved to overdress until she was stiff with finery—a whole brood of handsome, golden-haired children played round her knees and romped with Puss's kittens. Tom, having flung his fling, had settled down admirably—he was even glad that Pamela preferred her stiff high-necked taffetas and brocades, for if she had gone about as Constance had, in clinging silks and velvets, would not all the world have known what a beautiful body lurked inside? And perhaps some other likely lad would have got her away from him! He was glad now that Pamela did not flaunt herself, reserving her improprieties for those long lovely hours when the door to their bedchamber was securely latched and a fire burned warmly on the hearth, and she, in the sheerest of chemises or night rails, flung herself invitingly upon the bed and opened her arms to him.

And the Archers would evermore be known—and muttered about—as a family in which resurrections were quite commonplace: not only the Squire's sister, "dead" these many years past, but his brother-in-law as well, "dead" in the Taunton jail and now sailed home from Holland! But then the Archers always were a daring lot and left a spellbinding trail of glamour and adventure wherever they trod.

And Margaret, who had so long ago lost her way and had known so much of tragedy, knew at last the deep bittersweet ecstasy of a love that had transcended time and trouble and won out over all. Lonely Dartmoor was forgotten. She had transported Clytie and Lys and big purring Tiger, along with her unworn trousseau, to Somerset. She was back again at Warwood, where she had long lived in her dreams, and gallant Captain Warburton roamed abroad no more. Indeed he was too busy siring children these days and growing rich, his brother-in-law and old friend, the Squire of Axeleigh, was apt to taunt him. The irises that Constance came and planted with her own hands flowered purple over Ned's grave every spring, the color of her eyes. Ned rested there in the walled family plot along with other valiant Warburtons who had ever ventured, ever dared.

At Warwood, following his old friend Clifford Archer's sage advice, Captain Warburton's fortunes flourished and he was able to restore the great house to its former grandeur. There he and Margaret reared a whole new brood of wild Warburtons to astound the county—and the lads had their father's dash and the lasses their mother's recklessness and her beauty. The Masked Lady had thrown away her mask and faced the world at last, viewing it from her beautiful green eyes—for Tony Warburton's yearning glance told her every day that she would always be beautiful to him. They gave great balls which the whole county attended and when Margaret rode out none dared ask her where she had been all these years, for the most dangerous blade in the West Country rode beside her and his cold gray eyes suggested that any who tried to bait his wife might soon be leaving this world for another.

Even roaming Tiger Lilies find their garden spot!

The Daffodil was firmly rooted in the Valley of the Axe and by adding Huntlands had merely extended her flowery domain, and the flaming Tiger Lily had come home at last to valorous Warwood with its long and thrilling tradition of chivalry.

But the Iris had found new soil in the garden land of Kent and a country seat that was every girl's dream.

For Constance—Lady Roxford now—strolled almost unbelieving through the vaulted corridors and sumptuous rooms of Wingfield, on the arm of her husband, handsome, debonair Lord Roxford, who was so well thought of at Court now that William of Orange had come to the throne. Sometimes she asked herself by what miracle it had all come to pass? For she had loved Dev when he was a stableboy, and when he was a highwayman, and now that he was a peer of the realm she loved him still—and always would. Their tall slim son would inherit Wingfield—and the title. Their flower-faced daughter would one day marry a duke—oh, nothing was impossible, not to such as they who had won through against such awful odds!

And at Wingfield, beneath a stone that says only "Gibb, a

good man who got his wish at last,'' a one-time highwayman, transferred from a grave in Somerset, lies buried—upside down in a deep shaft—awaiting the Resurrection. Dev had kept his word to an old friend.

And sometimes Constance, brooding over that grave and thinking back to Somerset, remembered gallant Captain Warburton who had swept like a fury into her life and nearly unhinged her senses. She remembered then the last look he had given her as he gripped her hand, just before he and Margaret rode for Bristol—and Holland. There had been relief in his gray eyes—and gratitude. And a kind of consternation at how close he had come, all unknowing, to betraying Margaret.

We so nearly took a wrong turn, she told herself. *And we would never have forgiven ourselves—never. It would have ruined all our lives.*

But fate must have been watching over them, for they had won through—to this.

At Wingfield, that glorious mansion in Kent, the Earl of Roxford and his countess presided over their estate and rarely left it—not because they feared the dashing Earl would be recognized as a former highwayman, for he looked so distinguished now with his great full-bottomed black periwig that he clapped over his russet hair when they went out, and she with her piled-up powdered hair, and both of them dressed in the latest French fashion—no, they stayed at Wingfield because its great echoing halls were filled with their love, and the vista from the big carved and canopied bed in their gilded bedchamber with its mighty bay windows overlooking the reflecting pool was to them the finest view on earth. They seldom bothered to lock their doors, for was not the young Earl the deadliest shot in all of England? And the Countess twined her white arms around his neck and thought how thin had been her chances and how narrowly she had won through and marveled. But it was over now, she was clasped in the arms of—in truth—her only love.

The Girl With The Wrong Father had come home at last.

But on summer nights the Earl and his countess sometimes lifted their glasses and their laughing eyes met and they drank a toast to all that they had been. . . .

> *When desperate loves and lives must clash,*
> *Each seeks to claim his own,*
> *And through the fire and dark and sword*
> *Win safely back to home!*

The *BEST* of Romance
from WARNER BOOKS